THE
TEMPLAR
PROPHECY

Mario Reading is a multi-talented writer of both fiction and non-fiction. His varied life has included selling rare books, teaching riding in Africa, studying dressage in Vienna, running a polo stable in Gloucestershire and maintaining a coffee plantation in Mexico. An acknowledged expert on the prophecies of Nostradamus, Reading is the author of eight non-fiction titles and five novels published in the UK and around the world.

THE
TEMPLAR
PROPHECY

MARIO READING

CORVUS

Published in Great Britain in e-book in 2013 and paperback in 2014 by Corvus, an imprint of Atlantic Books Ltd.

10 9 8 7 6 5 4 3 2 1

A CIP catalogue record for this book is available from the British Library.

Paperback ISBN: 978 1 78239 317 7
OME ISBN: 978 1 78239 385 6
E-book ISBN: 978 1 78239 319 1

Printed and bound by CPI Group (UK) Ltd, Croydon, CR0 4YY.

Corvus
An imprint of Atlantic Books Ltd
Ormond House
26–27 Boswell Street
London
WC1N 3JZ

www.corvus-books.co.uk

For my beloved granddaughter Éloise – Baba's
best little girl in the whole world.

I would like to thank Michael Mann for his seemingly innate capacity to steer me towards interesting and esoteric ideas without appearing to do so. Nick Robinson, for advising me to 'keep it simple' when my fervid brain would have had it otherwise. My agent, Oli Munson of A. M. Heath, for relentlessly guiding me in the direction of my readers rather than towards the rocks. My secret reader, Michèle O'Connell, for her unerring insights into my elusive psyche and her ability to remind me to play to my strengths rather than to my weaknesses. And finally my beloved wife, Claudia, without whose presence in my life this would all be mush anyway.

'We are awake. Let others sleep. What today is known as history, we will abolish altogether.'

Adolf Hitler

'Nor can we ever know what visions sweeten the dreams of the crocodile.'

John D. MacDonald, *One Monday We Killed Them All*

'So I ask myself the question: could the religions I study teach us the art of killing the dragons in our flesh? This diabolical presence, buried within us yet constantly surfacing: is this the original sin I was taught as a child?'

François Bizot, *The Gate*

ONE

Homs, Syria

16 JULY 2012

The peace demonstration was spiralling out of control. John Hart had been a photojournalist for fifteen years, and he was attuned to outbreaks of negative energy. He could sense when things were about to turn bad. It was why he was still alive.

Hart elbowed his way to the front of the crowd and began taking pictures, switching focus and emphasis as instinctively as he switched cameras. There was a time limit to this one, and he needed to get his material in the can before the mob began to search for scapegoats. He had hidden his Kevlar vest and flak helmet behind a wall, but he still stood out from the pack. He had three different cameras slung around his neck and a separate rucksack for his iPad and lenses. If even one man singled him out for special notice he would need to run. Hart was nearing forty, and he couldn't run as fast as he used to.

Shots rang out. They were single spaced and ordered, as if whoever was firing had a specific agenda – a sniper, or

1

someone firing a sequence of warning shots. The crowd surged in their direction.

Hart had seen such a thing before. It was a bad sign. It meant that people no longer cared what happened to them. That they were relying on the sheer force of their numbers to protect them.

Hart allowed himself to be swept towards the side of the avenue. He smelt tear gas. He veered down a side street that ran parallel to the main avenue. Almost immediately he found himself running alongside a gang of about thirty young men, their faces covered. Some were talking into mobile phones. There was organization of a sort here, he decided. And intent. He would shadow them and wait to see what happened.

Hart and his companions emerged onto a semi-derelict square. The area had recently been subjected to either a bombardment or a concerted tank attack. Sheet metal and crumbling concrete amplified the moonscape effect. The sun glistened off a field of broken glass.

Hart sidestepped alongside the young men, taking pictures all the time.

A yellow Peugeot 205 breasted the far corner of the square at breakneck speed, struck a lump of concrete and flipped over.

The group changed direction like an animal scenting prey.

A man climbed out of the shattered front door of the Peugeot. Blood masked his features. When he saw the crowd surging towards him he made the most disastrous decision of his life. He took out his pistol.

2

There was a collective roar. The group turned into a mob. Their focus, once random, became explicit.

The man fired three shots into the air. The mob stuttered a little and then regrouped. It began hurling bricks, stones and lumps of concrete as it ran. Hart realized that no one was in the mood to pay any attention at all to the word PRESS stencilled onto the Peugeot's roof in both English and Arabic.

He positioned himself on a pyramid of shattered concrete and began taking photos. He knew better than to involve himself in what was happening. He was a veteran of the siege of Sarajevo. Of the troubles in Sierra Leone and Chechnya. Of the war in Afghanistan. Photographers didn't make history – they recorded it. That was set in stone. You kept your nose the hell out.

It was then that the woman stumbled into view and overturned all his certainties. She had been sitting in the back seat of the Peugeot typing copy onto her iPad, which she was clutching to her chest like a talisman. Hart recognized her despite the Kevlar vest and the padded helmet with her blood group stencilled onto the front in indelible white ink. It was journalist Amira Eisenberger.

Hart had known Amira for ten years. They had slept together in Abidjan, in Cairo and in Baghdad. Once they had even shared a fortnight's leave on the Kenyan island of Lamu, following which Amira had briefly fallen pregnant. The on/off nature of the affair had suited them both. No ties. No commitments. Falling in love in wartime is painless. The hard part was to pull it off when peace broke out again.

Hart shifted his cameras onto his back and sprinted towards the mob, shouting. The driver was dead. The mob was focusing all its attention on the woman.

One youth made a grab for Amira's iPad. She tried to hold onto it, but the boy cuffed her across the face with the back of his hand and sprinted off with his prize. He loosed a kick at the battered body of the driver as he ran past.

Another man, slightly older than the others, picked up the driver's pistol. He forced Amira onto her knees, threw off her helmet and put the pistol to her temple.

'No!' shouted Hart. 'She is a journalist. She is on your side.'

The mob turned towards him as one.

Hart waved his Press Pass above his head. He spoke in halting Arabic. 'She is not responsible for what her driver did. She supports your revolution. I know this woman.' He was counting on the fact that some of the men would have seen him shadowing them and taking pictures. That they might be used to him by now. Might sense that he didn't work for Assad or the CIA. 'I know her.'

They made Hart kneel beside Amira. Then they took his cameras and equipment bag.

Hart knew better than to argue. Three cameras and an iPad weren't worth a life. He would buy them back on the black market when things quieted down again. That was the way these things were managed.

'You are spies dressed as journalists. We shoot you.'

'We are not spies,' said Amira, also in Arabic. 'What this man says is true. We support your revolution.'

Amira's use of their language wrong-footed the men.

'Show us your Press Card.'

Amira felt in her breast pocket and took out her pass.

The older man raised his glasses and held the pass so close to his eyes that it was clear that he suffered from extreme myopia. 'It says here your name is Eisenberger. This is a Jewish name. You are a Jew.'

'My first name is Amira. My father is Arab.'

'But your mother is a Jew. You have chosen to carry her name. You are a Zionist. You are an Israeli spy.'

Hart knew that he and Amira were doomed. Nothing could save them. The man holding the pistol had a thin mullah's beard and was an acknowledged leader. As Hart watched, he cocked the pistol.

The snap and fizz of incoming machine-gun fire echoed around the square. The crowd unfolded in all directions like a flower in the wind.

Hart threw himself onto Amira just as the man with the pistol took aim. Why did he do it? Instinct? Knight errantry? Because Amira had briefly – ever so briefly – carried his child? The bullet would probably pass through his unprotected body and kill Amira anyway. What a stupid way for both of them to die.

The pistol clicked on an empty chamber. The man with the beard called on Allah to witness the uselessness of the dead driver's gun.

Hart turned round and looked at him.

The two men locked gazes.

Hart stood up and approached the man.

The man put the pistol to Hart's forehead and pulled the trigger a second time.

Nothing happened. The magazine had contained only three bullets, and the dead driver had exhausted them with his warning shots.

Hart put his hands round the man's neck and began to squeeze. Amira told him later that he had been shouting, but he had no memory of this. He only knew that a red mist descended on him and that his gaze turned inwards, like a man on the verge of death. Like a dead man living.

Syrian government soldiers dragged the two men apart a few moments later. At this point the man who had tried to kill both him and Amira was still very much alive.

Afterwards, when he and Amira passed through the square again on their way to the airport following their formal ejection by the Syrian authorities, they saw the man's body crumpled against a wall as if he had been washed there in the aftermath of a tsunami. When they asked the military driver what had happened, he told them that the man had tried to escape and had been inadvertently crushed to death by a lorry.

Hart sat back against the side of the van and closed his eyes. What is this madness? he asked himself. Why am I here? Why am I still alive?

When Amira reached across to touch his arm, Hart shook his head.

TWO

The Saleph River, Cilician Armenia, Southern Turkey

10 JUNE 1190

Johannes von Hartelius had never seen a man in full armour fall into a raging river before. Much less the Holy Roman Emperor.

Dressed only in a linen undershirt and a pair of sheepskin breeches, Hartelius sprinted to the riverbank and plunged into the icy water. He was instantly swept towards the central current, fifty feet above the spot where Frederick Barbarossa and his wounded horse were still struggling to stay afloat. The king's charger was no match for the combination of man and armour that was clinging in deadweight to the pommel of his saddle. Added to which the crossbow bolt in the stallion's neck, from which blood now jetted, was weakening him by the minute.

Hartelius, a poor swimmer at the best of times, spooned the water towards his chest, alternately lunging forwards and then throwing out his arms like a man welcoming a loved one back to his bosom. Both the king's squires, swiftly separated from their own mounts, had already succumbed to the river.

7

Hartelius was alone with the sixty-seven-year-old monarch, but still more than twenty feet to his rear. Behind him, he could sense the clamour of the ambush diminishing, to be replaced by the greedy roar of the river.

Riding parallel to him, and on opposite sides of the bank, were the two Turkish crossbowmen who had targeted the king. Hartelius swung onto his side as first one and then the other crossbowman let fly. The first quarrel ricocheted off the surface of the water a few feet from Hartelius's head, whilst the second quarrel sliced through the gathering twilight in a looping downward arc. Hartelius threw himself backwards in an effort to avoid the missile, but the bolt split the skin on his right cheek as cleanly as a hatchet splits wood.

Hartelius sank beneath the surface of the river. He could feel the water's icy grip numbing his wound; see the crimson spread of his blood being snatched away by the current against the sky's fading light. When he resurfaced, the king's horse was swimming alone – the king was nowhere to be seen. Hartelius arrowed downwards, but the cold and the shock from his wound were beginning to tell on him. He tried three more times to force himself towards the river bottom, but at each attempt his dive was shallower and less effective than before. He now knew himself to be well beyond the place where the king had become separated from his horse. And there was no possible way back against the current.

Hartelius let his head fall forward between his arms and allowed the river to take him. Thirty feet away he could see the bracketing crossbowmen hesitate and look backwards.

Their main target was dead – no man could withstand the actions of such a current whilst dressed in full armour. With darkness falling, was an injured and half-naked knight with no accoutrements worth their further efforts, when the real plunder lay back at the camp? The Turks reined in their horses and retraced their path along the opposing banks of the river, first at an amble, then at a canter.

Had the crossbowmen really not recognized that their victim had been the Holy Roman Emperor himself? Hartelius concluded probably not. The ambush had commenced just a little before dusk. And for a good three days now the king had no longer been accompanied by the telltale flock of ravens whose sudden absence, for many, had portended his coming death.

The ravens and the Holy Lance of Longinus had between them constituted unimpeachable proof to the faithful that the king's authority was directly vested in him by God. The sacred Lance was the very one used by the half-blind Roman centurion, Longinus, to spear Christ's side on the Cross. History had construed this as a final act of pity to prevent the symbolical breaking of Christ's bones by the followers of the Israelite High Priests, Annas and Caiaphas. Since then, the Holy Lance had served as emblem to all the great leaders of Germany and the Western Kingdoms. Now the ravens were gone and so was the king. And the Holy Lance had doubtless sunk to the bottom of the Saleph River, never to be recovered.

Hartelius had little choice but to submit to the current and allow it to carry him along. Far ahead he saw the king's stallion struggle towards the far bank and collapse onto a sand spur. The horse's body spasmed once, its legs sweeping the air like those of a newborn foal, and then it died. He struck out towards the spur. He was beginning to die of cold himself. There was only one possible solution to his condition.

Hartelius crawled onto the spur and dragged himself towards the horse. The king's sword was still attached by its scabbard to the saddle. He levered it out and used its blade to disembowel the stallion. The hot blood and stomach contents of the horse gushed over his feet. He tore out the Turcoman's gut sack and intestines, and then, still gagging, he eased himself inside the animal's vacated belly. He could feel the heat from the Turcoman's body enveloping and cradling him as if he were a child.

In this way, through this symbolical rite of passage, was Johannes von Hartelius, celibate Knights Templar and proud wearer of the white mantel of purity, *frater et miles*, and oath-sworn servant of the German kings, reborn.

THREE

Morning came, and with it, the sun. Hartelius, noisome and fly-infested, crawled from his hiding place and looked around. In the distance he could see smoke – whether from cooking fires, or as the result of carnage, it was impossible to tell.

Hartelius glanced down at the Turcoman. The stallion had harboured him well. All night its residual warmth had protected Hartelius from the cold, as well as from being spotted by any Turkish scouts or outriders on the lookout for stragglers. Now, having long ago sacrificed his shirt to bandage his wounded face, Hartelius decided that the caked blood and gore that still coated his body might serve to protect his armour-pale skin, at least for a little while, from the rays of the morning sun. He had lived with the offal-stench all night – he was pretty near immune to it by now.

Hartelius hefted the king's sword and turned to go. But a fleeting memory caused him to pause. Some years before, as a very young knight, he had seen the king ride past him during an investiture at Speyer Cathedral. He remembered asking his companion what was in the finely tooled leather pouch that hung from the opposite side of the king's saddle to his sword.

'But that is the famous Lance. The Holy Lance of Longinus. The king carries it everywhere with him.'

'That is no lance. It is less than a foot in length.'

His companion had laughed. 'The Holy Lance is more than a thousand years old, Hartelius. The wood on its haft has long since rotted away, leaving only the blade, and a single nail from Christ's Cross, which has been bound to the bevel with gold thread.'

Both men crossed themselves at the mention of the Redeemer's name.

'You have seen it, Heilsburg? You have seen the Holy Lance yourself?'

'No. No one but the Holy Roman Emperor may look upon it. But whilst it is in his possession, or that of his successors, God is with us. Everything is possible.'

Sick with anticipation, Hartelius cut the leather girth and levered the saddle away from the Turcoman's carcase. Yes. The pouch was still there, hanging from the pommel straps just as he remembered it.

Hartelius reached down to unlatch the retaining buckles and reveal the Lance, but some power outside himself stayed his fingers six inches from the hasp.

'No one but the Holy Roman Emperor may look upon it,' Heilsburg had said.

Hartelius snatched his hand back as if it had been burnt. As a Templar he had taken many vows. Foremost amongst these was his oath to the Grand Master, and, above this even, to his Liege Lord, the Holy Roman Emperor. Such oaths might not be broken, even in the exceptional circumstances of the death of a king, without the oath-breaker risking eternal damnation.

Hartelius used the girth to fashion himself a harness strap, from which he hung the king's sword and scabbard, together with the leather pouch containing the Holy Lance. When he was satisfied with his arrangements, he secreted the king's saddle inside the Turcoman's still reeking stomach, drank his fill from the river, and started in the direction of the camp. Whether it would be his companions he found there, or a triumphant enemy, was entirely in the hands of the Lord. One thing he knew, though – he would smash the Holy Lance to pieces with the pommel of the king's sword rather than let it fall into any Saracen's hands.

It took Hartelius three hours to retrace the distance it had taken the river a mere twenty minutes to sweep him. He was in bare feet. Even with the remaining parts of his undershirt wrapped around each foot, every step he took was agony. The ground was rocky and unrelenting. The sun, even this early in June, was fierce. Many times he was forced to stop and re-tie the Saracen-style turban he had fabricated to protect his facial wound from the flies that hovered eternally around him.

Hartelius only realized that the encampment had been abandoned when he ascended a hill a quarter of a mile short of where the original site had lain. He stared out over the mayhem the crusader knights had left behind them and felt his heart clench inside his chest with shame. He could read the signs as if they were seared across the sand in Gothic script.

Crushed and unmanned by the unexpected death of their king, the knights had gone home. There was no other explanation. The course of their retreat was clear. Hartelius shaded his eyes and tried to discern some further narrative from the chaos left behind by the panicking army.

Yes. A smaller trail did indeed lead on in the direction of Acre. Surely this meant that the Emperor Barbarossa's son, Frederick VI of Swabia, might nonetheless be pressing onwards to Jerusalem with his remaining knights? Or was this trail the one left behind by the retreating Turkish skirmishers after they had attacked the camp and killed the king?

To retreat at this point seemed to Hartelius an impossibility. If he walked into a trap, so be it. But his duty now lay with the king's family. He needed to return both the king's sword and the Holy Lance to its rightful owners. He also needed to explain where and how the king's body might be retrieved from the river, if such a thing had not already been done.

Hartelius had acted so much on the spur of the moment in following the king into the water that he was still unsure if anyone else had seen him in the confusion caused by the first Turkish onslaught. The attack had occurred near sunset. Most of his companions had been at evening prayers. Hartelius had been excused from attending vespers through being outwearied from guard duty. Such exonerations were customary on campaign, where military realities had long since overcome excessive dogma. Hartelius had been preparing for bed when the Turks struck.

Now, perilously close to despair, Hartelius foraged amongst the detritus left by the retreating knights for some item that he might wear over his sheepskin breeches, which were now in a lamentable condition. He found only a lady's *bliaut*, belonging, no doubt, to one of the noble handmaidens being sent from Germany to serve at the court of Sybilla, Queen of Jerusalem, and Countess of Jaffa and Ascalon.

Grimacing at the sun, Hartelius hacked off the ludicrously extended sleeves of the *bliaut* and abbreviated the ground-scraping hemline of the garment with the point of his sword. Then he rinsed himself clean in the river and slipped the *bliaut* over his head and into place. The discarded sleeve-cloth could serve as further head protection.

If he must die dressed as a woman, thought Hartelius, so be it. At least he would not die of sunburn.

FOUR

The four horsemen approached him at a gallop, with the sun behind them.

Hartelius freed the king's sword from its scabbard and took up the port arms position. He decided that he would attempt to bring the lead horseman down and then take cover behind the dead horse. He had been taught this technique as a young squire and had used it numerous times on the battlefield when deprived of his own mount. It felt good to Hartelius to be about to die as a martyr should, protecting the Holy Lance, and with a guaranteed place in heaven as a result. No knight could wish for a better end. At the last possible moment he would slide the Holy Lance under the dead horse, where it would hopefully rot, quickened by his own and the horse's body fluids, unseen and unrecognized by the enemy.

He was disappointed, therefore, when he recognized the first of the four approaching horsemen by the cant of his silhouette. Its rider was constrained to lean at least thirty degrees off the upright, thanks to a congenitally foreshortened leg. Einhard von Heilsburg was unmistakeable, even in battle.

'Heilsburg. Put up your weapon. It is I, Hartelius.'

Heilsburg pulled up his horse thirty feet from where Hartelius stood.

'Hartelius?'

'Yes.'

'You are alive?'

'So it appears.'

'Why are you wearing a turban? Do you have toothache? Or have you decided to become a Saracen?'

'I shared a quarrel with a Saracen crossbowman. He instigated the direction of the quarrel and I received its after-effect on my cheek. I needed to protect my wound from the sun.'

Heilsburg slapped his thigh with his gauntleted hand. 'Why are you dressed in women's clothing, then? Did the Turk offer to marry you after your temporary misunderstanding?'

'I am still celibate, Heilsburg. You may rest assured of that. My vows are intact.' Hartelius leant wearily on his sword. There were moments – and this was one of them – when Heilsburg's perpetual good humour became a little wearing. 'These women's clothes were all I could find to cover me back at the camp. When I dived into the river after the king, I was wearing only my shirt and my sheepskin breeches. Later I used the shirt for bandages and the breeches for decency. I still required protection from the sun, however. The *bliaut* seemed like a good idea at the time. I realize now that you will never allow me to live this down, so I shall unfortunately have to kill you.' Hartelius straightened up and made as if he were about to take off the *bliaut* before engaging in combat.

The three knights with Heilsburg burst out laughing, but Heilsburg's expression turned serious. 'Are you telling me you followed our king into the river?'

'Yes. But I could not save him from drowning. I recovered his sword, though, and the Holy Lance. The king's Turcoman fetched up on a sandbar some way downstream, and I was able to retrieve these objects from his majesty's saddle.'

'You have the Holy Lance?'

Hartelius held up the leather pouch.

The four knights crossed themselves.

Heilsburg unhitched himself from his horse and limped towards his friend. 'Here. You are tired. Take my mount. The king's son is encamped a mile down that track. We were sent out in posses of four to check for further marauders. It is lucky we ran into you, Hartelius. The Turks are everywhere. They can smell the scent of carrion on the wind. You would have been dead meat. After they had raped you, of course. The *bliaut* sets off your beauty very well.'

Hartelius made as if to strike his friend. Then he eased himself into Heilsburg's vacated saddle. It felt good to be on a charger again. 'Come, Heilsburg. We can ride like Bactrian camels from Turkestan. You can be the front hump and I the rear. Surely you trust me in this rig?'

Heilsburg forced back a smile. 'No, Hartelius. You are the bearer of the Holy Lance. I will walk below you, as is fitting. Our Seneschal was killed in the raid. We have only a Marshal left. The Holy Lance's return will be a cause of great rejoicing to him and to all the remaining knights.'

Hartelius turned to his companions. He was grateful to them for their instant acceptance of a story that other non-knights might have found catastrophically far-fetched. 'I saw a slug trail leaving the site of our camp. How many men did we lose?'

'Three-quarters of our fighting force have deserted. There are less than a thousand knights remaining. And only a scant few thousand followers left to minister to our needs and those of our mounts. Many knights committed suicide when they heard of the death of the king. Their bodies are scattered in unmarked graves along the Silifke-Mut road. They will be eaten by turtles, or so the priests tell us. And then basted by demons in the eternal pot.'

'You have not lost your sense of humour, I see, Fournival.'

'You neither, Hartelius. But I have to tell you. You make a piss poor woman.'

FIVE

By the time Hartelius and his posse arrived at the outskirts of the fresh camp, they were surrounded by at least fifty knights, all clamouring for news of their dead king. Each moment that passed brought more knights, so that it soon proved impossible for Hartelius to break away from the throng, far less dismount.

The charivari flowed inexorably towards the tent of the king's twenty-seven-year-old son, Frederick VI of Swabia. Whilst his elder Minnesinger brother, Henry VI of Staufen, was running their father's kingdom from Frankfurt during the crusade, the as yet unmarried Frederick had been taken along by the Holy Roman Emperor as battle companion and fallback leader. Having just lost three-quarters of his effective fighting force in the panic following his father's death, Frederick was both fearful for the future and in mourning for a dominant and charismatic father lauded throughout Europe as the greatest Christian king since Charlemagne. If this was a test of his mettle, Frederick was little prepared for it.

'What is this? What is happening?' Frederick strode out of his tent, accompanied by his ally, Prince Géza of Hungary. A small group of noblewomen, destined for the Queen of Jerusalem's court, shadowed the two men.

Hartelius now found himself shunted to the forefront of the mass of mounted knights. He eased himself from the saddle and prostrated himself on the earth. A vast muttering swept over the throng like the reverberation from a flight of starlings, and then fell silent.

'What is this? Why is this man dressed as a woman? And what is he doing here?'

Some of the ladies began to laugh behind their hands.

Heilsburg limped forwards. To kneel, he first needed to corkscrew his body to one side and then compensate by a second counter-screw, accompanied by a deft backward flick of his leg. The entire performance seemed to fascinate both the crowd and the two paladins facing it.

'It is Hartelius, Sire. One of your Knights Templar. He has come to tell you of the exact manner of the king's death. He also wishes to return to you your father's sword. Together with the Holy Lance.'

Bedlam erupted from the crowd encircling the tent. Cheers became mixed with wailing and weeping and guttural shouts. Frederick Barbarossa had been Germany's beloved king – a legend both to his family and to his people. His death had been perceived as a sign from God that all was not well in Europe. Might this be God's countersign?

Hartelius moved towards the Duke of Swabia on his knees,

bearing Frederick Barbarossa's sword in front of him like a talisman. He laid the sword carefully on the ground. Then he unhitched the Turcoman's girth from around his neck and placed the pouch containing the Holy Lance beside the sword.

'You retrieved these from my father's body?'

'No, Sire. I failed to reach the king before the river took him. Instead, I followed his horse to its place of death. The king's sword and the Holy Lance were still attached to the saddle.'

'How was my father killed?'

'Turkish crossbowmen, my Lord. A quarrel struck the king's horse. The horse plunged into the river to escape the pain. The king was in full armour. He hung on for some moments whilst the crossbowmen dogged him. I tried to catch up with him but I am a weak swimmer, and I was almost immediately struck on the face by a second quarrel.' Hartelius revealed his wound. 'But the cold water revived me and served to numb my pain. When I regained my wits the king was gone. Only his horse remained.'

'So you know where my father's body can be found?'

'The certain place, my Lord. We can dredge the river and retrieve the king's person, I guarantee it. I will show you exactly where he has fallen. I marked a *sosi* tree – what we call a plane tree – on the riverbank as I was swept past. It is unmistakeable.' Hartelius prostrated himself on the ground behind the sword and the Holy Lance.

Frederick inched forward. He was uncomfortably aware that the many mounted knights and their followers were watching his every move. Nobody dared dismount. Only the nicker of the horses and the swishing of their tails against the flies disturbed the pregnant silence. It was as if the throng was waiting for a revelation.

Frederick understood that he was facing his moment of destiny. Whatever he chose to do now would dictate the future progress of the crusade, together with the honour, or dishonour, that would subsequently adhere to his name.

He picked up the pouch containing the Holy Lance. Then he grasped the pommel of his father's sword and cradled the weapon across his chest. 'You have done well, Hartelius. What is your full name and noble title?'

'Johannes von Hartelius, Lord. I have no noble title. That belongs to my elder brother.'

'Where do you come from?'

'Bavaria, Lord. Near Saint Quirin.'

'Which is near Tegernsee Abbey, is it not? Where the *Ruodlieb* was written? And the *Quirinals*? And the *Game of the Antichrist*?' Frederick found himself smiling. 'My grandmother, Judith, was Bavarian. I have family there.'

'Yes, Lord. Your grandmother was the daughter of the Black Duke. My great-uncle was briefly Abbot of Tegernsee before his death. He was accorded the great honour of baptizing her.'

Frederick raised his father's sword. 'Rise to one knee, Hartelius.'

Hartelius did as he was bidden.

Frederick brought the flat of the sword down on each of Hartelius's shoulders in turn. Then he twisted the sword in his hand and lay the virgin side onto the crown of Hartelius's head and the opposing side against his own forehead. 'Now stand and take back the pouch that you have brought me.'

Hartelius stood and took the pouch.

'I dub you Baron Sanct Quirinus. From this moment you and your descendants will be Guardians of the Holy Lance. In perpetuity.'

Hartelius squinted into the sun. 'In perpetuity? Descendants? But, Lord, my vow of chastity. As a Templar Knight I am constrained not to marry. I can therefore have no children.'

For a moment Frederick looked crestfallen. He briefly closed his eyes. 'I have done what I have done.' He turned his full gaze onto a knight standing to his right. 'Marshal. Can this man be freed from his vows?'

The Marshal stepped forward. He was still in shock following the Seneschal's unexpected death the day before, followed so swiftly by that of the king. As if that were not enough, he was also smarting from the disgrace brought upon the Templars by the desertion of a significant number of their knights, and the suicide of others. The Marshal was determined not to rock the royal boat before he knew the full extent of his duties, responsibilities and even liabilities. The actions of this young Templar might very well be enough to redeem the honour of the brotherhood.

'Your action has freed him, my Lord. You stand here as representative of your father. This knight's oaths were taken, first to your father, then to the Templar confraternity. Such an oath may only be negated by the perception of a greater duty than that owed to the brotherhood. You have pointed to such a duty. The way is clear.'

'Good. He is exonerated, then. Now we need to find him a wife.' Frederick turned to the noble ladies behind him. As he did so, he winked at Prince Géza. Both men had long ago chosen mistresses from amongst their number, for, needless to say, the vows of poverty, chastity and obedience taken by most of their followers could hardly be deemed to apply to princes of the blood. 'Can any of you ladies suture a wound?'

One of the young women had been looking fixedly at Hartelius from the moment he dismounted from his horse. It had become clear to her from the outset that it was her own abandoned *bliaut* that the knight was wearing. Thanks to this fact she had been one of the first to laugh in delight at the ridiculous picture he made. This alone was her connection to him. But it was enough. She knew this as if a weight were pressing from outside her chest and hard upon her solar plexus. 'I can suture a wound, Lord.'

'What is your name, my Lady?'

'Adelaïde von Kronach.'

'So you are also Bavarian?'

'Yes, Lord. From Upper Franconia.'

'How old are you?'

'Fifteen, Lord.'

'Perfect. If I were to suggest to you that you tend to the Baron's wounds, and if the two of you were to come to an understanding during this process – in terms of dowry, transfers of property, and suchlike – that you were then to marry him

25

in a binding *Muntehe* ceremony, might you be amenable to this? I would, of course, underwrite such an agreement in your father's absence. I am sure he sent papers of lodgement with you?'

Adelaïde could feel all her companions staring at her. Her face turned ashen white. 'I am your ward, Lord. As are we all until we reach the court of the Queen of Jerusalem. My father has placed me in your hands. And yes. I have my papers of lodgement. It was always expected that I would marry whilst at the Queen's court, and with the Queen's permission. But I am not as yet under her tutelage. I will do as you wish.'

'Excellent. Hartelius?'

Hartelius was struck dumb. In less than two minutes he had moved from being an inconsequential younger son, dedicated for the span of his mortal life to chastity, poverty and obedience as a Templar, to being a soon-to-be-married Baron and hereditary Guardian of the Holy Lance. He wondered for a moment whether his wound had become infected and he was imagining all this. Was he still lying inside the belly of the king's Turcoman and fever dreaming? But no. The icy waters of the Saleph had cleansed and anaesthetized his wound. There was no fever. And now this elegant young woman – his future wife – would soon be leaning over him and suturing his wound with hemp. Never – beyond his mother and his nurse – had any woman been allowed to touch his body. His battle wounds, his jousting knocks, even the care of his hair and beard and teeth, had all been vouchsafed to men. The prospect facing him was therefore quite extraordinary.

'Hartelius? What do you say? Will you agree to a *verba de praesenti* without the presence of clergy?'

Hartelius opened his eyes as wide as he was able. He feared that he might be about to plunge forward and measure his length on the ground. 'If my Lady will agree to tend to my wounds. And if she is not put off by this proximity to my person, who am unused to women. And if she respond positively to my request for her hand at the *despontatio*. Then will I agree to the *verba de praesenti*.'

'Good. That is settled, then. In one week from now you and your wife will return to my brother's court. I will provide you with a suitable escort. You will take my father's sword and the Holy Lance with you, Hartelius, and you will personally place them in my brother's hands, together with a full account of what has befallen our father. One of our Turkish notaries will transcribe a record of all that has occurred to be given to my father's advisors. We remaining crusaders, meanwhile, will fulfil our holy vows. We will first take Acre, and then Jerusalem.'

The assembled knights cheered the Duke of Swabia. The feeling around the camp had changed, in an instant, from desolation to hope. Frederick felt more than satisfied with his morning's work.

Johannes von Hartelius, on the other hand, beset by wounds, blood loss and dehydration, drifted slowly to his knees. He appeared to hover for a moment between the earth and the air, almost as if he were estimating the potential value of each.

Then he yielded to nature and to the forces of gravity and pitched headlong onto the ground.

SIX

Syrian Air Flight 106
from Damascus

17 JULY 2012

'What in God's name made you do it?'

'Do what, Amira?'

'You know what I'm talking about.'

'No, I don't.'

'Yes, you do.'

John Hart and Amira Eisenberger were standing in the rear galley of the early morning Syrian Air flight from Damascus, via Aleppo, to London. It was the first time they had been alone together since their sequestration. They had been escorted onto the plane in handcuffs by the Syrian police. They had not been allowed to pack their own cases. But they had been made to pay for their flights in hard currency and encouraged to add a hefty tip on top of the ticket price to make up for the inconvenience they had caused their captors and to recompense them for the fuel used in ferrying them around town. It was made clear to them at the time that it was either that or spend another few days in one of Assad's jails, this time communally. Amira, who was on a significantly more advantageous expense account than Hart, had, under protest, divvied up for them both.

Hart filled two plastic cups with ice. He took out two of the whisky miniatures he kept hidden beneath the false floor of his holdall and cracked their caps. He poured the whisky over the ice. When Amira shook her head, he transferred her whisky into his own cup and threw the unused cup into the trash bin. He loved the crackle the whisky made when it kissed the ice and the scent of the Bailie Nicol Jarvie in his nostrils. One needed to be alive to enjoy such things. And free. And – against all the odds – he was both.

'By "do it", do you mean clatter in on my white destrier to your aid when I might have turned round and run away?'

'No. You were right to do that – I am a fellow journalist. I mean throw yourself across me when that man was threatening to shoot. What do you think that would have achieved? Apart from sending me to my grave covered in bruises?'

Hart took a sip of his whisky. He held onto it for a moment, letting the fumes filter through the roof of his mouth, then swallowed. 'I wasn't thinking. I just did it.'

'The story of your life, then.'

Hart took a second sip of his drink. This one he held for even longer. Amira was an Aquarius, he told himself. An idealist. She viewed humanity as a mass that needed to be saved. Not as a collection of individuals, each with their own eccentricities and modes of behaviour. Hart, a Robin Hood Aries of the old school, thought he understood this. But it blindsided him every time.

His phone buzzed, saving him from having to respond. He retrieved it from his shirt pocket and squinted at the display. 'I need to take this. It's my mother.'

'We're on a plane, John. Using mobile phones is forbidden.'

'My mother doesn't know that.'

Hart moved away from Amira and went to stand by the porthole. He stared at the passing clouds as if they might hold the answer to some question he had not as yet managed to formulate.

'Yes, Mum. I'm all right, Mum. The Syrians just decided to throw us out, that's all. Nothing heavier than that. No, Mum. They didn't imprison us. They didn't torture us. They didn't hold us to ransom.'

There were pauses in between each answer whilst Hart attempted to digest the question. His mother was crowding the line in her panic. She was in the early stages of dementia, and still frighteningly aware. He could feel Amira staring at the back of his head, but he refused to turn round.

'I'm sorry? What did you just say? You're handing me over to Clive? Why would you do that, for Pete's sake?'

Hart sighed. He signalled to Amira for a pen and paper. He stood with the phone trapped between his ear and his shoulder and began to write.

'Yup. Okay, Clive. Yup. I got that.' There was a long pause whilst he scribbled something down in longhand. 'Thank you for passing on the message. Yes. Thanks. I'm glad my mother's all right. Seriously. Yes. I know you're doing everything you can in the circumstances. I appreciate that. And yes, I'll send you the cheque as we agreed. Thank you, Clive. Thank you. Would you please pass me back to Mum for a moment?'

The connection ended and Hart stared at his phone.

'Who is Clive?' said Amira.

'My honorary stepfather. Or so he likes to call himself.'

'Did he just hang up on you?'

'No. He hasn't got the imagination. The connection broke. Or Clive pressed the off switch before he had time to listen to what I was asking him. I'm used to it. He does it all the time.' He blew air out through his lips. 'Both of them are off their trolley. Only in subtly different ways. My mother chemically, Clive genetically. But it no longer matters. The damage has been done.'

'What damage?'

Hart shook his head. He motioned for Amira to precede him back to their seats. She eased her way through to the window and he sat down beside her. He spent a long time rearranging the cup on his tray whilst Amira stared at him.

'John. What is this damage you're talking about?'

Hart rubbed his forehead, his elbows outspread like butterfly wings. 'It concerns my father.'

'Clive?'

'No. My real father. My American father. James Hart.'

'Your American father? I didn't know you were American. You never told me you were American. You don't sound American. You don't even look American.'

'That's because I'm not American. My mother is English. I was born in the Bristol Royal Infirmary. My father left my

32

mother when I was three years old. Some sort of breakdown, apparently. But then I no longer know what to believe when it comes from my mother. Half of what she tells me stems from memories she can't be sure she ever really had. One thing I do know, though: my father now lives in Guatemala. Under a false name.'

'Why would he use a false name?'

'Maybe he's become one of those nutters who thinks the CIA is after him? Or the Internal Revenue Service? Or the Child Support Agency? I haven't seen the man for thirty-six years, Amira, so I really don't know. He's calling himself Roger Pope, according to Clive. Well, at least the bastard has a sense of humour.'

'John. Stop joking please. You joke about everything.'

Hart closed his eyes. He let out a ragged breath. 'My father is dying. Clive tells me he phoned my mother and told her he needs to see me. Urgently. To pass some kind of message on to me. Something of crucial importance that has only recently come to light. And my mother, being my mother, promised him that I would go.'

'And she's sure that it was him?'

'She's not that far gone, Amira. She was married to the man for seven years.'

'And you're planning to go?'

Hart shrugged. 'Yesterday, before that stuff happened in the square, I'd have said no. That nothing on earth would get me out of Syria. That my father could go fuck himself. But suddenly, for the first time in years, I'm a man with no

33

assignment. And no cameras.' Hart made a phantom pass towards his chest, as if he was responding to some ancient muscle memory known only to photojournalists. 'Staring down the barrel of that pistol has shaken me up. Last night I dreamt of the kid we might have had together. That he was talking to me. Urging me towards something. But I couldn't make out what he was saying. Maybe my father feels the same way about me? Maybe he has the same nightmare? Maybe he wants to apologize for leaving me when I was three? I suppose I should be grateful that he didn't persuade my mother to have me aborted.'

Amira grasped Hart's arm. Her face was ashen. 'I had to abort our baby, John. You know that. I've told you over and over why I never wanted to bring children into this filthy, stinking world. Why I never wanted to be a mother.' She struck her chest with her fist. 'I'm a journalist. And a good one. That is who I am. Nothing else. My career is the whole of me. You knew that right from the start. I thought we were agreed on that? That the rest was just icing?'

'You might have asked me. About our baby.'

'I know what you would have said.'

'And what's that?'

Amira turned her face away from him and refused to answer.

34

SEVEN

The Hitlerbunker,
Reich Chancellery, Berlin

29 APRIL 1945

'We're dead.'

Inge von Hartelius stared at her husband. 'What do you mean?'

'I mean that we're dead.' The colonel held out the palm of his hand. Two blue ampoules nestled in the valley formed by his headline, his lifeline and his mound of Venus. 'The Führer gave these to me. He assures me that he has had them tested out on his Alsatian, Blondi, and that they work. Actual tears sprang into his eyes as he told me. Now he's handing them around to his people as if they are lollipops.' Hartelius gave an involuntary shudder, as if someone, somewhere, had just walked over his grave. He glanced up at the ceiling of the anteroom and raised his voice. 'It is a great honour to be asked to die with the Führer.' He lowered his voice to little more than a whisper. 'They're potassium cyanide. Two hundred milligrams. Bite one and you lose consciousness in seconds.'

'How…'

'Heart attack.'

'I mean how long will it take for us to die? If we're desperate enough, or stupid enough, or frightened enough to bite on one of these things?'

Hartelius pocketed the pills. He reached for his wife's left hand, squeezed it in both of his own, and kissed the ring finger. It was a long-standing ritual, and each recognized its significance. 'The actual time span is irrelevant, *Schatzi*, because we will no longer be conscious of the process once it has begun. In reality, between thirty minutes and three-quarters of an hour. But even if the Ivans burst in just as we are taking them, they will not be able to resuscitate us or avenge themselves on our bodies in any way that we will notice. From the moment we bite into these we will be freed from any such nonsense.'

'But what about –'

'Inge. No.' Hartelius pressed a finger to his wife's lips. His gaze travelled round the upper corners of the anteroom. He cleared his throat and raised his voice. 'Ever since the July plot the Führer has become justifiably suspicious.' He rolled his eyes to show that he was in deadly earnest about the possible presence of microphones. 'All of us are searched. Nobody is immune. Not even our generals. Yesterday he had the traitor Fegelein brought in. His own brother-in-law, I tell you, accused of conniving with that sewer rat Himmler. The Führer has brought in Müller of the Gestapo to question him personally. This is happening as we speak. Then he is to be taken out and shot. Good riddance, I say.'

Colonel Freiherr von Hartelius raised his hands in mute supplication as if to apologize to God for the gulf between his words and their meaning. He was a Wehrmacht officer. A career soldier. Instinctively non-political. For the past two years he had seen Adolf Hitler steadily arrogate all military power and all strategic decision-making solely onto himself. First it was the fifty-six-year-old and otherwise healthy General Guderian who had been overruled and forced to take sick leave; now it was General Krebs's turn. Everybody knew that the daily strategy meetings held in the bunker had become little more than a screaming match in which Hitler blamed everybody but himself for the imminent collapse of the thousand-year Reich. He was the *Gröfaz*, after all – the greatest commander-in-chief of all time.

'But Johannes. Why did the Führer order me to fly you out here if all he intends for us to do is to die with him? It's grotesque. And why us? What significance do we have? We are little people compared to the Bormanns and the Goebbels of this world.'

Hartelius shrugged. 'Because they couldn't spare any male pilots, I suppose. And you just happen to be number two on the Führer's favoured list of celebrity female test pilots. You also happen to be my wife, *Schätzchen*, and I'm not able to fly a plane to save my life. Lieutenant Colonel Weiss just explained to me that we were called in as last-minute replacements for another husband-and-wife team. Any guesses who they might be, in the light of what I've just said?'

Inge von Hartelius rolled her eyes.

'Yes. General Ritter von Greim and Hanna Reitsch. Who are unfortunately a little higher up in the pecking order than we are. Even though they are not, strictly speaking, married.' Hartelius's laugh was almost a bark. Test pilot Hanna Reitsch, alongside film-maker Leni Riefenstahl, was the most famous woman in wartime Germany, and her affair with von Greim was an open secret. 'The pair flew in on the twenty-sixth. But just as Greim was landing his Fieseler Storch on the East–West Axis, they were hit by a Russian artillery shell. It blew out the bottom of the plane and damaged Greim's foot. I got all this verbatim from von Loringhoven, who is one of Krebs's aides. Hanna Reitsch had to take the controls herself and land the plane. But Greim has since recovered and the Führer has sent them away again. Greim has been promoted to Field Marshal, apparently, and is now in charge of the Luftwaffe.'

Inge began to mouth the words 'what Luftwaffe?' but her gesture was swamped by the crump of incoming Russian shells landing on the nearby Chancellery.

The vibrations in the Hitlerbunker were more or less constant now. Water trickled everywhere – down the corridors, down the walls, from the ceiling – and the smell of un-evacuated waste was overpowering. As Hartelius and his wife waited for the shelling to diminish, the emergency lights began to flicker. Smoke and dust drifted underneath the doors and through the ventilation shafts as if strobe lit.

Inge von Hartelius could no longer control her outrage. 'That whore Reitsch didn't steal my plane, did she, Johannes?

You understand why I am asking you this?' She glanced up at the ceiling in an echo of her husband's acknowledgment that there might be listening devices. 'As one of the few women left in this house of fools, everybody treats me as if I am invisible. Even the secretaries refuse to acknowledge me. I would like to crack their simpering heads together.'

'I understand very well why you are asking me this.' Hartelius begged her with his eyes to be discreet. 'Von Loringhoven informed me that the lovebirds flew out in an Arado Trainer, not a Fieseler Storch. And from the far side of the Tiergarten. Also that they landed safely at Rechlin Airport. So it is still possible to get out of here if one is allowed to purchase a suitable lottery ticket.' Hartelius pointed up at the light brackets and then to his ear. 'Your plane is still on the Charlottenburger Chaussee. The Führer has ordered his men to keep it on standby.'

'For him and Eva Braun?'

'Absolutely not. The Führer has made it very clear that he means to die here with his wife.'

'His wife?'

'He and Frau Hitler were married last night. Things move fast here in Berlin.' Hartelius lowered his voice again. 'Though not as fast as the Ivans, apparently. They are within two hundred metres of the bunker as we speak. Only the two thousand men of the SS Mohnke Brigade stand between us and *Götterdämmerung*. Normally, I wouldn't trust the SS further than I can spit. But for once we must be grateful for their crass stupidity.'

Inge von Hartelius took her husband's hand. 'Why don't we make a break for it, Joni? If we can somehow reach the plane I could still fly us out.'

'What? You mean bluster our way through?'

'Yes. You've always been particularly good at that.'

Hartelius gave another of his barking laughs. He loved it when his wife made fun of him. He lowered his voice to match his wife's. 'Impossible. These *fanatisch glaübig* SS diehards who stand between us and Armageddon also stand between us and freedom. And all officers have been disarmed on the Führer's direct order. If he doesn't want us to leave, we don't leave. It's as simple as that.' He squeezed his wife's hand. 'We have been allocated a bedroom in which to rest after our flight, *Schatzi*. May I suggest that we withdraw there, barricade the door and go to bed? When we hear the first grenades going off in the corridors, we can say our farewells to each other and crack down on our pills. In the interim, I know exactly what I would like to do with my remaining time on this earth. If you are agreeable, that is?'

'But how can we…'

Hartelius lowered his voice to a hoarse whisper. '*Schatzi*. No. He is safe for the time being. I promise you this. We cannot think about him. We cannot even talk about him. Saving a miracle, we are both going to die in this place. It is a certainty. I beg you, please, to believe what I am telling you. And to make your peace.'

EIGHT

The fourteen-year-old boy had been watching the gap between the two buildings for twelve hours now. His stomach felt as if rats were gnawing at his entrails. Each hour, the hunger pains got worse. But he had been told by the SS sergeant to wait until the first Russian tank rounded the corner, fire his Panzerfaust, and only then retreat. Failing that, he would be shot. If he knocked out the Russian tank, on the other hand, the Führer would congratulate him. Personally. And give him a medal. For he would have helped save Germany.

The boy glanced down at his Hitler Youth uniform. He rubbed the brass belt buckle with the back of his sleeve. Then he took off his crusher cap and looked at the badge. He began polishing the buttons on his blouson.

Yevgeny Lebedintsev grinned as he watched the boy through the telescopic sight of his Mosinka sniper rifle. He had been watching him for more than an hour, ever since he had slithered along the upper floor of the abandoned warehouse

41

and taken up his position covering the square. When the first friendly tank approached the turning he would have to take the boy out. It would make him sad to shoot such a young boy, but it was his duty. Take him out earlier and another would replace him, but possibly in a less amenable position. This Yevgeny could not countenance. It might lose his people a Betushka or, God forbid, a T-34. And such tanks, in the battle for Berlin, could mean the difference between stalemate and victory. Meanwhile Yevgeny would wait and see if a better target came along first. If that happened he could spare the boy with a clear conscience.

The boy reminded him of his younger brother, Valentin. Valentin was thirteen. He was the apple of their mother's eye. If the war ran on for another two years and Valentin was taken as a soldier, their mother would pine away. It was as simple as that. So it was Yevgeny's duty to foreshorten the war as far as it was in his power to do so. To this end he had killed 143 men. Of these, 117 had been in Stalingrad, the remainder in the seemingly endless run-up to the battle for Berlin. His teacher, Vasya Zaytsev, whom they all looked up to, had killed many more: 257 in total. But 143 was good. Good enough for one of the master's *zaichata* – one of Vasya's 'leverets', as his sniper students were called.

Yevgeny caught movement out of the corner of his eye. He waited ten seconds, and then swivelled his head at considerably less than what Vasya used to call the 'speed of a rutting tortoise'. He saw the SS lieutenant colonel dart from one ruined doorway to another. Yevgeny swore under his breath, but the expletive stemmed more from astonishment than anger. What was a shit-kicker SS officer with a briefcase and no weapon in his hand doing alone on the battlefield? Collecting for the German Red Cross?

Yevgeny inched the Mosinka round so that the 3.5 power PU fixed-focus sights bracketed the last doorway which the shit-kicker had entered. He waited with indrawn breath.

The officer burst from the doorway and Yevgeny shot him. The shit-kicker spun wildly round and plunged back through the threshold.

'Fucking acrobat.' Yevgeny checked the ground outside the doorway through his telescopic sight. Yes. There were gouts of blood on the ground. The bastard was probably lung shot. He wouldn't last long.

The boy sprinted through Yevgeny's field of vision, almost slipping on the blood, and then disappeared into the doorway. Yevgeny grunted. 'You're a brave little squirrel.' He had already reloaded. The good news was that the boy had abandoned his Panzerfaust, so that danger was at least past.

Inside the ruined house the boy crouched over the wounded officer. 'Sir. Sir. What can I do?'

Obersturmbannführer Baldur Pfeidler knew that he had only minutes left to live. The sniper had got him through both lungs. Already the pain of breathing was threatening to make him delirious. He coughed up some blood. It tasted like the scrapings from a metal pannikin. It struck him as strange that his body could change from functional to dysfunctional in the space of a few seconds.

'Your name?'

'Scheuer, sir.'

'Age?'

'Seventeen, sir.'

'Don't shit with me, boy. I haven't the time.'

'Fourteen, sir.'

'Anyone out there with you?'

'No, sir.'

'So you're the front line?'

'Yes, sir.'

Pfeidler sighed. So this was how it was going to be? Pfeidler was the sole survivor of six officer volunteers whose task it was to carry an important dispatch from the Tiergarten to the Hitlerbunker and place it directly into the Führer's hands. As luck would have it they had stumbled into a Russian patrol within five minutes of starting out and been massacred. Pfeidler, the only survivor, had been on the run ever since with the briefcase he had liberated from a gutshot Wehrmacht major whose name he did not even know.

'You are to take this.' Pfeidler canted his head towards the briefcase. 'The sniper who shot me will be covering that doorway waiting for you to emerge. You must exit by another route.'

'But sir? Where am I to go with it?'

'You know where the Reich Chancellery is?'

'Yes, sir. Five hundred metres behind us. My mother used to clean there.'

'And the bunker?'

'Yes, sir. Below the Chancellery.'

'Take this briefcase to the Führer. Place it directly in his hands. No one else's. Take the Luger from my holster. If anyone tries to stop you, kill them.' Pfeidler coughed up some more blood. This time it was lighter in colour. Bright red rather than crimson. Pfeidler knew that this was because it was mixed with oxygen from his lungs. He had only moments left. 'When I die, take the ID tag from around my neck. You will need this to show to the SS guards surrounding the Führer. Listen to me, boy. Don't look away. Take my medals too. These will prove to the guards who I am. They will let you through. Give them my pistol when they ask for it. You will not be allowed into the presence of the Führer bearing it.'

Pfeidler felt a great pressure on his chest, as if a heavy man was standing on him with the full extent of his weight.

'Gerda,' he whispered.

Then he died.

The boy burst into tears. For a long time he sat beside the officer, weeping. His father had been killed during the Battle of Kursk nine months earlier. Now he wept both for his father and for the man lying beside him. He wept also for his childhood, and the loss of it. For his mother, and her widow's grief. For his sister, and the broken country that she would inherit. Hans Scheuer did not understand that he was weeping for all these things. If such a thing were explained to him, he would have made a face and ducked his head to one side, laughing.

When he was finished crying, he stood up. He had forgotten all about the sniper. He ran out through the same entrance he had entered by.

Yevgeny Lebedintsev let the boy pass. He knew it was a stupid thing to do, but there it was. The boy resembled his brother, Valentin, too closely for comfort. Someone, somewhere, might one day spare Valentin just as he had spared the boy. Such things happened. He knew it. His mother had the second sight. She had brought him up to believe that certain things were fated.

He watched the boy darting through the rubble but did not vary his rifle's position. The boy's own people would probably kill him on the assumption that he was running away. Yevgeny had seen this happen many times now. Even the Red Army's own Commissars had been ordered to do similar things to Russian troops who funked battle. Such was warfare. Yevgeny was pleased that he had let the boy live and instead killed the shit-kicker SS officer. This was the correct way of things. He inched his way back from the blasted-out window and took up a new position further along the building. Someone would soon come to claim the boy's abandoned Panzerfaust and he would kill them. That, too, was the correct way of things.

The boy, Hans Scheuer, zigzagged through the rubble like a hare pursued by gazehounds. At every moment he expected to be shot in the back. At the very last instant before hurtling through the door he had remembered the lieutenant colonel's warning about the sniper, but by then it was too late. He stopped thinking about the sniper and began thinking about the SS sergeant. He had left the Panzerfaust behind him in the trench. Such a thing was tantamount to treason. He deserved to be shot.

Hans ran and ran. He ran until his lungs burned with the effort. He was running towards the Führer. He had been tasked by a senior officer with an important mission. The Führer would realize that he was not running away and give him a medal. He would show his mother the medal and she would be proud of him. She would rub his hair the way she did when she was particularly pleased, and then give him a gingerbread man, which he would eat with a tall glass of creamy milk, straight from the cow. All the neighbours would turn out to see his medal. Arthur Axmann himself, the national leader of the Hitler Youth, would come by to admire it. The mayor would tell Hans to take the medal back to his school and show it off in front of his class.

Young Hans Scheuer never felt the bullet that killed him. It was fired by SS Master Sergeant Friedhelm Eberhard. He had warned Scheuer not to abandon his post until the Russian tanks came calling. Scheuer deserved to die. If everybody behaved as he did, there would be chaos. As it was, things had already descended into a state of anarchic disorder. Eberhard considered himself one of the final bulwarks of civilization against the Red Army hordes that threatened the Fatherland. Killing cowards was a necessary part of his duties. The traitor Scheuer was lucky not to have been hanged from a lamp post like the three men Eberhard and his gang had encountered the day before. The bastards had even changed into civilian clothes. But Eberhard knew a military haircut when he saw one. The court – of which he was the only functional member – had condemned the men out of hand. They had been strung up within minutes, with signs hung round their necks as a warning to others.

Eberhard turned the boy over with his foot. He was taken aback by how little he weighed. Where had the snivelling tick found a Luger and a briefcase? And what were these? Medals? The identity discs of an SS lieutenant colonel? Had Scheuer been plundering the dead as well as running?

Eberhard broke open the hasp of the briefcase with his combat knife. What he saw turned his skin as cold as if he had inadvertently swum through an ice current. The documents inside the briefcase were marked 'For The Führer's Eyes Only'. Eberhard looked around. Some of his men were watching him. Eberhard could see disgust at his action in killing the boy written all over their faces.

'This traitor has been plundering the body of an SS officer. Look. He has stolen the medals and identity tags of one Obersturmbannführer Baldur Pfeidler. Here. This one is a Knight's Cross. And this one a Close Combat Clasp in gold. The man he stole from was a hero of the Reich.' Eberhard held out the medals as proof. He glanced down at the boy's body. Maybe the boy had been running back to bring him the briefcase? Maybe he had made a mistake in shooting him?

Eberhard forced the thought from his mind. In war, everything was justified if it led to victory. That's what they had taught him during training at Bad Tölz, and that's what he believed. Whichever way you chose to look at it, the boy had died for his Fatherland.

'You. You are not one of mine. What is your name?' Eberhard asked of one of the men standing near him.

'Gerlacher, Sergeant.'

'Go and take over Scheuer's Panzerfaust, Gerlacher. The first Russian tank that rounds the corner – *paff*. No need to tell you what happens to cowards. You've just seen.'

'Yes, Sergeant. There is no need.'

'I shall be gone for a while. I am needed at the Führerbunker. This briefcase Scheuer stole contains a document of the utmost importance to the Reich. A safe pair of hands must deliver it.'

Eberhard didn't wait for a reply. He started off immediately in the direction of the bunker. When next he turned back to look, some of his men were clustering round the body of the Hitler Youth boy.

Well. They could transform themselves into sitting targets if they so desired. He had other fish to fry.

By the time he had rounded the first corner, Eberhard had convinced himself that what he carried in the briefcase would garner him at the very least a commendation. Possibly even a promotion. Perhaps even a medal.

But best of all it carried with it the chance of meeting the Führer himself.

NINE

Adolf Hitler looked like an old man. At fifty-six years and nine days old, he was developing the beginnings of a dowager's hump from stooping, dropping his head, and hunching his shoulders. His skin was ash-coloured from lack of sunlight, and his eyes and expression were dull. He wore blue-tinted glasses. When he walked he dragged his left leg and shuffled. During the past nine months he had developed the habit of favouring his left arm following the damage his right arm had received in the July 1944 assassination plot, making him seem lopsided when he approached people.

But for Master Sergeant Friedhelm Eberhard, the evidence of his own eyes was irrelevant. He had worshipped the Führer for so long from afar that the reality he saw in front of him bore no relation to the picture his mind succeeded in conjuring up. To him, as he stood there in the Führer's personal study, the man who took the briefcase from him seemed God-like. And to serve such a man was the equivalent of a divine commission.

'How did you come by this item?' There were stress lines on Adolf Hitler's cheeks, and dried spittle at the corner of his mouth from a recent outbreak of shouting.

'I took it from a dead Russian soldier, Mein Führer.' Eberhard had pocketed Lieutenant Colonel Pfeidler's medals and wasn't about to give them up. After the war was over he could claim them as his own. Failing that, they might be worth money. He had tossed Pfeidler's ID tag into the rubble, where it belonged. And to hell with the boy he had killed.

'Extraordinary.' Hitler exchanged his blue-tinted glasses for a pair of reading glasses, painstakingly checked the condition of the official seal on the document wallet, then sliced through it with a penknife. He drew out the covering letter and read it. The hand holding the letter shook like that of a drunkard, so that the letter flapped limply, like a handkerchief farewell. 'Quite extraordinary.' As Hitler read further, a smile crossed his face. The smile steadily grew, and Hitler seemed to grow with it, until he resembled a partially inflated caricature of the man who had ordered the invasion of Poland in 1939. 'Bormann!' he shouted. 'Bormann and Goebbels. I want them in here. Now.'

One of the SS guards standing by the study door saluted, swivelled on his heel and left the room.

Hitler began to laugh.

Eberhard stood aghast. What was going on? Why was the Führer in such high spirits? What could possibly have been inside the briefcase to cause such jubilation? For even Eberhard, a past master at wishful thinking, saw little or nothing to be jubilant about in the present crisis confronting the Reich.

As Eberhard watched, Adolf Hitler cut what amounted to a caper on the carpet in front of him. In reality it looked more like the uncontrolled gyrations of a madman. To Eberhard, however, Hitler's dance resembled nothing so much as the victory jig he had seen the Führer do on newsreels after receiving news about the capitulation of Paris to German forces in June 1940.

'You.' Hitler pointed to the second guard. 'Fetch me Colonel von Hartelius and his wife.'

'They have retired, Mein Führer.'

'Then un-retire them. They are to bring everything necessary for a journey. A long journey.' The Führer clapped his hands together like a child impatient for his Christmas present.

Eberhard was left alone with his leader.

'You know what is in here, Sergeant? What is on this piece of paper? What it says?'

'No, Mein Führer. Of course not. It was marked for your personal attention only. I would have cut off my right arm at the shoulder rather than open it.'

'Good. Excellent. You shall be rewarded for this. And you may keep your arm for the time being. I wish there were more men like you, Sergeant. Then we wouldn't be in this pretty pass. Instead I have to deal with roomfuls of blithering incompetents.' Hitler's attention wavered. He stared for ten seconds at the skirting board. Then he slapped the paper in his hand and focused all his attention back on Eberhard. 'As of this instant I am promoting you to sergeant major. My housekeeper will sew on your new collar tabs. Go to the armoury and procure yourself a weapon. Also two officers' pistols and spare clips. One of my adjutants will see that you have all you need. Then wait outside until I call you.'

Eberhard saluted. He felt as if Hitler's gaze had pierced his very soul.

'Wait. You know how to get to the East–West Axis, don't you?'

'Of course, Mein Führer. I have been there many times.'

'Can you get there still? Given the prevailing conditions? You can assure me of this?'

'Yes, Mein Führer. We are dug in like moles out there. The Tiergarten is still very much in our hands, and is likely to remain so. Which means the Charlottenburger Chaussee is too. At least as far as the Victory Column.' If Eberhard felt uncomfortable mentioning the Victory Column, he hid it well. Even so, his voice ended on a dying fall. There was a limit to the amount of self-deception even a dyed-in-the-wool Panglossian like Eberhard could conjure up.

Hitler had heard what he wanted to hear. 'You will leave the bunker by the *Kannenberggang*. You will guide Colonel von Hartelius and his wife to their Storch. The plane is being held in readiness for them on the East–West Axis, one hundred metres due east of the Brandenburg Gate. When they reach it, you will see them safely aboard and into the air before returning and reporting to me personally.' Hitler slapped the desk with the paper he was holding. 'Into the air.'

'Yes, Mein Führer.'

'Now go and fetch the weapons. Then wait outside.'

As Eberhard left the study, he could hear Hitler cackling behind him. To Eberhard's ears the sound resembled not the pathetic croaking of a beaten man but the triumphant cawing of a hawk, stooping onto its prey.

Not for the first time in his life Eberhard thanked whatever forces controlled his destiny for providing him with such a forceful and charismatic leader as the Führer. Germany could never be beaten when led by such a man. It was inconceivable. Something would always turn up. And Eberhard suspected that the documents contained within the briefcase he had just delivered constituted exactly that expected miracle.

TEN

Hartelius had just finished making love to his wife when the knock sounded. It was a military knock – forceful, ordered, and impossible to ignore.

Inge von Hartelius, whose real pleasure lay in the series of post-coital orgasms her husband nearly always provided her with, gave one final shunt of her hips and dismounted.

Hartelius wriggled out from underneath her and padded to the door. He threw aside the barricade he had constructed from two library chairs and flipped back the bolt.

The SS guard standing in the corridor affected not to notice that Hartelius was stark naked, and his member still semi-erect. 'The Führer requires your presence and that of Frau von Hartelius in his study immediately, Colonel. You are ordered to prepare yourselves for a long journey. Bring all that you need with you. You will not be returning to this room after the interview.' The direction of the guard's gaze flickered briefly over Hartelius's shoulder, and then shifted once again to neutral.

Hartelius gave a snort. He knew better than to prod the guard for any additional information. In the prevailing circumstances it would be absurd. 'We'll be ready in ten minutes. No. Make that fifteen. There is a lady involved.' Hartelius slammed the door in the guard's face. He couldn't abide the SS. He could scarcely even bring himself to acknowledge their absurd uniforms. Far less their Ruritanian customs and ersatz mythology. The man had been unpardonably abrupt, given the differences in their rank. 'You heard?'

Inge von Hartelius was already slipping into her underwear. 'Of course I heard. You were both shouting at the tops of your voices.' She finished attaching her stockings to her garter belt and slithered into her favourite Lucien Lelong dress.

Wearing a dress and stockings when you expected to be flying an aeroplane within the next hour, might not, at first glance, make sense. But Inge had come prepared. She understood men. And the Führer was a man like any other. The publicity pictures she had seen of Eva Braun in the follow-up to her sister's society wedding to General Fegelein showed her elegantly and femininely attired, often with exotic furs draped over her shoulders. Inge had therefore deduced that the clothes Eva wore were a direct reflection of the Führer's taste – how could it possibly be otherwise, when it was an open secret that the two of them had been lovers since 1931?

'Wear your smartest outfit, Joni. Medals and all. This may be our last chance to make our mark.'

'My smartest outfit? Who do you think I am? Marika Roekk?' Hartelius grinned. Unlike many professional soldiers, he relished the differences between men and women, and the sometimes competing polarities of their thought processes. Despite his pretend outrage, he pulled his best uniform out of his kitbag and began putting it on. His wife was generally right on such matters. 'What does the carpet-eater want, do you think?'

'I don't care what he wants. But I know what I want. I want my plane back.' She glanced around the room and lowered her voice. 'And everything that is inside it.'

Twenty minutes later, externally immaculate but still reeking of sex, Johannes and Inge von Hartelius were shown into the Führer's study.

Martin Bormann and Joseph Goebbels were standing beside the Führer. All three men were laughing in that artificial way men have when they know they are the centre of interest. The SS guard who had escorted the Harteliuses from their quarters saluted and backed out of the door. He took up position in the corridor alongside his companion-in-arms and the frightened-looking female SS-*Gefolge* guard who had been called in to conduct the mandatory weapons search on Inge. Beside them, his face impassive, stood the newly promoted, and now heavily armed, Sergeant Major Eberhard.

Hartelius snapped out a Hitler salute. Inge did the same. The salute had only been imposed on the Wehrmacht after the July 1944 assassination plot, and it sat badly with the army. Its pragmatic use, however, was mandatory. People had been put into concentration camps for mocking or refusing to use it. Given the top echelon audience in front of him, neither

Hartelius nor his wife dared not conform. Both shouted, 'Heil, Mein Führer!' in enthusiastic voices.

Hitler gave a lazy crook of his right arm in response. His attention seemed focused elsewhere. His expression, behind the forced levity he and his minions had seen fit to impose on themselves, was dark.

'A thousand congratulations on your recent marriage, Mein Führer. Please pass on our compliments to Frau Hitler.'

Hartelius raised an eyebrow at his wife's forthrightness. Well. At least she knew what to say and when to say it. Looking at her, he felt a surge of pride and possessiveness. Twenty minutes ago he had been making love to the beautiful woman beside him, and she had been whispering endearments in his ear. Now they were standing in front of their country's certifiably insane leader, and two of his equally insane henchmen, bandying social niceties. Fate was a curious thing.

Joseph Goebbels stepped forward. His eyes were red-rimmed and bloodshot. His face was covered with red blotches. He wore a rictus grin like a man already dead. 'You are Colonel Freiherr Johannes von Hartelius, hereditary Guardian of the Holy Lance?'

Hartelius did a double take. The Guardian of the Holy Lance? Was that what all this nonsense was about? The Holy bloody Lance? The object itself was in the basement of an infant school in Nuremberg. On the Panier Platz. Near the entrance to the Oberen Schmied Gasse. Either that or it was at the bottom of Lake Zell, near Salzburg. Depending on which army rumour you had listened to last. But who gave a damn any more about the bloody thing? Or who its hereditary guardian was? The Ivans were at the gates of Berlin. The so-called magic Lance wouldn't save anybody from them.

'Are you the person this speaks of?'

Goebbels held out a document. On it were the seals of Frederick VI of Swabia and Henry VI of Staufen. Hartelius noticed that Goebbels's fingertips were yellow with nicotine. Something of a paradox, as the Führer formally prohibited the smoking of cigarettes in his presence.

Hartelius took the document and held it up to the light. The emergency generator picked exactly that moment to respond to a more than usually concerted Katyusha rocket salvo on the Chancellery. It faltered for ten seconds and then regained its equilibrium. Hartelius had already recognized the document, despite the temporary blackout. It was an exact copy of the one his father had shown him a few weeks before his suicide in October 1938, following the annexation of the Sudetenland. It was painstakingly dated 1190 in Gothic Blackletter.

'I have seen this document before. Or at least one similar to it. It refers to my namesake, Johannes von Hartelius. The Baron Sanct Quirin.'

'I know who and what it refers to. Are you this man's direct male descendant? According to semi-Salic law?'

Direct male descendant? Semi-Salic law? Hartelius forced back a baffled smile. 'Yes. I suppose I am. Twenty generations later. Maybe more. But yes. I also carry the Uradel title of nobility mentioned in the text. It actually predates the oldest Uradel title, but that is beside the point. I would need to engage in a twenty-year court battle to prove it.' Hartelius was playing for time. Before this, he had simply looked upon himself as nothing more than a high-ranking courier – albeit with the priceless additional convenience of a test-pilot wife. In the light of what Goebbels was asking him, he was rapidly being forced to reassess the situation in which he found himself.

Goebbels made an impatient gesture. 'So you are indeed the Guardian of the Holy Lance? What is otherwise known as the Maurice Lance? You are certain of this?'

Hartelius was tempted to burst out laughing. Was this really what these maniacs had brought him and Inge five hundred kilometres to Berlin for? In the final stages of the war to end all wars? To ask him if he was hereditary guardian of some stupid lance that had probably been faked up nine hundred years before by an overzealous priest in order to galvanize recalcitrant crusaders? Were these really the people for whom he had been risking his life these past five years? The comedian in front of him was hardly Frederick Barbarossa now, was he? More like Cruel Frederick in Heinrich Hoffman's *Struwwelpeter* stories, who loved to tear the wings off flies, and killed the birds and broke the chairs and threw the kitten down the stairs.

Hartelius could feel Inge's eyes boring into him. Urging him not to spoil their final chance of freedom. Urging him to respond with caution. 'Yes, I am certain of this. I am indeed Hereditary Guardian of the Lance.'

'Excellent.'

Goebbels withdrew and Bormann stepped forward. It was as if the trio had rehearsed their respective moves prior to their appearance in a Marx Brothers movie, thought Hartelius. A nice irony.

'Do you have children, Freifrau von Hartelius?' Bormann appeared to be making a specific point by the use of Inge's honorific title. It didn't sit well with his butcher's face and peasant's body, however. In the haphazard light from the emergency generator he looked more like a character from a painting by Pieter Breughel the Elder than a German Party Minister and de facto General Secretary of the Nazi Party. He was the only one of the three leaders present who did not carry the aura of imminent death about him.

'Yes. One.'

'Boy or girl?'

'A boy.'

'How old?'

'Six.'

'And where is he now?'

Hartelius saw the maternal panic begin to flare on his wife's face. He cut into her dialogue with Bormann, aping the role of the stern professional soldier with little time for small talk. The paterfamilias. 'Johannes is with his grandparents in Darmstadt.'

'Ah. Darmstadt. The first city in Germany to force its Jewish shops to close. We executed Leuschner and Hauback there. Two of our home-grown terrorists.'

'No,' Hitler cut in. His voice had a querulous quality, like that of King Lear on the heath talking to his fool. 'They were executed here in Plötzensee. They came from Darmstadt, though. You are right on that score, Martin. They are in the photo collection. You used to have a better memory for such things in the old days.'

Hartelius was beginning to wonder whether Hitler might be working himself up to passing round the Schnapps? The atmosphere in the room was lurching towards the sentimental and nostalgic. He offered up a silent prayer of thanks that Bormann had veered off the subject of their son. He tried not to think to what the photo collection might refer.

'Now. To business.' Hitler pointed one shaking hand at the mid-sized leather suitcase resting on a painted table in the corner of the room. 'This case contains two things, Colonel. One: the true Holy Lance. Not the ersatz model my people mocked up to fool the idiot Americans. And two…' Hitler hesitated for a moment. He rubbed at the corners of his mouth with the sleeve of his tunic. 'Suffice it to say that it contains something of crucial importance to the future of the Reich. Of equal importance – of equal significance even – to the Holy Lance, and in strategic terms, superior even to the V-2 rocket.' Hitler's eyes flashed. He resembled, for a moment, a magician who has just withdrawn an enormous lop-eared rabbit from a very small hat.

Hartelius could only nod. He hadn't the remotest idea where the Führer was heading with his declarations.

'Tomorrow morning I intend to offer up my life as a final sacrifice to the German Reich.' Hitler's gaze turned inward. 'Frau Hitler, of course, will die alongside me, just as Isolde died alongside Tristan. I shall use the same cyanide tablets I gave to you, Hartelius. But in addition I shall use a pistol.' Hitler's bleary eyes gleamed with self-pity. He held up one shaking hand. 'No. It is pointless to protest.'

Hartelius had not been about to protest, but Hitler was plainly at the stage where he saw only what he chose to see. Hartelius found himself wondering why the Führer was still intent on killing himself moments after taking possession of the plans for a new, all-conquering super weapon? This was, indeed, a house of fools, just as Inge had suggested.

'To make entirely sure that the Russians will not be able to make use of our bodies in the same way that the communist filth made use of Il Duce's, two days ago, I have ordered that our corpses be immediately incinerated. Reich Minister Goebbels and Magda, his wife, together with their six children, have requested permission to accompany me.'

'To accompany you?' Inge von Hartelius couldn't help herself. The thought of the six Goebbels children being forcibly killed was too much to bear. She, like everyone else in Germany, had seen perennial images of this perfect Aryan family in endless propaganda magazines and newsreels. 'Do you mean accompany you to die?'

'What did you think I meant, Freifrau von Hartelius? Honour to the point of destruction. That is the only possible answer to the dilemma our nation faces. Reich Minister Goebbels and his family, to their eternal credit, have refused my direct order that they leave Berlin and help form the new government. They have chosen to accompany me in death.

Head of the Party Chancellery Bormann will represent me in their stead. My decision is final. I have already made my will. Everything is left to the German people. The Reich expects nothing less.'

Hartelius's eyes flickered towards the leather suitcase. Was Hitler anticipating a round of applause? Hartelius knew that he needed to get everybody back on track and away from their Wagnerian *Ring des Nibelungen* fantasies, or he and Inge would be doomed along with the rest of the asylum inmates in the impending *Götterdämmerung*. 'Where are we to take the suitcase, Mein Führer?'

'The suitcase. Yes. This must be our number one priority.' Hitler took off his blue glasses and handed them to Bormann. Bormann inspected them for a moment and then began to clean them on the sleeve of his uniform. 'The sergeant major – I forget his name, the one you passed outside in the corridor – he will guide you back to your Storch. He has pistols for you both. Also a packed lunch and thermoses of coffee made by my butler. I'm not allocating you extra guards. That would simply draw attention to what you are doing.' Hitler took the glasses back from Bormann, checked that they were clean, and replaced them on his nose. 'You will take the suitcase and fly it to Gmund in Bavaria. There you will be met by my representative, Heinrich Rache.' He glanced at Bormann, who nodded. 'You know Rache, I believe?'

'Yes, Mein Führer. I met him before the war. Our parents are near neighbours.'

'Good. That will make things easier. This is why we have chosen you for this duty. You will hand Rache the suitcase. He will hand you a receipt.'

'Then what must we do?'

Hitler snorted. 'If it's still possible, save yourselves. Failing that...' He made a scything motion with his left hand. 'Swallow the pills.'

ELEVEN

Eberhard handed over the pistols unwillingly. But he had very little choice. The colonel had been told to expect them.

'Come, sir. We must press on. The Ivans are getting closer by the minute.'

'No, Sergeant Major. Stop. First I must change.' Inge halted just before the *Kannenberggang*. She rummaged in her holdall and brought out some overalls and a pair of Luftwaffe pilot's boots. 'Avert your gaze please, Sergeant Major.'

Eberhard did as he was told. But he didn't like it. He'd never in his life been ordered about by a woman. He muttered something under his breath. He could smell the colonel's wife from nearly two metres away. A mixture of perfume, woman and sex. He heard the whisper her dress made as she slipped it over her head. It sent another gust of scent in his direction. Eberhard desperately wanted to ease his crotch. But he didn't dare do it in front of the colonel – especially now that he'd been forced to arm the bastard. But somehow he'd have the stuck-up bitch. Somehow.

He glanced down at the suitcase the colonel was carrying. There was more in it than simply the document he had brought with him in the dead colonel's briefcase. It was filled with cash, no doubt. Swiss francs, probably. Maybe even gold. Bribery money. Why would the Führer send this pair of clowns out of Berlin for any other reason?

A plane. Money. A woman. Eberhard decided that he'd been gifted Christmas, Easter and New Year all in one.

'What are your specific orders concerning us, Sergeant Major?'

Ah. The colonel had been watching him, then? Eberhard straightened up. Pretending to obey whilst withholding his real character was second nature to him. 'To see you both onto your plane. Then to report back to the Führer.'

'Remember that. If I see you staring at this suitcase again, I will shoot you. For you, it doesn't exist.'

'No, sir. I didn't know where to place my eyes, sir. That was all it was.' So. His suspicions were confirmed. 'The colonel's wife, sir. She is ready.' And so are you, you Wehrmacht shit.

Eberhard led the way to the surface. Each step brought them nearer to the war. Explosions rocked the night. Firelight lit up the sky. Eberhard signalled to an SS soldier sheltering behind a pile of rubble. He made a cutting motion with his hand. The soldier nodded. His face looked grotesque in the half-light. He seemed half-starved.

'This way.' Eberhard led Hartelius and his wife into the night, his black uniform blending into the shadows. 'Stick close behind me. Go where I go. Do what I do. We are five hundred metres from the Brandenburg Gate. Your plane is due east of there.'

'I know very well where our plane is.'

'Good. Good. Then if anything happens to me you will be safe, sir.' Eberhard put all the emphasis he could on the word 'sir'. He grinned as he said it, knowing that neither of them could see his true expression in the darkness.

Halfway along the western border of the Tiergarten they came to a barricade manned by a detachment of six Hitler Youth. The oldest was perhaps fifteen years old. The youngest, ten. The boys' eyes widened when they saw the colonel's bars on Hartelius's collar.

'Is this way still open?'

The oldest boy nodded. He swallowed and tried to speak, but he had not had any water for eighteen hours, and his throat seized up on him. He began to cough.

A younger boy held up his hand as though he was still at school.

'Yes? What is it?'

'The Ivans. We've heard their women soldiers cut off our…' He ducked his head and looked towards his companions.

'What? What do they cut off?' Eberhard pushed forward.

The boys huddled together when they saw that Eberhard was SS.

'They won't cut anything off if you kill them first. That is my suggestion to you. Kill the enemy first. That is the secret to survival. You have your weapons. You have your orders. What else is there to discuss?'

Hartelius caught his wife's gaze. He rolled his eyes. He gave a marginal shake of the head as if to reassure her that this madness wasn't any of his doing. 'Sergeant Major. Can't we send these children back to their mothers?'

Eberhard's outraged look came straight from silent pictures. 'If they move from these positions, I will shoot them. Sir. They know this. They will do their duty. This will make their mothers proud. Sir.' Eberhard forged ahead as if the boys had already ceased to exist.

Hartelius shook his head again and followed his wife. As he passed the last of the boys he whispered, 'Get out of here when we're gone. All of you. Ditch your uniforms and go back home. Tell the others. That's an order.'

The boy stared back at him, naked fear in his eyes.

'A direct order. Do you hear me? Don't listen to that turd. I outrank him four times over. Go and see to your mother. She will need all the help she can get in the next few days. We have lost this war. The Ivans own Berlin now. Your duties here are over.'

Once, when the shelling approached too close for comfort, they were forced to hide in a bomb crater until the salvo diminished. Hartelius took his wife's hand. He pressed both the cyanide tablets into it. 'These are in case anything happens to me or the plane. Think of them as backup. The Ivans are going to behave like ravening beasts when they break through. No one will be safe from them. No one.'

Eberhard was trying to eavesdrop on their conversation, but Hartelius didn't care. A feeling of impending doom was overwhelming him. He felt like a man reaching the end of a long journey whose destination he neither knew nor cared about. A pointless journey that had been sprung on him as the result of a practical joke.

When he first saw the Fieseler Storch standing on the concrete sidings of the Charlottenburger Chaussee, Hartelius thought that he was seeing a mirage. How could this possibly be? How could the discipline needed to maintain a plane in satisfactory condition have been upheld in a hellhole such as this? How come no one had made off with it in the seemingly endless fourteen hours since they had landed? How come it hadn't been struck by a mortar or an incoming shell? Set alight by phosphorous? Broken up for spare parts?

'You are lucky,' said Eberhard.

'I know we are.'

'No. I mean you are lucky that nobody around here knows how to fly. How long do you think your precious Storch would have lasted, then?' Eberhard showed his pass to the head of the SS detachment guarding the plane. The man snapped out a Hitler salute when he saw the Führer's personal seal.

'Now we get on board.'

'We?'

'Yes. We.'

'But you told me the Führer ordered you to see us safely into the air and then report straight back to him.'

'That's what I was told to say. This was a test of your loyalty. I am in fact ordered to come with you. To guard you until you reach your destination.'

Inge von Hartelius stepped forward. She was frowning. This was her plane. She was its captain. Not this SS worm. As a test pilot, she was used to dealing with men who were her inferiors in rank.

'You can see the size of the cabin, Sergeant Major. Look at it. Three of us will not fit in. Our maximum take-off weight is 1325 kilograms. It will be impossible to lift off with both you and the overload tanks on board. The landing strip is too short. We will need more than the usual hundred feet to get into the air. Not to mention the utter waste of fuel.'

'But still. You will do it, Freifrau. These are the orders of the Führer. Somehow you will take off. Somehow you will get us to our destination.'

Inge stared at her husband.

Hartelius gave a brief inclination of the head. The men guarding the plane were SS, not Wehrmacht. They would obey Eberhard, not him. Now was not the time to make a fuss, he told Inge with his eyes. Once safely in the air, he would use his pistol on Eberhard. Knock him out. Inge could land in a field somewhere and they could dump him. Save fuel that way. The bastard could look after himself from then on in. They would probably be doing him a favour.

Eberhard caught the look that passed between them. He twitched the barrel of his Schmeisser. Better to be hanged for a sheep as for a lamb. 'You will hand me your pistols. Now.'

'What?'

'You will no longer need them once we are in the air. They will simply weigh you down. They will be safer in my care.'

The three men of the SS detachment guarding the plane snapped to attention when they saw what their sergeant major intended. They, too, were cradling Schmeissers. As far as they were concerned, a Wehrmacht colonel had about as much clout with them as a Russian commissar. An SS sergeant major was another beast entirely. They would obey him without question. And to the death.

Hartelius drew his pistol from his holster and handed it to Eberhard. Inge slipped the Luger from the specially made pouch in her flying jacket and did the same.

'Thank you. Now I get in first. The colonel and I will share the twin passenger seats behind you. This way I can better protect the plane. You may have your pistols back when we land in Bavaria. You have only to ask.'

Eberhard ducked under the struts and swung himself up into the cockpit. The plane creaked on its hinges. Inge and Johannes von Hartelius followed.

Inge strapped herself into the pilot's seat. She leant out of the staggered door and addressed one of the SS guards. 'No one has tampered with this plane?'

'No, Frau Flugkapitän. We did exactly as you requested when you landed. Both wingroot tanks have been filled to the brim with fuel – seventy-four litres in each. We have also filled the self-sealing overload fuel tank under the fuselage with a further three hundred litres. We brought the fuel in by hand, twenty litres at a time. Two of our men were killed doing it.'

'I am sorry. You have all been very brave. The Führer is proud of you.'

The guard acknowledged her words with a brief inclination of the head. 'Using the details you gave me, I have calculated that you will have a potential range of between eight hundred and one thousand kilometres, if you fly at no more than four thousand metres altitude and at a steady speed of circa one hundred and thirty kilometres per hour. No one has been inside the cockpit or tampered with the luggage compartment in your absence. Whatever you brought in with you is still safe. Just as you requested, Frau Flugkapitän.'

Inge wanted to weep for all the doomed and indoctrinated young men who were so earnestly defending what remained of her country. Instead she slipped on her leather flying helmet and goggles and gave a curt signal with her hand. 'Fold down the wings.'

The SS guards did as she asked.

'Now prep the engine by turning the propeller six times anticlockwise. Slowly. Then circle the fuselage and check all the flaps manually for freedom of movement.'

The soldiers split off into units and ran to obey her.

'It is done, Frau Flugkapitän.'

Inge glanced at Eberhard. 'If you didn't insist on coming with us, we could manage an almost vertical take-off. As it is we shall have to launch ourselves over the Russian lines. This is an absurd extra risk, Sergeant Major. I beg you to reconsider.'

'Then order your husband off the plane. That would lighten us up considerably.'

Inge turned back to her instruments. 'He is the reason we

are making this flight, Sergeant Major. Not you. You know that very well. He stays on, or I don't fly.'

'As you wish, Freifrau. You have a machine gun in the nose, don't you? Use that on the Ivans.'

'No. There is nothing in the nose beyond the propeller. The MG 15 is usually behind you. On a swivel. It was taken off in order to lighten the plane. It may have escaped your notice, but I am a test pilot, Sergeant Major, not a fighter pilot. Women in the Third Reich are not permitted to fly on combat missions. Although you wouldn't know it to look at me now.' Inge laughed and flipped the electric starter. The Storch burst into clattering life. 'I suggest you view this plane as a woman, Sergeant Major. You can hit her, but she cannot strike you back. But I am sure that, given the particular qualities you have demonstrated to us on the way out here, you have encountered such a situation already in your life?'

Now that she was in charge of her plane again, Inge was feeling the first clear return of hope. She had seen her son Johannes's Max and Moritz marionettes dangling from the control stick and knew that all was well.

'Take away the chocks.'

'They are clear, Frau Flugkapitän.'

Inge pulled back the throttle and the Fieseler Storch surged forward. She knew the plane intimately. She had been exaggerating when she had told the sergeant major that they would have to encroach over the Russian front line in order to take off. If she couldn't take off within a hundred feet, and pretty much vertically, she didn't deserve to be called a pilot.

The moment the Storch was fifty feet off the ground and rising, Inge swung the plane away from the flak towers and north across the Spree River towards the Moabit District, which she had been assured was still held by forces loyal to the Führer. One thing she knew for a fact: the southerly Tempelhof Airfield had been taken by the Russians on 24 April, and the even more southerly Schönefeld had fallen on 22 April. Both had originally been mooted as possible landing points for the Storch and been as quickly discarded. Travel in that direction and she would be shot down by low-flying Soviet P-39 Kobrushkas. At least this way they would have an outside chance of catching the Ivans napping. Who, after all, would be expecting any more German planes out of Berlin at this late stage in the game? And at night?

The ruins of Berlin opened out below them. The whole city seemed on fire. Little was left to the imagination thanks to the outstanding all-round visibility from the Storch cabin. Buildings burnt, or cast great shadows across other bomb-damaged skeletons of buildings. The fretwork of streets below them was thrown into even greater prominence by the retreat into rubble of the edifices and shop fronts that had once overlooked them. It seemed impossible that anyone or anything could still be living down there. The place was a wasteland.

Inge banked left in the direction of the Havel River. As she did so, languid tracers arced towards them, fizzing past the Storch's wing towers like streamers fired from a shotgun. If just one round struck the overload fuel tank underneath the fuselage, the plane would brew up like a tank struck by a white phosphorous shell.

'My God.' Eberhard was gazing out of the window, his eyes wide with shock. 'This is a tragedy beyond all imagining.'

Hartelius, who had already seen the devastation on the flight in, gazed fixedly at Eberhard. When the sergeant major bent forward to obtain a better view of the carnage, he struck.

But Eberhard was a street fighter and a former SS boxing champion. It had been Eberhard's prowess in the ring, rather than any intellectual acumen or leadership skills, that had led to him being promoted master sergeant. And he had been fighting, in one way or another, ever since the invasion of Poland on 1 September 1939. He had been expecting Hartelius to make a move – even hoping for it.

As Hartelius attempted to ram Eberhard's head against the metal surround of the window, Eberhard raised the cocked Luger he had been surreptitiously concealing beneath his greatcoat and shot Hartelius through the neck. The shot severed Hartelius's spine and he died instantly.

Inge von Hartelius reacted from pure instinct. She swung the steel lunchbox containing the two vacuum flasks backwards over her seat. The lunchbox struck Eberhard on the temple. He fell to the floor of the aircraft and lay still. Inge hammered and hammered at his supine body with the lunchbox, but the position of her seat in relation to the seats behind her made any formal attempt at accuracy impossible. Every time she struck out at Eberhard she screamed her husband's name. But he did not answer.

The Storch dipped to one side and then swung back across its own wake in a jerky arc. Inge let the lunchbox fall. She knew that she had to regain control of the aeroplane or she would never get her husband to a hospital. The Storch had performed a near perfect semi-circle during the fracas and was now heading directly back towards the Charlottenburg flak towers. Another sixty seconds' flying time would see her and the plane ripped to shreds.

She levelled the Storch and took it down to just above roof height. For the next five minutes Inge flew by prayers and adrenalin alone, until she felt that they were safely out of the danger zone. Only then did she crane her head back over the seat and look down into the cabin's semi-darkness.

Hartelius lay in an impossible position, his head at right angles to his body. No one still living was capable of such an unfeasible contortion. Inge began to wail.

The next fifteen minutes were lost to her. Somehow she continued to fly the plane, but it was not through any effort of will. Speed and direction appeared to have no meaning for her. Tears and mucus flowed unchecked down her face. She was as unaware of her flight position as she was of the Russian soldiers below her, targeting the Storch with their rifles, submachine guns and, in one case, a plundered Panzerfaust.

Instinctively, intuitively, when Inge first caught sight of the moon reflecting off Schwielow Lake, muscle memory caused her to ease back on the control stick and gain a little height.

Five minutes passed, during which her hearing slowly returned. She ripped off her flying goggles and mopped at her face with her sleeve. When she could see properly again, she set her course along the luminous strip of the Havel River, which she knew would carry her eastwards towards the American lines. Rumour had it that the US Ninth Army had reached Tangermünde. That's where she would make for.

As a German woman, Inge knew that she could expect no mercy from the Russians. But the Americans were a different matter.

Now, with her husband dead, her country raped, and all her former allegiances null and void, Inge had nothing left to lose.

TWELVE

Eberhard regained consciousness just over an hour into the flight. This coincided exactly with the Storch's crossing of the Elbe River into US-held territory. Eberhard, however, was aware of little more than that they were still flying in the dark – that his vision had in some way been impaired – and that a significant amount of time had elapsed between his execution of Hartelius and his return to full awareness.

He lay still and endeavoured to work out just how badly he was injured. It would be pointless to rear up in search of his pistol only to find that his limbs were not functioning correctly – or that he wasn't able to see what he was looking for. The madwoman flying the Storch would hit him again with her metal lunchbox. And this he could not tolerate.

He needed the bitch alive, unfortunately, as he had not the remotest idea how to fly a plane by himself. Plus she was his now. He intended to take her at his leisure and inflict the maximum possible humiliation on her in the greatest possible time span. He might even fuck her on top of her dead husband's body. There. That would be something to see, now, wouldn't it?

The only thing Eberhard could not fathom about his condition was why he kept on hearing voices. Was he hallucinating? He began to probe around himself for the pistol. Slowly. Steadily. His fingers acting as feelers. It was an impossibility that the woman could have struggled across from the front seat whilst the Storch was still in motion and retrieved the weapon herself. The cabin was not designed for that sort of in-flight movement. Once the pilot was strapped into the bucket seat, that was the end of it – they were in there for the duration.

Eberhard muttered under his breath as he searched for the weapon on the cabin floor, but the muttering was lost in the Storch's engine clatter.

At one point during his fingertip search, Eberhard glanced up at Hartelius's dead body. The colonel's cadaver loomed over him like the Hindenburg Zeppelin. A bullseye, straight through the neck. Eberhard had participated in the execution of hundreds of men as part of an SS Einsatzgruppe in Russia, and he knew exactly how it needed to be done. The last thing you wanted was for your victim to come back at you when they had nothing left to lose. So if they weren't completely dead, you wanted them at the very least quadriplegic. So that your assistant could give them the *coup de grâce* without any slithering around on the victim's part.

Eberhard's hand closed gently around the barrel of the

Luger. He allowed his fingers to palpate it, as though he were measuring the firmness of his own penis.

Power. Weapons gave you power. All his life Eberhard had sought to exercise power over others, just as his father had exercised power over him. That was the only way you could keep the bastards off. The only way you could stop the nightmares from returning to haunt you. He remembered his victims tumbling into the waiting slit trench like an endless rank of dominoes. He remembered the buzz it gave him. The total sense of control. It had been the highlight of his life. The meaning of his life.

Eberhard jerked to his knees and wrenched himself upwards, using the back of the pilot's seat for leverage. What he saw when he straightened up stopped him dead.

Inge von Hartelius threw the Storch into a nosedive.

Eberhard was thrown backwards, the Luger skittering from his hand.

Incensed by her idiocy, and as good as blind, Eberhard lunged forward, using gravity as his aid. He got his hands round Inge's neck. He was screaming incoherently, no longer rational.

Inge tried to force his hands away from her throat, but Eberhard both outweighed and outmatched her. She kicked wildly at the rudder-control pedals in an attempt to gain some traction, but she was unable to break Eberhard's hold.

The Storch continued its nosedive.

Fifty feet from the ground, Inge managed to grab the joystick and wrench it backwards, forcing the plane into a vertical stall. It banked sideways, and then began to helicopter down, turning onto its side at the very last moment and ploughing into a field of corn.

Inge and Eberhard were catapulted through the windscreen. Inge was decapitated by the final turn of the propeller; Eberhard was speared through the chest by the port-side wing strut, which had shattered on landing.

Two and a half hours later, when a group of American GIs located the burnt-out wreckage, all they found alive was a six-year-old boy with a badly broken arm and three shattered ribs. He was clutching a battered leather suitcase and a set of Max and Moritz marionettes to his chest. The boy kept repeating that his name was Johannes von Hartelius, and that his mother and father were on the plane.

When one of the GIs made as if to lead the boy away, the boy refused to let go of either the suitcase or the marionettes. He kept on repeating his name – Johannes von Hartelius – just as his mother had told him he must do if he ever became separated from her.

The GI shook his head and let the boy keep the suitcase and the puppets. What the hell? He had seen the bodies in and around the wreckage. The boy's escape, with so little obvious injury, was nothing short of a miracle. His parents and their mystery companion were no longer recognizable as human beings – the three of them had been fried when the overload tanks blew. All that remained to show that they had once been alive was a shattered wristwatch and a barely functioning Luger, shy one bullet, that had somehow been thrown clear. The rest was ashes.

'Johannes von Hartelius, Johannes von Hartelius,' cried the boy.

The GI pretended to cuff him round the ear. 'From now on, son, you speak English. We're through with this Johannes von Hartelius shit. I got a new name for you.' The GI hesitated. 'James. Not Johannes. James. James Hart. Now how about that? That's close enough, isn't it? That's not so hard to remember?' The GI pointed to his chest. 'My name is Abe. Abe Mann. A good American name, see? None of this foreign garbage I been telling you about.'

THIRTEEN

Calle de Chipilapa,
Antigua, Guatemala

19 JULY 2012

James Hart's house was surrounded on all sides by churches.
San Pedro. Santa Clara. San Francisco. La Concepción. The
house itself sat back a little from the road, as if it had broken
ranks from the other houses and decided to go its own way.
John Hart approached it through an untended garden, under
an unruly trellis of dog roses, tiger flowers and Heliconias.

Hart had flown in that morning via Miami to Guatemala
City, and then taken the forty-minute cab ride on to Antigua.
The difference between the two places was stark. Guatemala
City was modern, grimy and lovelorn, whilst colonial Antigua
seemed a throwback to a gentler, more idealistic age of faith,
calm and spirituality. Hart could see why his father had chosen
it. But why, in that case, had he felt the need to change his
name to the quasi-iconoclastic Roger Pope? In a city which
was home to the most frenzied Holy Week celebrations in all
the Americas? And in a house surrounded by churches? It just
didn't make sense.

No one answered the door when Hart knocked. And there was no possible way round the house. Hart retreated a few paces and stared up at the frontage, trying to discern signs of life through the partially shuttered windows. He had telephoned ahead a number of times, but on each occasion he had been met by an engaged tone. Was this some gigantic con trick, he wondered? His father's idea of a practical joke? You don't see your son for thirty-six years, and then you call him out of the blue and invite him out on a wild goose chase to the other side of the world whilst you leave for a holiday in Europe, from where you summoned him in the first place? A post-Freudian variation on the game of vice versa, perhaps?

Hart stepped out into the street. The house on the right had been turned into a Casa de Huespedes for tourists – he could see people taking coffee in the morning room and preparing for their day's sightseeing. The house on the left was still a private dwelling, however. He knocked on the door. An old woman answered. Before he had time to utter a word she pointed her fist at him and burst out laughing.

'Ah. *El hijo del* Señor Pope.'

Hart summoned up his best schoolboy Spanish. 'Yes. I am Señor Pope's son. Is it so obvious?'

'Oh, yes. There is no mistaking. He is expecting you.'

'Could you please speak slower?'

'He is expecting your visit. He knows you are coming.'

'He asked me to come, yes. But he is not answering his door.'

'But I have seen him.' The old woman thought for a moment. 'Yesterday. He was with a friend. A close friend.

They entered the house arm-in-arm. This was in the morning. Since then, no sign.'

'I'll try once again then, shall I? He may be having a siesta.'

'This is possible. He is an elderly man. Though not nearly so old as I. I shall come with you, Señor Pope, if you will allow. There is a spare key. I know where it is hidden.'

Hart accompanied the old woman back to his father's house. When they reached the front door she stretched out her hands and shrugged. They were paralysed with arthritis. Hart inclined his head. He knocked five times. They waited. There was no answer.

'The spare key is here.' The old woman pointed downwards, using her hand and arm in concert, as if they were fused. 'My daughter cleans for Señor Pope once a week. She also does his laundry and cooks when he has guests. But most of the time he…' She stopped, looking forlorn.

'He what?'

'The key is under the stone, Señor. See? I cannot pick it. Please raise it yourself.'

Hart lifted the stone and retrieved the key. 'Are you sure he won't mind me entering the house without his permission?'

'You are his son. Why should he mind?'

'I am his son. Yes. But we have never spoken to one another.'

'I am sorry?'

'We don't know each other, Señora. My father left home when I was three years old. I celebrated my thirty-ninth birthday three months ago. I am thirty-nine years old, Señora.' Hart thumped his chest like a child. He was astonished to find

86

himself on the verge of tears. 'This is the first occasion he has been in contact with me in all that time.'

'*Dios mio*. And still you came?'

Hart could see the pistol pointing at his head in the square at Homs. He could hear the click of the trigger as it fell on an empty chamber. Twice this had happened. Twice someone had tried to kill him and failed. What else did he have to do with his life but afford his errant father the courtesy of a hearing? For what other purpose had God decided to spare him? He didn't have a wife. His mother was in the early stages of Alzheimer's. And the woman who had aborted his child, and whose life he had just saved, was more interested in where her next scoop was coming from than in maintaining any sort of a relationship with a washed-out photojournalist with a death wish.

'Yes. Still I came.'

Hart turned the key in the lock and entered the building. The stench was overwhelming. It made his eyes smart and his gorge clench in panic. It was an odour he was entirely familiar with. The odour of death and decomposition.

Hart crooked his forearm across his mouth. 'Señora. Please wait outside.'

The old lady crossed herself. But still she came on in.

Hart's ears were hissing with tension. It felt as if his head was being stuffed full of cotton wool and chloroform. He threw open the door to the first room and looked inside.

The old lady swept past him and down the corridor. She knew exactly where she was going. The pervasive stench

87

didn't seem to bother her at all. 'Come, Señor Pope. Come with me. This is your father's room. This is where he will be. This is where he always comes.'

She led Hart towards the far end of the house. She stepped back from a door and bade him enter, almost formally, as if she was already familiar with what might lie on the other side. But her eyes belied her certainty.

Hart hesitated. He felt like a drunken man on the lip of a precipice. One false step and he would pitch forward into boundless space and be lost for eternity.

He turned the handle of the door and allowed it to swing open ahead of him. He was sweating, and his heart was pulsing inside his chest. The room was in intense gloom. Hart tried the light switch. Nothing. He could hear the buzzing of a thousand angry flies in the darkness.

Hart clamped a handkerchief to his nose. He felt his way towards the solitary crack of light that was revealing itself via an interior shutter. The room had no access at all to the outside world. The interior shutter simply opened into another, marginally more enlightened, room. Hart tripped the latch and threw the slats aside.

The old woman let out a stifled groan and began to pray.

Hart turned round.

His father was nailed to the wall, stark naked, in the style of the crucifixion.

FOURTEEN

It took Hart a little less than twenty-four hours to arrange for the funeral and secure the release of his father's body from the authorities. The local police made a desultory search of the premises, and the chief faithfully promised Hart that they would hunt down his father's killers and bring them to justice, but that, if Hart were to ask his personal opinion, he would have to tell him that he believed the killers had come in from outside the country and had returned home the same way. They were probably Mexican. Or maybe from Honduras. Or possibly even El Salvador. Guatemalan criminals, in his experience, did not use the symbol of the crucifixion when they conducted their killings, as this would show a lack of proper respect.

When Hart asked him why, if the killing had been conducted by criminals, nothing was missing from the house – a fact attested to by the old lady's daughter, Eva, who regularly cleaned there – the chief suggested that Señor Pope may have been involved in drug-trafficking activities into the USA, and that this was an honour killing. That the assassins were not after plunder but revenge.

'Have you any proof of that?' said Hart.

'It is a supposition only. But if true, it will lead to the requisition of Señor Pope's house by the authorities and a fire sale of all its contents.' The chief flashed Hart a grin from beneath his Zapata moustache. It was a sad comment on life, the grin seemed to be saying, but everyone – even luminaries such as he – must at some point acknowledge existential reality. 'Is this a direction in which you wish to go, Señor Pope?'

Hart steeled himself for the formality of the lie he knew that he must utter. 'Absolutely not. I agree with you about the fact that my father was undoubtedly killed by outside elements. That is self-evident. I am sure the police department will do its utmost to find the killer and secure a conviction. Thank you, Chief. Thank you for your courtesy in this matter. It is much appreciated.'

Hart and the chief of police shook hands. Hart left the building.

Hart had been dealing with corrupt officials and unprincipled servants of the state for most of his working life, and he knew when he was facing a brick wall. The best thing to do on these occasions was to make a graceful retreat without drawing too much attention to oneself in the process.

He was in a country he neither knew nor understood. A country in which the murder rate, at forty-six per hundred thousand, was twice as high as Mexico's. A country in which nearly half the children – most of whom spoke only Mayan and benefited, if that was the word, from less than four years of schooling – were chronically undernourished, and via which 350 tonnes of cocaine passed through to the US every year. A country in which the Zetas, Gulf and Sinaloa drug cartels were taking a significant interest. A wide-open country in which crimes went unpunished and in which heads were turned in whatever direction was the most profitable and the least amenable to risk. In this way it was like ninety-five per cent of the other countries that Hart visited professionally, and he felt curiously at home. He would have had less of a grasp of the situation in federal Germany or metropolitan France, where graft, jobbery and official corruption took on more subtle colorations.

He returned to his father's house. Eva had taken it upon herself to clean up what she too called 'Señor Pope's special room' after the mess left by the police and the paramedics, an act which struck Hart as above and beyond the call of duty. But the Maya, as he had learnt from her and her mother, accepted death as quotidian. Even violent death. The dead were of our world, not beyond it – they deserved consideration, not exclusion. They deserved respect.

Hart forced his eyes upwards. The marks of his father's crucifixion were still visible on the wall; only drastic redecoration would mask them. The room reeked of fly spray, bleach and insect repellent. If his father had left any odour in the room at all during his life – cigars, good whisky, medication even – it was no longer apparent.

Hart sat down in his father's library chair and lowered his eyes. A profound emptiness overwhelmed him – a deep sense of the hopelessness and futility of all human endeavour. In the entirety of his life Hart had never consciously spoken a word to his father. He'd no doubt gooed and gaahed and gagaahed at him as an infant, and maybe stuttered out the occasional 'dada', but he had no single memory of the man, nor any key to his nature or to his identity. And yet here he was, sitting in his father's study, close to tears.

Hart looked at his watch. Two o'clock. The funeral was scheduled for three. He forced himself up and into action. He had set himself the task of going through all his father's things, and he was now at the penultimate stage in which lateral thought was being called for. He had already checked every conceivable cupboard, wardrobe and storage box throughout the house. Now he would search along the tops and bottoms of things in case anything had evaded his eye during the first few sweeps.

It took him forty-five minutes to locate the photograph. It was taped beneath a drawer in his father's desk – and relatively recently, for the Scotch was still fresh. The photograph had been cut from a book, as the black-and-white image bore a printed description beneath it and was blank on the back, as if it might have formed the frontispiece to something, rather than figuring within the double-sided bulk of the main illustrations. Hart upended the drawer and leant over to investigate the image.

It was of two people: a man and a woman. The woman was in her early thirties, the man perhaps a little older –

possibly Hart's age. The woman was wearing a white flying suit, which must have been designed and cut especially for her, as it had a fox-fur collar that no male pilot would have tolerated for an instant. The woman had taken off her flying helmet and goggles and was squinting at the camera, one hand pushing back her blonde hair, as though the photographer had snapped her a split second before she was quite ready to be photographed.

The man standing beside her was dressed in the uniform of a senior officer in the wartime German Wehrmacht. He, too, was looking directly at the camera. His visor hat was pushed well back from his forehead, revealing a widow's peak of pale-coloured hair, suggesting that the photograph had been taken whilst he was nominally off duty. The logo, in English, read: 'Wartime Luftwaffe test pilot Inge von Hartelius and her husband, Johannes, posing in front of the Messerschmitt 262A in which she first broke the sound barrier.'

Hart's hand rode automatically to his hairline and touched his own widow's peak. It was an entirely pointless gesture. The evidence was laid out in front of him. He and the Wehrmacht officer might have been identical twins.

FIFTEEN

Hart was barely aware of the funeral service. It was at the old woman's insistence that he had finally agreed that she and her daughter might contact the local priest and arrange for a Mass, following her repeated assurances that his father was, on paper at least, still a Catholic. He also gave her permission to invite along any of his father's friends who might care to swell the congregation. Nobody turned up. It was at this point that the old woman had tried to persuade Hart to consent to a *novenario*, which she explained was a sequence of nine daily memorial services that traditionally followed the inhumation, and which were crucial to the safe and speedy arrival of the defunct in heaven.

Hart had thrown up his hands in horror. 'This is absurd. I believe in God, not in what people have made of him. I'm not going to sit in a strange church for nine days, all alone, mourning a man I've never met via a series of rites I don't believe in. It simply doesn't...' he had hesitated, fearful of alienating his only ally in Guatemala even further … 'punch my ticket.'

Hart had privately convinced himself by now that his father had been assassinated by rogue elements of the local Catholic Church, incensed at his choice of a pseudonym that implied the Pope be shafted. Who else would mimic the crucifixion to the extent, even, of mirroring the spear thrust in Jesus's side, midway between the fourth and the fifth ribs? Failing that, maybe someone had uncovered the fact that his father was originally German and had taken revenge on him for some alleged atrocity his grandfather had committed during the war?

That idea was so far-fetched that Hart discarded it out of hand. His grandfather had been Wehrmacht, not SS – that much was clear from the photograph. And people didn't revenge themselves on the children of people who behaved badly towards them but on the people themselves. And anyway, the American continent was stuffed full of the descendants of former Nazis. The place would have become a bloodbath long ago. No. Here in Latin America people were killed because of drugs, money, religion, politics or sex. Nothing else counted. And certainly not the Second World War, which had avoided the place entirely.

Hart was gradually coming to terms with the fact that he would probably never find out who killed his father, and that all he would derive from the whole benighted trip was that he wasn't quite the half-English, half-American straight-down-the-liner he had thought he was – in fact, he wasn't

95

American at all. He wondered if his mother had known about his father's German background when she married him? He decided probably not, as his mother was an honest being and would undoubtedly have told him. Now, given her condition, he would never know for sure.

Hartelius? Johannes and Inge von Hartelius? The names made perfect sense, Hart supposed, given his own variation on the theme. Johannes von Hartelius to James Hart to John Hart in three generations. He couldn't see himself using the von Hartelius name, however, tempting as it might be to style himself as a wannabe German aristocrat in order to wrong-foot some of his more irritating colleagues. He'd been John Hart for nearly forty years now and it suited him. Plus he couldn't speak German and knew next to nothing about the country and its history. It was odd, though, to realize how much cultural preconceptions dominated one's life, when, in reality, it was genetic predetermination that probably ruled the roost. The males in the von Hartelius family were clearly prepotent. Peas in a pod. Each one looked like the other regardless of who the mother was. It was one of nature's object lessons, and it had just reared up and stung him in the eye.

Hart walked into the hotel bathroom and stared at his face in the mirror. Yes. He could pass as a German at a pinch. But then he could pass as an American, or as an Englishman, or as a Dutchman, or as an Australian as well, if called upon to do so. So what significance beyond the mildly intriguing did his father's ancestry hold for him? Probably none at all.

Hart was on his way out to an early dinner when the shakes overwhelmed him. The movements were so convulsive, and so far beyond his ability to control them, that he was forced to sit down on the edge of the pavement or risk collapsing.

Hart had never experienced anything quite like it. Not even following his first major bombardment in Sarajevo, when he had found himself subject to tremors and half-tremors and soarings and swoopings of the stomach for what had seemed like days, but which were probably only hours. Or even minutes. For normal time seemed to have eluded him in the aftermath of the bombing.

This time the shaking was largely confined to his hands, arms and upper body. Hart hugged himself as tightly as he was able, but the juddering would not stop. Sweat poured down his face and back, drenching his shirt and trousers. His teeth began chattering, and he was forced to clamp his mouth shut with one dancing hand or risk a splintered tooth.

Hart wondered for a moment whether he wasn't having a recurrence of the malaria he had once contracted during the bush war in Sierra Leone, after he had managed to mislay his chloroquine in a spate ditch, but he soon discarded the idea. He was far too war-wise not to recognize the signs of post-traumatic stress. He had seen it in others many times and had pitied them for it, whilst still going on to plunder their images for his camera. Now he, too, was a victim of the syndrome. It was an object lesson in humility.

Hart hunched forward and tried to overcome the shaking by a process of rationality. The whole thing was hardly surprising, he told himself. A pistol had been aimed – first at his body and then at his head – and two botched shots had been fired. Shots that he had been convinced, in his essential being, would kill him. He had wilfully ignored the after-effects of these and had travelled halfway across the world only to find his father crucified, stark naked, on the wall of his study. What had he expected? That he would be able to soldier on with his life as if nothing had happened?

Gradually – despite the shaking and juddering that was inhabiting his body – Hart became aware that he was being watched. A woman was staring at him from the far corner of the square. She was sitting on a bench, her legs zigzagged beneath her. When it became clear that he had seen her, she started up from her place and headed towards him. Hart's fevered imagination came up with a picture of a dog that has been forced to sit for too long and has finally resolved to anticipate its master's command to come to heel.

The woman approaching him was around fifty years old, of Maya descent. She did not wear the traditional floor-length *huipil*, however, and neither did she have a head covering of any sort, but instead she wore a Western-style dress of a black silk material, set off by a black jade necklace of a strange geometrical design, with gold and coral inlays. Her manner of walking, too, was at once elegant and knowing, as if, long ago, she had made a study of its effect and was no longer able or willing to shake off the habits of youth.

If she had been younger, Hart might have assumed that she was a streetwalker, on the lookout for evening trade – in

Central America, the *zocalo*, or central square, was where such women often approached you. But this lady was no streetwalker. Maybe she had seen him collapse onto the kerb and was concerned for his welfare? But Hart doubted it. There was intent in her walk.

He rose, meaning to give her the slip, but his legs gave out on him at the halfway point and he lurched backwards onto the kerb in a muddle of arms and legs. He put out a warding hand to slow her down. 'I'm fine, Señora. Absolutely fine. I've had a little too much to drink, that's all. I'll be right as rain in a minute.' Hart realized that he was babbling to the stranger in English.

The woman halted two yards from where he sat. She, too, replied in English. 'You must come with me, Mr Hart. My name is Colel Cimi. There are things you should know about your father. Things that only I can tell you.'

Her English was American-accented and oddly imprecise, as if she was being forced to act as both speaker and interpreter for want of an assistant. Hart suspected that she had once been fluent in the language but had fallen out of the habit of speaking it. He tried to gauge the expression on her face but failed.

'Why should I come with you? You're a total stranger to me. And what should I know about my father?'

Colel Cimi fluttered her hand. A 1972 Lincoln Continental glided towards her from a distant part of the square. The car shone with a combination of Turtle Wax and four decades of elbow grease. The premium-grade whitewalls rumbled over the cobbles. The burnished trim gleamed in the reflection of the streetlamps. The chrome glistened like shot silk.

'And how do you know my real name? Tell me that? How do you know I'm not called Pope? I've told no one that here. I've just let them make their own assumptions.' Hart realized that he was sounding petulant and needy, like a fatally compromised man in a street brawl trying to act tough.

The Lincoln drew up behind Colel Cimi and its driver got out. He was wearing a white Guayabera shirt and a simple pair of dark trousers, not the chauffeur's uniform, peaked cap and polished boots Hart might have expected given the immaculate condition of the car. He held the rear door open, his expression indicating that he didn't much care whether Hart got in or not.

Hart allowed Colel Cimi to help him to his feet. He was shaking like a man with the ague and was thus far too weak, or so he now managed to persuade himself, to effectively resist her ministrations. The truth was that he found her presence – and her offer of unfolding secrets relating to his father's life – tantalizing.

Hart sank back onto the rich burgundy leather seats. Despite the twitches and jerks emanating from his central core, Hart's photographer's eye noted that the seat covers were not original but had been installed at some later date. As had the leather on the dashboard console and the French polished walnut inlays. Money had been lavished on this car.

The chauffeur reached across and tucked a blanket, patterned with geometric Maya designs, around Hart's legs. It, too, was a work of art.

Hart noted that Colel Cimi did not help tuck him in. Maybe she thinks that what I have is catching, he told himself. Or maybe she lacks the maternal touch? There was something about the woman that was as icy cold and polished as the black jade pendant that she wore around her preternaturally elegant neck.

The car started out of town. Hart decided that he no longer cared what happened to him. Kidnap? Extortion? Murder? It was all the same in the end.

His shakes were getting worse. He began to pitch and buck against the seatback as if he were tackling Niagara Falls on a lilo.

'Take one of these, Mr Hart. It will calm you down.' Colel Cimi inclined towards him. In her hand was a pill and an open bottle of mineral water.

'No, thanks. I never take pills from strange women.'

'As you wish.'

Hart clutched his knees. He began cursing his runaway body. What was wrong with him? Had his system decided to take a nosedive after twenty years of accumulated tension? Or had the shock of his father's unexpected death finally flipped his off switch for good? He had a sudden image of himself as a drooling, juddering, straitjacketed zombie being forcibly sectioned inside an asylum for bewildered photojournalists.

'I'm okay, you know. Really. It's probably only a touch of malaria.'

'I thought you said you'd been drinking?'

'I lied. I wanted to put you off. I thought you were playing the Good Samaritan.'

'Hardly that.' She laughed. 'Hardly that.'

The rest of the journey was conducted – apart from the occasional litany of curses from Hart – in silence. By the time they drew up at the back of Colel Cimi's isolated ranch house, Hart's shivering was in temporary remission. He staggered out of the car with the blanket still wrapped around his shoulders. Despite the residual heat of the day, he felt chilled to the bone.

'You have sweated though your clothes, Mr Hart. Would you like to put on something of your father's? He was about the same size as you.'

'I'd rather not.'

'Ah. "I'd rather not." I recognize the quote. It is from Herman Melville's *Bartleby, The Scrivener*. One of your father's favourite stories.'

Hart stared at her in horror. 'I never knew my father, Señora Cimi. So I don't know what he read. I don't know if he went to the cinema or to the theatre. I don't know if he preferred dogs to cats. I don't know if he was gay or straight or bisexual. Preferred classical music or rock and roll. Not to put too fine a point on it, Señora, I know fuck all about my father, and even less about you. You could be the person who killed him for all I know. Or you could be an escaped nutter with a passion for pimpmobiles and for picking up stray gringos on whom you will later conduct grotesque experiments in a bid to give yourself eternal life. Why don't you tell me who you are and what you know about my father and let's be done with it.'

Colel Cimi laughed. Behind her the chauffeur rolled his eyes and pretended to clap his hands in polite applause.

'I was your father's mistress, Mr Hart. If that is the correct word for the condition of a paid concubine. I am certainly not his killer.'

'My father paid you for sex?'

'He bought me this house. Settled a monthly allowance on me. Gave me presents.' Her hand flicked towards her necklace. 'So, to all intents and purposes, yes, I was paid for sex. But it was more than that in reality. Much more.'

'Are you telling me you were in love with him?'

'No. How could I have been? He was twenty-five years older than me. He bought me from my father when I was fifteen.'

'Bought you?'

'Came to an understanding. Does that sound better? My family was very poor. And your father wanted a virgin. A person he could shape to his will.' She motioned Hart to a chair.

Hart sat down with a thump. He huddled forward in his blanket and stared at the woman in front of him as if she might at any moment burst from behind a curtain in yet another elusive guise. 'I suppose you're going to tell me next that the house in Antigua belongs to you as well? That it forms part of some grotesque bride price? And that I'd better not be getting any wrong ideas about inheriting the damned thing? Is that what this is all about?'

'No. The house belongs to you. You are James's only child. There are laws about such things. It is only proper.'

'You can take it, then. With my compliments. You can add it to your property portfolio. I don't want charity from a man I never knew. A man who didn't speak to me for thirty-six years. A man who bought virgins.'

'He loved you, Mr Hart. Your father thought the world of you.'

That silenced Hart for a moment. He tilted his head to one side like a cat listening for birdsong. 'He had a very curious way of showing it.'

'Still. He did. He followed your career. Got me to trawl the internet for mentions of your name. Endlessly planned on meeting you.'

'It was one heck of a meeting when he finally pulled it off. I'll give the old man that.'

Colel Cimi leant forward, her expression suddenly bereft. 'I would have come to the funeral. You believe that, don't you? I would have been there. But I am not liked by the Church. By decent people. Women like me are scorned in Guatemala. This is still a very Catholic country.'

'You weren't the only one not to attend. The congregation consisted of exactly three people. The woman who cleaned his house, her elderly mother, and me. Oh, and the priest. Who I had to pay sixty dollars for the use of his church, and who was pissed off that I wouldn't agree to a *novenario*.'

Colel Cimi gave another of her laughs. They were curious eruptions that sounded more like coughs than laughter. 'You and your father were more alike than you think. You were both prepared to pay to get the things that you want.'

Hart was not in the mood to cut either himself or his hostess any slack. 'Pay how? With the shakes? With what happened to me out there in the *zocalo*? Maybe that is payment of a sort, come to think of it.'

'For the shock of your father's death, you mean?'

'For surviving when I should have died. For using other people's grief as the fuel for my ambitions as a photojournalist. For the two empty chambers in the gun a complete stranger pointed at me a few days ago in Syria, which should have put paid to me for good. These shakes are probably God tapping me on the shoulder and saying, "Straighten up, John Hart. Get a grip."'

'You believe in God, then, Mr Hart?'

'I know God. I fear God. It's no longer a question of belief with me. It's way too extreme for that.'

'You are a lucky man.'

'No, I'm not. I'm cursed. Because I am utterly incapable of living a good life. God despises me. I despise myself.'

Colel Cimi got up. 'You may not have noticed, Mr Hart, but you have an erection. This is a sign that the shaking you have is malarial, and not due to PTSD or shot nerves. That it is simply a reminder of an illness that lurks in your bloodstream, and not a full-blown repeat attack. Trust me, Mr Hart. You must go to bed now. Santiago will show you the way. He will give you quinine and sleeping tablets. Tomorrow, when you are feeling better, we will have our talk.'

SIXTEEN

Hart slept for three days. On the first day the shakes came back again, harder than ever. He was half aware of Colel Cimi by his bedside, feeding him pills, urging him to drink. Sometimes it would be the driver, Santiago, who visited him. Who sat him up. Bathed him. The man was unexpectedly tender, despite his initial air of detachment, and Hart soon gave up struggling and allowed himself to be ministered to. Each time he pissed his piss came out the colour of black Camellia tea.

The second day was worse than the first. Hart knew that he must be running a fever, but beyond that fact lay nothing. No concept of time. No purpose. Just entropy.

On his third day of fever Hart woke to find himself lying in a cold bath with ice cubes floating in it.

'Can you stand up, Mr Hart?' Colel Cimi was proffering him a towelling bathrobe. 'You must try. I think the worst of the fever is over. We need to warm you. Quickly.'

Hart levered himself out of the bath, his knees cannoning together as if he were dancing the Charleston. When he glanced down at his newly emaciated body he realized that he had yet another one of his spasmodic erections. He ignored it. He and his hosts were way beyond embarrassment by now.

Colel Cimi enveloped him in the bathrobe. She called Santiago in from the corridor and the pair of them escorted Hart down the stairs and into a small room in which an open fire was burning.

'Sit here. You will soon be warm. Santiago will bring you something to eat.'

'Chicken soup? Isn't that what you feed people after they've been involved in train wrecks?'

'We have *menudo rojo* instead. Made from the tripe of the cow. We have been feeding it to you for three days, Mr Hart. Don't you remember?'

Hart's physical body might be in abeyance, but his mind seemed crystal clear. 'Three days? I've been here three days? You've got to be kidding me.'

'Three and a half days to be precise.'

Hart realized that there was no one in the world who gave a damn whether he lived or died – no one who would even notice that he had been out of circulation for eighty-four straight hours. Amira? On another assignment probably, busy burnishing her career. His mother? In a world of her own where no one could ever join her. His mute, prodigal father? Crucified by unknown parties before he had even been able to stutter out a first, tentative 'hello, son'. Hart decided that he had drifted through life for thirty-nine years without making any mark on it at all. He might as well have been a will-o'-the-wisp.

'Why are you doing this for me? Why are you and Santiago looking after me? My father is dead. You don't owe me anything. In fact, you've got no earthly connection with me at all. You could have dumped me back at the local hospital and still felt noble. Nobody would have blamed you. Nobody called you to book. I'd have been just another visiting gringo who got sick.'

'Listen to me, please, Mr Hart. Listen closely.' Colel Cimi held Hart's gaze with her own. For a split second Hart thought that she might be about to strike him, but she didn't. 'Your father is the only man I have ever known. He may have bought me from my own father, which is a bad thing, I agree, but from the outset he was good to me and gave me much freedom. Your father loved me very strongly. I would almost say he had a passion for me. He saw to it that I was properly educated. He never struck me. He never abused me. He waited until I was eighteen, and old enough to give my informed consent, before he took my virginity. We travelled everywhere together as a couple. He helped my village when times were bad, and protected us during the civil war. I owe him much. In Guatemala, women of my age and cultural background are usually dead by now. Or they are prostitutes. Or they've had ten children and their breasts sag to below their knees.' Colel Cimi made a cutting gesture with her hand, akin to a person shooing away a fly.

'And that's why you're looking after me? Because my father was kind to you and stopped your breasts from sagging? Why didn't he marry you, then? Tell me that. Why didn't he make an honest woman out of you if he loved you so much?'

Colel Cimi laid her hand on her chest. 'I know what you are trying to do, Mr Hart. You are lashing out at me because I have seen you at your weakest and most vulnerable. And because you are still angry at your father's memory. Angry, too, that he allowed himself to be killed before you were able to come to terms with him. But you need to understand something about your father. Something very important. Your father was a Catholic. As am I. And we Catholics marry only once. Your father believed that he was married to your mother in the sight of God – divorce was therefore out of the question for him. I accepted that. It was the least I could do for him.'

'So that's why you had no children?'

'We did have a child, Mr Hart. A daughter. She died of meningitis when she was seven years old.'

Hart stared at Colel Cimi. His face was bereft of colour. 'You and my father had a child together?'

'Yes.'

'You're telling me I had a sister? For seven years I had a sister, and no one thought to tell me?'

Colel Cimi closed her eyes in a God-give-me-patience kind of a way. 'I am telling you now, Mr Hart. Without being asked to. And without any need that I can see to provide you with this information.' She got up and walked to a table in the corner of the room. 'Here is a snapshot of your sister. She was called Carmen.' She handed Hart a framed photograph.

Hart glanced sheepishly at Colel Cimi. He had been unforgivably rude, he knew that now. She was a lady still in mourning for her lover and their only child, who had welcomed him into her house and seen him through a violent malarial flashback. She was also the lady his father had chosen to share his life with for more than thirty years, and he owed her a little respect. Added to that was the fact that she was his one remaining link to a past he was as yet unaware of, and she had offered, out of simple kindness, to share that with him. He was the one at fault here.

He accepted the photograph and looked at it for a very long time. Tears collected on his eyelashes and began to fall unheeded onto his cheeks. He handed the photograph back.

'She's so beautiful. My sister is so beautiful. She looks like you.'

Colel Cimi took the photograph from Hart's hands and inclined her head.

Hart began to sob – deep, wracking sobs that outwitted all his efforts to control them. He glanced at Colel Cimi in consternation and saw the echo of his own tears in her eyes. 'I'm sorry, Señora. I don't know what's come over me lately. I'm not usually this emotional. I'm not usually emotional at all.' Hart could scarcely get the words out.

Colel Cimi smiled at him. 'What is happening is that you are discovering truths about yourself and about your life, Mr Hart, that you never knew existed. This is a hard thing for any man to deal with. Much more so for somebody who has just survived their own near death. For a man such as you, who has been wound so tightly for so many years, the process must be overwhelming.'

Hart sank his head in his hands. 'I'm sorry for what I said just now and for the way that I said it. You have been more than generous to me. You deserve better.'

She reached forward and touched him lightly on the wrist. 'You look just like your father when you put your head in your hands like that. He would do the same when he wished to apologize to me. An infrequent occurrence, I have to admit. But there it is.' She sighed. 'You want to ask me something more, Mr Hart? I can see it in your face.'

'What else do you have to tell me, Señora? What other bombshells do you have in store? I think I'm ready now.'

Colel Cimi set the photograph tenderly back in its place. 'Oh, much, Mr Hart. I have much else to tell you.'

SEVENTEEN

Haus Walküre,
Bad Wiessee, Bavaria

21 JULY 2012

Elfriede 'Effi' Rache had blonde hair that cascaded to her shoulders in gentle waves. She had wide-apart blue eyes framed by a heart-shaped face, high cheekbones, and a cupids' bow of a mouth with a prominent underlip that gave her a slight air of childish obstinacy, as if, were you not to do her bidding, she might withhold both her approval and her favours until you did.

Udo Zirkeler – or 'Fat Udo' as he used to be called before he discovered the joys of competitive weightlifting – craved Effi's approval. He had just gone to considerable lengths to do her bidding, and now he was counting on some of those favours in return. Once, some months before, Effi had briefly allowed him into her bed, and the thought of her body, and her smell, and a particular trick she had of tightening her vagina when you least expected it, had driven him crazy with lust ever since. Not to mention the matching red underwear she had worn at the time and which Udo now pictured, with goatish certainty, nestling beneath her summer dress.

But after that all-too-brief sexual interlude, Effi had scarcely looked in his direction. This was why Udo had offered her his services with such alacrity when she had asked for a volunteer to travel to Central America and collect something crucial to the future of the *Lanzen Brüderschaft* – the Brotherhood of the Lance – whose leader, by de facto inheritance via her father and grandfather, Effi Rache was. Effi was a National Socialist blue blood – the equivalent, to all intents and purposes, of Nazi royalty – and Udo was in awe of her. To repeat the ecstasies he had achieved that one time in her bedroom was his highest aim in life. Which was exactly what Effi had intended when she let him fuck her.

When Effi admitted to Udo that the object she sought was the actual Holy Lance itself, mislaid for nearly seventy years, and just now waiting to be reclaimed by the Brotherhood and to serve once again as its talisman, Udo had recognized his chance to shine. Now Effi was holding the broken spear he had brought back from Guatemala – at considerable risk to himself – as though it was contaminated with dog shit.

'And this is it? This is the Holy Lance? You are sure?'

'Absolutely sure. This is the sacred object Johannes and Inge von Hartelius were transporting to your grandfather at the Führer's direct request when their plane was shot down. According to the version Pope gave me, his father was the first GI on the scene and simply snatched the case, thinking it was loot that he could sell on after the war. Papa Pope didn't speak German, however, and when he opened the case and found only a broken bit of spear and a sheaf of illegible papers, he shut it up again and buried it in his attic. Pope only received the thing, along with a mass of other stuff, on his father's death, aged ninety, back in January. Pope speaks a bit of German so he was able to make out your grandfather's name and address, together with the Führer's unbroken personal seal on the main envelope. He thought about it for a while, decided that what was past was past, trawled the internet for your grandfather's heirs, found out that the only heir left was you, and that you were living at the very same address that was on the covering letter, and got in touch. The rest is history.'

'And Pope was happy to volunteer all this to you, Udo? He didn't want anything in return? This American patriot was simply happy to restore the Holy Lance to its rightful Nazi owners and not sell it on eBay? Do you seriously expect me to swallow this truckload of manure you have transported me?'

'No.' Udo made a sour face. 'No, I don't expect you to swallow it. I'd much rather you swallowed something else, Effi.'

Effi Rache slapped him. 'My name is Elfriede. Either that or Fräulein Rache, depending on who is addressing me and in what context. Only my friends and my equals are allowed to call me Effi. And you are neither. You are merely an instrument for me to use when and how I see fit.'

Udo stared hard at her but he did not retaliate. He had taken the Führer Oath to obey whoever happened to be leading the Brotherhood at whatever time they happened to be doing the leading, and Elfriede Rache was, in consequence, his lawful superior by direct right of birth. Udo's family had served the Raches, and shared their politics, for close on a century. Obedience to a central organizing authority was so deeply ingrained in Udo's nature that not even sex and a hefty dose of misogyny could shake it. 'Pope wasn't happy to tell me anything. He played up from the beginning and pretended that he no longer knew what I was talking about. When I remonstrated with him, he tried to tell me that he was mentally ill and that he'd changed his mind and didn't want to hand over the Lance after all.'

'What did you do?'

'I changed his mind back for him.'

'How did you do this?'

'I have my ways.'

'Is he going to be a problem for us? This is what I need to know.'

'No. He's retired from public life. Permanently.'

'You mean you killed him?'

'Of course I killed him.'

'How?'

'I nailed him to the wall, questioned him, and then I killed him. With that, actually. With what you are holding in your hand. I whacked it in with a book. It wasn't easy. The thing has lost most of its edge over the years, but I still managed it. That's why it's got all that gore stuck to it. Just at the spot where you are holding it. You see? There.'

Effi didn't actually scream. But she did throw the Holy Lance onto the table beside her as if it had transformed itself into a centipede in her hand. 'Why did you do that? Why did you kill him that way?'

'I thought it would look like Pope was killed by fundamentalist Christians. Or maybe by some homosexual drug-crazed nutcase with a Christ fetish. I don't know. It was fun. It seemed like a good idea at the time.'

'You cretin. You utter imbecile.'

'I'm not an imbecile. And I'm not a cretin. In fact, I'm not even Fat Udo any more, as you might remember if you cared to think back to a few months ago, when you allowed me, ever so briefly, inside your knickers. I did exactly what you asked of me, Effi Rache. I got you the Holy Lance. I got you the papers. Thanks to me you now hold in your hands exactly what the Führer intended for your grandfather sixty-seven years ago. What did you think I would do when you sent me out there? Offer the man a pension? I was in Guatemala, not Luxembourg. Do you expect the local police to throw up their hands in panic and call in Interpol? The per capita murder rate in Guatemala is worse than in Mexico, and the clean-up rate is maybe a tenth of one per cent. They'll bury it, and bury it deep. Anyway, I needed the practice. Murders in Germany are far too risky these days. And I must keep my hand in. As we both know only too well.'

Effi closed her eyes. She recognized Udo Zirkeler for exactly what he was. A foot soldier. A useful robot. The contemporary equivalent of a not very intelligent master sergeant in one of her grandfather's SS Einsatzgruppen units. Udo was someone who loved killing for killing's sake. He was the modern-day equivalent of the young man who had beaten fifty people to death with an iron crowbar in Kaunas, Lithuania, on 25 June 1941, at her grandfather's bemused instigation, and who had then sat down and played the Lithuanian national anthem on his accordion for the further edification of his cheering audience.

Effi knew that she had made a catastrophic mistake in ever allowing Zirkeler into her bed. She had hoped that the brief act would cement his dedication to her. When in fact all she had succeeded in doing was to drive him wild with lust and guarantee that he would dog her everywhere she went in a single-minded desire to repeat the exercise. Now she felt compelled to use every excuse she could to send him away and keep him separate from the conventional, political wing of the Brotherhood. Men like Zirkeler were necessary fifth columnists if one ever wished to attain real power – but it was a clear case of lighting the touch paper and standing well back. She ran him, yes. But she was also afraid of him.

'And what about the mistress?' Effi said.

'What mistress?'

'The mistress Pope has been living with for the past thirty years.'

Udo made a face. 'There is no mistress. He lived alone. I went through his belongings with a toothcomb. There were no women's clothes in any of his cupboards. Not even a hairbrush.'

'They have another house. A ranch. He keeps her safely out of town.'

Udo threw his head back in a movement he had learnt from watching endless film clips of Benito Mussolini. 'How do you know this?'

'Because I asked one of our people in Guatemala to check up on any comeback we might receive thanks to your morbid enthusiasm for high theatre. They came up with this.'

'So you knew I'd crucified him all along? You were simply playing with me? Pretending to ask me questions to which you already knew the answers?'

Effi picked up a paper knife from the table beside her and held it a few centimetres away from Udo's right eye. 'You can function equally well with only one eye. I am this close –' she pricked the bridge of his nose with the point – 'from pushing it all the way in.'

The smile froze on Udo's face, but he refused to move. He was in the grip of two conflicting, though equally powerful, emotions. One side of him recognized that he might, after all, have gone a little too far in crucifying the man in Guatemala, and that Effi might have a point in being irritated with him. The other side was filled with admiration at her boldness in standing up to him. He was nearly a foot taller than her and outweighed her by at least sixty kilograms – which meant that he could break her neck with one sweep of his hand if he wanted to. But he didn't want to. This was a woman worth following to hell and back. A woman who acted without compunction. A woman after his own heart.

Udo felt an overwhelming testosterone surge – the sort of rush he usually only felt when he was beating up on somebody, or imposing his will on them in some way. If Effi hadn't been who she was – and been related to who she was related to – he would have raped her there and then, and to hell with the consequences. Then he would have made her eat her red silk underwear and throttled her with the leftovers.

But she was who she was – that much was set in stone. And a man needed order in his life. Someone and something to fight for. Someone to think things out for him. A hierarchy. And Effi fitted that bill perfectly. Plus there was still the outside chance that she would one day relent and take him back into her bed. Women were always changing their minds, weren't they? Then he would really make her suffer. He would send her out into the world bowlegged, and with his mark upon her. And if anyone else tried to get near her in the meantime, he would kill them.

'So what do you want me to do about it? Write the woman a sympathy note?'

Effi let the paper knife fall away from Udo's nose. 'What I want you to do about it is this, Udo. I want you to go back to Guatemala and finish what you started. Search the woman's house from top to bottom. Find anything that might link her either to Pope or to the contents of this suitcase. Then eradicate her. Wipe her from the face of the planet. Do I make myself clear?'

Udo snatched the paper knife from Effi's hand and speared his cheek with the point. Then, never leaving Effi's eyes with his, he threw the knife onto the table and smeared the blood across his face until he looked like a Tsenacommacah Indian chief.

'That is grotesque, Udo. And very childish.'

'So is going back to Guatemala. Are you telling me this stupid Lance thing is so important that you want me to go all the way back to the other side of the world and kill someone else for it?'

'This stupid Lance thing is important because it is a symbol, Udo. The symbol of the resumption of our struggle. It has served as the emblem of all the great leaders of Germany and the Western Kingdoms throughout history. Constantine. Justinian. Charles Martel. Charlemagne. Henry the Fowler. Otto the Great.' Effi ticked them off on her fingers, aware that she was talking to a man with little or no historical perspective, and with an IQ that probably hovered around the low eighties. 'Napoleon Bonaparte was prepared to kill to possess it – to overturn entire kingdoms for it – so why shouldn't we? The Führer valued it so highly that he had copies made and scattered all around Germany to fool the Americans. Now we hold the real thing in our hands. And with the Führer's very own seal of approval attached to it. If used correctly – in other words if we allow it to go viral on the internet, via mobile phones, word of mouth – it will unite our people just as it did in the Führer's time. The people who really count. The pure people. So yes. No one must be left alive to question how we got hold of it.'

'If all this is true, then why are you waving that other envelope that was in the suitcase at me? What is in that?'

'Something far more important than even the Holy Lance.'

Udo made a sceptical face. But he could feel the fires of

hope burning in his belly. 'And what can that possibly be?'

'Armageddon for our enemies, Udo, and for those of our own people who betray their race. It means death to all the Jews and the Muslims and the Turks and the Gypsies and the Africans and the rest of the hoi polloi who are filthying up Europe with their putrescence. It means death to the cultural Marxists. Death to multiculturalism. Death to chaos. The envelope you brought me contains the formula for the super weapon the Führer spent the entire war years searching for. The Führer's scientists perfected it just as the Russians were entering Berlin. All we have to do is to put it together and use it. With it we can strike at the very heart of the enemy and leave our own hands clean.'

Udo's face had gone numb. His bloodied cheeks shone with a faint sheen of sweat. His mouth gaped open like a bloodhound's. 'Why did the Führer not use it himself, then, and save Germany?'

Effi closed her eyes. 'Because it is chemical, Udo. It needs to be made up before it can be promulgated. And when the Führer received the formula he was surrounded on every side by enemies of the Reich. Just as we are, Udo. Just as we are. But there is one difference between then and now. We have time. And the Führer didn't. We have time to choose our targets. There will be no more Breiviks for us. No more lone wolves. Winston Churchill said only one true thing in his entire life – that "the fascists of the future will call themselves anti-fascists". Anders Behring Breivik quoted exactly this in his manifesto. He is now in jail. We will not make the same mistake he did. Where he killed seventy-seven, we will kill millions.'

'Here? In mainland Europe?'

'No, Udo. Not in Europe. This time we shall take the war to the enemy.'

EIGHTEEN

Rancho La Virgencita, Antigua, Guatemala

23 JULY 2012

This was the bit Udo liked the best. He laid the SS uniform tenderly across the bonnet of his car. It had been his grandfather's, but his mother had let it out for him some years before and now it fitted him like a glove. Udo ran his fingers lovingly over the thick black material. Then he leant forward and buried his face inside the fabric, snorting in its odour like a truffle pig.

His father's father, Hanke, had been an *oberscharführer* – equivalent to a Wehrmacht sergeant major – in the Julius Schreck Regiment of the General SS. He had fought with distinction throughout the entirety of the war, and had blown his brains out the day General Jodl and Grand Admiral Dönitz signed the German Instrument of Surrender on 7 May 1945 in Reims. On his body had been a handwritten note quoting from Heinrich Himmler's speech to the SS Generals at Poznan on 4 October 1943:

A war has to be won spiritually. By willpower and via the spirit. He wins the battle who goes on fighting for even one hour after the armistice has been declared. I consider it crucial for the life of our people to teach our grandsons to enter into this same life and to understand the difficulties of their ancestors. There can be no doubt that it will be our Order, the racial élite of the German people, which will have the greatest number of progeny. Woe to us if the Germanic people cannot win this battle! It will be the end of beauty, of culture, and of creative thought on this earth.

Mouthing Himmler's call to arms to himself – the call to which both his grandfather and father had dedicated their lives – Udo stripped naked and began the ritual. First he poured water from a bottle of Salvavidas onto a flannel and scrubbed his face, neck and armpits. Then he dried himself on a clean napkin he had brought especially for the purpose and put on the black silk boxer shorts and vest he so enjoyed wearing next to his skin. Next he slipped on his grandfather's khaki shirt and black SS issue tie, the winged breeches and the black patent leather riding boots. After that came the tricot jacket, the belt and shoulder strap, the accompanying SS dagger, and the non-commissioned officer's crusher cap. Last of all came the red swastika armband.

When he was ready, Udo leant inside the car and adjusted his hat in the rearview mirror. He viewed the result with profound satisfaction. His jaw was clean and his nose was straight. He no longer carried an ounce of excess flesh on his body. He was a true Aryan. One day he would have sons and, like his grandfather, he would teach them the ways of the world – tell them exactly what they needed to do to protect the natural order from outsiders. Meanwhile he would serve the Brotherhood with a true and honest heart. Perhaps it would be Effi who would bear his children one day? Now there was a thought. That would be the correct way of things. The peasant Zirkelers and the blue-blooded Raches combined into one. She would not be able to fend him off forever. What else was a woman for but to breed with?

Udo slid the machete he had bought at a hardware shop in Antigua out of its leather scabbard. They were sold blunt, so he had honed it to within an inch of its life with a diamond chip sharpener he had brought expressly with him from Germany. He eased the car door lightly shut behind him so that he would not warn the enemy of his arrival, straightened his tie, and marched towards the ranch house. Night was falling and the lights had been switched on inside the house, with the occasional silhouettes of a man and a woman smudging across them. Udo tried the back door. It was unlocked.

He smiled and inclined his head, as if he were performing in front of an audience. For in Udo's mind there was always an audience present on these occasions. It was a large audience made up of his ancestors, both known and unknown, certain Norse Gods, and a dozen or so carefully chosen figures from German history. This audience watched every move Udo made. Approvingly. Paternalistically. Encouragingly. They were the chorus to his hero. The witnesses to what Udo understood to be Nietzsche's 'tragic joy even in destruction'. They were Udo's secret sharers.

He pushed open the door. A man in a white Guayabera shirt and a pair of dark trousers was straightening a painting on the far wall. The man left off what he was doing and started up the corridor towards Udo, a quizzical frown on his face. He came to an abrupt stop when he caught sight of what Udo was wearing.

'Salgase, Señora. Afuera. Rapido!'

The man ran straight towards Udo, his face livid with fear.

Udo smiled. He knew just what the man was about to do. He had encountered such situations before. He termed them 'the instincts of sacrifice'.

Colel Cimi's chauffeur, Santiago, pulled down the bookcase that almost blocked the narrow hall corridor, causing the books to tumble out in an untidy pile between himself and Udo. By doing this it was clear that he intended to hamper Udo's progress towards the main part of the house, allowing his mistress the chance to escape.

Udo backed out of the door. The man could wait. It was the woman he wanted.

'No!' shouted Santiago. He fought his way across the obstacle he had just created and ran after Udo.

Udo stepped back inside the house. He brought the machete down in a full sweep from left to right, allowing the weight of the blade to carry the power of the blow, just as he had learnt from the numerous books on samurai swordsmanship he had studied as an adolescent. He was back out of the door even before Santiago's body hit the ground.

In the distance he could see Colel Cimi's pale face and forearms flashing in the moonlight. He gave chase. Speed was of the essence on such occasions. Speed scared people. Speed and certainty of action. Certainty of will.

Colel Cimi looked behind her and saw the black-clad figure briefly silhouetted against the luminous white of the ranch-house walls. She recognized the SS uniform. Saw the glint of the machete. Knew what was about to happen to her. There would be questions. Force. Pain. Disfigurement.

Colel Cimi had spent the greater part of her life keeping herself beautiful for the man who loved her. Now, in this penultimate moment of her existence, she understood that she, too, had loved him. She looked up as she ran, half expecting to see her lover and their daughter beckoning to her from beyond the stars. Calling her back to them.

She launched herself off the edge of the barranca and into thin air. There was no forethought. No remorse. It was something she knew she must do.

She fell fifty feet, her arms and legs spiralling, before she hit the ground. She rolled for a few paces and then tumbled off the lip of the waterfall that overlooked the valley. She was dead before she struck the water.

Udo stood at the edge of the barranca and watched Colel Cimi's body resurface. She looked like a rag doll some child had cast away – a loose-limbed piece of jetsam drifting on the swell. He watched her for some time with active interest, as one would watch the carcase of some unknown species of fish roiling in the surf.

He turned round and headed back towards the ranch house. Things weren't usually this easy, he told himself. Fate and his audience must be smiling on him for a change. Looking with approval on his destiny. Humouring him.

NINETEEN

Hart finished packing for the airport. He checked his watch. His taxi was due in twenty minutes. He still had time.

He left his bag with the hotel clerk and hurried the two hundred metres to La Casa Del Jade. Once there he picked up the black jadeite necklace he had ordered for Colel Cimi as a thank-you present for seeing him through his attack of malaria. The necklace was made to his own design, and he was thrilled with it. Colel Cimi was not a woman who showed emotion easily, but Hart could imagine her delight when she opened the package – a particular look she would get on her face when she was taken with something you had said or done. The prospect pleased him enormously. He had become very fond of her during his days under her and Santiago's care.

He had fleetingly toyed with the idea of having a second piece designed for Amira as a peace offering, but he was no masochist. Amira was still so angry with him for attempting to save her life that she would probably throw it in his face. And then throttle him with his camera straps for good measure. No. Better to let sleeping dogs lie.

Hart sat back in the taxi and mulled over everything that Colel Cimi had told him. The process made him feel oddly content. As though she had unwittingly supplied the key to something that had hitherto been missing from his consciousness. A crucial part of an impossible to unravel thousand-piece jigsaw.

That his father suffered from bipolar disorder – which Hart understood to be the same as manic depression – had come as a profound shock to him. But it answered many questions. The baffling 'Roger Pope' alter ego that his father used only in the house in Antigua when he was in the throes of mania, for instance. Or the crazy plan his father had come up with to contact the descendants of the man to whom his parents had been entrusted to deliver Hitler's suitcase. Colel Cimi had confirmed that rationally, when he was taking his medication, such an idea would never have occurred to the James Hart she knew. But to Hart's alter ego? When he was in a manic state? Roger Pope was capable of any idiocy.

Colel Cimi had gone on to describe how his father had once sold a twenty-five thousand dollar SUV for one hundred dollars cash to a passing stranger. Later, he had given away most of his clothes and cut up his credit cards and passport because he had felt threatened by perceived enemies – enemies who existed nowhere but in his imagination. He had been located by Santiago, a week later, living rough near San Andres, on the shores of Lake Peten Itza, being fed and clothed by some American tourists who had taken pity on a fellow countryman so down on his luck that they had felt constrained to contact the US Embassy about him as a matter of urgency.

Such psychotic episodes usually lasted for between two to six weeks, she told him, depending on the strength of his mania. During these periods Pope felt that he was in direct communication with God and took to acting like a man possessed. Colel Cimi had long ago realized that only medication and Santiago's watchfulness could control him during such episodes, but there were times when Pope had managed to elude both the medication and his minder and go AWOL.

There were times, too, when Colel Cimi temporarily gave up on her lover and returned to her village to renew herself. It was during one of these periods that Pope had made the disastrous mistake of contacting someone – Colel Cimi did not know who – concerning the Holy Lance and the other material in the suitcase.

When Hart had pressed her as to what additional material she might be referring to, Colel Cimi had explained that she had no idea, as it had remained under Adolf Hitler's unbroken personal seal. When Hart questioned this, Colel Cimi explained that it had become an article of faith with Pope not to fracture the seal under any circumstances, for he was convinced that to do so would be to negate his parents' blood sacrifice – a sacrifice that Pope felt his parents had made in order to protect him.

'It was a superstitious delusion, you mean?' said Hart.

'You might call it that. Your father would have called it something else. A moral imperative, perhaps.'

'I see.'

'Yes. I believe you do. Your father was a good man, John. It was his illness that made him seem foolish.'

Colel Cimi had only learnt about the Holy Lance and the seemingly unbroken von Hartelius family connection to it because Hart – in full Roger Pope mode – had begun obsessively reading up on his ancestry and, being something of a Luddite, had been forced to ask for her help in obtaining books via the internet. Ancient books on the Knights Templar, on Frederick Barbarossa, on the Grail Legend, and on the Third Eye. Books on Second World War female test pilots and on the Battle for Berlin. Biographies of Adolf Hitler and of Dietrich Eckart, the occultist to whom Hitler had dedicated the second volume of *Mein Kampf*. Books on secret groups like the Vril or Luminous Lodge, and on the Thule Society, which had welcomed the young Adolf Hitler as a member and had helped form his public persona via séances related to the Secret Doctrine. It was through the Thule Society – at least according to Roger Pope's version of events – that Hitler had been inculcated into the irrelevance of personal morality and the strategically inverted importance of the Manichean Struggle between Light and Darkness. Later she had caught the fatally obsessed Pope reading August Kubizek's *Young Hitler: The Story of Our Friendship*, in which Kubizek described the Luciferically possessed Hitler's first viewing of the Holy Lance.

'So my father was a closet Nazi? Is that what you are telling me?'

'No. No.' Colel Cimi had laughed. 'Nothing like that. But when he was in a manic state he didn't know who or what he was. He would enter into what he described as a condition of Karmic Transformation. A communion of spirit with the past. What he called being bathed in astral light. When he was in his "normal" state, he was, if anything, of an advanced liberal persuasion. What in the United States one might call a democrat. That is certainly how he voted.'

'My father voted democrat?' The thought struck Hart as a little surreal. He was grateful, though, for small mercies. The prospect of both his father and his grandfather being fascists was too dreadful to contemplate. He could imagine the terminally socialist Amira's withering contempt. She would probably never talk to him again.

Hart's train of thought was broken by the taxi driver slapping lightly at his steering wheel and making a cutting gesture with the edge of his hand. 'These people you are visiting must be very rich, Señor. Very rich indeed. They leave their lights burning even in the daytime.'

Hart glanced towards the ranch house. The man was right. It was broad daylight but the lights were still on and the back door open.

'They've been holding an all-night party perhaps? I'm sorry, Señor, but you have missed all the fun. There is only the cleaning up to do now. The drink is drunk and the girls are gone.' The taxi driver slapped the steering wheel again, this time with a downward flicking motion, as if he was shaking excess water off his fingertips. He grinned, showing three widely separated teeth. '*Asi es la vida*, eh? Such is life.'

Hart felt the first faint stirrings of unease. 'Stay here, please. I'll be back in twenty minutes. My plane leaves in two hours. We shall have to hurry if my visit takes any longer.'

'*No problema*,' said the taxi driver. 'I have my newspaper. I have the capacity to sleep. And I sleep like a baby whenever the meter is running, that I promise you. Tick, tick, tick, tick.'

Hart started towards the house, leaving the man cackling at his own joke. It was an odd thing about the lights, though. The day was sunny – not overcast at all. Maybe the electrician was testing the circuits? Or maybe there had been a power cut and the juice had just been switched back on again?

Hart stepped into the hall. He half opened his mouth to call out but he got no further. Santiago was sprawled lengthways across a pile of books. He had been slashed across the face and down one side of the chest with a sharp weapon. Hart could see the white of exposed bone through the gristle. The blow must have nicked Santiago's intestines because the stench was overwhelming. Hart steadied himself against the wall and began to dry retch.

This couldn't be happening. Not twice. Not twice in one week. Hart drew a hand down his face. It came away covered in cold sweat.

He stepped over Santiago's body and hurried down the hall. He searched anxiously through the familiar bedrooms but they were all empty. Pillaged, but empty. The French windows leading to the garden were wide open.

Hart ran towards the barranca. Had Colel Cimi managed to escape? Was she hiding in the grounds? Should he call out to her? Or was Santiago's murderer still on the premises?

Some instinct drew Hart to the lip of the gully leading down to the falls. Colel Cimi had shown him the place the afternoon before. It had been her special spot. The place she went to when she was upset or worried. The place she called 'the gateway to my soul'.

He stood at the edge of the barranca and looked down. A body floated face downwards in the pool below the falls. Long black hair spread out in a starburst all around it.

Hart plunged down the scree slope, arms akimbo, not caring when he lost both of his shoes in his flailing downhill progress. When he reached the pool he plunged in. It took him ten strokes to reach the body.

The instant he took hold of Colel Cimi's head, he knew that she was dead. Her neck was loose and her eyes were closed. Her mouth was pursed as if in prayer.

Hart pressed her body to his chest and kicked backwards towards the shore. Colel Cimi seemed as light as air in his hands.

He carried her up the path towards the house, hardly noticing that his bare feet were being laced to shreds on the volcanic stones. Once inside, he carried her to her bedroom and laid her on the bed. He stood over her, gasping and choking, his face contorted with grief.

Slowly, tentatively, Hart began to return to a state of rational consciousness. First he remembered the taxi and its driver waiting for him outside. Then he recalled the original purpose of his journey, which was to get him to the airport in time for his plane back to London. He realized that if the taxi driver decided to venture into the house for some reason – to use the lavatory, say, or to check how much longer he was going to be – he could not fail to spot Santiago's body. Then Hart would be forced to remake the acquaintance of the chief of police. And this time he would not get off so lightly.

An *Inglés* accused of murder in Guatemala? The chief would clean him out. Together with any friends and family who were foolish enough to cough up even the smallest portion of the *mordida* bribe that would be the only way to secure his acquittal. That was the way things worked in countries like Guatemala. Hart knew how it went down. He'd witnessed it for himself just a few days before in Syria – and many times further down the line.

He looked down at the bed. Colel Cimi was dead. Santiago too. Nothing could change that. Nothing could bring them back. But at least he now understood why they had been killed. One look around Colel Cimi's bedroom answered that question for him. The place was a wreck. Every drawer and cupboard had been torn open. Each pillow slit. Even the mattress had been eviscerated, as if whoever had done it enjoyed the mayhem and the effect it would leave behind. But why had they waited so long after his father's murder? Why hadn't the murderer come whilst he was still there and added him to the bag? Hart shook his head in despair.

The reason for all three deaths must lie in the suitcase his grandfather and grandmother had spirited out of Berlin in April 1945, just hours before the victorious Russian Army had begun violating the city in revenge for the Siege of Stalingrad. The person or persons responsible for their deaths must be linked to the descendants of the man to whom the suitcase had originally been consigned. These were the people his father had contacted in his manic state. These were the people responsible.

But that was as far as his logic managed to carry him. Hart had neither a name nor an address for the perpetrators. And any clues left behind in his father's or in Colel Cimi's house were long gone. Where should he start looking? What should he do? How should he respond?

Hart hobbled into the drawing room. He searched through the detritus littering the floor until he found the photograph of his sister that Colel Cimi had shown him. The frame was broken and the glass was cracked, but Carmen's photograph was blessedly intact. Hart took it out of its frame and flattened it carefully between the pages of a discarded magazine. He slipped the magazine inside his shirt, making sure that the photograph was snug against his belly and in no danger of being creased.

He picked his way down the corridor and into Santiago's bedroom. He scrabbled around in the mess left by the murderer until he found a matching pair of open-backed mules and some socks. He put them on over his bloodstained feet. Then he swept an eiderdown off the floor and shook it clear of dust. He covered Santiago's body with it. He returned down the corridor and did the same for Colel Cimi. Then he stepped into the sunlit yard.

The taxi driver was sleeping. He was using his newspaper as a sunscreen.

Hart eased himself into the back of the cab. He propped the door open with his foot whilst he swept the damp hair back from his forehead. Then he allowed the door to fall shut.

The driver straightened up, his newspaper disintegrating into leaves around him.

'I am ready, Señor,' said Hart. He passed a fifty dollar bill across the seatback. 'My plane leaves in less than an hour. And it is a matter of the greatest possible urgency that I get on it.'

TWENTY

Hart called Amira Eisenberger from one of the few remaining payphones at Miami Airport.

'Ah. The prodigal son returns,' she said. 'Have you saved any more damsels in distress recently? Leapt in front of any more bullets?'

'Where are you, Amira?'

'I'm in London. In bed. With my lovers. Both of them. They have promised to intercede if anyone tries to shoot me again. No bullet will be able to penetrate their muscle-bound bodies, so I am safe at last. Ah, the perils of being a woman. Where are you?'

Hart rolled his eyes. So it was going to be like that? 'I'm in Miami. Between planes. I thought you'd be on a new assignment by now.'

Amira sighed. 'Before they send you on a new assignment, John, you have to suggest a story to them. Or have one suggested to you. That's the disadvantage of being an actual journalist rather than a glorified paparazzo. I am researching four possible stories as we speak. When I find one that suits my editor, she will encourage me to research it in more depth. Then, if I am very lucky, she will buy me a ticket and allocate me some expense money. Only then will I be going anywhere. But I forget. I'm talking to a photojournalist. Someone who hasn't put pen to paper since he left high school. You just aim your thing at them and then you press the trigger, don't you? And then they pay you. Typical man.'

Hart closed his eyes. So Amira was still angry with him? And perfectly capable of hanging up if it suited her mood. He needed to go for the jugular. 'I've got a story for you. You can junk your other leads. This one is big.'

'Don't tell me. Boy reunites with father after thirty-five years. That'll guarantee me a double-page byline, won't it? I can see the headlines now. *A tender reunion took place in Central America between photojournalist John Hart and his errant father. Tears were shed and promises exchanged. Hart's father apologized for his many years of mutism: "I am so moved at seeing my son again that I can't find the words to express it."'*

Hart squinted at the phone. Jesus. The situation was worse than he'd imagined. He mustn't lose his temper. That would play straight into Amira's hands. She was the sort of woman who took her own time with everything. Obstinacy was a political statement with her – things were only done and dusted when Amira Eisenberger decided they were done and dusted.

'How about this for a headline? Photojournalist's father crucified. Lethal spear wound discovered on right of ribcage.

140

Two further deaths believed connected to the first. Victim's son on the run.'

Amira broke in on his litany. 'That's not funny. I don't write for the tabloids, remember? I am what passes for a serious journalist. If you want to play those sorts of games, why not chat up Martha Ferret, or whatever her stupid name is. She's just your sort of woman. Winsome, mincing, and the exact age to settle down and raise a family. She writes just the sort of sensationalist tripe you are talking about, too. I don't.'

'Did you listen to anything I just said?'

'Unfortunately, yes. I suppose you want me to collect you from Heathrow and save you the taxi fare? Is that why you are calling me? I can't imagine for what other reason.'

Hart counted slowly to five before he answered. 'No, Amira. I've decided to come in through Paris, not London. After that I'm going to travel as a foot passenger on the ferry from Dunkerque to Dover. There's more chance they won't scan passports that way. I really may be wanted for murder in Guatemala, and via that through Interpol. So I can't afford to take any chances.'

'Have you gone mad? Cross-channel ferries? Murder? What did they feed you over there in Guatemala? Ayahuasca?'

'Sorry, Amira. They're just calling my flight. I've got to hurry. Work your way back through the conversation we've just had and think about it. Particularly what I told you about the killings. And you might want to research something called the Holy Lance whilst you're at it – the one that pierced

141

Jesus's side and possibly my father's. And then link it somehow to Adolf Hitler. When you've done that, drag whatever you find back into the present day. You're good at that sort of thing. *Sayonara.*'

TWENTY-ONE

Richmond, England

26 JULY 2012

Amira picked Hart up near Richmond Hospital. She drove silently for some time and refused to look at him.

'It's nice to see you too,' said Hart.

Amira swivelled round in the driver's seat. 'You *are* wanted for murder in Guatemala. You weren't joking.'

'No. I wasn't joking. But I didn't kill anybody.'

'Would you like to explain that?'

Hart threw his head back against the headrest. 'Explain? I wish I could.'

Something flashed across Amira's eyes. She switched into journalistic mode without skipping a beat. Her eyes took on the piercing stare with which a cat will mesmerize its prey. 'You've lost weight. Have you been ill?'

Hart groaned. Amira was right on the button as usual. He knew just where she was coming from. He'd been on a number of assignments with her as her photographer. There was an art to the give-and-take of asking questions – a necessary rhythm – that Amira possessed in spades. It was a sort of questioning by numbers. It was accompanied by a hefty dose of professional detachment and an even sharper eye. What had he expected? Sympathy?

'You remember the malaria I picked up in Sierra Leone?' he said. 'Well, it came back. The woman and her chauffeur that were killed saw me through the relapse. She was my father's mistress. She told me many things.' Hart faltered. 'She told me I had a sister, Amira. She was called Carmen. She died when she was seven years old. Of meningitis. Look. This is her picture.' He scrabbled in his jacket pocket. 'I wish I'd known her. Why didn't my father tell me? I could have travelled to Guatemala and met her. Maybe I could have done something? Helped her in some way? Even just been there?'

Amira stopped the car in a lay-by. She turned to Hart and laid her hand on his arm. But there was caution in her action – as if she might pull back if Hart responded inappropriately to her touch.

She studied the picture. 'She's beautiful. And she does look a bit like you. But I'm sorry. You can't go on like this. Go to the police. Explain things. It will soon become clear to them that you are innocent.'

Hart slid the photograph back inside its protective cover and put it into his holdall. His expression turned to granite. 'Do the UK and Guatemala have an extradition treaty? Come on. I know you'll have done your homework.'

Amira reached into her handbag and fished out a cigarette. She lit it, cracked open the window, and wafted the smoke out with one hand. 'Yes. They do. Since the thirteenth of January 1883. For the Mutual Surrender of Fugitive Criminals.'

'Great.'

'But you didn't kill anybody.'

'We're talking about Guatemala, Amira, not the European Union. Everything points to me. I even left my shoes at the scene of the crime. There are prints from my bloodstained feet all over the ranch. My DNA will be everywhere. Over the beds. In the bathroom. In the kitchen. The police chief will be beside himself with joy thinking of all the extra income he will earn in bribes. He simply can't afford to let this one pass.'

'DNA? In Guatemala? You must be kidding.'

'There were three murders, Amira. Three.'

'In a country of thirteen million people? Which boasted 5681 murders last year, with scarcely a single killer brought to justice? You see? I have done my homework. Have you ever tried to find an ant in a bowl of wild rice? That's what it'll seem like to whoever inherits this case. Your father was dead before you even arrived in the country. They can't pin his murder on you unless you dropped in by balloon.'

'They'll still contact Interpol. They'll still flash my name up on their Most Wanted list as a possible suspect in the final two killings. I left by plane and in a hurry. My name appears in black and white on the passenger list. My taxi driver will be able to identify me and testify that I spent three-quarters of an hour in a house containing two dead people and then tipped him fifty bucks to speed me to the airport.'

'Then go to the police first. Before they come to you.'

Hart shook his head. 'No. I won't do that. I'm going to pursue these people myself. To the grave, if necessary. I owe that much to Colel Cimi. I owe that much to Santiago. And in a curious sort of a way, I owe it to my father, too.' Hart stared out of the window. His face was bleak. 'What else did you discover?'

'About what?'

'About the Holy Lance, Amira. And all the other stuff I asked you to check out. Don't kid a kidder.'

Amira gave a long sigh. 'This isn't the right place for it. We'll use my flat as yours is probably surrounded by a SWAT team. The actual debriefing had better wait, though. You're jet-lagged, post-malarial, and probably still in shock. When did you last eat?'

'I don't need food. I need answers. And quickly.' Hart cast her a sidelong glance. 'Are you sure you want to risk having a possible murderer on your premises? Becoming an accessory after the fact? It could mean the end of your career.'

Amira laughed. 'You must know me better than that by now, John.' She crashed the gears as she changed up. 'It could mean a story.'

TWENTY-TWO

Amira sat across from Hart in the kitchen area of her flat and watched him not eating. Instead he drank coffee. Mug after mug of coffee. Until his hands shook from the caffeine, and his eyes stared out of red-rimmed shells.

She tried to put herself in his shoes, but she found it impossible. Hart was the most tender-minded man she had ever met, and she was a tough-minded woman who detested 'niceness'. It was a disastrous combination. Her decision to abort their child hung between the two of them like a rotting corpse.

'They call their association the *Lanzen Brüderschaft* – the Brotherhood of the Lance. Despite its name, their leader is a woman. Elfriede Rache. She's the thirty-three-year-old granddaughter of Heinrich Rache, who was one of Adolf Hitler's first lieutenants. Rache began in the SA under Ernst Röhm, then betrayed Röhm to Hitler on the Night of the Long Knives in 1934. Röhm was a true revolutionary – meaning he wanted a redistribution of wealth from rich to poor. Rache and Hitler were as far from revolutionaries as you could get. Hitler because he understood that power and loyalty needed to be bought and paid for, and Rache because he was a multi-millionaire by inheritance and despised homosexuals, which Röhm was.'

'No more Mr Nice Guy, then.'

Amira ignored him. 'The Raches were Bavarian industrialists. They still own a small chemical factory in Gmund that makes spa products, but most of their holdings were bought out in the 1960s. Rache Junior then went on to found the LB in 1970, subsidizing it out of his newfound wealth. Rache Senior had left him a mansion and extensive landholdings in Bad Wiessee and the surrounding area, which his granddaughter has now inherited following her father's death, together with all their accumulated loot elsewhere. And there's a lot of it, believe me. Grandfather Rache was entertaining some of Röhm's cronies in the same house when Hitler came calling on the Night of the Long Knives. The whole thing was pre-planned. A trap. After that he was Hitler's man until the end. The Americans inherited him, but for some reason his name was never put forward for the Nuremberg Trials. Which probably means he collaborated with his American interrogators and named names. Whatever. For some reason he was allowed to hold on to both his fortune and his landholdings after the war and pass them on to his son.'

'And these people have the Holy Lance?'

'Yes. It's clear they don't know about you, or you would already be dead. I don't know what happened, but there was a reason for the gap between the murders. My own suspicion is that they did not at first know about Colel Cimi's role in your father's life. When they found out about it, they acted. But you slipped between the cracks.'

'So they're publicizing their possession of the Lance?'

'They've been looking for it for years. Now they've got it they intend to use it as a symbol. It's all over the internet like a rash. They are claiming one of their number dug it up in a field whilst metal detecting. The field belongs to the Raches, of course. Under Germany's law of Treasure Trove, half belongs to the finder, half to the owner of the field. Convenient.'

'Aren't the LB illegal? I know how strict Germany is on Nazi revisionism.'

'Far from it. The LB is a bona fide political party. Effi Rache, as she popularly styles herself, is its figurehead. She's blonde and beautiful and magnetic. In public, she disdains her grandfather's Nazi past and points to her father, Hans Rache, who was a Christian Democrat MP and a major philanthropist. In private, those in the know suspect she's a chip off the old block. That her father's philanthropy and moderation were just a cover for far more sinister goings-on. But no one can prove it. She's fast becoming a major political force. But it's clear to anyone with even a modicum of sense that she's much further to the right than even Marine Le Pen in France. She's against all immigration. She supports the death penalty. She's Eurosceptic. She believes in traditional culture and in raising incentives for homemakers. You remember Hitler's KKK mantra for women? *Kinder*, *Küche*, *Kirche?* Children, kitchen, church? Well, Effi's one hundred per cent for it. Except not in her particular case, of course. The LB are fielding four candidates for the next round of European Parliamentary elections. Effi Rache is one of them.'

'Neat.'

'Yes. She's all about normalizing the LB. De-enclaving it. Making it electable.'

'But in private?'

'Nobody knows for sure.'

'But she interests you?'

'I think she stinks. I think she needs bringing down. I believe she ordered the murder of your father, his mistress and her chauffeur in order to get hold of the Holy Lance. She's the sort of woman who'll stop at nothing to get what she wants.'

Hart was tempted to say, 'it takes one to know one', but didn't. 'Did you just come to all this? Magically? Thanks to me?'

'No. I've been monitoring her for years. Looking for a way to crack her armour. Just like I monitor all leaders of extreme right-wing parties in Europe. The Front National in France. The British National Party. The Freedom Party in the Netherlands. The Progress Party in Norway. The Northern League in Italy. The True Finns in Finland. The Golden Dawn in Greece. España 2000 in Spain. There are reams of the bastards. But until now, I've never found a way in.'

'And now you've got one?'

Amira hesitated. Then she shook her head. 'No. I don't think I have. Everything you've told me about your father is unprovable. We've just got your word for it. I believe you, but the police won't. When they find you they'll simply arrest you for murder and go through the usual processes. If you give yourself up voluntarily there will be considerable publicity and some of it will stick. I'll make sure of that. But it won't be enough to bring Effi Rache down, or to change the minds of the idiots who follow her. I still can't see any way to get to her and put the LB out of business.'

'I can.' Hart put down his coffee cup. 'I've thought of a way.'

TWENTY-THREE

'But you don't speak any German. What are you going to do? Knock on Effi Rache's front door, wave a fake passport at her and say, "I am Johannes von Hartelius, hereditary guardian of the Holy Lance, and I have come here to fulfil my destiny?" Only you'll be saying it in English, of course.' Amira cracked one of her rare smiles. 'You'd better hope she's a polyglot.'

Hart stared out of the window. It was raining. Hart liked the rain. It might serve to keep the police indoors. 'I can learn.'

'What? An entire language?'

'Enough to get along with. I can use my own father's backstory to explain why I was brought up in England and speak hardly any German. My father's parents famously died in a plane crash and he was left an orphan. There was utter chaos in Germany immediately after the end of the war so records are hard to come by. I can say the Yanks farmed him out to a US couple, but he didn't take their name because he still had his German passport. Then, as an adult, he came to work in England and married an

Englishwoman. They had me. Then he died. And so did she. But before he died he told me about the origins of the von Hartelius name. How my ancestor had been made hereditary guardian of the Holy Lance by Frederick Barbarossa's son. I'm the spitting image of my grandfather. And pretty close to the same age he was when he died. Maybe your researcher can find more pictures of him? Any taken during the war years will do. Once they see those, I'll be home dry.'

'You really think so?'

'No. But it's all I've got. Can you get me the passport, Amira? Without it, I'm dead in the water.'

'Johannes Freiherr von Hartelius.' Amira squinted at her iPad. 'That's the way it says German titles have to be written on official documents. They are part of the surname since 1919, not a prefix to it. You're actually a Reichsfreiherr, because your title was awarded under the aegis of the Holy Roman Empire, but that doesn't have to go on your passport. In Germany they will call you Baron.'

'Why are you frowning?'

'Because I never suspected you were an aristocrat. I hate aristocrats. I would never have slept with you if I had known you were an aristocrat.'

'Thanks. I know you're joking, but thanks.'

'I'm not joking.'

'Well, I'm not an aristocrat.'

'By birth you are.'

'I didn't know about my birth until I talked to Colel Cimi. So it doesn't count.'

'Still. The fact is there.'

Hart stood up. He was tired. Deep-down tired. With the sort of tiredness he used to get as a young man after a day spent climbing in the Cuillin Hills. He was nearing forty, though, and the tiredness needed to be placated, not ignored. 'I can't argue with you any more, Amira. I need my bed. Where am I sleeping?'

'In the spare room.'

'I thought as much. Is it because I am an aristocrat?'

'No, John. It's because I need to work. I'm going to arrange to get you your passport. I know a man who knows a man. I'm going to explain the situation to my editor, *sub rosa*, and trust that she doesn't pick up the telephone and dial 112. The passport is going to cost us, and I'll have to do it clandestinely, not through the newspaper. If I'm lucky, she'll allocate me expenses with no questions asked. If I'm unlucky, we'll have to pay for it ourselves. Do you have any savings?'

'No.'

'What do you mean? You can't spend everything you earn?'

'My mother is in the early stages of dementia, Amira, and the NHS aren't interested in her. It takes nine months to get an appointment with a consultant, and they're few and far between. So I'm paying for her care privately. There are new drugs out there that can slow things down, but they haven't been passed by NICE yet, so I buy them for her on the open market. That doesn't leave me with much to play with by the end of the month. Plus I'm a freelance photojournalist, not even a stringer – you don't get closer to the bottom of the food chain than that. And I've been out of work since Syria. Maybe I could go back to Guatemala and put my father's house on the market? Would that do? Or ask your editor for a salary? Or sell my sperm to a sperm bank?'

'Just go to bed, John.'

TWENTY-FOUR

Udo Zirkeler looked at the twelve young men surrounding him with an active, avuncular interest. He called them his 'apostles', and he was ridiculously proud of them. All of them were over six feet tall – some as tall as six foot six. All were neatly turned out, with short hair, clean-shaven faces, good skin and good teeth. All except one.

'Why have you shaved your head, Jochen?'

Jochen Sturmeier blushed. He was sixteen years old and a new recruit to Udo's little band of brothers. 'I thought that's what was wanted?'

'I explained what was wanted when we recruited you from the orphanage. We want you to look normal. Not like a skinhead or a skullhead or a slaphead. No tattoos. No studs. No rings. No chains. No Dr Martens. No Lonsdales. And no fucking razor cuts. What part of that didn't you understand?'

Jochen was already red. He turned redder.

'I'm tempted to leave you behind.'

'But it's Friday night.'

'You should have thought of that before you told the barber to set the switch to zero on his electric razor.'

'Please, Udo.'

'We'll take a vote on it. How many of you want Jochen with us on our outing? Bearing in mind that his decision could put us all at risk?'

Not a single hand went up.

'Excellent. You can come, Jochen.'

'But no one put their hand up.'

'Exactly. I am in command here. Whoever told you this is a democracy needs their head examined.'

There was an explosion of laughter from around the room. Udo beamed. He held them in the palm of his hand now. 'Get out the bottle.'

One of the young men hurried out of the room and returned with an old-fashioned narrow-waisted Coca Cola bottle.

'Now spread these pieces of paper out in a circle for me.'

Another of the young men laid the papers out in a tight circle on the floor, leaving just enough room for the bottle in the centre. Each piece of paper had a word written on it. Homo. Turk. Jew. African. Black. Asian. Journalist. Gypsy. RFWDL. Muslim. ZOG. Pole.

'What's RFWDL, Udo?'

'Random Fuckers We Don't Like.'

'Ah.'

'What's the difference between Africans and Blacks, Udo?'

'Africans are Africans – they can include Maghrebins,

Arabs, Libyans, Tunisians, Egyptians, what have you. Blacks are any other Blacks. We split them up because it gives them two chances of being chosen. Just like with the Jews and the ZOGS.'

'What are the ZOGS?'

'Jews who are members of the Zionist Occupation Government.'

'What's that?'

'Nothing to trouble your head about. It'll all be explained when the time comes. Spin the bottle, Jochen. Let's see who we hit tonight.'

Jochen spun the bottle. It stopped at Homo.

Udo looked disappointed. 'We did Homos two weeks ago. Did you spin it properly?'

'I did, Udo. I spun it hard.'

'Then the gods want us to hit Homos again. That's all there is to it.' He handed the first young man a further sheaf of papers. 'Destroy that lot and put these down instead.'

The young man did as he was told. The papers all held the names of towns. Altomünster. Bruck. Dachau. Ebersberg. Erding. Freising. Fürstenbruck. Gräfelfing. Grünwald. Ismaning. Kirchseeon. Markt Schwaben. Obershleißheim. Pullach im Isartal. Sauerlach. Schäftlarn.

'Why these, Udo?'

'I chose them at random. They are all in the Munich area, but poorly policed and with little or no CCTV. The internet will give us the addresses of Homo clubs in whichever one we choose. Lenzi, spin the bottle.'

Lenzi spun the bottle. Everyone in the room followed it with their eyes.

'It's Ismaning, Udo.'

'Good. Any of you ever been there?'

'No,' said one. 'I only know it's got a river.'

'Perfect. We can sail in.'

Everybody laughed.

'Shall I destroy these papers too, Udo?'

'Why? They only have towns written on them. Who could make anything of that? We'll hold them over till next time. Sibbe, have you got the pickaxe handles?'

'Yes, Udo. Thirteen of them. Packed together in a clump, like for a garden delivery. Zip-tied with nylon. Easier to cut that way.'

'Lighter fuel?'

'Two sachets.'

'Matches?'

'A plastic lighter.'

'I want matches, Sibbe. Plastic lighters carry fingerprints.'

'Yes, Udo.'

'You all ready?'

Each man stood to attention.

Udo eyed them one by one, the same way his father used to eye Udo's outstretched fingers before every mealtime to make sure they were clean.

'Excellent, lads. *Banzai!*'

TWENTY-FIVE

They parked the vans at three separate spots on the outskirts of Ismaning, transferring from one van to the other as each was dropped off.

'Every one of you has the keys to all three vehicles?'

'Yes, Udo.'

'Then put on these brown T-shirts and brown work trousers over your other clothes. And the polythene shoe covers.'

There was silence whilst the young men dressed.

'Now pass out the pickaxe handles.'

Sibbe handed each man one of the handles. They were three feet long and made of hickory wood, with a flared, weighted base. Each weighed two and half pounds.

'Time check?'

'Ten to one.'

'What time does the club close?'

'Three o'clock. Sometimes they have a lockdown. Probably when they are having a sex orgy.'

Everyone laughed. There was a palpable air of expectation amongst the group.

'Arms and legs only. No blows to the head or back. No blows to the heart. No blows to the neck. We don't want anyone killed. We just want them discouraged. Got it?'

'Yes, Udo.'

'And we do it at a run. Fast in, fast out. Each team leader is responsible for ensuring his team get back to their designated van.'

'Yes, Udo.'

'Are we ready?'

Each man tapped the head of his helve on the ground.

'Put on your dust masks.'

Each man slid on his white plastic dust mask.

'Now go!'

There was a swish and patter as Udo's gang ran down the street.

TWENTY-SIX

Hermann Ewarden was kissing his boyfriend Jürgen out by the Leather Bar car park when he heard the strange swishing sound. He straightened up, frowning.

The next thing he saw was half a dozen men wearing dust masks breasting the corner. They ran in phalanx, with what looked like baseball bats held across their chests like rifles.

For a split second Hermann found himself unable to move. An unwanted mental image came to him of something he had seen in a documentary. The image he remembered was of a long unbroken line of police running towards some rioters. They looked unstoppable. The image had frightened him at the time. The reality frightened him even more.

Hermann took Jürgen by the hand and began to run. Two of the men broke off and began to pursue the couple. Hermann upped his speed but Jürgen soon dropped his hand and began to fall behind. Hermann was a jogger and Jürgen was not. Jürgen spent most of his time in front of the mirror.

'Go, Hermann. Go. Call the police.' Jürgen was crying.

Hermann pulled up. He waited until Jürgen caught up to him, then turned to confront the two men. He pushed Jürgen a little to the rear of his right shoulder. 'Why are you chasing us? Why do you want to hurt us? What have we done to you?'

One of the men slowed down. The other man, seeing his partner falter, slowed down too. The men faced each other at a distance of five metres.

When Hermann saw that the men in dust masks were carrying pickaxe handles, something died in him. He watched the two men across from him with a sense of deep sadness. 'Please leave my friend alone. If you have to hit someone, hit me.' Hermann could sense Jürgen feeling for his hand. He grasped Jürgen's hand and squeezed it back. In the distance, screams could be heard, and the smashing of glass. 'Why are you doing this?'

One of the men confronting them began to back away. 'I can't do it, Sibbe. Not like this. I say we leave them.'

'Don't use my name, you fool.'

'I'm sorry, Sibbe.'

'Jesus. You're such an idiot. They'll call the police if we don't nobble them.'

'Someone will be doing that already. You can count on it. One of the others.'

Jürgen moved fractionally further behind Hermann's arm. 'Please don't hurt us.'

The second man – the older, more angry one, Hermann decided – cast a look back over his shoulder.

'Place your phones on the ground and back away.'

Hermann and Jürgen placed their phones on the ground and backed away from them. 'Thank you. Thank you both.'

The man stepped forward and brought the butt of his pickaxe down on the phones. For a moment it looked as though he would change his mind about not hurting them. Then he stepped backwards again. 'Now run. The only reason we haven't broken your legs is because we did Homos two weeks ago. We're ahead of the game.'

Hermann and Jürgen eased away from their aggressors, their eyes moving from their broken phones to the pickaxe handles and back again.

'You're not such bad people,' said Hermann. 'But you shouldn't be doing this. Why hurt people you don't know?'

'Shh, Hermann. Shh. Please,' said Jürgen. 'They'll change their minds.' He was sobbing uncontrollably now.

Jochen and Sibbe turned on their heels and began to jog back towards the bar.

'What are we going to say to Udo, Sibbe?'

'What do you think? That we caught them and broke their elbows. No one will know any better if neither of us cracks.'

'I won't crack.'

'Neither will I.'

'Why didn't we hit them, Sibbe? Why did you let me persuade you?'

Sibbe shook his head. 'Because my brother's a pretty boy too. Just like the younger one of those two. And my mother loves him like crazy. I just couldn't do it. Not when they turned round and faced us like that. I can do it in the heat of the moment. Or when Udo is watching me. But I can't do it cold like that. They suddenly became real people. I have a nightmare that we're going to do my brother and his lot one day. Then what do I do?'

'I don't know, Sibbe.'

'Neither do I.'

TWENTY-SEVEN

Udo smashed the last queer left standing and then gave him a second belting across the hind quarters for good measure. His pickaxe handle was splintered and he was sweating with the effort of fag-bashing. 'Right. We're out of here.' He signalled to Lenzi. 'Your whistle.'

Lenzi blew his whistle.

The LB Sonderkommando pulled back. One man stepped sideways and raised his helve over a crawling man.

'No more bashing, you silly cunt. That's it.'

The man lowered his pickaxe handle.

Once outside they began to run.

'Anybody hurt?'

'No, Udo. We took them completely by surprise. We fucking wrecked them.'

Those amongst the Leather Bar's clients who were still conscious groaned and wailed in pain. Legs, arms and hips were broken. Hands had been crushed. Knees shattered. The landlord, who had been caught telephoning, had a smashed ribcage and a fractured femur. Men were dragging themselves around the floor as in the aftermath of a major traffic accident.

Udo looked at Sibbe. 'Did you get those two who were running away?'

'Yes, Udo. We smashed their phones too.'

'Good. This was an excellent operation. Excellent. You are all getting better. Working like a team for a change.'

'Thank you, Udo.'

'Now you see what we can accomplish when we work together. No one can stand against us.'

They drove slowly out of town, each in opposite directions. Then they curved back towards the pre-arranged rendezvous, which was at the fourth angle of an imaginary square.

'Pickaxe handles down.'

The men laid their pickaxe handles in a grid on the ground.

Udo squirted lighter fuel on them, fired up the matchbox and threw it onto the grid.

The pickaxe handles burst into flame.

'Take off your over-clothes and masks.' Udo waited until the handles were well alight. 'Now dump the clothes on top.' Udo took the second sachet of lighter fuel and squirted it over the clothes. He threw the empty sachets onto the bonfire. 'Right. We're out of here.'

Udo's Sonderkommando dispersed back into their vans. Two of the vans started straight off, but Udo waited behind for a moment, watching the bonfire. It reminded him of archive film he had seen of the Brown Shirts on the night of the Burning of the Books in 1933. His grandfather had been present at the Munich burning. In Berlin, forty thousand people had gathered at the Opernplatz to hear Joseph Goebbels's speech denouncing decadence and moral corruption, and twenty-five thousand un-German books had subsequently been torched.

'This time we will do it right,' Udo said to his silent audience.

When he was sure that the bonfire was roaring, he gunned his engine and followed the others.

TWENTY-EIGHT

'The police have been to see my mother and Clive.'

'And?'

'And nothing.' Hart shrugged his shoulders. 'As far as Clive is concerned I am still in Central America. As far as my mother is concerned, I may as well be in Greenland. I didn't disabuse either of them of their notions. I hardly think their phones will be tapped yet.'

'I'm sorry, John.'

Hart gave a long sigh. 'Why has all this happened? Ever since Syria my life seems to have gone to shit.'

'Sorry to add insult to injury, but the police have been to your flat too.'

'You sent someone along to check?'

'I asked Wesker to sniff around a little. See if you were home. It was clear he thought I was suffering from withdrawal symptoms – that I thought you were cheating on me.'

'Does he still think that?'

'No.'

'What else did you tell him?'

'Not a lot. Wesker will have worked it all out for himself by now. He doesn't need me to baby him along.'

'Lovely lot, journalists.'

'They're your only friends.'

'Only because I'm part of a story.'

'There is that.'

Hart and Amira looked at each other. The tension between them was palpable.

'Does Wesker know I'm not even seeing you at the moment? Far less anyone on the side?'

Amira ducked her head as if Hart's words might leave a scar behind them if they struck her. 'I got you your fake passport.' She tossed it onto the table between them. 'It's good for most things. But I wouldn't try travelling to the US if I were you.'

'I've no intention of travelling to the US. It's way too close to Guatemala. Like two thousand miles close.'

Amira laughed. Hart smiled back. Both were hyper-aware how things stood with them. But neither dared address the underlying issues.

'How did you get it?'

'Through a crypto-anarchist network. I stumbled onto them once during an investigation, and I've used them a few times since when I've wanted to cover my traces on the internet. Muddle up search patterns. Use what they call cypherspace. It's a great resource when one encounters copyright problems in the real world. Because in cypherspace no one can hear you cream.'

'That's a dreadful pun.'

'It's not mine.'

'I didn't think it was, Amira.'

They were both silent.

'I got the passport in exchange for information and immunity, if you really want to know. The cryptos now feel protected because they hold details of your false identity, which they have vowed to give up at the first sign of double-dealing. And we're protected because they need me to cover their backsides and give them warning in case they are ever investigated by the newspaper. Which I've promised to do.'

'That's comforting. So they don't know who I actually am, but only my pseudonym? What a relief. I was anticipating blackmail. It would have made such a welcome change from being a murder suspect.'

'Why is everything a source of amusement to you, John? These people aren't criminals. They really believe in what they are doing.'

'As do you. Obviously.' Hart tried on a grin, but it was a poor substitute for how he really felt. 'Tell me, is there any nutcase-anti-statist-anarcho-looney-counter-capitalist-cyberpunk-hacktivist type group out there that you wouldn't support at a pinch and hand my identity over to?'

'No. There isn't. And it's not your identity anyway. Your name is really John Hart and not Johannes von Hartelius, in case you've forgotten.'

A shadow crossed Hart's face. 'Actually, it is my real identity. Johannes von Hartelius is the name I would have been born with if my father had known where he truly came from. It's the oddest feeling. I don't think I've quite come to terms with it yet.'

'Well, you'd better come to terms with it soon. The LB are upping their game. Or at least we think they are. Racist and homophobic attacks are on the increase all around the Munich area. There have been the usual tit-for-tat reprisals from amongst the Turkish community against random whites, and angry street demonstrations by the gay community, with the equally inevitable backlash from "out of sight, out of mind" Joe Citizen. Which is exactly what the LB wants.'

'What do you think the LB are after in the long term? Is it anarchy, do you think? The same as your friends the cryptos?'

'No. It's not anarchy they're after. It's political power. With the main population as sandwich meat between them and the opposition. It's exactly what the SA Brown Shirts and the communists did in Germany during the 1920s, when they faced up to each other in the streets. Each side thought they would come out the stronger. That the main mass of the public would attach itself to their bandwagon. And look what came of that. Adolf Hitler. Talk about unintended consequences.'

'But these people are marginal. The situation isn't comparable, surely?'

'You don't think so? The LB – or one of their offshoots – are already killers. Killers and maimers. The parallels with how the Nazis went about it is striking. It doesn't take much to set people off during a Depression. They're frenetically keying into people's fears of being swamped by immigrants and gays and Jews.'

'Jews? In Germany? After all that's gone before? You can't be serious.'

'Yes, the Jewish thing is still up and running. It always is. And always will be.'

'But I thought you sat astride that particular argument? Being half Jew and half Arab? Last I heard you were pro-Palestinian and anti-Zionist.'

'Anti-Zionist doesn't mean anti-Semitic. I may be against a Jewish state built on someone else's land, but I'm Jew enough to resent being singled out because I am Jewish, and Arab enough to resent being singled out because I am Arab.'

'Bloody heck.'

'It's not funny, John.'

'You're always telling me things aren't funny. But laughter is sometimes the only possible answer when one bumps up against mass insanity.'

Amira shook her head. 'For as the crackling of thorns under a pot, so is the laughter of the fool: this also is vanity.'

'Where does that come from?'

'Ecclesiastes. I think it hits the mark, don't you?'

TWENTY-NINE

'The lads are getting better, Effi. All except Sibbe and the new boy, Jochen.'

'What's wrong with them?'

'They lied to me yesterday, at the gay bashing.'

'How do you know?'

'They told me they smashed up two queers who ran away from the car park as we arrived.'

'How do you know they didn't?'

'When they handed me their pickaxe handles to burn there wasn't any blood on them. All the other pickaxes were dripping with it. Split and shattered. I could have sold theirs brand new.'

'Do you think they're undercover?'

'No. I think they're scared. And squeamish. I think they should be put on special duties.'

Effi looked at him. 'You know what that means?'

'One's an orphan, the other might as well be. His brother is queer. I know that for a fact. I think that's why he held back.'

'It's not his fault his brother is queer.'

'But it's his fault he held back.'

'Yes. It is.'

'Special duties?'

'Yes. Tell them they've been chosen out of all the others because you're so impressed by their commitment.'

'They'll like being postmen. Foreign travel and all that.'

'Jochen will have to let his hair grow out a bit.'

'We've got time. They'll need training.'

'When's your next outing?'

'Saturday.'

'Who is it this time?'

'We won't know until the actual night. It's better that way.'

'You enjoy all this, don't you, Udo?'

'No. It's not about enjoyment for me. It's about setting the record straight.'

THIRTY

Hart was slowly getting to grips with the basics of the German language. He was studying for up to six hours every day. He was studying so much his brain hurt.

Amira was still not inviting him into her bed. And he wasn't pushing for it. He couldn't quite understand why.

Sometimes he went out, heavily disguised in a trilby that Amira's Egyptian father, Nassif, used to wear in a bid to appear more conventional when he went to visit his wife's Jewish relatives in Swiss Cottage. It hadn't worked. According to Amira, her mother's family had viewed being a Coptic Christian as akin to being a golem. In their view, the New Testament was an abhorrence, and those who believed in it abhorrent in turn. Such people – Catholics, Protestants, Copts, Russian Orthodox, Eastern Orthodox, etc. – were behind every evil thing that had happened to the Jews in the twenty centuries that had elapsed since the Crucifixion. Nassif hadn't dared argue.

In an effort to exact compensation of sorts, Amira's grandparents had pressurized Nassif into agreeing to Amira carrying their surname, arguing that in the Jewish tradition descent was guaranteed by the female line. The ever-tolerant Nassif had gone along with it in a doomed attempt to keep the peace and be accepted by his wife's family – which was something that a less gullible man might have realized was never going to happen. Amira had abominated 'niceness' ever since.

No wonder she's so mixed up, thought Hart. Being part of a family like that must have been worse than being brought up in a convent. Religion had a lot to answer for, he decided, and those who hid behind it as an excuse not to think for themselves were the worst offenders. Wasn't there enough strife in the world without adding to it by default?

In the end they both agreed that Hart should wait at least another week before travelling to Bavaria, by which time any interest the British police had in him might have dwindled. The Holy Lance was being endlessly talked about on the internet, and there was much toing and froing of experts opining on this and that. Germany's leading dendroarchaeologist had agreed to travel to Bavaria and pronounce on the newly discovered Lance's possible age, and then compare it in detail to pictures taken of the original Vienna Lance before it fell into Hitler's hands. The LB's claim that the Holy Lance at present held in the Hofburg Imperial Palace Treasure Chamber in Vienna was actually one of Hitler's forgeries – and that General Patton had been fooled into assuming it was the original one – had thrown the cat amongst the proverbial pigeons.

It would no longer seem so surprising, therefore, if Hart, in his von Hartelius guise, heard about it and came calling. The LB were busy claiming that 'manifold destiny' intended them to have the Holy Lance, which is why it had been dug up on their leader's land. Insane as it all sounded, there were many people out there both willing and able to swallow the lie.

'And what is your plan after that, John? After you go knocking on Effi Rache's door saying, "Look, it's me!"?'

'There is no plan after that. I'm going to wing it until I discover what I need to know.'

'I see. Good thinking. And I just sit here and play backstop to your forward?'

'I'll pass you on any information I find out.'

'That's big of you. I hope you've got your backstory down pat, or they'll skin you alive.'

'Why are you always so pissed off at me? You only have to look at me to become aggressive.'

'I'm not aggressive.'

'You could have fooled me.'

Amira scowled at him. 'I don't like to be owned.'

'Owned? How can I possibly own you? I don't even get to fuck you any more.'

'Oh, that's what it is? Fucking? Not even making love. Just fucking.'

'I would be scared to make love to you in your present state. You might think I was trying to own you.' Hart ducked the tea towel Amira threw at his head. 'Amira, why do you always make life so bloody complicated?'

'Because it is complicated.'

'How?'

'If you don't know, I can't tell you.'

Hart hunched forward. He folded the tea towel and laid it carefully on the table between them like a peace offering. 'Maybe you should have an affair with Wesker? He's an alcoholic. That would complicate matters nicely, wouldn't it?' He raised an eyebrow to show that he wasn't being serious. Wesker looked like a cross between a gurnard and a bullmastiff, and he didn't want to risk Amira launching the teapot at him. 'Where is the great man, by the way? I have a funny feeling we haven't heard the last of him.'

'He's in Bavaria.'

'Ah. Poodling around for you again?'

'Yes. Poodling around arranging a safe house for us in Rottach Egern. Wesker and I have agreed to collaborate on the LB story.'

'Cosy. And where's Rottach Egern?'

'Across Lake Tegernsee from Bad Wiessee. Which is where Effi Rache lives, in case you've forgotten.'

Hart sat back in his chair. 'So you're serious about all this? You're really going for the big story? You're not going to cut me loose and move on to the next thing?'

'No. I'm not going to cut you loose.' Amira looked down at her hands. 'I love you, John. That admission may surprise you, because you have me down as such a cold fish, obsessed with my career and my politics to the exclusion of all else. But I love you so much it hurts.' She raised a hand to prevent him interrupting. She refused to look him in the eye. 'My heart flutters like a teenager's when you enter the room. When you make love to me I feel like I am dying and have gone to heaven. I love the look of you. I love the smell of you. I love the sound of your voice.'

'So where's our problem, then?'

'I love you but I can't live with you.'

'That's crazy, Amira.'

'No, it's not. I can't live with you because I know that part of you still wants me to knuckle down and become a sort of glorified *hausfrau*, whilst you go off gallivanting around the world. Oh, you wouldn't want me to grind completely to a halt. You'd like me to go on writing a few articles for the girlie bits in the magazines – get myself a picture byline and an audience gleaned from the *Daily Telegraph* culture pages. Live in a cottage in the country. Raise a brood. But I'm better than that.'

Hart sat back in bewilderment. 'When have I ever said that?'

'You don't need to say it. All I have to do is look at your face when we talk about children and my whole future is spread out in front of me like a roadmap. You're never going to forgive me for aborting our child, are you? It's always going to be there between us.'

Hart closed his eyes. 'It's not a matter for forgiveness. But you should have asked me. Allowed me the chance to sway you.'

'There. I told you. We're no further forward.'

Hart stood up. His chair crashed onto the floor dramatically, though he hadn't intended for it to do so. 'Right. That's it. I'm not hanging around here for another week, whilst you resent me and imagine I'm trying to ground you. I'm leaving for Germany now. We can't go on like this – hot and cold, cold and hot. You're not going to change and neither am I. We either accept that and agree to a compromise, or we're finished. You go your way and I go mine.'

'But –'

'Listen to me, Amira. I've no intention of curtailing your career. Or telling you what you ought to be doing. Or turning you into a *hausfrau*. I've never done that and I never will. I'm not your father and I'm not your mother and I dearly wish you'd stop projecting them onto me. My only concern at the moment is to find the people who killed Colel Cimi, my father and Santiago, and make them pay for it. If that brings you a prizewinning story, all well and good. If it doesn't, I'm sorry, but I'm still going to do it. If your crypto-arsehole friends cut up rough about getting me my passport, they can hand me over to the police and have done with it.'

Hart began shovelling his clothes directly from the coffee table into his holdall.

'John, you can't allow emotion to sway you in this.' Amira was as close to tears as she was ever likely to come. 'You're not nearly ready yet. The LB are dangerous. Far more dangerous than you suspect. Your cover needs to be perfect.'

'What can be more dangerous than premeditated murder?

I saw my father nailed to a wall and speared. I saw Santiago degutted. And Colel Cimi floating face down in a lake with a broken neck. I'm fresh from my own botched execution and a repeat bout of malaria. And still I can't speak German. Look at me.' Hart raised his hands into the air and let them fall. 'I'm about as ready as I'm ever likely to be.'

THIRTY-ONE

Hart took the overnight Stena Hollandica Superferry from Harwich to the Hook of Holland, leaving Harwich at 23.15 and arriving in Holland at 07.45 the next morning. He used the same logic he had used coming over from France two weeks previously – namely that foot passengers were less likely to be booze or cigarette smugglers and therefore more likely to be waved through passport control without their identity papers being scanned.

This time he wasn't so lucky. British customs officers were monitoring all passports heading for the continent. Hart stood in the queue wondering whether he should pull out and head back to London. But then he noticed the CCTV cameras. The film would be checked. Someone would be watching. Passengers leaving the line would be routinely photographed and their faces held on record. And he'd already bought the original ticket using his von Hartelius alias. The fact that he'd paid cash for it was irrelevant. He had still been forced to give the name exactly as it was written on his passport. When he didn't turn up for the trip, his name and photograph would be flagged up. He might as well send customs a letter denouncing himself.

He handed over his passport and watched as it was placed on the scanner. He tried to unclench his jaw. He could already envision the gaggle of customs officers rounding the corner to confront him. Should he run? But the place was crawling with uniforms. Maybe Amira could make a story out of it yet? *Inept photojournalist caught on first leg of revenge journey. Fake passport tripped him up. Crypto-anarchists must have seeded it with fatal flaw, declares felon.*

'Next, please.'

Hart took the passport and continued towards the ferry. He was through. The relief of the moment was immediately overtaken by the realization that he was committed now. On his way. Bloody well launched.

He sat on the deck of the ferry and tried to gather his thoughts together. He'd left Amira on a terminally bad note. He'd refused her offer of a pay-as-you-go phone on the pretext that he didn't want anything that could incriminate him when he eventually made contact with the LB. He'd also refused her offer to allow him back into her bedroom. He'd aggravated the refusal by implying that her proposal might be principally motivated by her desire to stay with the story, rather than any belated desire for him.

If he'd had the sense to accept the phone he might have called her up and apologized. Instead he sat on the boat and watched the sun set over the remnants of their relationship. Then he went to sleep in a chair rather than in a cabin, as that way he would at least get some warning if the authorities decided to come for him during the night.

Next morning he took the train via Amsterdam to Munich. He had cleared out all his accounts, including the full extent of his overdraft allowance, before posting his credit and debit cards back to himself at his mother's address. He had a little under two thousand euros in cash. Hardly enough to sponsor a major campaign against the LB, but enough to last for a couple of weeks if he spent the money frugally. He'd had a rough moment at the bank wondering if the police had closed down his accounts, but then he remembered that Scotland Yard did not even know for certain that he was back in the country. His paper trail only led as far as Paris. And maybe the relationship between the UK and Guatemala didn't stretch to monitoring people's bank accounts? That took manpower – something the British police were notoriously short of. Maybe he should turn to identity theft and thievery when he eventually ran out of cash? It wasn't as bad as being a murderer, after all. And he seemed to be getting rather good at it.

After the seven-hour trip from Amsterdam he switched to a local train from Munich to Tegernsee. Tiredness nearly persuaded him to give up and get himself a stopgap hotel, but he was so near to his goal that he felt it would be counter-productive to bottle out at this stage. He walked the five minutes from the station to the lakeside Ducal Brewery at Schloss Tegernsee. He drank a litre of beer and ate a plate of local white sausage with rye bread and sweet mustard, followed by some Kaiserschmarrn pancakes with powdered sugar, rum-soaked raisins and a plum compote, which he'd seen other people eat and fancied the look of. His German, he discovered, wasn't remotely up to translating the menu.

After his meal, he took the ferry across the lake to Bad Wiessee, where he knew Effi Rache lived. He sat with the wind in his hair and stared at the mountains all around him. The lake, with him at its centre, was held within the bowl of the mountains as if in a pair of outstretched hands. He had never been to Bavaria before, and yet he felt a curious sense of homecoming as he looked about himself. Almost as if he were expected.

He walked up from the ferry terminus at Bad Wiessee towards the Freihausweg. He asked an elderly local woman in halting German where the Haus Walküre was, and she pointed up a narrow road backed on one side by a pine forest, and on the other by lush hay meadows.

He walked for ten more minutes until he crossed a small bridge over a trout stream. He stood for a while, unable to tear his eyes from the shadows of the fish beneath the bridge. Then he walked through a span of overhanging trees. On the left, straddling the hillside, were a number of houses with wooden terraces, sloping roofs and ornately carved balconies. One of them had Hotel Alpenruh painted in discreet lettering on its terrace wall. Two hundred yards below the hotel, Haus

Walküre was set back from the road and held within its own great meadow, dotted with brown and white Pinzgauer cattle. The farmhouse was constructed in the old Bavarian style, with the house directly attached to the main barn into which the cattle would be shunted via a ramp, their residual warmth heating and insulating the house during the long winter.

Effi Rache's house was on three levels, its balconies festooned with hanging baskets full of flowers. Each window was framed by green shutters, whilst the window surrounds boasted intricately painted decorative borders. The main frontage of the house was also painted, this time with religious iconography – Jesus carrying a scroll, angels with musical instruments, and assorted saints. The upper balcony area was decorated with non-religious themes – men in lederhosen and leather breeches chopping wood, whilst milkmaids in dirndl dresses brought them refreshments. A blue and white Bavarian pennant hung from a flagpole in front of the house.

Hart continued up the hill until he came to a stone staircase leading to a slope, and then on to another staircase that would take him to the Hotel Alpenruh's terrace café. He turned and looked once again at Haus Walküre. It was perfect. Immaculate. Even the Pinzgauer cattle looked as though they had been currycombed and then given a buffing with a straw wisp for good measure. How could a place of such exquisite beauty possibly house such evil?

He walked onto the hotel's empty terrace, hesitated for a moment, and then made his way through an open door marked 'office'. An elderly woman, nearer ninety than eighty, sat behind the desk. She was writing by hand in a ledger. Hart thought he could smell coffee and spices and salami and vanilla and possibly plum cake wafting towards him from the kitchen area behind her. For a moment he wondered if he hadn't stepped through a time gap into the 1950s.

'Good afternoon, Gnädige Frau. Forgive my poor German. But might I have a single room with a balcony and a view? Facing the front if possible? So that I can overlook the lake?'

The old lady burst out laughing. She regained control after a few seconds and replied to Hart's question in heavily accented English. 'I'm sorry for laughing at you, young man. But nobody has called me Gnädige Frau for over thirty years now. And your grammar is truly shocking. What primer have you been using?'

The old lady's good humour was infectious. It was impossible to take offence at anything she said. Hart was relieved to be able to continue in English. 'Ah. You have me there. I bought it at a second-hand bookshop and didn't think to check the date.'

'Well, the use of Gnädige marks a welcome return to formal politeness. Please continue using it.' She put on a pair of reading glasses and lowered her head over her schedule. 'Yes, you are in luck. We have a room. And it has a balcony. And a view of the lake. In fact, we have many rooms. Since the closure of the main Bad Wiessee spa, we seem to have nothing but rooms, and no one to put in them. No one wants spas any more. They want adventure holidays, and kayaking, and

bungee jumping. This is to be our final season. And you, Mr…'
She took off her reading glasses and hesitated, looking at him
more closely.

'Johannes von Hartelius.' Hart handed her his passport.

The old woman sat back in her chair, her arms gripping
the sides. She ignored the passport. Her startled eyes, milky
with cataracts, never left Hart's face. 'And you, Baron Sanct
Quirin, are our only guest.'

THIRTY-TWO

'Why did you call me Baron Sanct Quirin, Frau Erlichmann?'
Hart was seated across from the old lady at one of the dining-
room tables. An elderly waitress in a Bavarian pinafore dress
had just served them coffee.

'Because that is who you are.'

'May I ask how you can possibly know this? You did not
even glance at my passport. And the barony you speak of
doesn't appear there.'

Frau Erlichmann bowed her head. 'At first I did not know it
for certain. My eyes are bad, you see. And you spoke execrably
poor German. But then I saw you. This happens sometimes. It
is like a curtain lifting. Soon the surgeons will operate, then
I shall see properly again. Or so they tell me.' She laughed.

'So you thought you recognized me?'

'Thought? Doubt doesn't come into it, young man. You
are the image...' She hesitated. 'The double, I should say,
of your grandfather. Not your father. Your grandfather.

Sometimes I forget how very old I am. In my head I am still a young woman.'

'You knew him? My grandfather?'

'Knew him? Certainly not. It was more what you would call a schoolgirl crush. I was ten years old, and already serving table at my parents' hotel. Your grandfather was a dashing young officer in the Reichswehr. An aristocrat. A "celebrity" you would probably call him now. He came here many times with your grandmother for coffee. She was very glamorous. She looked like the actress Brigitte Helm. I hated her and wished she would die, so he might notice me and we could get married. I would spy on them and their friends from below the counter. I was so small the guests couldn't see me. But I could see them. I can't tell you how many times I imagined sprinkling a little rat poison over the baroness's *zwetschgenkuchen*. But then, of course, you would not be here. So I am grateful I did not do it. How very brutal little girls can be when they are in love. No?' Frau Erlichmann laughed.

'So they lived here? In the neighbourhood?'

'But surely you know this? This is why you have come back?'

'Know what?'

Frau Erlichmann watched Hart closely. It was clear that she suspected he might be trying to make fun of her after her embarrassing admission. 'For your grandfather's castle. After the war the Americans took it over for a military barracks. They have been there ever since. In two years they are leaving. I assume you are here to arrange for its transfer back into your family?'

Hart leant forward, his coffee cup poised halfway between his lips and the table. 'Where is this castle?'

Frau Erlichmann stared at Hart as if he had taken leave of his senses. She shook her head as though she was dealing with a simpleton. 'Behind us. Through the forest. About two kilometres due west. But how can you not know the location of your own castle?'

'Ah,' said Hart. 'That is a very long story…'

THIRTY-THREE

'But the Raches are filth. You must have nothing whatsoever to do with them. You know the expression "the apple never falls far from the tree"? Well, this applies to them. The father was bad. The grandfather was worse. The daughter is worst of all.'

'I've heard the expression, yes. But I must ignore it. For the time being at least. I can't tell you why.'

'Then you are a fool.'

'You sound as if you have a personal grievance against the Raches.'

'You could call it personal. Heinrich Rache denounced my parents to the Gestapo in 1942. I know this for a fact. But I cannot prove it, because the records have mysteriously disappeared. Such things happened after the war. The Americans did what they wanted. If somebody helped them, they helped him. And Heinrich Rache helped them a lot. So his records were erased.'

'What happened to your parents?'

'They were ordered in front of a *Sondergericht* court. They were condemned as "enemies of the Reich". They were sent to Dachau concentration camp, which is just outside Munich. They were immediately separated. My father committed suicide in 1943 after he heard that my mother had died in the women's camp of malnutrition. I suspect that it wasn't malnutrition that killed her, but a broken heart. My parents were very close. Separation would have been an abomination to them both.'

'What were they accused of?'

'My mother had been heard changing the Hitler salute from "Heil Hitler" to *"zwei liter"* – meaning "two litres". This was considered un-German. When my father was confronted with this fact, and asked if he took responsibility for his wife's actions, he gave the court a piece of his mind. The result was foreordained. The real reason behind the denunciation was that Rache wanted to buy some land my father owned, and my father refused to sell it to him. The Raches of this world aren't used to taking no for an answer.'

'I am very sorry. What happened to you?'

'I was nineteen years old when my parents were taken. I was given a choice. I could either enrol in the German Red Cross or accompany my parents to the camp. My father persuaded me to enrol in the German Red Cross. It is a decision I regret to this day.'

'What happened to this house?'

'It was turned into a girls' school. The land, of course, went to Rache. After the war, when the Americans found out what had happened to my parents, it was returned to me. For that much, at least, I am grateful to the Amis.'

'And you?'

'I served first in Norway, then later in Czechoslovakia. My girlfriend Trudl and I ran away when the Russians entered the country. We were afraid of being raped. We walked all the way home. It took us three months.'

'Did you know that your parents were dead?'

'I knew. The Third Reich was very efficient in such matters. A letter was sent to me where I was serving saying that my parents had passed away whilst imprisoned by the state, and that all their assets had been confiscated.' Frau Erlichmann glanced towards the window. 'So you see, Baron, I sit here in my parents' house, and I look out across that meadow, and I see the granddaughter of the man who was responsible for my parents' ruin and death trying to bring back the very same regime that destroyed them. Only this time she is doing it by stealth. Preaching moderation with one hand, fomenting civil unrest with the other. And I can do nothing about it. Absolutely nothing.'

Hart leant across the table between them. He grasped Frau Erlichmann's hand and squeezed it. 'But I can. If you will help me.'

THIRTY-FOUR

Effi Rache sat between her two girlfriends at the Gasthof zur Hirschtal and tried not to look at the man dining alone at the window table ten feet away from her. But each time she looked away, her attention was drawn back to him again. There was something familiar about him. Some distant memory associated with the way he looked.

'Do you know who he is?' she whispered to her friend, Margrit Hanauer. 'I've seen him before. I know it. Is he an actor?'

Margrit leant to one side and opened her handbag. As she did so she glanced across at the man. 'No. But he's handsome enough. He looks like Brad Pitt. Only with a widow's peak instead of a straight hairline. Do you fancy him, then? Do you want me to go over and fetch him for you?'

Effi punched Margrit lightly under the table. 'Don't be so stupid.' But she kept on looking at him. It would come back to her eventually, this elusive memory. But why didn't he look up?

Everybody knew who she was. The other diners had clocked her straight away. But he seemed lost in whatever he was reading and didn't appear to know that she was in the room.

A flurry began on a table at the far side of the panelled dining room. Effi glanced over. Three young men were eating Sauerbraten and drinking steins of beer with schnapps chasers. One of the young men was pointing across to her and saying something in a loud voice to his companions, who were trying to restrain him.

Effi was used to this. People either supported her or hated her. There was no middle ground. This meant that she encountered an equal mixture of anger and adulation everywhere she went. It rarely got out of hand, though. The Bavarians still held to the habits of formal courtesy that they had inherited from their forebears. But politics fuelled by drink was another matter entirely.

The boy made as if to get up from his seat but his friends dragged him down again. Margrit rolled her eyes, and Effi's other friend, Alena, made a face and took out her phone. 'Shall I call Udo?'

'God, no. We involve that little shit and our name is mud. He'd probably wreck the place and lose us fifty votes. Let these people dig their own grave. They don't need any help from us.'

The uproar was getting worse. The other diners had become aware of the problem and were glancing across the dining room with a mixture of disapproval and apprehension. The manageress was preparing to involve herself. One of the chefs had emerged from the kitchen and was monitoring proceedings.

The young man broke away from his companions and made across the floor towards Effi's table.

'Oh God. Maybe you had better call Udo after all.'

Alena ducked down and began making the call.

'You fucking fascist whore.' The young man was shouting as he walked. He was pointing his finger at Effi. 'You know who this bitch is, everybody? She's the person who is trying to send Germany seventy years into the past. She's trying to turn back the clock to the good old Hitlerzeit.'

The manageress had reached the young man by this time and had put out a hand to calm him down, but he shrugged her off and kept walking.

'She wants all the Turks out. The Poles out. The Romanians out. She wants the Jews out, and the Muslims out, and the gays and lesbians out. She probably wants you all out too. She wants to keep Germany for herself and her cronies. Well, I know her little plan. We're not going to let her in. You mustn't either. We've been here before. We don't want to go down that path again.'

He had reached Effi's table by this time. He hammered on it with his hand.

Effi and her girlfriends stood up. Effi's face was white with rage, but she refused to back away. Her girlfriends stood a little behind her and to one side. Alena had finished making her call and slipped her phone back into her handbag.

Effi took a step forward and made as if to walk past her aggressor towards the exit.

It was then that the young man hit her. It wasn't a hard

blow – more like a lazy slap. But the sound echoed through the dining room like a thunderclap.

Hart stood up. He approached the young man from the rear, snatched his arms from behind him, and eased upwards, so that both arms were straightened out to their full extent and pushing against the shoulder sockets.

'Do you understand English?'

'Ja. Ja.' The boy seesawed his head. His eyes were wide open and his lips drawn back in pain.

'If you move a muscle I'll dislocate your arms. I mean this.' Hart looked towards Effi. Their eyes met for the first time. 'This man struck you without provocation. There are witnesses. Do you intend to prosecute?'

Effi shook her head. 'No. He didn't really hurt me. He only surprised me, that's all. It was nothing.' Her English was lightly accented and fluent. Finishing-school English. She spoke deliberately, with an emphasis on the consonants. The tone she took made it clear to everybody that she wished to avoid a scandal, whether they understood English or not.

Hart ducked his head towards the young man's companions. 'One of you pay the bill. The other one come over here. Hands held out where I can see them. Then you take him and you leave. If you turn round before you get to the door, or begin shouting again, or cause any trouble at all, the manageress will call the police. We'll see which car you leave in. We'll have the number. So it won't take long for them to come calling.'

Both boys nodded. One of them got out his wallet and began counting out some money on the table. The other couldn't seem to decide whether to make for the door or go and rescue his friend.

'Don't spend too long thinking about it. Come over here and take him off my hands. And I repeat, if either of you makes a single aggressive move, this thing will escalate to the next stage. There'll be no comeback from that. Is that clear?'

The boys put on surly faces, but neither showed any hint of intended aggression. One of the boys walked towards Hart and stopped a few paces away from him.

'Here. He's yours.' Hart released the boy with a light shove.

The boy turned round. For one moment it looked as though he intended to continue his rant.

Hart opened his hands expectantly. He never took his eyes off the boy's face. 'You're what – seventeen? Eighteen? Take this any further and you'll wreck your life. Walk out the door and you can make up any story you want about today. Show off to your friends. Play the hero. But in here, things are real. There are witnesses. Why not pretend you're a grown-up for a change?'

Hart turned round and walked back to his table. He picked up his book and began to read. From time to time he spooned a forkful of food into his mouth. He could feel the atmosphere simmering and seething around him.

It was only when the clapping began from the other diners that Hart realized the boys had taken the hint and made good their escape. He ducked his head a little in acknowledgment of the applause, and then went back to reading his book. The boys glared at him through the window as they passed by outside.

'Excuse me.'

Hart looked up.

'I want to thank you. For what you did.' Effi Rache was looking at him intently.

Hart could feel the testosterone triggered by the altercation still surging through him. Effi Rache was a beautiful woman. Physically – apart from her hair colouring, for he had always mistrusted blondes and favoured brunettes – she was close to his ideal. Deep-blue eyes, an emphatic waist, small breasts, and a pronounced bottom, which her spray-on jeans did little to conceal. She stood beside him, flanked by her two clones, and he could literally smell the sex on her. The feeling astonished him. He wanted to grab her by the hair, force her head back, and claim his prize. The feeling was both primitive and overwhelming.

Hart stood up. He allowed no shadow of what he felt to pass over his face, but the sexual chemistry between the two of them was palpable. He was aware of Effi's girlfriends looking quizzically at her. If this was the woman responsible for the deaths of his father, Santiago and Colel Cimi, then fate had afforded her a very efficient form of camouflage.

'You are English. So you probably do not know who I am. My name is Elfriede Rache.' She held out her hand.

Hart took it. 'I'm English, yes. But of German descent. My name is Johannes von Hartelius. And of course I know who you are. Our grandparents were neighbours once upon a time.'

'So you've come back to visit?'

'No. I've come back to claim my castle.'

THIRTY-FIVE

Udo Zirkeler had only been able to gather up Sibbe and Jochen out of his usual gang at such short notice – his two weakest reeds. This was typical. There would come a time when he'd have a barracks-full to choose from, like his grandfather had had before him. But that was far into the future. For the time being, he would have to make do with what he had.

He drew up in front of the Gasthof zur Hirschtal and ordered his men to pile out. It wasn't often that Effi called on him personally any more, and he wanted to milk the moment for all it was worth. Effi's friend Alena liked him, he knew. If he stayed close to her he would stay close to Effi. Then he could dump Alena when things got interesting.

Effi and the two women were talking to a man in the parking place of the Gasthof. Was this the guy who was causing the trouble? Udo took an instant dislike to him. The man had the patrician look that always hit Udo's top note. Tall, limber, good-looking. The sort of man who knew the world was his oyster, and wanted champagne with it. Officer class.

Udo ran towards the group, Sibbe and Jochen trailing in his wake.

Alena broke away towards him, one hand held high to slow him down. 'It's all right, Udo. They're gone. This man chased them off for us.'

Udo pulled up near the group, panting. He was not a tall man, but he was heavily muscled, thanks to endless workouts and protein mixes, and running was no longer his forte.

'Chased them off?'

'There were three of them. One of them gave us a lot of grief. The baron saw them off.'

'The baron?' Udo's heart sank. The man was a fucking baron. Good-looking and a baron. And he'd seen off Effi's assailants. Jealousy flared through Udo's body like a poison. 'Where are the bastards? I'll follow them home and turn them into rissoles. Do you have their number plate? I'll call Munter at police HQ. He owes us a favour.'

'No, you won't.' Effi turned away from the baron to concentrate on Udo. As she did so she flared her eyes at Udo in a clear message that he should shut up.

Udo was immune to messages. He could see the man looking at Effi possessively. See his eyes travelling across Effi's bottom. Resting on the back of Effi's head. Udo knew just what to look for in his competitors. Knew just how their minds worked. His own worked in exactly the same way. When men did gallant things, they expected prizes.

'Why won't I?'

'Because we can't afford bad publicity before the European elections. And any public episode where someone turns against the LB is bad publicity. We can't win. Our opponents rub their hands in glee and applaud our aggressor. That's the sort of logic we must put up with. We must remain whiter than white.'

'I'll drive you home, then. Sibbe and Jochen can accompany your two friends.'

'No, thank you, Udo. Margrit will take Alena back in her car. The baron is going to drive me home in mine. It seems we are neighbours again.'

'Neighbours again? What are you talking about?'

'I'm sorry, Udo, my mistake. May I present Johannes Freiherr von Hartelius. He is staying at the Alpenruh whilst he negotiates about the future of his castle. I believe his great-grandfather employed your great-grandfather in his Freikorps after the First World War, so you two will have a great deal in common. Life is strange, isn't it? The baron is the very man I have been wanting to meet.'

THIRTY-SIX

'Why are you staying at the Alpenruh with that ghastly old woman? You could be staying at Bachmair's. Or the Überfahrt.'

'It's an odd thing to do, I know, but my grandparents loved the place. They used to go there in its heyday, during the 1930s. I thought it would be amusing.'

'But she's a communist.'

'She must be nearly ninety. I suspect she's no longer a threat to the German state. But I'll keep my eyes and ears open nonetheless.'

'Now you're teasing me. But I'm serious.'

'I know you are. And so am I. I really will keep a watchful eye out in case she's passing messages to the Russians. I suspect she'll do it by hanging out sheets in a certain order. Like Morse code. I think I saw that once in an early Hitchcock film. It's a cast-iron technique, I gather.'

Effi had been evaluating and then matching her response to

what she believed men wanted all her life. This was how she got what she wanted. She knew better, therefore, than to follow that line of argument any further. 'May I ask you another question? But you give me a serious answer this time. Agreed?'

Hart smiled. 'You can ask me anything you like. But I can't promise to be serious.' He was stretched out in an original 1950s Charles Eames armchair, his feet up on the rest. He had a glass of Delamain XO cognac in his hand. He'd passed on the Second World War vintage SS *Stumpen* cigar from her late father's humidor, which Effi had offered him with an ironical laugh. No point in overdoing it at this stage. But he didn't feel as relaxed as he looked.

Effi Rache's drawing room ran the full length of the main floor of the house. Everything in it was either black or white. White carpets, freshly painted white walls, black furniture, black ornaments. The kitchen had been shunted downstairs, where the cellars had originally been. A swooping open staircase led up to what Hart assumed were two further floors of bedrooms and an attic.

'The question I want to ask is how do you speak no German? Your family is one of the oldest in Bavaria. And this is a country of old families. Our Wittelsbach kings first ruled in 1180. Your title stems from ten years later. Your grandfather was a war hero. Your grandmother one of our greatest female fliers. Where have you been all this time? What happened to your father, for instance?'

Hart had known it was coming, but he was still unprepared for it. He was not a gifted actor. His forte had always been humour.

The light riposte that deflected attention from more serious underlying issues. The sort of wit that went down so badly with Amira. There was a part of him now that wished he hadn't broken off contact with her quite so abruptly. She'd been right on the button when she'd told him preparation was everything in these cases. It would have been comforting to know that she was somewhere in the background, watching out for him.

'But how do you know I am who I say I am?' He shrugged. 'I might be an impostor. I might have made up my name on the spur of the moment just to impress you.'

Effi burst out laughing. She stood up and walked towards the floor-to-ceiling library section at the far end of her drawing room. 'Did you see me looking at you oddly before that little brat started shouting at me?'

'No. I was reading. I didn't notice you at all.'

Effi gave Hart a little pout from across her shoulder. She was aware of Hart's sexual interest in her, and was pleased to be able to display herself to him in a domestic setting. She held no illusions whatsoever about the effect of her beauty and desirability on men. They were a given. But it was Alpha males that appealed to her. Effi had no time for losers. 'Well, I was. Staring at you, I mean. Because you reminded me of someone. Someone I have been looking at all my life.'

Hart leant forward. What was she talking about? How could she have been looking at him all her life? He dropped his feet off the Eames foot-rest. Then he stood up, placed his glass of cognac on the table, and followed Effi through to the library section.

It didn't take him long to realize that Effi's way of walking – the movement of her hips, the sway of her bottom, the bounce of her hair – was having the most ridiculous effect on him. Maybe it was the mixture of cognac and beer after a long spell of virtual teetotalism? Maybe it was the fact that he hadn't had sex for more than three months and he missed it badly? Or maybe it was sheer bloody perversity? Whatever the reason, Hart found himself speculating on what Effi might look like beneath her spray-on jeans, and her boots, and her Cracker Barrel blouse. Looking at her, as she walked in front of him, it was inconceivable that she'd had anything to do with the murder of his father. The thug who had come running up with his two acolytes when they were in the car park? Him, yes. But her? Never.

A vision of Amira flashed through his consciousness and he felt a momentary pang of guilt. But she'd made it clear she didn't want him any more. Thought he wished to own her, when nothing was further from his mind. And their affair had been something of an on/off concern over the last ten years. Off more than on, lately. In fact, in the past twelve months it couldn't even be called an affair. More a sort of extended farewell.

Effi stopped at a gap between two floor-to-ceiling book-shelves. The actual wall was invisible from the rest of the room, so that one had to stand directly in front of it to see inside. And it could be covered, at will, by a sliding bookcase. The wall space itself was festooned with photographs, almost like a shrine. Hart recognized Goebbels, Himmler, Bormann and Speer, all posing unsmilingly and in official black and white. In each photograph they stood near a black-haired man in civilian clothes. He, too, was unsmiling, as if there were more important attributes to life than surface charm. In just one photograph – the near-ubiquitous one alongside Adolf Hitler – was the man wearing what amounted to a uniform. And this time he was grinning broadly. As if the Führer had just cracked a very good joke.

Maybe Hitler had just explained to him about the Wannsee conference? Hart squinted at the snapshots over Effi's shoulder. All I know for certain, he told himself, is that when she turns round to look at me I must pretend that such a wall and such photographs are part of the normal fabric of my life. My grandfather and my grandmother inhabited this world. I must act as if I am used to it. That I have come to terms with it long ago.

'That is my grandfather, Heinrich Rache. This is the memorial my father made to him.'

Despite all his resolutions, Hart found himself lost for words. He blurted out the first thing that came to mind. 'But he is dark-haired, and you are blonde.'

'My grandmother was a Jargenried. Jargenried women always throw blonde children. That is why my grandfather chose her.'

'Ah.'

'But my grandfather's photo is not the one I want you to see.' She bent down.

Effi's perfume floated up to him in waves. Hart suspected that she had taken the time to freshen up whilst she was out in the kitchen getting his drink. The position she was now taking, crouched beneath him and hunched a little forward, was inflammatory in the extreme, and plainly done with intent. It meant that Effi's jeans were stretched tightly across the rounded swell of her buttocks so that Hart could just make out the braided top of her red silk underwear poking over the hem. He moved a little closer.

'Here it is. I knew I would find it.' Effi stood up.

Hart had virtually boxed her into the shrine by this time.

When Effi realized how close Hart was standing to her she gave a triumphant little smile. 'It was on the very bottom row. Just where a child would be able to see it.' She swivelled the photograph round and held it to her chest like a school prize.

It was a wider-angled copy of the same photograph Hart had found beneath his father's desk in Antigua. This was the uncropped version, however, with four figures on it instead of two. An out-of-uniform Heinrich Rache was standing off to one side with a grotesquely fat, exotically uniformed Hermann Goering. Both men were beaming possessively at the two beautiful people standing by the aeroplane.

Effi touched the photograph with her fingernail, carefully picking out Johannes von Hartelius's head. 'Your grandfather.' She placed the same finger on the bridge of Hart's nose. 'You. No difference. Two peas in a pod. What do you say to that, Baron?'

Hart caught Effi's finger in his hand and bit down on it, as a cat will bite down on its owner's hand when it wishes to play. Effi pretended to snatch it away, but Hart held onto it, making a tunnel of his own hand. The symbolism was explicit and unmistakeable. Hart held Effi's gaze with his own in order to drive the message even further home. 'You have me bang to rights. Did you like this photograph when you were a child?'

Effi backed a little tighter against the wall. She canted her hips marginally forward so that she wouldn't disturb the photographs behind her. Just far enough, in fact, to confirm that Hart was genuinely excited by her closeness to him. When she was satisfied that she had his complete attention, she said, 'I thought it was the most romantic thing I had ever seen. I wanted to be your grandmother. In that exact same flying suit she is wearing. With all the fur around the collar. But naked underneath. And I wanted to have a man like your grandfather loving me.'

'That doesn't sound like a little girl talking.'

'I matured early.'

'I can see that.'

'Do you like what you see, Baron?'

'I don't know yet. I must see more of it before I decide.'

'How are we going to arrange that?'

'I can think of one approach that might work.' Hart leant forward. He cradled Effi's head in his hand and ran the fingers of his other hand through her hair, smoothing it away from her forehead. Then he guided her gently towards him.

Effi let him take the lead. Dominant in her public life, she enjoyed feeling dominated in private. Men who were afraid of asserting their masculinity disgusted her. She allowed Hart to kiss her. Then, after only a moment's expedient submission, she kissed him passionately back.

He responded instantly, crushing her against the wall, not caring if her grandfather's photo collection fell off in a heap or was smashed to smithereens.

Effi writhed beneath him, her hands entwined in his hair.

Hart ground his hips into hers, the full length of his body measured against hers as if she was already on the floor, and he on top of her.

Outside the house, Udo Zirkeler circled like an angry lion. As the minutes and then the hours ticked by, he became more and more incensed. When the lights went on in the upstairs bedroom, he kicked out at the nearest thing he could find, which happened to be a birdhouse. The birdhouse snapped in two. Udo stamped on it, then heeled what remained of the birdhouse into the ground.

There was little chance of anyone hearing. Haus Walküre, like all well-made Bavarian homes, had double-paned windows against the long winters. And Effi's windows were firmly sealed against Udo. Just like her heart.

THIRTY-SEVEN

'You're fucking that fake English baron.' Udo could control neither the sneer in his voice nor the contortions on his face. The anger he felt went deeper than he would ever have believed possible. He felt betrayed. Used and betrayed.

'It's no business of yours who I fuck, Udo. And he's not a fake. I have a photograph of his grandfather and he is the image of him. Not just near, but dead on. You can't fake that. Not even with the best plastic surgery in the world. It's all about bone structure and hairline. The width of the eyes and the shape of the nose. Things you wouldn't understand. And why should he be trying to fake anything? He's over here for a very good reason: to get his family's castle back. He met me by accident.'

'I don't think it was an accident. I think it was a set-up. To get to you.'

'I want him to get to me. So it was a lucky set-up, wasn't it?'

'You're besotted. You're not thinking straight. He's fucked you witless.'

'Don't you speak to me like that. You've got no right. Remember who I am? I'm your employer, Udo. And your superior. You take my orders. For which you are paid vey well. That can all change with a click of my fingers. Then you'll be all alone out there in a ghetto of your own choosing. How long do you think you will last before they reel you in? One month? Two?'

'Pah. You're throwing all we are working for away. What do you think the English baron will do if he finds out what you're really up to?'

'He won't find out. I'm perfectly capable of keeping my private life separate from my public persona. And my public persona separate from our hidden agenda, should it come to that.'

'You would be the first person in the history of the world who could pull that one off.'

'Nonsense. We Raches have done it for years.'

'Your father and grandfather were men. You are a woman. Women are made differently.'

'You really think so?'

Effi's ironical tone was lost on Udo. 'I know so.'

'You really are a sexist pig, Udo. An unregenerate.'

'That's why you find it convenient to use me. You should use me more.'

'I should be with you, you mean? Not him? Keep it all in-house? Protect the fort?'

'Yes. You should be with me. I know all your secrets. I do anything I'm asked. Even down to killing for you.'

'That's just it, Udo. You do anything you're asked. I want a man who doesn't ask. Who just takes. When I decide to give it, of course.'

'And the English baron is such a man?'

'Stop calling him the English baron. He's German. His family have been here for more than a thousand years. He's an Aryan through and through. He has more true German nobility in his little finger than you have in your whole body.'

'Then why does he have an English passport?'

Effi whirled round. 'What are you talking about? How do you know that?'

'Because whilst you were busy fucking him last night I visited his room at the Alpenruh. The old biddy is deaf as a post. And the place is empty. They are shutting down for good at the end of the season. I could have camped out in the *Speisezimmer* and no one would have noticed.'

'Are you crazy? What if he had caught you?'

'I'd have killed him. I still might. I'd bear that in mind when next you see him.'

THIRTY-EIGHT

'You never answered my question about why you speak English and not German?'

Effi was lying across Hart's stomach. She knew he liked to look at her bottom, so she was exhibiting it freely for him. She loved the look of herself, and she loved even more being looked at by a man. When the man who was doing the looking was as virile as her English baron was, it was doubly satisfying. She'd never known a man who could hold out for as long as he could without coming. Nor one whose penis was so thick that it made her gasp whenever he entered her. She meant to hold on to him, whatever that degenerate Udo said. Effi enjoyed living dangerously.

Hart was better prepared for her question this time around. 'You know my father was made an orphan in 1945? In a plane crash?'

'Whilst your grandparents were bringing a suitcase out of Berlin to give to my grandfather. Yes.'

Hart sat up in the bed, causing Effi to tumble ingloriously over onto her back.

'To your grandfather?'

Effi sat up too. If she was put out by Hart's unexpected reaction to her revelation she didn't show it.

'Yes. Didn't you know? Your grandfather and grandmother were ordered out of Berlin by the Führer the night before he committed suicide. They were to bring a suitcase containing the Holy Lance to my grandfather in Gmund. Only their plane was shot down by the Americans before they could get here. The Lance was found by a GI. He and his family kept it for –' Effi counted on her fingers like a child – 'sixty-seven years. Then their ancestor contacted us and gave it back because he felt guilty keeping it. It was addressed to my grandfather at this house, you see.'

Hart was having a hard time disguising his shock. He hoped that Effi would assume that it was shock at her first bombshell announcement, and nothing more than that. He needed to gather himself together again. Fast.

'But I thought someone dug up the Lance on your land? Quite recently? Given my family's long connection with the Lance, this was a matter of some interest to me. I've been following it online and in the newspapers. I did think it extraordinary at the time that the Lance had simply been buried here.'

Effi slithered up the bed and snuggled herself into the crook made by Hart's legs. This time she made sure he got a good long look at her breasts and her depilated mound. 'It wasn't. That was all a lie to allow my political party, the LB, to keep hold of the

217

Lance whilst investigations took place. And these investigations will take years. You can count on it. If we had simply admitted the Lance had been given back to us by a well-wisher, the state would have confiscated it and interviewed the man about the Lance's acquisition. As it is, what we have is treasure trove. And there are rules about such things. Nobody can take it away from us unless it can be proved that the Lance in the Vienna *Schatzkammer* is a fake, and that ours is therefore the original. And that will be hard, as Uncle Adolf got his best technicians to counterfeit it, using the original as a template. He used two thousand-year-old wood from a Roman shipwreck. An ancient nail from the same source. Wire from a Vandal sword hilt. Tenth-century silver and fourteenth-century gold. The two lances are as similar as you and your grandfather. But theirs is fake and ours is real. Our people know that, and they are passing the knowledge around that we are the ones who have been chosen to hold the Lance, and not those Viennese strudels at the Imperial Palace.'

Uncle Adolf? Hart decided to assume, for the time being at least, that Effi meant the title ironically, given that she must have been born at least thirty-five years after Hitler's death. 'Where is this man? The one who found it?'

'He didn't find it. He inherited it. He's in Portland some-where. Or so I believe. Portland, Oregon.'

Hart watched Effi's face as she told the lie. Nothing showed. No emotion. No fluttering of the eyelids. No facial tics. She was either telling the truth as she knew it, or she was the most consummate liar he had ever encountered.

'Did he send it to you?'

'Yes. Extraordinary, isn't it? That there are such honourable people left in this world. When you think that a thing as valuable as this can languish in someone's attic for nearly seventy years, and then come straight back to the place it was originally intended for. It's like a miracle.'

'It's really valuable?'

'In money terms? No. It would be unsellable. A court order would be slapped onto it straight away. But in political terms? It's worth more than diamonds to us. You know about my party, don't you?'

'A little. It's like the Front National in France, isn't it?'

'And how do you feel about that?'

'Neither one way nor the other. I'm fundamentally non-political. I believe in people, not political parties.' The lie was almost truthful, so Hart could say it without flinching. 'Anyway, I'm making love to you, not your politics.'

'And you're happy to leave it at that?'

'Perfectly happy. As long as I don't have to make love to you in front of a roaring crowd.'

'You'd find that off-putting?'

'Somewhat, yes. But I'd probably forget all about the crowd once I got into it.'

'Probably?'

'Definitely.' Hart rolled Effi over onto her stomach. 'You've been exhibiting yourself to me for the past twenty minutes, Fräulein Rache. Now you're going to have to pay the piper.'

'How, Baron? With what?'

'Just you wait and see.'

THIRTY-NINE

Hart watched Frau Erlichmann from across the *esszimmer* table. They had agreed to meet for coffee every afternoon at three, but Hart had missed their first two appointments because he had been in bed with Effi. This third appointment, he suspected, might prove a little awkward.

Frau Erlichmann enjoyed making a ritual of her 'coffee time'. First she got Hart to grind the coffee beans by hand, because that was the only way they stayed fresh. Then she boiled a pot of water and placed the white porcelain coffee jug in it to heat. Next she placed a porcelain filter and an unbleached filter paper over the pot. When the water from the kettle was going marginally off the boil, she wet the grounds, and then continued pouring.

'This way the coffee is kept hot, but the grounds aren't poached.'

Then the coffee pot was placed onto a tea light to maintain the heat. Milk wasn't used to dilute the coffee, as that might curdle and spoil the brew, but instead Frau Erlichmann used what she called 'coffee cream' – a secret mixture of her own making. To accompany his coffee Frau Erlichmann offered Hart a choice of homemade *nusskuchen* (nut cake), *zwetschgenkuchen* (plum cake), or *sauerkirschkuchen* (sour cherry cake).

'I shall put on weight.'

'You are underweight as it is. You must be over-extending yourself. I noticed you did not come back to your room last night, nor the night before, as your bed did not need to be made up. I assume you were with the Rache girl both nights? And perhaps yesterday afternoon as well?'

Hart made a face. Damage limitation was needed. 'I'm sorry I missed our coffee times. I really am. I wanted to tell you that the boys did a splendid job. I hope I didn't hurt your grandson when I grabbed him like that in the restaurant? He had me convinced, I can tell you. He had Effi and her girlfriends convinced too.'

'His politics are his own. He knows where he comes from. I was only afraid he might overdo it in the heat of the moment. He is still young.'

'No. He acted his part perfectly. As did the other two. But are you sure Effi will never have seen them? Nor that brute she keeps as her unofficial bodyguard? Will he know them?'

'The Raches of the world are not interested in the likes of us. My son and his family live on Lake Würm – what they now call the Starnberger See. I visit them there. They do not come here. Too many bad memories.' Frau Erlichmann gave Hart an old-fashioned look. 'Talking of the Raches, it is difficult to separate physical attraction from emotion. Even for a man. Are you sure you can keep the two apart?'

'Answer a question with a question, eh?' Hart looked a little sick. 'I know you don't like Effi Rache. And you have every reason not to. But it wasn't she who denounced your parents. It was her grandfather. Her politics might stink, but I don't think she had anything to do with killing my father, Santiago and Colel Cimi either. I've had lots of time to watch her...'

'I'm sure you have.'

Hart didn't rise to the bait, but it was hard. 'I'm convinced others are using her.'

'The brute she keeps as an unofficial bodyguard – Udo Zirkeler, you mean?'

'Well, yes. Probably.'

'I'm sure you are right.'

'You are?'

'Yes. About Zirkeler. Someone broke into your room the first night you were away.'

'How do you know?'

'I have lived in this house, apart from the three years during the war that I told you about, for nearly ninety years. I know every nook and cranny. Every scratch on every lock. I also know my maid doesn't leave wood chippings on the floor of the hall and in the bedrooms after she has vacuumed. Did you carry wood chippings into the room on your boots when you weren't there?'

'Of course not.'

'Then Zirkeler searched your room. Do you have anything in there that could be construed as suspicious?'

'No. I don't think so. What could there be? I don't have a phone. I don't have a computer. I've got no family pictures with me.' Hart slapped his top pocket to make sure the photograph of his sister Carmen was still safely in place. He tried to conjure up a clear picture of his room and his belongings in his head, but he had spent so little time there that it was difficult. 'Ah. I know what they might have found. My fake passport. In a drawer in my dresser.'

'Is it obviously fake?'

'No. It's pretty good, actually. Enough to survive a visual check. The only snag is that it's British, not German. We had to get it in a hurry. We didn't have time for frills like that.' Hart rolled his eyes. 'So that's why Effi kept harping on about why I can't speak German.'

'Did you have a suitable explanation ready for her?'

'Yes. I did. But we never quite got round to the punch line.' Hart managed a sheepish smile. He couldn't pull the wool over Frau Erlichmann's eyes, however myopic or misted by cataracts they might be. 'Each time she asked me we got sidetracked.'

'Fräulein Rache is a desirable woman. Her beauty is perhaps a little shallow, if you want my honest opinion, but I know well enough after all these years what men are satisfied with.'

Hart looked as if an apple core had lodged in his throat.

'You are playing a dangerous game, John. These are people one should not toy with.'

'I've been in some rough places during my career as a photojournalist.'

'Yes. I'm sure you have. But this is another animal entirely. This is your animal. Not someone else's. And you are not here simply to take pictures.' Frau Erlichmann felt in the pocket of her cardigan. 'A man came visiting this morning. A fat Englishman with an ugly face who reeked of alcohol and tobacco smoke and looked as if he might have a heart attack at any moment. He asked after you. I told him I did not know what he was talking about. He handed me a letter and said, "Please give this to the person you don't know I am talking about". I thought that was very funny for him to do this, so I took the letter. I trust I did the right thing?'

Hart nodded. 'Wesker. His name is Wesker. If he's here, it means the woman I told you about, Amira Eisenberger, is also here. Or on her way over.'

'This is the woman you used to be with?'

'Yes. Used.' Hart blushed. It was not a condition he was accustomed to. But Frau Erlichmann appeared to have the innate capacity to see through whatever he said to the kernel of truth lurking beneath, and then hold him to account for it. 'Amira aborted our child without asking me. That's why we're no longer together.' Hart could feel his face tightening up. 'I don't know why I just told you that. Nobody knows about that. I don't know why I said it.'

'To justify yourself? To justify what you are doing with Effi Rache?'

Hart stood up. He let out a deep breath. 'Thank you for the coffee, Frau Erlichmann. I'm going somewhere to read this letter. Then I'm going down to visit Effi. I may not be using my bedroom tonight, so you'll be saving on the maid service once again.'

Frau Erlichmann bowed her head. 'You must do as you see fit, John. You are a good man. But you are carving a bitter road for yourself.'

FORTY

Hart took the ferry back across the lake from Bad Wiessee to Rottach Egern. He hadn't gone to visit Effi immediately after leaving the Alpenruh – Wesker's note had precluded that, as it set down a specific time for their meeting. The same hour every day. On the hour. At the Gasthof zur Post. But he felt the absence of Effi's physical presence in a way that he had not anticipated.

Frau Erlichmann's final warning had unsettled him, despite all his posturing. He liked and respected the old lady, and her good opinion mattered to him. Now he found himself checking everyone coming aboard the ferry in case he was being followed. He would have no problem recognizing Zirkeler again. The man was a true one-off. A grotesque. A human mountain. Pit him against a silverback gorilla, and Zirkeler would be odds on favourite to win. He would also recognize Zirkeler's two young companions from the Gasthof zur Hirschtal car park. But there might be others he wouldn't be able to identify so easily.

Hart wondered for a moment if he wasn't seeing reds under the beds. Or whatever colours modern-day Nazis had chosen as their own. Browns beneath the eiderdowns? Blacks beneath the tie-racks? Would he really come under suspicion just because he held a British passport? Or was he becoming paranoid?

He turned things over in his mind as the ferry glided across the lake on its silent electric motor. No. There was no possible way anyone could know that the man who had been killed in Antigua was his father. No way he could be linked to Colel Cimi or Santiago. And Effi must be convinced by now of his bona fides as Johannes von Hartelius, thanks to his grandfather's prepotent genes, and the photograph she grew up with from childhood.

He'd been gifted the perfect alibi, too, in the matter of the Hartelius's ancestral castle. It was absurd to think that he might have a genuine stake in the issue, but he probably had, given his lineage. It could take a year or two to sort out in the courts, though, assuming he wasn't arrested for murder before the case could be brought to trial. But halfway-true alibis were always the best. And this one was more than halfway true. There was no reason for Effi to question it. He couldn't see himself contacting the Americans any time soon, however. That would really throw the cat amongst the pigeons.

Udo Zirkeler was another matter entirely. He had taken an instant dislike to the man when they had been introduced in the Gasthof zur Hirschtal car park. The repulsion had been a chemical one, as though the two of them were linked by past actions neither could possibly know about. Hart shook his head angrily. Was there such a thing as inherited cell memory? Of course there bloody wasn't. The concept was absurd. That Zirkeler's family and his own family had been connected in the past was simply a sick coincidence. No more than that. The fact remained, though, that Zirkeler was just the sort of brute who would kill three innocent people. And then lie to Effi about where he found the Holy Lance. Hart had seen the look on Zirkeler's face as he had come running at him in the car park. If the women hadn't vouched for him so swiftly, he'd have been dead meat.

Effi, Hart felt, had been telling him the truth about how the Lance had come into her possession. All he would need to do to be absolutely sure that she hadn't been involved with the murders was to sneak a look at her passport, just as Zirkeler had sneaked a look at his. Hart remembered from his own passport, now safely back at home with his mother in England, that the Guatemala *migracion* entry and exit stamps took up close on a full page all by themselves. There was no way to expunge them, short of razoring the page out and burning it. And that left traces. Sneaking a look at Zirkeler's passport would be another matter entirely, and could prove conclusive. But that, Hart knew, would never happen.

Hart threw open the Gasthof zur Post doors and looked around for Wesker. He walked up and down the booths, and then checked his watch. Ten past the hour. Maybe the bastard had gone back to his lair? But Wesker would never knowingly pass up the chance for a drink. He'd need to be levered out of a place that could boast its very own brewery a mere two kilometres away.

Hart sat down to wait. He ordered a beer. He'd give Wesker half an hour and then head back to see Effi. She'd promised to cook him *geschnetzeltes* for dinner, with a cream and mushroom sauce and *spätzle*. Hart already knew what he would request for dessert.

Amira tapped him on the shoulder.

Hart sprang up, nearly oversetting the table. 'Christ. I thought you were Zirkeler.'

Amira kissed him on both cheeks, and then once, lightly, on the mouth. When Hart didn't respond as she expected, she gave him a searching glance, then sat down opposite him in the booth. 'So you've met Udo Zirkeler, then?'

Hart flagged the waitress down to mask his agitation. 'Yes. Effi introduced us.'

'Oh. So it's Effi now?'

Hart went through the motions of ordering Amira a drink. Then he began to feel around in his pockets, for a pencil or a notebook or something. If a total stranger had offered him a cigarette at that precise moment he would have taken it, just to be able to have something to do with his hands.

'I'm a trained journalist, remember? Nothing escapes me.' Amira flashed him an artificial smile. She waited patiently for Hart to look up from what he was doing and meet her eyes again. 'I've checked Miss Rache out on Google Images. A Marlene Dietrich clone without either the charm or the talent.'

Hart knew where this was going. Amira and Frau Erlichmann would get on very well, despite the fifty-year age gap. 'That's why I'm over here. To cultivate Effi. That's what we agreed I would do when we last spoke in London. So I don't see what's so surprising about it. And I'm hardly likely to call her Elfriede, now, am I?' He wasn't getting anywhere. Amira knew him far too well. 'Where's Wesker, by the way?'

'I sent him in ahead of me to check out whether you were here. You were daydreaming about something, so he didn't disturb you but came straight back to the house to fetch me. We're just round the corner from here: 134 Bergstrasse. You could do worse than remember that address. You may need it one day. If you're really as thick in with those two as you pretend to be.'

'I suppose the house is being paid for by the newspaper?'

'Yes. We're onto the story big time. Committed. Everyone's fired up about what Golden Dawn are doing in Greece – blood banks for true Greeks, the targeting of restaurant owners to employ only locals, and so forth. But we think the danger's much nearer home. We think it's here, in fact. Racist violence and terror attacks on immigrants and gay people have increased tenfold in Bavaria over the past few months. And the recession only aggravates it. People who wouldn't normally dream of joining a far-right party are jumping onto the bandwagon. Remember what happened in Germany between 1923 and 1933? Well, it's happening all over again. Fear and resentment breed exclusion. But I'm teaching my grandmother to suck eggs, aren't I? You've been there, haven't you? You've seen what happens. Remember Syria?'

Hart leant back in the booth, his hands thrust in his pockets. 'Are you sure you still want me to help you, Amira? You and Wesker? The team? You both still think I've got a part to play in this? That I might be of some use to you? I remember what happened last time I stepped in where I wasn't wanted.' Hart tried to inject a little irony into his voice, but he was far too wound up to pull it off. He knew he was babbling.

'That all depends on how committed you are.'

Hart swayed forward. He took his hands out of his pockets and gripped the table. 'I'm committed, Amira. You'd better believe that. I'm not going to stop until I find out who killed my father and his people. I saw them dead. All three of them. It's something I'll never forget.'

'I know that, John. I know that.'

'I've already got an ally in the old woman who runs the Alpenruh. She hates the Raches. She believes Effi's grandfather had her parents sent to Dachau, where they both died. It's through her and her grandson that I've managed to make friends with Effi. Effi believes I'm over here to wrest my family castle back from the Americans. They've been using the place as an army barracks for the past seventy years. That bit just fell into my lap, actually.' Hart wanted to bite his tongue off the minute the words came out.

'It fell into your lap?' Amira sat back in the booth. 'From my reading of Effi Rache, she doesn't seem like the sort of woman who just makes friends. Are you fucking her? Has she fallen into your lap as well?'

Hart could feel himself colouring up. This was absurd. He wasn't a teenage girl. And he had nothing whatsoever to feel guilty about. Despite this fact, he could think of nothing constructive to say.

'You *are* fucking her, aren't you? It's written all over your face. You couldn't even bring yourself to kiss me when I came in. Well, I suppose I should have expected it.' Something flashed across Amira's face, but whatever the emotion behind it had been, it was gone in an instant. 'And has your fucking of the main suspect in your father's death allowed you to come to any conclusions?'

Hart closed his eyes. 'Effi did not kill my father. Or Santiago. Or Colel Cimi. I can guarantee you that. And tonight I'm going to prove it. I'm going to check her passport.'

'Quite the Sherlock Holmes. You fuck her rigid, then you sneak into her study and rifle her drawers.'

'Amira, don't.'

'What do you expect me to do? Pat you on the shoulder and say well done? I told you I loved you in London…'

Hart held up his hand. 'And that you couldn't live with me.'

'But I said I loved you. Do you know how much it cost me to admit that?'

'Don't tell me you haven't cheated on me in the ten years we've known each other, Amira. Don't tell me you're as pure as the driven snow.'

Amira slapped the table between them. Two nearby drinkers took up their glasses and moved to a table a little further away. Amira ignored them. 'Why have you never asked me that before? Why only now? Because it would be convenient for you? Salve your conscience?'

Hart shook his head. He didn't know why he'd asked her either.

'Actually, I haven't.'

Hart felt the walls begin to close in on him. 'You haven't what? Slept with anyone else?'

'No. I haven't. I thought we had an understanding. That we were both mature individuals who chose to be together from time to time, but understood that any long-term plans had to be put on hold because of our careers. But that we still needed to cherish each other and build up some sort of trust. That included giving each other the freedom to be free if we wanted to. And because you gave me that freedom – gave it willingly, I should add – I didn't use it. Because right from the beginning I knew that you were the only man for me. So I didn't want anybody else, even though there were a good few who tried, believe me. I still don't.'

Hart met her eyes. 'I didn't know, Amira. I really didn't know.'

'And that's our tragedy, isn't it, John? Because you don't really know anything.'

FORTY-ONE

Udo looked across at Jochen and Sibbe. The half-hearted ones he and Effi had decided to allocate as postmen because they were useless as storm troopers. Udo wondered for a moment whether this was a good idea. But the two of them were entirely disposable. If things went wrong, there would be no comeback. Jochen was an orphan – the perfect patsy. No mother or father to kick up a stink if something happened to him. And Sibbe was a faltering neo-Nazi with a gay younger brother who deserved whatever he got. In the war, Udo would have had them both shot for recalcitrance.

The upside was that if they could get away with it once, they could get away with it again. Udo couldn't afford to lose any of his more committed 'apostles'. He needed to keep up – even increase – the race attacks. They were happening once a week now, and they were having an outstanding effect. Extreme right-wing parties from all over Europe were emulating his methods. It was all so simple. Isolate people, marginalize them, and you were home dry. Sheep always follow the flock.

'You are to take these two suitcases to where I tell you. You will be allocated first-class tickets, spending money, a cover story and a clothes allowance. You need to look neat and unexceptionable. Which shouldn't be difficult for either of you. You will each be going to different cities. You will not – I repeat not – be travelling together.'

'What is in the suitcases, Udo?'

'That is none of your concern. You are merely couriers.'

'It's not a bomb, is it?'

'Don't be absurd. We are not Jihadists. We don't expect people to blow themselves up in futile gestures. No.' Udo appeared to hesitate, as if he was making up his mind about something. In fact, he was adhering to a prepared script. 'You will be transporting jelly.'

'Jelly?'

'Jelly. Yes. Fruit and vegetable jelly. Made from bones, bovine hides and pig skins. And some other crap I can't remember.'

Sibbe and Jochen looked at each other.

'Does that answer your question?'

'What are we to say if our suitcases are searched?'

'That you like jelly, you fool. That you need jelly. That you have a stomach condition – we shall provide you with a doctor's certificate to prove this – which necessitates that you eat only jelly. And that you fear you cannot get it in the country concerned, so you are taking along your own supplies for added security. It's all perfectly legal.'

'But jelly is a liquid. It wobbles. They'll take it off us.'

'No. You mix it with liquid to make it wobble, but it is not a liquid per se. And you will be carrying it in your hold baggage, not in your hand. No one will be interested in it, I can promise you that.'

'Are you sure it's not a bomb?'

'It's gelatine, not gelignite. And how can jelly be a bomb? It's transparent, you idiot.' Udo forced himself to calm down. He was used to dealing with cretins. Most of his 'apostles' were cretins. How else could one hope to get people to do whatever one asked of them if one didn't filter and categorize them correctly in the first place? Cretins and sheep. Breed the two together, and that was how you constructed an effective nation. 'Are you going to follow orders? Or shall I give the task to someone more deserving? It will mean a considerable number of trips for both of you. Always in first class. Always with different airlines. In each city you visit you will leave the sealed containers of jelly – undiluted and unopened – in a particular location in a particular apartment. When that is done, you will go sightseeing. Visit museums. Frequent brothels. I don't care what you do. But you will stay three days in each place in a hotel of our choosing. Then you will come home. Rest for a day or two. Then go out again. This is the task you have been chosen for. This is the task you were born for. Are you both comfortable with this?'

The two boys looked at each other again.

'It's a test. To get them used to us. The jelly is entirely innocent. This way, when we want to transport something that looks similar, but is very different indeed in constitution, they won't bother to check us. I repeat, are you both comfortable with this?'

'Yes, Udo.'

They really were as stupid as he suspected. 'Excellent. I knew I could count on you. You are hereby forgiven for botching your gay-bashing the other week, and letting the two queers escape.'

'You knew about that?'

'I know about everything.'

FORTY-TWO

Udo wasn't sleeping well. The thought of the English baron making out with Effi was too much to bear. So he had taken to teaming up with Lenzi and Frischl, two of his keener 'apostles', and going out on the town. This involved travelling to areas they hadn't already hit and looking for random Turks to bash. If you wore a long overcoat with feel-through pockets, it was an easy thing to conceal a pickaxe handle inside the skirts. You just had to make sure you didn't give yourself away going through the narrow doorways of kebab houses.

But even this form of entertainment was starting to pall. Udo hadn't put on his grandfather's SS uniform since his little outing to Guatemala, and he missed the thrill. Just bashing people, or blackmailing them into conforming to his demands, didn't cut the mustard any more. Udo needed action. And action involved death. Not the breaking of a bone or two that could easily be mended again. But death. The permanent solution to all problems.

And the man Udo most wanted to kill was the fake English baron.

Udo stood outside Haus Walküre and gazed up at Effi's bedroom window. He had seen Hartelius enter the house at seven o'clock. He had seen him embracing Effi. He had seen Effi cooking, like a proper German woman should, and wearing an apron. But she hadn't been cooking for him – she had been cooking for the English prick.

Later, after dinner, he had seen Effi and Hartelius playing a sort of game. At first Udo hadn't been able to work out what they were doing. Were they pretending to be children? Hartelius was covering his eyes, but Effi wasn't going anywhere to hide. She was standing in plain sight in the middle of the room.

Then Udo saw Effi begin to undress. He could see her mouthing words. Probably telling Hartelius to keep his eyes closed. She stripped down to her red silk underwear whilst Udo watched. She looked like a goddess. Why had she let him fuck her once, and then closed down the gate? He was the one who knew her best. Who had the same aims as her. What did this idiot with the fancy title know of the real Germany? He couldn't even speak the language. That was how close he was to the country of his ancestors. And the man's grandfather had been a hero of the Third Reich – his grandmother a flying ace. And between them they had produced this – this thing. The thought made Udo sick to his stomach.

Now Hartelius had his eyes open and Effi was turning round and letting him take a good look at her. She was behaving like a whore. With no decorum whatsoever. Bending over. Flashing him her breasts. Wriggling a little way out of her panties so Hartelius could have a view of her down there. Front and back. Like a striptease artist. Udo began grinding his teeth.

As he watched, Hartelius strode towards her, hefted her over his shoulder, slapped her playfully on the rump a few times, and carried her towards the stairs. If Udo didn't know that Effi's outside doors were on a timed security lock, and that the whole house sealed itself automatically when anyone was inside it, he would have marched through the door then and there and had it out with them.

But it was a good thing he didn't. Udo needed Effi. Without her and her money and her father's friends in high places who secretly supported the LB – not to mention her chemical factory in Gmund – nothing would go forward. He would remain a thug whose sole use was to beat up on people, and then Germany – the Germany he loved more than anything – would slide into the hands of foreigners.

Udo watched the light go out in Effi's bedroom. He could imagine her cries of joy as the Englishman porked her. He remembered her cries the one time she had been with him. They had driven him crazy with desire. How much more would she give to Hartelius now that she was in love with him? Because Udo wasn't a fool. He knew Effi in real life and Effi after she met this clown, and the two bore no resemblance to each other. He'd watched them together for many hours now. For days, it seemed. He'd seen the way Effi looked at Hartelius. Let him do whatever he wanted to her. Submitted to him, despite her dominant position in real life.

Maybe she secretly wanted to become a baroness? A Freifrau? How good that would look on the party billboards. Effi Rache, head of the Lanzen Brüderschaft, marries the hereditary Guardian of the Lance. It would be like a royal wedding. German high society might shun the occasion because of the political dimension – half the natural right-wingers in Germany didn't dare come out into the open about their true beliefs because of the carry-over from the war – but it would still be a major event. A publicity overload. Udo wondered if Hartelius knew what Effi had in store for him. Maybe the man thought he was just having a rollicking affair with an upmarket bit of tail? Well, he would soon find out the truth of the matter.

Udo walked the three kilometres back to his house in Abwinkl. At first he followed the Simperetsweg bicycle trail, then later he cut through the fields. At one point he chased what looked like a stray dog, but he couldn't catch it. Later, when he was about a kilometre from home, he passed through a field of cows. He picked up a heavy stone from the side of the track and hefted it in his hand. He picked out a cow that stood apart from the others and edged up to it. It was dark. The animals were half asleep.

Before the cow was able to react, Udo brought the stone down on its star – the apex of an imaginary triangle between its eyes and its poll. The cow fell to its knees and toppled over onto its side. Its legs windmilled for a while and then became still.

Udo grinned. Yes. First time. One blow. It was how you killed horses when using a pistol. But he had never done it to a large animal like a cow. And with simply a rock.

Udo turned to his audience for approbation. In recent days his 'secret sharers' – the chorus made up of his ancestors, his chosen Norse Gods, and Germany's greatest kings – seemed to have been avoiding him. Now they were back in force. Watching him. Approving him. Urging him on.

Udo felt vindicated. The night, he decided, had not been entirely wasted.

FORTY-THREE

Hart waited until Effi was asleep before padding downstairs to her writing desk. The desk was situated in the library section of her open-plan living area – the section that housed the photo museum dedicated to her grandfather.

Hart switched on the desk lamp and began checking through the drawers. At one point he caught sight of himself reflected back from the study window. He looked furtive. Like a sneak thief at a boy's school. He straightened up and listened for any sound that might suggest Effi was waking up. But apart from the ticking of her ridiculously ornate rococo desk clock, there was only silence.

What was he doing here, in this strange house? Making love to the woman who headed Germany's most powerful far-right political party? Was he really so naïve as to believe that she had nothing whatsoever to do with the three murders in Guatemala? Well. Yes. He was. Otherwise why was he down here in the dead of night going through her things?

His meeting earlier that day with Amira had begun as a catastrophe and ended as a disaster. Beforehand, he had found no difficulty in convincing himself that he was adhering to Plan A – the plan which he and Amira had agreed in London, and which involved inveigling himself as close to Effi Rache as he possibly could and passing on any information that he found. In the original scenario he would have become magically transformed into a hero by these actions, and finally worthy of Amira's love.

But he hadn't counted on his own susceptibilities in the matter. The sheer physical magnetism of Effi Rache had blindsided him. She was far and away the most purely carnal being he had ever encountered. In Effi's mind sex seemed an entirely natural function one enjoyed in any way one chose to enjoy it. It was uncomplicated. Innocent, even. Hart had seldom, if ever, known the delights of pure sex – of carnality without complications. Sex with Amira had been like jogging through a minefield naked. Sex with Effi was like diving into the Mediterranean Sea in mid-summer from the highest rock you could find. The whole thing was baffling.

He took Effi's passport out of its black leather folder and held it up to the light. It was still in date. He flicked through the pages. Visits to Romania, the Seychelles and the United States. Hart wondered who Effi had gone to the Seychelles with, but then thrust the thought into the far recesses of his consciousness. More visits. To the Ukraine. Moldova. Even Transnistria, wherever that was. But nowhere in Central America. And no pages, that he could see, had been cut out, as each page was numbered one to thirty-two, and they were all intact.

Could she have driven down from the United States and done it? Crazy, but possible. He checked the dates again. No. Effi had visited the United States in July 2010. On a visa waiver. And with a visa waiver you got only one bite of the cherry. If you wafted back across the border on anything but a transit flight, you'd have to have a very good reason for your return visit.

Hart replaced the passport, then stood there looking down at the desk. Well, nothing ventured, nothing gained. He sifted through the remaining drawers but found little apart from a sheaf of bank balances. He held them under the light, and then did a double take when he saw the figures – 6,433,171 euros in various investments. Hart tore a piece of paper off a pad on the desk and wrote down the account numbers, the figures and the bank names. But there was nothing illegal here that he could see. The accounts were in Munich and Berlin, not Zurich, and no doubt entirely aboveboard. One had only to look around to realize that Effi was a very rich young woman. Her father and her grandfather had left her well provided for. Alongside the Bad Wiessee house, Effi had already admitted to him that she possessed a house in Deia, Mallorca, and a four-bedroom apartment on the Île St Louis in Paris. He could imagine Amira's disdain when he told her.

Hart wondered about Effi's mother. Why did she never figure in Effi's narrative? What had Effi called her? A Jargenried? No. That was her grandmother – the one who came from the family where the women only gave birth to blonde children. Hart wrote that name down too. At least all this information would provide him with something to take to Amira. A sort of peace offering. Something to get her teeth into, whilst he – yes, he might as well admit it – carried on his affair with Effi.

As he started towards the stairs, an object tucked under an occasional table tight against the side of the desk caught his eye. It was an old-fashioned fireproof box – the sort with a lock, not a combination. Hart hesitated for a moment, and then retraced his steps. He slid the box out and tested the lid. Tight as a drum. He sat down on the floor and looked at the box. Was there any point trying to pick the lock with a paperclip or something similar? No. That only happened in the movies.

He flicked at the lid with a finger and it bumped open.

Hart sat staring at it for a moment, lost for words. The lock was down, the mechanism committed. How had he been able to open it?

He dragged the box towards him and focused on the lock. It was an old box – probably 1950s vintage – and the lock's reverse seat had simply worn away over the years until it rested on a diminishing lip. One tug and it would hold. Two, and it would pull free. The thing must have sentimental value for Effi, he decided, because it served no useful purpose whatsoever.

Hart sifted through the papers inside. Share certificates, a will, some American Express dollar travellers' cheques that had probably been forgotten about as they were already curling at the edges and, underneath them all, an old, browned envelope, with the remnants of a wax seal adhering to it. Hart held the envelope under the banker's light on Effi's desk. There was a slip of paper inside. Hart looked at the signature.

To term it higgledy-piggledy would be to accord it a compliment. The signature ran from above to below, with the H of Hitler done in a ridiculously ornate style, and the R at the end of the name finished off in a descending mouse's tail, similar to the Snakes & Ladders boards of his childhood. The single sheet of paper was headed by a raised bevel in the top left-hand corner with the German Eagle standing atop a circled swastika; the words ADOLF HITLER were printed in upper case beneath it. On the upper right-hand side the words '*Berlin, den*', meaning 'Berlin, on the', were printed for the convenience of the sender. Hitler had filled in the date below: 29 April 1945. The day before he committed suicide. The day he had ordered Hart's grandfather and grandmother on their final, doomed flight out of Berlin. The note was addressed to '*Mein Lieber Heinrich*' – 'My dear Heinrich'. Effi's grandfather.

Hart tried to disinter the meaning of the note using his rudimentary German, but it was impossible. The note was handwritten, and virtually illegible. Dots were transposed to slashes, and each sentence ended on a downward falling spiral, as if Hitler had been unconsciously mirroring his own imminent doom in the way he wrote. Old German was hard enough, but old German written by an elderly man with shaking hands who had decided to kill himself the very next day was an impossibility.

Hart could hear the sound of Effi's voice calling him quizzically from the bedroom. He stood up, his senses on full alert. He looked down at the note in his hand. Did he dare keep it and simply return the envelope to the box? Could he count on the lock snapping open a second time when he wanted to put the note back?

He heard the squeak of Effi's bare feet on the old wooden floorboards at the top of the stairs.

Hart slipped the empty envelope back into the strongbox and clicked it shut. Then he slid the box back underneath the table. He looked first at the letter and then down at himself. He was buck-naked from bed – the house was far too well heated and insulated to even consider wearing pyjamas or a nightshirt. So where should he put the thing? And what could he use as an excuse for being down near Effi's desk in the middle of the night?

Hart ran to the Heinrich Rache picture gallery and snatched the photograph of his grandfather off the wall. He felt around the back of the frame and sliced into the mount with his thumbnail. He slipped Hitler's letter inside.

When Effi reached the bottom of the stairs, all she saw was Hart standing in his birthday suit, staring at the photograph.

'What are you doing, Johnny? It's the middle of the night. Why are you standing here naked?'

'I couldn't sleep. So I decided to come down and visit my grandfather and grandmother. I have no copy of this photograph, Effi. In fact, I have no photographs of either of them. Would you have it copied for me one day, please? I'd be really grateful.'

Effi came up to him. 'You are a sentimental old beast, aren't you?' She took the photograph from his hand and carried it to her desk. 'I'll do it for you tomorrow. I promise.' She glanced down at his midriff. 'You may be up, but he looks like he's gone to sleep.'

Hart laughed. 'Don't worry. He's only resting.'

Effi put on a broad smile. 'Well, then. Shall we see if we can wake him up again?'

FORTY-FOUR

When he and Effi had finished making love and she was safely asleep again, Hart spent the remainder of the night worrying how he might get the Hitler letter out of the photoframe before Effi had time to ask her private secretary, Frau Schwirk, to make a hard copy of it for him on the MFP in her office. Frau Schwirk's office was situated in what used to be the cattle byre attached to the house, and was far too convenient for comfort. Hart knew the way Effi's mind worked by now in terms of giving him pleasure. It would be the first thing she would ask Frau Schwirk to do when she came in for work at ten o'clock.

In the end, he needn't have worried. Effi insisted on making him an early breakfast of scrambled eggs, oven-crisped bacon and fresh *mohnsemmel* rolls to make up for the shenanigans she had involved him in the night before. He had ample time, whilst he was waiting for her to squeeze the orange juice and make the coffee, to go back to her desk, pretend to be perusing his grandparents' photograph in broad daylight, and slip the letter into his pocket.

There were definite advantages to being involved with German women, Hart decided. Amira never made him breakfast. In fact, it was usually him who ended up preparing necessities like that – in the rare absence of hotel staff – whilst she prodded and poked at whatever variety of laptop, tablet or phone she was enamoured of at that particular time. Amira also smoked wherever and whenever she felt like it, which Effi didn't. And Amira was subject to moods – ecstatic, depressive or seething – whereas Effi always seemed bright and cheerful. Hart supposed it was what came of being beautiful, blonde and a millionaire, rather than half Arab, half Jew, and irredeemably intense. Further than that he didn't care to go.

'I need to go and sort out my stuff at the Alpenruh. They must be wondering where I spend my nights.'

'The old cow knows, don't you worry about it. She'll even have our bed plan sketched out by now. She's used the same maid for the past forty years. And her maid knows my maid. And maids gossip.' Effi shrugged the shrug of a woman who has been used to staff catering to her every whim all her life. 'It would be much easier if you came to live here, Johnny. There's enough room, and it's the political dead season. I'm entitled to a summer holiday. And if I want to take it at home, who's to stop me?'

'You want me to live here with you?'

'Only if you want to? If you think it would be comfortable enough for you? Convenient enough?' Each sentence ended on an upward lilt, turning it into both question and tease.

Effi was entirely confident by now of Hart's sexual interest in her. She stood up and walked over to the kitchen counter for more coffee. She knew how much Hart liked to watch her. It was one of his major attractions, for Effi needed a male audience. And Hart was far and away the best audience she had ever encountered. Plus he never said no to anything she suggested. In fact, he dreamt up new things all the time by himself. She'd never met a man who relished women and their ways as much as he did, and she was not about to let him escape.

'You really mean that?'

'Why waste money paying for a room you never sleep in? Breakfasts you never eat? Maid service you never use? I will service you for free, Johnny.'

Hart burst out laughing. 'How can I say no to an offer like that?'

'Yes. It's an offer you can't refuse.'

'Like in *The Godfather*?'

'Just like that.'

FORTY-FIVE

'You're going to live with her? You're going to live with Effi Rache? In her house?' Amira was unable to hide her dismay. Her face was drawn, her expression sallow, and she smelt of stale cigarettes. She looked as if she hadn't slept for the past few nights.

Hart shifted on his now familiar bench at the Gasthof Zur Post. In the past ten minutes it had begun to feel like the miscreant's bench at the Old Bailey. 'I think it's the best way to get the information we need. It's a gift.'

'It sort of fell into your lap, you mean?'

Hart closed his eyes. 'It means I'll be right where I need to be if anything happens.'

'What if nothing happens? You'll just force yourself to go on sleeping in her bed until something does?'

'Amira. Please don't make this any more difficult than it already is.'

Amira attempted to light a cigarette. A passing waitress

pointed at the No Smoking sign on the table and made a sad face. Amira thrust the pack back into her satchel, and then threw the still smouldering cigarette and the lighter in after it. 'What if I started an affair with Wesker? What would you think about that?'

Hart groaned. Part of him wanted to fish around in Amira's handbag and turf out the cigarette before it set something alight. Another part of him recognized that such an act might, in the present circumstances, prove suicidal. 'I'd think you and Wesker were made for each other. I'd hang the Do Not Disturb sign on your door myself.' Instead of the expected slap, Hart saw Amira's eyes clouding up with tears. 'Oh, for God's sake, Amira. I'd feel wretched. How do you think I'd feel?'

'Well, at least you'd be feeling something. Rather than this numbness you seem to be feeling now. I can't understand you any more, John. How can you pretend with that woman? How is it possible for you to do that?'

Hart had arrived at the unknown frontier. The point of no return. He'd known it was coming, but he was still unprepared for it. 'Because I'm not pretending.'

Amira's pent-up tears finally overflowed and cascaded down her cheeks. She ignored them, as if the tears were being shed by some other woman, sitting in the same place, and facing the same man.

'What do you mean you're not pretending? She's a Nazi. Pure and simple. A bigot. A racist. She's the filth stuck in the filter at the bottom of the sink. The crud the cat leaves behind after he has eaten the mouse. You can't be so blind. You must see her for what she is?'

'I don't think it's as easy as that. I think she's the partial victim of her background.'

Amira dashed at her eyes with her sleeve. 'So your blow-up sex doll is a partial victim, is she? Quite unlike those people who get firebombed out of their homes by her people? Or who get their bones broken on her say-so? Or who get blackmailed out of their jobs by her thugs? No. Those aren't the true victims. But Effi Rache is.'

Hart offered Amira his handkerchief. She gave him such a wrathful look that he hastily replaced it in his pocket. He had an unwanted vision of himself sprinting for the emergency exit, with the chairs toppling behind him like dominoes.

'She's not involved in any of that. I'm sure of it. Plus she played no part in the murder of my father and Colel Cimi. I checked her passport, just as I told you I would. She hasn't been to Guatemala. Or anywhere close.'

'You've got a fake passport. Why shouldn't she have?'

'Because she hasn't. She's not who you think she is, Amira.'

'She isn't a whore, you mean? The sort of woman who steals other women's men?'

'She doesn't know who you are. She doesn't even know you exist.'

'Well, that's a surprise.'

Hart took the letter and the torn-off piece of notepaper out of his jacket pocket. He decided to hold the letter back in case he might need something to bargain with further down the line. There were moments when Amira scared him with the intensity of her feelings – with her utter lack of self-control – and he needed to think strategically, not in response to passion.

'This is a list of Effi Rache's investments and bank account details. I copied them from documents in her personal safe. At considerable personal risk, I should add. I thought they might be of interest to you.'

'So you're still pretending you're on the side of the good guys?

'Yes. I'm still pretending.'

'Then what's that other piece of paper you are hiding in your hand?'

Hart laid the single sheet on the table. 'It's a letter from Adolf Hitler to Effi Rache's grandfather. Dated twenty-ninth of April 1945. The day before Hitler committed suicide. The day he ordered my grandfather and grandmother to fly the Holy Lance out of Berlin a few hours ahead of the final Russian push. I found it in Effi's portable safe. I need to get it back there tonight, or my cover will be blown. The letter's probably meaningless. But I can't even start to interpret it. My primer didn't teach me how to read German Gothic script.'

'Spread it out for me.'

Hart spread out the letter.

Amira set her phone to 'photographing documents'. She took a series of shots, with and without flash. 'Now turn it over.'

'There's nothing on the other side.'

'Turn it over. Then hold it up against the light so I can get the watermark.'

Hart did as he was told. Sometimes he forgot how professional Amira was.

'I'll forward this to my editor. She'll get a specialist to translate and authenticate it. At least as far as we can from a photograph. But the provenance is spot on, I'll give you that much. From one Nazi to another.' Amira glanced up from her phone. 'I'm going to take you at your word. About being with us on this.'

Hart raised an eyebrow, but he kept his mouth shut. The storm appeared to be over. For the time being at least. He didn't want to risk rekindling it with one of his snap remarks.

'I want you to take this spare phone. If your Marlene Dietrich clone asks you where you got it, say you bought it today. That you wanted to be able to send her lovey-dovey text messages, or something equally inane. Here's the receipt. I'm sure she'll be grateful to have some means of contacting you when you're out of her sight. Or video calling you when she gets the itch. If you have to phone either me or Wesker, wipe the record. Don't keep us in your contacts either. If you text us, wipe the text. Here are our numbers. Memorize them on your way back across the lake and then destroy them. And use a password. Something complicated. Not your birthday. Or the anniversary of your first fuck-a-Nazi day.'

Hart's face was stiff with the strain of not responding to Amira's barbs. 'You're talking as if I am a spy. As if I belong to some Mission: Impossible team.'

'You are a spy, John. And in the enemy's camp. I'm giving you the benefit of the doubt here. Of believing you when you say you are still with us. Please don't let me down. Effi Rache isn't worth the spit on your toecap. You'll realize that some day. Probably when it's too late.'

Hart stood up. He took the phone from Amira's outstretched hand. As he did so she turned his hand over and brushed him lightly with her fingers across the knuckles. Hart snatched his hand back as if her touch had burnt him. His muscles ached and his temples throbbed. He felt as if he had just passed through an Iroquois gauntlet line.

'Do you have any money left?'

'More than I should have. Around four hundred euros. Frau Erlichmann refused any payment for my room. I feel wretched about that. But it helped the exchequer. Considerably.'

'You'd better take this, then. In real life, barons are rarely broke. I have a strong suspicion that your mincing little Barbie doll will be high upkeep. I would hate for her to go short of the basic necessities.' Amira handed him a roll of notes.

Hart accepted it because he knew she was right. But it cost him to remain silent.

'You charmed Frau Erlichmann, John, just as you charmed me and the Barbie. You're a serial charmer. That's just the way it is. But charm can only take you so far in this life. You'd best watch your back from now on in. Wesker tells me he's seen Zirkeler lurking outside the house at night spying on you both through the windows.'

'He's what?'

'You heard me. Wesker's taken the room next to your old one at the Alpenruh. He has night-vision glasses. I told him to note whoever goes in and out of the house. But don't worry. He tells me he can't quite see inside your bedroom.'

Hart stood frozen to the spot, too stunned to utter a word.

'Oh, and Frau Erlichmann is being paid this time. By the newspaper. Wesker isn't nearly as charming as you are, apparently.'

FORTY-SIX

Frau Erlichmann took the grinder from Hart's hand. She transferred the ground coffee into the filter with a scoop, levelling each measure punctiliously. 'I've baked a *käsekuchen* for us today. What you would call in England a cheesecake. I thought it would be nice to ring the changes.'

'How did you know I would come, Frau Erlichmann?'

'I didn't. But I take my coffee at this time whatever the season. With the benefit of company or without. And your associate, Herr…?'

'Wesker.'

'Yes, Herr Wesker. It doesn't seem to me that he is the sort of man to drink coffee.'

'Only after a hangover. And instant, probably.'

'Oh.' Frau Erlichmann looked shocked.

Hart suspected that Frau Erlichmann's shock was less at the thought of the alcohol and more at the prospect of the instant coffee. 'I have to be honest with you. I came here for a purpose.'

'You always do, Baron.'

'You know I'm not a real baron. You shouldn't call me that.'

'I know that you are. I had a schoolgirl crush on your grandfather, remember? You have the same eyes he had. The same hairline. The same nose.' Frau Erlichmann smiled. The expression behind her cataract-clouded eyes seemed unutterably far away. 'We are all the products of those who bred us. And those who came before them. We cannot escape who we are. It is lunacy to try to do so.'

'But I am not that person you describe.'

'Not yet. But you are fast becoming him.'

Hart sipped his coffee. He ate a forkful of cheesecake. Then he took another sip of his coffee. He was aware that the old lady was watching him. Weighing him up. Measuring him in the balance. 'I have something I would like you to look at, Frau Erlichmann. Something written in what I take to be old German script. I cannot come near to translating it myself. I was hoping you might help?' He held up the letter.

Frau Erlichmann fixed Hart with her gaze. It was impossible to tell what she could see and what she couldn't. How much of his facial expression she could make out, and how much of it faded away into the woodwork behind him. 'You should pass it on to your woman friend – the one you were involved with before you met the Rache girl – and not to me. She will arrange to have this done for you far better than I. And it will please her to do it. Of this I am sure.'

Hart hid his discomposure with a shrug. 'I've done that. She's photographed it from every angle. She'll have already sent a copy back to England to be investigated and verified. Watermarks and so forth. But all that takes time.' Hart took a deep breath. 'I need to know what it says now, Frau Erlichmann. For myself. Before I return to Haus Walküre tonight. Before I put the original back in Effi Rache's strongbox.'

Frau Erlichmann looked at Hart for a long time. 'Will I really wish to see this letter, young man?'

Hart shook his head. 'Probably not. I will fully understand if you refuse my request.'

The old lady held out her hand. Hart handed her the sheet. She raised the glasses that hung around her neck and held them to her eyes. 'I see badly today. I can make out nothing. This is impossible.' The hand holding the letter began to shake. Frau Erlichmann offered the letter back to Hart.

Hart stood up. He could see from across the table that Frau Erlichmann's glasses were thickly encrusted with egg white, flour, icing sugar, and whatever else she had been baking with that morning. 'Please. May I?' He lifted the glasses gently from around her neck, spat on them, and cleaned them vigorously with his handkerchief. 'Now. Please. Try again. I'm very sorry to have to ask this of you, but it may be important.'

Frau Erlichmann gave a long, successive sigh. If Hart had heard the sound coming from inside a locked room, he might have been fooled into thinking it was sexual. But the expression on Frau Erlichmann's face was gaunt, not ecstatic. She looked like a woman who has just happened on a massacre. 'I recognize the signature, John. That much goes without saying. In fact, I recognized it even before you cleaned my glasses for me. It is burnt into my memory like a brand. I saw it printed on a thousand official documents and proclamations.'

'This is the real thing, though. Not a simulacrum.'

'Are you sure of this?'

'I'm sure.'

'And the date is?' Frau Erlichmann held the letter very close to her face. 'The lettering is far too small for me to read.'

The movement Frau Erlichmann made echoed that made by the bearded man in Syria when he was trying to read Amira's press pass. Hart froze in the act of raising his finger to the page. For a split second the train of events that had led him to this precise moment threatened to overwhelm him.

'The letter is dated the twenty-ninth of April 1945. The day before Adolf Hitler committed suicide.'

'And sent to?'

Hart hesitated. This was the part he had been dreading. 'Your neighbour. Heinrich Rache.'

Frau Erlichmann closed her eyes. The hand holding the letter drifted towards the table. She took off her glasses. 'It is nearly seventy years since my parents were murdered. But when I hear the name of the man who denounced them, it still turns my heart to stone. The pain is almost too much to bear.'

'I am sorry to ask this of you, but I have no one else. No one to turn to. You must see that.'

Frau Erlichmann smiled. She patted Hart's hand. Her skin had the colour and consistency of aged vellum. 'Yes. I do see it. And you need not be sorry, John. I am the right person to ask.' She hitched her shoulders. Then she threw back her head and took a succession of deep breaths, followed by a series of shallow breaths like a woman in labour. When she opened her eyes again, her face was calm. Reconfigured. 'Forgive me. I had a brief moment of cowardice after you mentioned that name. A moment in which I remembered the power such people used to have over us. It frightened me a little. I had thought I was beyond all that.' She settled the glasses more firmly on her nose and raised the letter so that it was about six inches from her face. 'There is a magnifying glass on my desk out in the lobby. Will you fetch it for me, please?'

Hart hurried out. He returned a moment later with the magnifying glass and placed it in Frau Erlichmann's hand.

'This is better. Much better.' Frau Erlichmann's head began to move with the action of reading. 'Yes. Modern-day Germans will have difficulty with this script. But I grew up writing like this. Even though *Fraktur* was replaced by *Antiqua* in 1941, it was already too late for me to change. I was taught *Kurrent* at school. Although they called it *Sütterlin* by that time.'

'I don't understand what you are saying.'

'I am speaking of the old Gothic script. The script we Germans have been using, without problem, since the sixteenth century. Hitler despised it. He called it un-modern. So the Nazis banned all black letter writing in 1941. Martin Bormann called it *Schwabacher Judenlettern* – Jewish letters Schwabach-style. From that moment on we were all to use *Normalschrift* – what you would call "normal script". And yet here, in this letter, we see Adolf Hitler returning to the sort of lettering he would have been taught as a child in Austria.' Frau Erlichmann allowed the magnifying glass to fall away. 'Don't you see, John? The man who wrote this was frightened, sick and angry. And he was reverting to old childhood mannerisms in an instinctive search for comfort.' She sat back on her chair. 'It pleases me very much to see how he was suffering. I am Evangelisch. What born Catholics like Hitler would term a Lutheran. We believe in a doctrine of justification. "By grace alone through faith alone because of Christ alone. *Sola Gratia. Sola Fide. Solus Christus.*" We also believe in heaven and hell. I hope this man is rotting in hell because of the torment he inflicted on millions of innocent people.'

Hart waited. There were times to talk and times to remain silent. This much he knew.

Frau Erlichmann drew the letter back towards her eyes. She slid the magnifying glass across its surface like a cursor. Slowly, in a surprisingly strong voice, she began to read.

Dear Heinrich,
This is a sad day for Germany. But all is not lost.
Though we seem beaten now, like the Phoenix and the
Salamander, we will arise from the ashes of our defeat.
I am sending you a package from Berlin through my
emissary, Colonel von Hartelius. If you receive it directly
from his hand, you will know that it comes from me.
By the time you read this note I shall be dead. But this
should be of no concern to you. What must concern

you is this. My scientists at Raubkammer have devised a new nerve gas. It is a mutant variation of Tabun and Sarin. Petscher writes to me that he has force-tested it on human guinea pigs at the Truppenhubuensplatz and it has proved itself to be infinitely more powerful than Trilon 83 and Trilon 146. And far more concentrated. He calls it Trilon 380. The process can be made into a jelly. In two separate sections. If kept apart, the jelly is harmless. The microbes will not multiply. If mixed, and subsequently waterborne, it becomes pathologically lethal within six hours. You know that until now I have always resisted using chemical warfare. This is due to my temporary blinding by a British mustard gas attack on the Ypres Salient on the 14 October 1918. To my eternal shame I only heard of Germany's false defeat whilst recovering at Pasewalk Hospital. Later, I vowed never to use such stuffs on the battlefield. I now believe that the rape of our country by the Russian hordes negates this vow. You will receive both the Holy Lance and the new formula for Trilon 380 alongside this letter. Use both in any way that you see fit. You have a chemical factory. You know where to find our buried stock of Trilon 83 and Trilon 146. Being a chemist yourself you will understand, thanks to this new formula, how to distil and concentrate these two entities into Trilon 380. You still have access to planes and to the men who can fly them. The ability to turn this war around is now in your hands, Heini. This letter is my final Führer command to you. If the actions you are forced to take mean the destruction of our own people alongside the enemy, you must do this. DO NOT HESITATE. I am dying for Germany; why should not they? It will be a sacrifice worth making. The Reich is doomed. Let us take our aggressors down with us. Let Frederick Barbarossa finally awake from his long sleep in the Kyffhaüser Mountains. Let the ravens fly again! My greetings to your beautiful wife Elfriede and to your little Hansi.

Your Führer,

Adolf Hitler.

FORTY-SEVEN

That evening Hart gazed at Effi Rache across the dining-room table with new eyes. The person he saw sitting opposite him was not a monster, but a desirable woman, in the prime of her life, blessed with large, startlingly intense periwinkle-blue eyes, framed by the longest natural lashes he had ever encountered. Her swept-back blonde hair cascaded over her shoulders like a waterfall, her heart-shaped face was set off by broad Slavic cheekbones, and a finely arched, slightly concave nose ended high above a heartwood bow of a mouth, whose pronounced underlip gave its owner the elusive air of forever needing to be kissed. Something deep inside Hart refused to associate the possessor of such treasures – of such a blameless face – with the bestial horrors contained in Adolf Hitler's letter.

Despite this inner conviction, he knew that he must still tread cautiously. The Effi he knew might be incapable of evil intent, but those around her might not prove so scrupulous. It was always possible that she was being used by others without her knowledge. The leaders and figureheads of political movements often were; Hart had covered enough foreign wars during his career as a photojournalist to be certain of this fact.

He leant in towards her, an intent look on his face. 'Look, I've no desire to alarm you, but when I looked out of this window last night, I saw the man who came running at us the other day in the car park. He was standing out there in the pitch darkness staring up at your bedroom window. It was only because the light was off that I was able to see him. I was deciding whether to run outside and confront him when it occurred to me that you might be employing him as a security guard. Are you? Or have I been a fool?' He smiled. 'I was stark naked at the time, so I felt at a marginal disadvantage.'

Effi laid down her fork. Normally she would have returned Hart's smile, for they both enjoyed flirtatious small talk. This time the face across the table was deadly serious. 'You saw Udo Zirkeler? Standing outside my house at night? Why didn't you tell me this before?'

Hart also laid down his cutlery. Bringing the matter up had been a risk worth taking, he told himself, even though it was Wesker who had seen Zirkeler, not him. The white lie was, at the very least, a believable one.

He had spoken to Amira on his new phone immediately after he had left the Alpenruh, and passed on to her the gist of the message Frau Erlichmann had translated for him. Her response had been immediate and unequivocal. It was Effi Rache who had received the letter, so it was Effi Rache they must go after. It was she who owned the chemical factory, and she whose grandfather was to be the original recipient.

Hart had immediately understood that if he wished to exonerate Effi from whatever might be going on without her knowledge, he would need to become far more proactive. There was no proof as yet that the formula even existed. Or if it did, that it had survived nearly seventy years of storage. And wasn't it reliant on buried stocks of the original Trilon 83 and Trilon 146? What were the chances of anyone knowing where they were buried now? The Americans had probably dug them up after the war and used them for their own purposes. Either that, or the chemicals were quietly leaching, unknown and unnoticed, back into the lithosphere. And beyond all that, who in their right minds would unleash such weapons on the modern world anyway, and risk their own destruction alongside that of their perceived enemies? It made no sense.

Amira was riddled with jealousy, he decided, and so she wasn't thinking straight. Hart suspected that it was only the prospect of a front-page news story that was stopping her from going straight to the authorities and blasting everything to kingdom come. Whatever Amira's susceptibilities as a woman, she was a professional journalist first and foremost. Her training would cause her to wait and see rather than act prematurely. But her emotions would be telling her a different story. He would need to act quickly to defuse the situation.

'I didn't think it was important. But yes, it was definitely Zirkeler out there. He is unmistakeable. Even after only one previous viewing.' Hart tried to make the tone of his voice as light as possible in order to conceal the lie.

Effi responded in kind. 'I use him as a guard occasionally. Him and a few of the others. Sometimes we get unwanted visitors. The party I lead tends to divide opinion. You saw that for yourself at the Gasthof zur Hirschberg.' She glanced at Hart to gauge his reaction.

'But your party is against all these outrages in the news, isn't it? I've been reading about Germany's problems with the Turks and so forth. The beatings. The clashes between rival gangs. Neo-Nazis and suchlike.' Hart found it surprisingly easy to pretend an ignorance and callousness that in real life would have been anathema to him. It brought home to him how much he was already playing a part.

'Of course we are against them. We are a mainstream political party, Johnny. We don't employ thugs. If anyone is caught indulging in that sort of behaviour, they are immediately ejected. It would be impossible for us to function within the democratic framework otherwise. We are committed to non-violence. I thought you realized that?'

'I knew that was the case. I just don't like the look of Zirkeler, that's all. Are you sure there's no more to it than that? He's just a security guard?'

Effi hesitated. Hart – hyperalert now to every nuance in her behaviour – could see her weighing up how far she was prepared to take him into her confidence. 'What else could there be?'

Hart decided to let her off the hook. He was sailing way

too close to the wind as it was. 'I thought he might be in love with you. Jealous of me, perhaps?'

Effi gave a relieved laugh. 'Oh, Johnny, really. I could never be interested in such a thug. What do you think?'

'I don't think you're interested in him. Of course not. But he might be interested in you.'

'Do you really think so?'

'I couldn't blame him. A frog can look at a princess, can't he? Look at me.'

'Are you a frog?'

'What do you think?'

'I think you're more of a bear. A big, cuddly bear. With hidden claws.'

Hart smiled. He knew the game well enough by now, and he enjoyed playing it. 'I hide them very well. I can't even find them myself sometimes.'

The moment passed with a hug and a kiss. Hart was relieved to let it go. He wasn't at his best saying one thing and meaning another. It was why both Amira and Effi could run rings round him whenever they chose to. It had been his mother – before she began her descent into dementia – who had said that women matured emotionally at puberty, and men in late middle-age. Well, Hart was a long way off late middle-age still.

Effi pulled away from their hug. She ran her hand through his hair just as a mother would do to a child. 'I have to go and meet some of our delegates tomorrow morning, early. They need a little encouragement from their leader in the quiet before the storm. Summer is always a bad time for us, politically. It's like being caught in the doldrums without a breath of wind. Do you think you will be able to entertain yourself here without me, Johnny?'

'I shall go on a long walk round the lake. I need some exercise.'

'Don't I exercise you enough?'

Hart grinned. 'That's a different sort of exercise altogether.' He gave her bottom a pat. 'Do you know what? I might even go for a swim. Isn't there a spa around here somewhere?'

Effi made a *moue*. 'There's a Badepark, but you might be overrun. Unless you like waterslides and squealing brats. And here in Germany we sauna naked, even amongst strangers, so I don't want you getting ideas about other women, do you hear me? I would go to the Strandbad if I were you. You get to bathe in the lake there, with a platform to swim out to. It's old-fashioned but nice. And utterly safe from predatory females.'

Hart pretended to look sad. 'Okay. No spas. And no predatory females. But I thought you still had a chemical factory that made spa products? Where are your markets then, if they're not over here?'

Effi's face turned serious again. 'I do still have a factory. Just down the road in Gmund. But our main markets are no longer in Germany. We produce chemicals for spas and swimming pools internationally. Chlorine. Bromine. Potassium peroxysulphate. Calcium hypochlorite. Cyanuric acid. That sort of thing.'

'I'd love to see the factory one day.'

'You want to see the factory?'

'Now that I'm living here with you, I'd like to involve myself a little more in your life. Get to know what you do with your days.' Hart cocked his head to one side. He knew he was on shaky ground. He decided to strike out laterally. 'What you say about your politics intrigues me too, Effi. You say you are using the Holy Lance to cement loyalty to your party? Well, I am supposed to be its hereditary guardian. And I have never even seen it. Would such a thing be possible, do you think?'

Effi looked at Hart for a very long time. The expression on her face passed through several disparate stages, varying from quizzical, through pensive, to hopeful. Hart felt as if he were watching the complex play of light across moving water.

'Would you really like to become more involved in my life? You're not just saying this to please me? Because it would please me, you know. It would mean a great deal to me.' For the first time since Hart had known her, Effi looked almost vulnerable. 'Because my one fear is that you will hold back on the way you feel for me because of who I am and what I represent. That there will come a point when you will cease to see me as a woman any more, and merely as the figurehead of my party.'

Hart laughed. 'I could never cease to see you as a woman. You must know that by now. In fact, it must be obvious for all to see. Even that goon, Zirkeler.'

Effi took Hart's hand in hers and kissed it. 'Then come. I will show you what you want to see. I will show you the Holy Lance.'

FORTY-EIGHT

'What were you doing outside my house last night? When did I give you permission to spy on me? What were you thinking of?' Effi struck Udo Zirkeler on the arm. It was like punching a slab of chilled meat.

Udo stared right through Effi. A part of him was still back in the field killing the cow with a single blow of his stone. The significance of the act had followed him throughout the day. If he could achieve such a thing with a cow, what more could he do to a man? What would his audience say, then? How would they respond?

'I'm sorry, what did you say?'

'You were standing outside my house last night. What were you doing there?'

'You saw me?'

Effi hesitated for a fatal fraction of a second. 'Yes.'

Udo grinned at her. 'You're lying. It was the Englishman who saw me. Admit it. He was probably cooling off by the window after fucking you.'

Effi turned her back on him and walked towards the glazed screen that separated the empty warehouse area of her chemical factory from the inner research laboratory. It would be pointless hitting Udo again, she decided. The oaf seemed insensible to normal stimuli. She was glad that he was on her side and not against her, however. Woe betide Udo's enemies. And heaven protect Udo's friends, because they must be few and far between.

She stood for a moment watching one of her technicians through the insulated glass of the laboratory window. He was wearing a Level A Hazmat fully encapsulating protective suit, with a full face-piece self-contained breathing apparatus. The suit was both gas-tight and vapour-tight, and boasted an internal two-way radio through which the wearer could communicate with those outside the laboratory. The whole outfit was set off by steel-toed boots, tunic shanks and chemical-resistant gloves. Its inhabitant looked like a spaceman, and moved nearly as slowly.

'It's irrelevant who saw you. But you admit you were out there?'

'Yes. I was out there. I was guarding you.'

'Guarding me? From what? And from whom? You were spying on me. And we both know why.'

'I wonder how well the Englishman would respond to you if he knew you'd fucked me?'

'Don't play games with me, Udo. We both know how things stand with us. You need me more than I need you.'

'Wrong. We both need each other. We both know way too

much. This thing has gone too far for either one of us to bow out graciously.'

'Nobody is bowing out, Udo. But you need to understand that I have plans for the baron. And they don't involve you. You have your role to play and he has his.'

'And what is his role? I would like you to explain this to me, please. You aren't thinking of taking him into your confidence, are you? You can't be as cock-struck as all that? Because I won't stand for it. What we are doing is world-changing. It will start the fall of the dominoes that will ultimately lead to the restitution of our country. The saving of our people. The restoration of the Reich.'

'Oh, shut up, Udo. Of course I am not taking him into my confidence. His role will be a different one from yours, that's all. A personal one. And it's none of your business.'

Udo wasn't satisfied. But he knew just how far he could push Effi. He was still reliant on her for the funding of his 'apostles' and for everything else concerning their venture, and he needed to be cautious. Theirs was a combative relationship that appeared to gratify them both, albeit on a surface level. It was based on family, and order, and innate natural hierarchies. At a deeper, more barbaric level, however, it remained inconceivable to Udo how Effi could favour an effete lightweight like the Englishman over a man like him. He hesitated a little before plunging back into the fray – but he couldn't let the subject go.

'What time last night did he see me?'

'I'm sorry?'

'I said what time last night did he see me. It is a simple question. Unlike you, I have no ulterior motives. I thought I had concealed myself well. I clearly had not. I need to rectify this so that, in the event of a crisis, I am at the top of my game.'

Effi stared at Udo. Sometimes he astonished her with his obtuseness. The difference between him and her baron was the difference between darkness and light. Last night, when she had shown Johnny the Holy Lance for the first time, she had watched his face carefully for any sign of equivocation. Instead, she had seen his expression transform itself before her eyes. The Lance, when she had handed it to him, had appeared to become a part of him. Then Johnny had turned to her, his face alight with something close to passion.

'This is extraordinary. Can you feel it, Effi? It's pulsing in my hands. As if it had a heartbeat of its own. Here. Reach across. Touch it.'

Effi had reached across. And yes, the Holy Lance had felt as if it were pulsing. But when she took it into her own hands, it had fallen dead again, like an expiring child. She had been almost afraid when she handed it back. As if the Lance had been attempting to communicate with her, but she had been unable to understand its message.

'What time?'

Effi looked up, surprised. 'What are you talking about, Udo?'

'What time did the Englishman see me?'

Effi shook her head to clear it of the memories and emotions conjured up by the night before. 'I don't know. Maybe three o'clock in the morning.'

'Are you sure?'

Effi shrugged. Then she stuck her tongue out at Udo like a little girl. 'Yes. It was three. Because when he came back to bed he fucked me twice more, and I reset the alarm at four-thirty to give us both some extra sleep. Some time to recuperate. Satisfied, Udo?'

Udo pretended to retch on the ground in disgust. But he was satisfied. He had left the grounds of Haus Walküre a little after midnight. He had killed the cow at around quarter to one. He had been tucked up in bed and asleep by two o'clock. Which meant the Englishman was lying through his teeth.

FORTY-NINE

Until now, Udo Zirkeler had only gone through the holy ritual of being inhabited by his grandfather's SS uniform on foreign soil. In Guatemala, to kill the three. Once in the outskirts of Izmir, Turkey, to put pressure on the wife and children of a gang leader. A single time in Paris, which he would rather forget.

On that occasion he had been intending to kill a Jewish columnist who had held the Brotherhood of the Lance up to ridicule in a leftist newspaper. Instead, he had come perilously close to walking into a Mossad trap. It had only been the necessity of hiding in a corridor alcove to change into his uniform that had enabled him to overhear the squeal from an agent's malfunctioning headset and save himself. Since then the uniform had become a talisman. A totem. Udo's lucky charm.

He had never risked wearing the uniform in mainland Germany. He had tried it on, many times. In front of mirrors.

Or modelling it to please his mother. But he had never used it completely. To its full extent, so to speak.

Udo's paternal grandfather – the original wearer of the uniform prior to his suicide on the final day of the war – had, in his grandson's view, been an unsung national hero. His father had often told Udo the story of how Hanke Zirkeler had saved Léon Degrelle's life near Cherkassy in 1944. At that time, Degrelle had been a lowly SS-*Hauptsturmführer* – the SS equivalent of a captain in the Wehrmacht – and Udo's grandfather an even lowlier sergeant. As a direct result of Hanke Zirkeler's intervention, however, Degrelle had gone on to command the 28th SS Volunteer Grenadier Division Wallonian, win the Knight's Cross, and become a propaganda hero, helping to recruit tens of thousands of foreign nationals into the SS when the Reich was most in need of them. Adolf Hitler had personally told Degrelle: 'If I had a son, I wish he'd resemble you.' The thought that such a man as Degrelle had been allowed to live and fulfil his destiny solely because of his grandfather's actions made Udo very proud. And it further reinforced his view, passed down to him via his father, that actions beget other actions. That fate was not a matter of happenstance, but a question of will.

Udo smoothed away the creases in his grandfather's uniform. He tugged the tunic down so that it fitted him snugly around the waist, adjusted his pistol belt, and made sure the SS dagger was tightly in place. He intended to look his best for his invisible audience. For tonight's campaign was to be a crucial test of his initiative.

Udo's father had taught him far more than mere family history. Jürgen Zirkeler had drummed into his son that, next to obeying orders, the capacity to show initiative was the true test of any soldier's merit. Udo smiled into the hand mirror he carried in the top pocket of his tunic. How his secret sharers would relish what he was about to do. And how delighted they would be with his spirit of enterprise. Udo was as convinced of this fact as he was of his own name. His excitement, and the usual gut-churning anticipation of action, began to mount. This was what Udo lived for. This was his Monte Cassino.

Udo chose to enter the Alpenruh via the beer-cellar door. As far as he knew, the place had not served keg beer to its customers for decades, but its cellar doors were still grandiosely in place, situated conveniently close to the road so that the beer-truck driver would have no difficulty de-crating.

Udo picked the simple padlock with a tortion wrench and a feeler pick. He inserted the wrench, put pressure on it, and then twisted the pick round. The click made by the deadbolt as it snapped open filled him with intense satisfaction. It was a big padlock, and pathetically easy to crack. Udo cast a look back over his shoulder. His watchers were still there. He would simply reverse the procedure on the way out, he informed them silently, and no one would be any the wiser. Grinning, he beckoned the watchers to follow him in.

Once inside the cellar, Udo made his way past crates of empty Coca Cola and apple juice bottles, fastidiously avoiding contact with any dust-ridden surface. He wished to look his best in this, his first uniformed foray on German soil. He did not wish to resemble a street cleaner.

He padded up the stairs to the ground floor on his felt-soled boots. He could smell the scent of the house now. It was a German smell, of sausage and spices and coffee. It was the smell of his mother's house.

He stopped by the concierge's desk and checked for keys. Yes. Just as he thought. Only one key out. The room next to the one the fake English baron had used. Udo snooped around in case a master key was hanging anywhere beneath the opened roll-top. No such luck. It would not be a problem. He had an alternative plan.

He eased his way up the main staircase, placing his feet on the outside of the stairs where they were flush to the walls. This was an old house. Some of the stairs were bound to creak if he wasn't careful. And Udo was no lightweight.

He made it to the first floor unannounced. The night-lights were on, throwing a strange blue tinge across the red carpets.

Udo crept to the door of the occupied room. He was briefly tempted to laugh, a sudden stuttering of breath inside his lungs that surprised him. He clapped his hand to his face. How absurd all this creeping around was. There was only a single guest here. And the old lady was probably deaf as well as blind. Udo knew that she lived in a separate apartment on the ground floor. There was no real danger of her overhearing anything. But still. It behove him to be silent. There would come a time when he and his people could come out into the open and display themselves. But not yet. Definitely not yet.

Udo tried the door. It opened beneath his hand. Now he would not have to imitate a cat. In his experience people were drawn to tiny noises. He had intended to scratch at the base of the door with a pen if it had been locked. Just a light scratching. With numerous hesitations. It would have worked. One hundred per cent. But now there was no need.

Udo stepped inside the room and closed the door gently behind him. No one in the bed. But the windows to the balcony were open, and the curtains pulled across. The inhabitant of the room was out there, in the darkness, watching Effi's house. This was the man who had seen him. This was the man who had warned the Englishman.

Udo tiptoed across the room until he was flush with the curtains. He breathed the night air deep into his lungs. He could hear rustlings on the other side of the curtain. The clink of a bottle. He would wait until the man had finished his drink. It was only courtesy. The whole thing would play better into his hands like this.

Udo heard the bottle being replaced on the floor. Now was the moment. He threw aside the curtains and stood, in the full glory of his transmutation, his arms outstretched.

Wesker turned. When he saw Udo, he ducked his head, open-mouthed, and made as if he would run away. But there was nowhere for him to run on the tiny balcony.

Udo took two steps forward and sank to his knees. He was used to moving quickly. He had trained himself for this.

The man in front of him was clumsy and overweight. He

was a heavy drinker, too, given the number of empty beer bottles littering the balcony area.

Udo grasped the man by his ankles and tipped him backwards.

Wesker had time enough for a single inhalation of breath before he toppled. He had no time to turn the breath into a scream. His body flipped once, in graceful slow motion, and then it hit the concrete paving of the terrace below with the thud a fertilizer sack makes when it is tossed from a barn loft.

Udo peered over the balcony. The man had fallen on his head and neck. Astonishingly, given the man's shape, these were probably the heaviest parts of his body. The single turn had done it. *Kraaak!*

Udo reached down and picked up the image intensifier the man had been using. A Swarovski NC2 with a camera adapter. Far too good to leave behind. Worth at least five thousand euros new; maybe four fifths of that in the open market. He took Wesker's phone too. Might prove interesting.

He checked the balcony area around him. Perfect. At least fifteen empty beer bottles lay scattered about. The police would assume the man had been drunk. He'd stumbled and toppled over the railings, which were low and wooden, and probably nowhere near to conforming with European health-and-safety regulations. With luck, the old cow who ran the place would be closed down and ruined. A double success, then. Maybe Effi could buy the Alpenruh at the distress sale and turn it into a barracks for his 'apostles'? Udo decided he would enjoy living in a house of murder.

He turned to his secret sharers and raised his hands into the air. Then he made a sweeping bow of prostration.

Now things were beginning. Now the future was under way.

Udo scrubbed the outside door handle of prints and hurried down the stairs towards the cellar. He would have loved to kill again – the old lady this time – but he knew that such a thing made no sense. Better to let sleeping bitches lie.

He let himself out of the beer-cellar door and relocked it. He checked his watch. Two in the morning. He was tempted to hurry down and check out what was happening at Haus Walküre. But the thought of Effi lying in the Englishman's arms made him want to puke.

He would take off his uniform and go to the Cosy Home Club instead. One of the girls there generally agreed to some spirited games if Udo paid her enough. And she looked sufficiently like Effi so that he could allow his fantasies free rein. And tonight, Udo sensed, he would surpass himself.

FIFTY

Hart learnt of Wesker's death from Amira over the phone, at around ten the next morning.

Amira had checked in with Wesker at eight, as previously arranged, to receive a progress report. She had been sent straight through to Wesker's voicemail. She had hesitated for a moment, nonplussed, and then some instinct had cut in and caused her not to leave a message. To her certain knowledge, she told Hart, Wesker never knowingly switched off his phone. Even if he visited the theatre, or a cinema, or the toilet, or, God forbid, a church, Wesker would still set the phone to vibrate just in case someone, somewhere, might be calling him with a news tip. Wesker and his phone were inseparable, to the extent that if the drink didn't scramble his brains, the phone signal would.

Now, face to face with Hart after their initial call, Amira wore a curiously blank expression on her face, like a woman still in shock in the direct aftermath of a bomb attack. Hart had suggested they meet at the Rottach Egern ferry terminal. They had taken a *rundfahrt*, which gave them the right to circumnavigate the entire lake by ferry without disembarking. Hart had been unable, off the cuff, to think of any better place for a rendezvous. But the lake air didn't seem to be doing either of them any good.

'Three minutes after I put away my phone I was in a taxi heading from our safe house to the Alpenruh. I thought Wesker might have overdone it with the booze and not been able to get out of bed. Don't shake your head. It's been known to happen. He's a drunk, not an alcoholic.' Amira lit a cigarette with nervous, staccato movements. She watched as the smoke was snapped away by the wind. 'He's been staking out Haus Walküre pretty much round the clock, whilst I've been off following other leads. He's not so good on his feet any more, so I thought a static job would suit him. But, being Wesker, he refuses point blank to live like a sensible human being whilst he's doing it.' Amira's voice faltered. 'I suppose I should use the past tense now. I'm talking like he's still alive. Like he'll stumble towards us at any moment with three bottles of beer in one hand and an unfiltered Gitanes Brunes in the other, grinning like a possum.' The frozen carapace Amira had been wearing for Hart's benefit was crumbling fast. 'Wesker lived every bloody moment as if it was his last. At least he had that. At least he got that bit right.' She put her face in her hands.

Hart didn't know what to say. He supposed he should comfort Amira, but the action somehow seemed inappropriate. The truth was that the news about Wesker had blindsided him, just as it had blindsided her. 'And? What then?'

Amira looked up. 'And there were police everywhere. What do you think? A man had just died, John.'

'You didn't make yourself known to them, did you?'

'Of course not. I spoke to one of the neighbours instead. They told me a drunk man had fallen off a balcony. They were surprised there were any guests at all at Frau Erlichmann's hotel. And certainly guests like that.'

'I'll phone Frau Erlichmann now.'

'Yes. You do that.' Amira turned away from Hart and stared at the onion dome of a church far across the lake. 'He was my mentor, John. My bloody mentor. He was renowned for not liking anybody. But for some reason he suffered me. Befriended me, even. He took me under his wing when I arrived at the newspaper and taught me all the wrinkles. Warned me who to avoid. Prevented me from stamping on too many toes.'

Hart glanced up in surprise. Generally speaking, Amira didn't do gratitude.

Amira threw her dead cigarette into the lake. She shot a glance at Hart over her shoulder. 'I still don't know why the bastard took pity on me. A cynical old hack like him; it defies belief.' Amira scrubbed at her eyes with the back of her hand.

Hart dialled Frau Erlichmann's number to give himself something to do. Amira's words had resonated with him – more than he cared to admit. They reminded him of who and what he had been. And what he was in the process of becoming.

'Maybe he recognized a kindred spirit, Amira? Someone who put journalism first?' Unlike me, he thought to himself. I put lust first, don't I? Lust and expedience. And to hell with the truth.

Hart let the phone ring for five minutes before hanging up. He was almost grateful that Frau Erlichmann didn't answer. It gave him an excuse for action.

'Nobody home?'

'Apparently not. So we need to go there. Now.'

'No, John. Not we. You. You must go alone. We can't afford to be seen together. It's far too dangerous.'

Hart straightened up from his slouch. 'I'm assuming, from that, that you don't think Wesker toppled off his balcony whilst blind drunk?'

'Wesker was never blind drunk in his life. He was simply a little bit tanked all the time. It was a way of life with him. He was old-school Fleet Street and proud of it. Canary Wharf, and all that it represented, disgusted him. There was no way that a man like that would topple backwards off a bloody balcony. He'd have gone out like his chum George Best. Or done an Ollie Reed and ruptured his aorta arm-wrestling with a bunch of sailors.' Amira turned away.

Hart stared over her shoulder across the lake. 'I think I killed him.'

'What are you talking about?'

'I told Effi that I'd seen that thug Zirkeler hanging around outside the house at night, spying on us.'

'How does that make you responsible for Wesker's death?'

Hart shrugged. 'I don't know. But I have a suspicion it does. What if Effi confronted Zirkeler about it? She seemed pretty upset when I told her, and tried to pretend he was a security guard or something. But it had clearly shocked her. I think Zirkeler has a thing about her, and Effi knows it. We already know that Zirkeler, or one of his cronies, checked out my room when I first arrived. Maybe when Effi confronted Zirkeler, he decided I was lying, and took matters into his own hands?'

'Do you mean you are finally coming to terms with the fact that Effi Rache may not be the shining little angel you take her to be? That she may be a rattler with wings?'

'No. I'm sure she had nothing to do with this, Amira. Positive of it, in fact. She just isn't like that. I'm more and more convinced that Zirkeler is acting on his own accord. The man is an animal. If you want to know who is leading the gang of thugs terrorizing half of southern Bavaria, I suggest you look no further. There is no way on earth that Zirkeler was guarding Effi's house in the middle of the night. He was spying on us. And I foolishly gave away that someone was spying on him. It wasn't Effi's work. She was just washing her own linen. Wesker's death is on me.'

FIFTY-ONE

Frau Erlichmann had not answered Hart's call because she had been taking her afternoon nap. This was a daily ritual during which she unplugged the telephone and used both earplugs and an eyeshade to reinforce her desire for solitude. She was wide awake, though, when Hart arrived at the Alpenruh.

'Thank you for your concern, Baron. But the police left two hours ago. Twenty minutes after that a female liaison officer turned up at my door. I sent her packing. I told her that I didn't need bereavement counselling, or social services, or meals-on-wheels. That a foreign guest I barely knew had fallen off one of my balconies while drunk, and that, whilst this was without doubt a tragedy for the person concerned, it wasn't a tragedy for me. I told her that I am still perfectly capable of looking after myself in this tragedy's aftermath in exactly the manner I have done for most of the past ninety years, during which I have had far worse disasters to face than the loss of my only paying guest.'

Hart sat opposite Frau Erlichmann at one of the *esszimmer* tables. He could tell, despite her nominally defiant words, that she was badly shaken up. 'Please. Tell me what really happened.'

'You will find a bottle of Niersteiner Pettenthal in the rear pantry. Will you fetch it please? With two glasses?'

Hart brought the wine. He poured Frau Erlichmann a glassful and watched her raise it to her mouth, using both hands to steady herself. The wine seemed to calm her, as if its familiar taste might be reminding her of the solid earth from which both she and it stemmed.

'It was the SS who killed your friend.' Frau Erlichmann placed her glass carefully back onto the table. She stroked the nap of the tablecloth with her fingers. 'I saw them. I heard a thump outside my bedroom window. So I put my dressing gown on and cracked open the door to my apartment. I saw the soldier passing. Even with my poor eyes, I saw the soldier passing on his way down to the cellar.'

Hart wondered for a moment if Frau Erlichmann wasn't beginning to suffer from the very same condition as his mother. But the old lady's gaze was clear, and bright with intelligence.

'There are no SS any more, Frau Erlichmann. They've been extinct for nearly seventy years.'

'This man was wearing an SS uniform. Please believe me when I tell you that. Sometimes my eyes work better in the semi-darkness. I could not tell his face. But the uniform, the boots, the hat, the swastika armband – they were all clear to me in the glow thrown by the night-light. I have seen such things a thousand times in the Red Cross during the war. I was not mistaken.'

'Did you tell this to the police?'

Frau Erlichmann stared at Hart as if he had taken leave of his senses. '*Quatsch*. Do you know what this word means in German? It means "total nonsense". That is what the police would have said if I had told them of this. I am a very old woman. They would assume I was demented. They would have ordered me to be sectioned by a brace of their tame doctors and then transferred to a nursing home for my own good. There is no sign of a break-in. Nothing was stolen. As far as the *Landespolizei* are concerned, your friend simply fell off his balcony whilst drunk. The *Kripo* in charge of the investigation counted more than twenty empty beer bottles in his room. Not thirds – litres. Twenty litres. And all with his fingerprints on them – of this I have no doubt.' Frau Erlichmann cocked her head to one side. 'Do you think I am suffering from dementia, John?'

'No. My mother has this condition. I would recognize it straight away. You are not suffering from anything resembling it.'

'Then come upstairs and visit Herr Wesker's room with me. The police are entirely satisfied that he fell off the balcony whilst under the influence of alcohol. Therefore the room is not a crime scene. They have requested that I have my maid collect up his belongings to be sent to Herr Wesker's family when they are able to contact them through the British

Embassy. You can help me with this, John. You knew him. Maybe we will learn something important?'

Wesker's belongings didn't amount to much. A few clothes, an old-fashioned nightshirt, a Kent washbag, and a beaten-up leather jacket. They fitted neatly inside his single suitcase. The only heavy objects were three bottles of Dimple Haig that Wesker must have bought at Munich Airport, if the duty-free bags were anything to go by. The bottles looked peculiarly forlorn, Hart thought, standing in line like promises of tomorrow.

Hart telephoned Amira from well inside Wesker's room. Amira had urged him not to go out onto the balcony just before they parted. It was at her insistence too that Hart had accessed the hotel via the rear woodland path, and not through the main entrance. It wouldn't do to underestimate Zirkeler, she had told him. The longer they could keep any connection between her, Wesker and Hart a secret, the better.

'I've been through all of Wesker's stuff. There's nothing out of the ordinary there. But Frau Erlichmann tells me she saw the man who probably killed him leaving the house. Listen to this, Amira. He was wearing an SS uniform.'

There was a heavy silence at the other end of the telephone. 'Zirkeler?'

'She couldn't tell. But it has to be.'

'So he likes dressing up when he conducts his murders? This gets weirder and weirder. Did she inform the police?'

'No. She was afraid they would certify her. But we can rectify that omission later on if need be. It won't take much to convince them that she was scared to death.'

'Then keep it under your own hat for a while, John. And please ask Frau Erlichmann to continue playing *stumm* as well. If she's game, that is? If Zirkeler thinks you bought the drunken fall story, he'll be that much further off his guard. Thank God he doesn't know about me yet.'

'What else do you want me to do?'

'Have you got Wesker's passport and wallet?'

'The police have taken it. Next of kin and all that.'

'What about his phone?'

'There's no phone here. Maybe the police have taken that too? That would make sense, because they'll need some way to contact his family.'

'It's encrypted. All our phones are. If it really was the police that took it, it won't do them any good. And if it was Zirkeler, it won't do him any good either. What else is there in his room?'

Hart listed Wesker's possessions.

'And the Swarovski?'

'What Swarovski?'

'Wesker was using an NC2 image intensifier to see across the valley at night.'

Hart made a final tour of the room with the phone in his hand. Then he dropped to his knees and cracked open the balcony door. He peered out at ground level, making sure that the wooden balustrade blocked any possible view from Haus Walküre.

'There's no intensifier here.'

'Then it was stolen. Along with his phone, I'm willing to bet.'

'That strikes me as incredibly dumb. Why cover your tracks, and then mess it up by stealing something you know will be missed?'

'These people aren't rocket scientists, John. Look at Breivik in Norway. They think they're smart, but they're all missing a few screws.'

'What if taking it was meant as a warning? A private warning to me?'

'That's giving Zirkeler way too much credit, in my opinion.'

'So where do we go from here?'

'You go back to your Effi Rache, and you say nothing. What happened here has nothing to do with you, at least as far as she is concerned. Learn about Zirkeler. Find out where he lives. What exactly he does for the Lanzen Brüderschaft.'

'And what are you going to do, Amira?'

'I'm going to pay a visit to Fräulein Rache's chemical factory.'

FIFTY-TWO

'Did you hear about the man who fell off Frau Erlichmann's balcony last night?' Effi was looking at Hart over her glass of wine. Her eyes were wide with excitement.

Hart glanced up from his Rindersteak. He met Effi's eyes. And then his gaze drifted down to her neckline, just as she had intended. She was wearing a gold lamé Marc Jacobs dress with a deep décolleté, more suited to a formal dinner party in a French chateau than to an intimate dinner *à deux* in a Mies van der Rohe dining room. The dress showed off the blonde lights in Effi's hair to their best advantage. It also emphasized the immaculate set of her shoulders, her alabaster skin, and the Venus indentations at her collarbone. When she stood up to fetch them a second bottle of wine from the kitchen, the dress hugged the contours of Effi's hips like a second skin.

'No. I hadn't heard. What man was that?'

'Oh, just some Englishman. He had been drinking heavily, I was told. The police found dozens of empty bottles in his room. He walked out onto the balcony for a breath of fresh air and simply carried on walking. What a pathetic way to go. I suppose it was suicide.'

'Where did you hear this?'

'Everyone's heard about it, Johnny. Bad Wiessee is a large village. Not the medium-sized town it thinks it is. Under five thousand of us live here all year round, so everyone knows everyone else's business. My friend Margrit phoned and told me about it. She got it from a friend of hers whose father plays golf with the *Land* chief. You remember Margrit, don't you? You met her and Alena the day I was attacked by that boy at the Gasthof zur Hirschtal. She's decided to throw a party for us so she can really get to know you. She and Alena are green with envy. She thinks you look like... now, who was it?'

Hart forced a smile onto his face. 'Brad Pitt? George Clooney? Ben Affleck? Johnny Depp?'

'No. Now that I come to think of it, it was that comedian. The one in *Dumb and Dumber*. What is his name? Jim Carrey.'

Hart pretended to draw back his fist. 'Very funny. Very funny indeed.' He watched Effi carefully as she sat opposite him, laughing. But there was no sign of duplicity on her face. She had brought the subject of Wesker's death up by herself, quite naturally, and with no prompting from him. It was the sort of event anybody might mention over the dinner table. It had happened in a neighbouring house, after all. And sudden death is always a subject worthy of comment, especially if the victim doesn't happen to be you. He decided to stir up the water a little.

'Did you ever get a chance to talk to Zirkeler, Effi?'

'Zirkeler? What about?'

'Him lurking around the house the other night.'

'Oh, that was all my fault.' Effi's face wore the wide-eyed look of a fallen angel who expects to be restored to heaven at any given moment. 'I'd forgotten I'd asked him to do the rounds of all my properties. He has quite a few people working under him. He and his colleagues specialize in personal security. I asked him to make sure someone checked out the house and the factory every hour on the hour throughout the night.' Effi touched the Caresse d'orchidées necklace her father had bought her from Cartier for her twenty-first birthday. Hart's eyes followed the movement. She smiled at him. 'That episode you witnessed in the Gasthof shook me up more than I thought. Udo Zirkeler may look like a Neanderthal, but he's actually a very responsible person. I think the night you saw him in the garden one of his people was off sick, so he decided to do the job himself. It's as simple as that. Nothing suspicious about it at all.'

'Do you really think someone would target your factory? A place that makes swimming pool chemicals and herbal bath foam? Is that why you're having it watched? It seems unlikely to me.'

'These crackbrained left-wing groups will target anything that may fetch them a little free publicity, Johnny. I've learnt this to my cost. It's always better to err on the side of caution. I've ordered Zirkeler to leave the house off his list now that I have you here with me, and to concentrate his attention on the factory and my farm at Schliersee. Does that satisfy you?' Effi cocked her head to one side as if she were weighing Hart up for auction. 'You'll protect me, won't you, Big Boy?'

Hart felt the look somewhere in the region of his hip pocket. It was Effi's intense femininity, he decided, that always wrong-footed him. There was something about the shape of her face, the swell of her brow, the configuration of her chin, which filled him with a baffling sense of wonder. Hart wasn't a fey man. He didn't believe in ghosts, fairies, guardian angels or spirit guides – and New Age blarney bored him rigid. So did people who wore their faith on their sleeves, or who claimed to believe in parallel universes. But when he looked at Effi, he knew, with an unshakeable certainty, that the two of them had been linked in a previous life. That they had once, long ago, been married. Or been brother and sister. Or father and daughter. Maybe she had been the man and he the woman? Who knew? But the feeling was total. Unassailable. And it coloured everything he did with her. Every response he made to her. Every suspicion he had of her. At this particular moment, discussing Wesker's murder with a detachment he didn't feel, he felt like a mother who hears that her son has been accused of a particularly grotesque crime, but who will not wear it, even though, in her heart of hearts, she knows it might be true.

When Effi left the table once more and walked into the open-plan kitchen to make them coffee, Hart excused himself and hurried down to the bathroom, ostensibly to wash his hands and freshen up. Once inside, he took out his phone and hit redial.

'Amira Eisenberger. Who is this?'

Hart made a face. He knew Amira had number recognition on her phone. She was giving him the cold shoulder on purpose. 'It's Colonel Gaddafi returned from the dead. Who do you think it is? Where are you?'

There was a brief hesitation on the line, as though Amira was wondering whether to take him into her confidence at all. 'I'm on my way to Gmund.'

'You're going to Effi's factory?'

'Yes. It's high time I did what I'm good at, John. I'm sick to my stomach of letting other people carry the load for me. I can cut my own cake.'

Hart knew all about Amira's mood swings. He'd suffered under them for years. It was pointless putting his head beneath the chopper when he didn't have to. 'But you need to be able to eat your cake, too. Don't forget that.'

There was an ironical snort on the other end of the line. 'I suppose you haven't learnt anything new about Zirkeler?'

Hart opened the bathroom door and glanced up the stairs. He shut the door again and put the phone back to his ear. 'Only that he has people patrolling Effi's house, her farm in Schliersee, and the factory in Gmund, every hour on the hour throughout the night. Is that of interest to you perhaps?'

'Why would they do that? They can't know about us yet. And there's no way they'll have cracked Wesker's phone. I'm sure of it. The newspaper employs encryption experts to protect our sources.'

'Left-wing groups are always looking for publicity, or so Effi tells me. And she makes a tempting target. So it's an ongoing problem for the LB. Nothing new, according to her.' Hart caught sight of his reflection in the bathroom mirror. He didn't like what he saw. He appeared to be betraying both the significant women in his life – Amira by commission, and Effi by omission. It wasn't a pretty picture. 'Who knows what to believe? Effi's not exactly a shrinking violet. She admits as much herself. And she does put people's backs up.'

'She's put mine up.'

'Then you'd better watch it, hadn't you? You're not thinking of breaking into the factory or anything stupid like that? You're just going to take a look at the place from the outside?'

'What do you care, John?' Amira almost spat the words out. 'Both of you are probably busy winding up for beddy-byes. I wouldn't want to put you off your stroke. I know how energetic you can be when you put your mind to it. Do you remember that hammock we shared on Lamu? Or has fucking Bianca Castafiore given you retrospective amnesia?'

Hart rolled his eyes.

When Amira spoke again, her voice came out as a hiss. 'Good night, then. Sleep tight. Don't let the bedbugs bite.'

When Hart tried to call her back, she'd switched off the phone and disabled her answering service.

FIFTY-THREE

Lenzi Hofmeier wasn't happy at all. He couldn't understand why Udo had detailed him for boring guard duty, whilst he'd allocated those two no-hopers, Jochen and Sibbe, glamorous international courier jobs.

The pair of them had been warned by Udo, on pain of excommunication, not to mention anything at all about what they had been ordered to do, but Lenzi was a past master at winkling titbits of information from otherwise recalcitrant parties. He'd soon learnt all he needed to know about their first-class air travel, their free days in a foreign capital, the exotic whores they would be tasting, and the slabs of stupid jelly they would be transporting.

Was this some kind of a joke? Had he put Udo's nose out of joint somehow without realizing it? Because here he was still pulling nightshift duty when he could have been out drinking with his friends and contemplating a little international travel. The whole thing stank to high heaven. Surely it was he, Lenzi, who was Udo's star 'apostle', and who truly deserved any sinecures going, and not that pair of dorks? It was he who was always at the forefront of any race attack. He who reconnoitred Turkish-owned businesses and decided when best, and how hard, to hit them. He who thought up new ways to make non-German Germans feel uncomfortable and unwanted.

Lenzi had hated all foreigners since his mother had been attacked and nearly raped by an Algerian in an abandoned building site fifteen years before. It was only his mother's quick thinking in inviting the man home to her apparently empty house that had saved her from being violated at knifepoint. She'd known that Lenzi and his father were at home, and had counted on male vanity to do the rest. When Lenzi's mother, pretending to unlock the front door, had shouted out their names, the Algerian had fled, closely pursued by Lenzi's father – with the ten-year-old Lenzi following some way behind.

Lenzi had arrived at the building site just as his father was smashing in the Algerian's teeth with a brick. His father had handed the brick over to him.

'Choose your spot. Then belt him with it.'

Lenzi had hesitated.

'This man was going to hurt your mother. You only get one shot at this sort of thing, boy. Do it or don't do it. Your choice.'

The Algerian was keening through his broken teeth.

Lenzi smashed his nose with the brick.

Then his father kicked the man's head in.

Now Lenzi was sitting in his car watching Effi Rache's chemical factory through some sort of night-vision device that Udo had foisted on him. He'd finished his Vollkornbrot and salami sandwiches, eaten his marzipan chocolate bar, drunk all his coffee, and now he wanted to go for a piss. But Udo had warned him that under no circumstances must he get out of the car, even with all the interior lights switched off. He must piss in the thermos if he had to, and call for reinforcements if anything out of the ordinary occurred. All the burglar alarms and automatic floodlights had been switched off to avoid involving the police. He was in sole charge of security.

So Lenzi unscrewed the cap of his thermos, slipped his cock inside, and began to piss. Only he'd drunk so much coffee and Coca-Cola that the thermos threatened to overflow. Cursing, Lenzi threw open the car door and shunted his hips to the edge of the seat, so that the excess urine stream would run off down the storm drain he'd parked beside. It was at this precise moment that he heard the sound of breaking glass. If he'd stayed in the car he wouldn't have caught it.

Lenzi thanked Christ for his full bladder. Now was his chance to shine. Zipping up his flies as he went, Lenzi hurried down the hillside towards the back of Effi Rache's chemical factory, forgetting both his phone and Udo's instructions in the process.

FIFTY-FOUR

Amira lay flat on her stomach on the hillside overlooking Effi Rache's factory. She wished she had the Swarovski NC2 night-vision glasses that she'd lent Wesker. Instead she'd have to make do with the pair of Silva portable binoculars she always carried in her kit. But the moon was high and getting higher. The light was as good as it ever got at night. Even better where it reflected off the lake. It was curious that the security lights weren't on, though. Might they be on an automatic switch? Would the whole place light up like a Christmas tree if she ventured beyond the periphery?

She focused her glasses on the buildings. They were odd too. The factory looked pre-Second World War vintage, with metal-framed windows, a brick outer shell, and a partially corrugated asbestos roof covered in lichen. The place looked unloved, like a fat boy in a playground wearing hand-me-down clothes. The only modern thing in the vicinity was a fifty-foot jetty jutting out into the lake, with a brand-new plankboard boathouse tucked in alongside it. An electro-boat and a rowing skiff were tethered to the end of the jetty, and a sailing boat with its masts shipped was moored thirty feet beyond it.

Amira wondered what Effi Rache kept in the boathouse. A hovercraft? A motorboat for waterskiing with? A fold-down seaplane? Anything was possible when you had that amount of money at your disposal. She forced her attention back to the factory. It was an odd thing, but when one compared it to the renovated splendour of Effi's house, it was almost as if she wished the factory to merge into the background and become invisible.

Amira crept closer. She squatted down in the lee of a juniper bush and tried to gee herself up for the job in hand. But she wasn't fully concentrating. Part of her was back at Haus Walküre, imagining Hart in bed with Effi Rache. She'd tried a dozen times to force the image from her mind, but each time she relaxed her guard it would come surging back. It served her right for making bitchy remarks to him over the phone.

A month earlier, if she'd been asked if she had a possessive or jealous nature, Amira would have scoffed at her questioner and quoted the line from her biblical favourite, the Song of Solomon, that 'jealousy is cruel as the grave: the coals thereof are coals of fire, which hath a most vehement flame'. She would have meant it ironically, of course, the implication being that it couldn't possibly pertain to her. Now she knew that it did.

She had no one to blame but herself. Hart had been the perfect lover. Tender and considerate – if a little wayward when the mood took him, but then you can't have everything. He had left Amira in peace most of the time to get on with her life, wasn't in the least possessive, and was always there on the occasions when she most needed him. He was also brave, ridiculously protective of her, and a five-star alpha male. As an alpha female herself, Amira couldn't have borne less in a man. It was her getting pregnant that had destroyed their harmony.

She'd always known that Hart was catastrophically tender-minded. As a tough-minded individual herself, she'd admired that about him, whilst assuming that it wouldn't apply in his dealings with her – except when it suited her, of course. She'd been taking the pill, after all. And she'd always made it clear that she wasn't in the least family-minded. Hart had appeared to go along with that.

But whilst they were on the island of Lamu, having a rare holiday together, she'd developed cystitis – probably from too much sex. The last thing she'd wanted at that point was to put up any barriers against intimacy, so she'd paid the maid who cleaned their bungalow to get her some off-prescription antibiotics. No one had told her that they could interfere with her birth-control pill. And, being Amira, she hadn't bothered to read the small print on the packet.

In retrospect her biggest mistake had been in ever telling Hart about the pregnancy. She should have kept her trap shut and sorted it out for herself. But she'd done it in a weak moment –

hormones, probably, post-Lamu – when they'd found themselves working together on a piece about the Gambia. She'd been on a deadline. Which meant that she didn't have time to research either abortion clinics or the attitudes of the predominantly Islamic medical authorities in Banjul to terminations. And when a colleague blindsided her with the fact that the agreement of two independent doctors would probably be needed before anything could be done, she became even more reluctant to chase the matter up herself and risk being lectured to by religious bigots. Hart was the father. He could bloody well do it.

The outcome had been a disaster. It had never occurred to Amira that Hart might be temperamentally and emotionally incapable of okaying an abortion. Instead, from the very first moment she had told him about the pregnancy, he had marshalled every argument in the book to persuade her to keep the child. She'd not taken him seriously, of course – after all, modern men were renowned for not being paternal, weren't they? Look at baby fathers.

She'd hurried to a Marie Stopes clinic on her first London stopover after Banjul. The baby hadn't been that far gone. Twelve weeks, maybe. Where was the harm? Hart would get over it, just like all men did. Just like she did.

But Hart didn't get over it. The Gambia had been the very last occasion they'd made love. By the time the Syrian crisis occurred, Amira was in full-blown denial that their affair was at an end, whilst Hart was still in emotional meltdown at the loss of his child. Amira had always assumed it would be the other way round. But it wasn't.

Now, with her head still churning out images of Hart and Effi in bed together, Amira ran through the factory car park and round the side of the building facing the lake. If the security lights came on, they came on – she would simply carry on running. If anyone stopped her she would say she'd fancied a jog under the full moon. What the fuck. If it was Zirkeler, she'd Mace him. On principle.

She reached a rear door topped with roofing glass. She looked around. The path to the lake was waymarked with whitewashed stone. She selected a stone she could lift and wrapped her Ascari bomber jacket round it. Then she smashed the stone against the door panel.

Time was everything in such cases. You had to get in and out quickly.

The safety glass made surprisingly little sound when it gave way. Amira was fairly confident she hadn't been heard much beyond a fifty-foot radius. She'd be long gone by the time the watchman made his rounds again. And, at the very least, by leaving a shattered door behind her, she might have succeeded in tossing a spark into the LB woodpile.

Using her bomber jacket as protection, Amira straddled the doorframe and eased her way inside the building. She checked around for a burglar alarm or flashing lights, but nothing was visible. Which didn't mean to say that an alarm wasn't going off in a distant office somewhere. If the police turned up, so be it. She'd make a dreadful stink, and still get her story. But somehow she suspected they wouldn't. The LB were not the sort of people who courted that kind of publicity.

The glass-sectioned doorway led into what appeared to be an old-fashioned clerk's office. In fact, the entire interior of the factory was curiously old-fashioned, as if it had been preserved in aspic as a sort of shrine. The windows were of the wartime Nissen hut variety, the floors were covered in 1960s linoleum, and the strip lighting resembled the sort they'd used in the Loftus Road football ground when she'd visited it with her father as a child.

Amira switched on her torch, shone it briefly around, and then switched it off again. She hurried across the floor to the main inside door, trying to keep the mental image of where everything was situated in her head. At the door she switched the torch on and off again. This one wouldn't be quite so easy to crack. She tried it first for give. Non-existent. She cast around for another possible entrance. None.

She thought for a moment, and then made her way to a desk situated in a nearby corner. Filtering the torch through her handkerchief, she checked through all the drawers. No keys. She took the drawers out. No keys taped underneath the drawers either. She walked back to the door. There was a filing cabinet situated an arm's length from the entrance, with a space left between its back and the wall. Amira cupped her ears and listened out for any extraneous noises. She realized she was sweating. She brushed the damp hair away from her ears and tried again. Nothing. No noise.

She inserted her hand deep into the gap. A key was hanging on a nail about six inches below the top of the cabinet. She rolled her eyes and tried it in the lock. Twisted once. The door opened. It never ceased to astonish her how lazy people could be in terms of security.

The smell of chemicals was stronger in this new room. Amira could see cardboard boxes piled high to the ceiling. Some had pictures of swimming pools on them. At the far end were bigger boxes. These were decorated with pictures of jacuzzis, Turkish baths and saunas. She was in a warehouse. No outside windows to give her away.

She began using her torch with impunity now, focusing on each section of the building in turn. But the part of her brain concerned with Hart wouldn't leave her alone. Did she still love him? Yes, she did. She'd admitted as much to him in England, but he'd been so resentful of her by that time that she wasn't sure he'd fully taken it in. Did she want him back? That also. Though not by any rational choice. More by emotional necessity. She couldn't get him out of her head. Whenever she thought about him, the image came to her of how he'd thrown himself across her body in Syria in an attempt to shield her from the bullets.

He'd been prepared to give up his life to protect her, even though they were in the process of breaking-up. Maybe she had been a little ungracious in her response to his heroism? Her feminism lever was set to the default position, and always had been, which got her into all sorts of trouble with male colleagues. Maybe she should just have said thank you, and left it at that? Rather than berating him for patronizing her, as she had done.

Amira sliced open a few of the cardboard boxes and checked inside them. Each one contained exactly what it said on the packet. She began to lose heart. Maybe she was on a wild goose chase? Maybe she was trashing a perfectly innocent chemical factory? She continued on her desultory rounds of the warehouse, her torch beam bobbing in front of her.

As she walked the length of the depository, she began speculating on how she might get her lover back. Simply appealing to his better nature wouldn't do it. Hart was a proud bastard at the best of times – all Aries were. Well then, how else? By proving to him that Effi Rache was pulling Zirkeler's strings, that's how. That she was a murderess as well as a whore. All Amira's instincts told her this was the case, but she would need to confirm it beyond a reasonable doubt. And way beyond Effi Rache's ability to sue her and the newspaper for libel – or soft-soap Hart into falling yet again for her Marlene Dietrich eyes and her gooey protestations of innocence.

Udo Zirkeler was the key, then. Amira had done her homework on him. She understood his psychology. Thugs like him seldom, if ever, acted alone. They needed the support of their peers. They needed someone to give them orders. Someone to look up to. Someone to work for. And that person, she was convinced, was Effi Rache. All she needed to do was to gather her facts together and publish them. Then Hart would come running back to her. And this time she'd find a way to make him stay.

Amira stopped what she was doing. She canted her head to one side like a dog listening for the return of its master's footsteps. Had she heard something? No. It had only been the gurgling of a radiator. As she listened out for a repeat of the

314

noise, the beam from her torch skated across a thirty-foot-long span of insulated glass. Amira played her torch beam across it a second time. Odd. What was such a vast expanse of glazing doing in a warehouse, where any idiot could smash through it with a misdirected pallet or an out-of-control forklift? She hurried forward and directed her light through the glass.

Amira's heart caught in her chest. It was a laboratory. But this was no ordinary laboratory – she could tell that much straight off. Treble doors with what looked like airlocks sealed the laboratory off from the outside world. Amira manipulated the torch so that its beam fell on the first of the two self-contained compartments. It contained a disinfection unit with shower nozzles and chemical cleanser tanks. Hardly necessary for making swimming-pool chemicals.

She swung the beam a little further. A pair of protective suits, each with a self-contained breathing apparatus and an internal radio, hung on a frame just inside the entrance to the lab. The bottom halves were designed in the same way as a pair of waders, to cover and completely seal the feet, so that the individual using it would have no possible contact with the laboratory atmosphere. Amira directed her torch beam downwards. Below the dangling feet of the body suits, two pairs of steel-toed boots stood side by side, with chemical-resistant gloves stuffed inside them.

Amira took the phone out of her pocket and began taking photographs. The flash was overwhelming in the enclosed area, but she was standing in a self-contained warehouse with no outside windows. It was a risk worth taking.

When she got back to her car she would forward the pictures to her computer at the safe house. Then she would show them to Hart. He might think a little differently about his lover, after that.

FIFTY-FIVE

Lenzi saw the flash from the phone camera just as he was climbing through the shattered door panel. He had no idea what the intruder was photographing, but he knew one thing for certain – thieves didn't take pictures during the course of a robbery.

Each flash lit up the direction he needed to take very nicely. Lenzi hurried forward and hid himself behind a pile of boxes three feet away from the open doorway that whoever was in the warehouse would need to exit through.

He felt in his pocket for his phone. Now was the perfect moment to text Udo, whilst whoever was in the warehouse was busy taking photos. Udo lived twenty minutes away. By the time he got to the factory, Lenzi would have everything under control. Maybe Udo would take him a little more seriously then?

Lenzi slapped at his clothes. Jacket first. Then trousers, front and back. No phone. He must have left it in the car

317

in his hurry to get to the break-in. Shit. That was typical. Bloody typical.

He flailed around in his head for what to do next.

Should he lock the door and run back to the car and get the phone? No. There might be another exit. Whoever was taking the photographs might slip out through there, and then Udo would use Lenzi's head as a punch bag. An ambush, then? Lenzi grimaced. He didn't even have a weapon. The crash of the broken glass had so excited him that he had left his pickaxe handle in the car.

He stood by the exit and listened for the sound of the intruder's shoes. Maybe if he toppled the boxes over onto them when they came through the door? That would give him the element of surprise, wouldn't it? Then he could overpower them and tie them up. That way he could run back to the car, get his phone and send Udo a fake message, effectively covering his butt.

Amira stepped through the exit before Lenzi had made up his mind whether to topple the boxes over or make a lunge.

Lenzi shouted and made a lunge.

Amira lashed back at him with her Maglite. She heard a satisfying crack as it struck home. Lenzi landed on top of her. She struggled to free herself from Lenzi's dead weight.

The rim of the torch had struck Lenzi on the upper corner of his right eye. Whoever was beneath him wriggled free and sprang to their feet.

Lenzi threw out an arm and tripped them up. His eye was hurting abominably. He hoped it hadn't burst in its socket. He hoped he wasn't blind.

He brought his fist down hard and struck flesh through clothing. Whoever was trying to pull away from him cried out.

It was a woman.

Lenzi grabbed the woman's leg and attacked with renewed vigour. He probably outweighed her two to one. This was going to be easy.

Amira lashed back with her torch a second time. Lenzi caught the blow on his forearm. In the same movement he brought his elbow down hard.

The woman cried out again.

Now Lenzi was on top of her. He knew where her head was. He remembered hitting the Algerian with the brick his father gave him. Remembered how sweet that had felt.

He brought his fist down as hard as he could.

FIFTY-SIX

Hart no longer understood himself. Nor did he care to understand. One part of him was insanely worried about Amira. This part knew that he needed to get through to her – to persist in trying to call her until she had the sense to switch her phone back on and take his warning about Zirkeler and the heightened security at the factory seriously. The other part of Hart had drifted into the habit of making love to Effi at every possible opportunity. On top of tables. Up staircases. Under the shower. In the bath. In Effi's private sauna. Even, on one notable occasion, in Effi's car. This part of Hart felt a distinct sense of entitlement. And even though their shared bedroom might seem a little mundane, the night has its own laws, as Hart had discovered to his delight. And one of those laws was that goodnight sex had become *de rigueur* between him and Effi, given the particular tenor of their relationship.

And Effi knew precisely which of Hart's buttons to press.

Which of his levers to pull. He had become like Punchinello to her doll mistress. Trilby to her Svengali. It took Hart less than the three-second span between the bedroom door and the bed to strip Effi out of her gold lamé dress and bury his head between her legs.

Now, twenty minutes later, the rhythm of Effi's breathing, just a few inches below the level of Hart's chest, seemed at the furthest possible extreme from sleep – and even further from what Hart had originally intended when he had followed Effi up to the bedroom. Hart grasped Effi's hair with one hand and her throat with the crook of his arm, and, using the frame of her body – which was splayed out on all fours in front of him, her rump in the air, her head cradled on the pillow – for support, he ground his hips between her legs until, to any remotely detached observer chancing upon their outline in the dark, there would have been little to tell between them. It was as if Hart wished to crawl inside her skin.

Effi cried out as Hart tightened his grip around her throat. But her cry wasn't fearful. It was full of joy. She wanted him to subjugate her. To force her to submit to his physical will. The sweetness of finally being allowed to give way – of being able to suborn oneself to a more powerful force, whilst at the same time trusting and knowing that that force would not abuse you – would not go beyond the irrational – was, for Effi Rache, the ultimate in sensual delight.

'Stay in me, Johnny. Stay in me, you bastard. Don't pull out yet.'

'I won't.'

Effi collapsed beneath him. Hart lay on top of her for the next ten minutes, the sweat drying between them, his hips spasmodically thrusting, as if through the inherited echo of what had passed before – the culmination of a tragically diminished muscle memory. Inevitably, inexorably, he felt himself stirring again.

'Can I pull out and go one higher?'

'Just do it. Do anything. Anything you want.'

'Has anyone done this to you before?'

'No. Never. Make me do it. Force yourself on me, Johnny. Put all your weight on me. Crush me.'

Hart eased himself out, tucked a pillow beneath Effi's hips, repositioned himself, and started the pair of them on their next ascent. I am an animal, he told himself. I am responding like an animal. Thinking like an animal. Reacting like an animal. There can be no possible harm in this. This woman does something to me. She makes me mad. I cannot help myself. She is a part of me. Has always been a part of me. Will always be a part of me.

He was matching Effi's cries with his own now. Sometimes, at the most extreme moments, his breath caught in his chest and his heart strained in its chamber like a man under torture. You are my sister, he chanted inwardly. My wife. My daughter. My mother. You are all women to me. I want to be in you. Part of you. I want to inhabit you.

Later, when Effi was asleep, Hart dragged himself downstairs to where he knew she kept the Holy Lance. He was exhausted – utterly spent. All he wanted to do was sleep, wake up, and fuck Effi again. He couldn't see beyond that point. But there was no question of will involved in the action he was undertaking now. It was something he had to do.

He hesitated for a moment, looking at the Lance. Then he picked it up with both hands and held it out in front of him.

The Lance began to thrum, just as it had the first time he had held it – just as he had known it would. But this time the thrumming seemed to resonate at a deeper, more profound level than before. Hart was no longer holding the Lance – the Lance was holding him.

He turned it over in his hands, marvelling at it in the detached way a man might marvel at a work of art. Slowly, despite his doubts, he began to discern that the object he was looking at was not an adjunct to his consciousness, but an aspect of his being. That he might be a part of the Lance. And that this connection was normal. Exactly as it should be.

Without knowing why, Hart set the Lance down on the table in front of him. He looked at it for a very long time. At first, he failed to realize that he was looking at the Lance with his eyes closed. That the image of the Lance was so seared into his consciousness that he no longer saw the reality of it, only the essence.

Steadily, in the invisible gap between his eyelids and his eyes, Hart began to experience random surges of the colour blue. The first manifestation was of a deep, pure blue, billowing out from its central point like diluted ink. This dispersed to reveal a brighter, almost cerulean blue – the blue of sunlit skies and the lost ecstasies of youth. This blue lightened in turn until it resembled cyan. Then it surged back to pure blue again, via cobalt, ultramarine, lapis lazuli and indigo. Hart watched in wonder, aware, all the time, of the Lance – at the farthest possible reaches of the visible spectrum – hanging, like an anchor, in the disembodied void at the outer edges of his consciousness.

He opened his eyes. As he contemplated the solid manifestation of the article in front of him, he heard a voice, quite clearly, from deep inside his head, saying, 'Open me.' And then, again, 'Open me.' It was Effi's voice.

Hart hurried into the kitchen. He selected a knife from Effi's Solingen block, tested its blade with his finger, and then returned the length of the house like a man intent on murder. When he reached the table holding the Lance, he tentatively stretched his hand towards the gold leaf encapsulating the shaft, as if it might burn him. Then, in one fluid movement, he turned the Lance over and levered through the single fold in its gilded carapace with the tip of his knife.

The sleeve parted. Hart slid the Lance from its protective capsule as you would a lobster from its shell. He held the Lance up to the light. A small glass phial, about four inches in length, was trapped inside the wirework securing the spearhead. Hart tapped it with the point of his knife. The phial shifted. Using the knife as a lever, Hart eased the phial past its supporting wire and along the grooved channel the Lance's maker had etched into its surface to prevent unwanted suction when the blade was removed from pierced flesh. The phial popped out of its graith and into his hand.

Hart raised the phial to the light. It was sealed with a wax stopper. The glass had clouded somewhat over time, but it seemed as if there was a manuscript of some kind concealed inside.

Hart levered at the wax, which crumbled the moment he touched it. He tapped the base of the phial so that the tiny manuscript fell out onto the palm of his hand. The rolled-up sheet was made of vellum, and still retained something of the spring it must have possessed when originally inserted. He opened the manuscript and pegged it onto the table using an ink pot, a Sellotape dispenser and a stapler. Then he bent down and looked at it.

FIFTY-SEVEN

Hart wound the gilt capsule back around the Lance and returned the object to its velvet-lined box. The Lance looked more or less as it had done before – as long as no one was tempted to pick it up and brandish it, upon which the whole thing would undoubtedly fall apart. Hart promised himself that he would return the phial to its rightful place and restore the Lance's integrity at his earliest convenience. He was its hereditary guardian, after all – he had a duty of care.

The vehemence with which he now held this conviction surprised him. A part of him even felt that the Lance might be grooming him in some way. Bending him to its will. And where had that voice come from, ordering him to 'Open me'? Was he going doolally like his mother? Was his relationship with Effi softening his head?

Hart keyed in Amira's number on his phone. He was transferred to her voicemail, just as he had been on his last two attempts. He shook his head, cursing Amira's notoriously short fuse.

He returned to the bedroom and bent low over Effi to check that she was sleeping. She was obviously in a brief cycle of REM sleep, her eyeballs dancing behind her lids. Hart knew that such a passage, especially early on in the night, was often followed by a lighter, less intense quality of sleep. He collected up his jeans as silently as he could, added a double layer of sweatshirts and his battered leather jacket, and hurried downstairs to dress. Then he wadded some tissue around the phial containing the miniature manuscript and slipped the package into his jacket pocket.

Once dressed, he tapped the exit code into the automatic security system and left the house by the back door, having first checked his surroundings for watchers. When he was satisfied that none of Zirkeler's men were posted within the vicinity of the house, he walked the two hundred yards up the main track towards the Alpenruh. The moon was up and he could see almost as clearly as day. He consulted his watch. Two fifteen.

When he reached the Alpenruh's terrace, he cut round the side towards where he knew Frau Erlichmann's ground-floor apartment was situated, passing the spot where Wesker's body had been found. The chalk marks were still visible in the moonlight. Looking at the outline of Wesker's body, with the blood marks seemingly sketched in like memorials to the placement of his internal organs, Hart experienced the same sense of semi-apprehensive, semi-exhilarating expectation he always got when venturing into a war zone – the unsettling recognition that he was approaching a point of no return.

He tapped on Frau Erlichmann's window, waited for a moment, and then tapped again. 'Frau Erlichmann. It's me. John Hart.'

Hart heard shuffling from inside the sitting room abutting Frau Erlichmann's bedroom. The curtains parted. Frau Erlichmann squinted at him through the glass.

'Please don't be alarmed. But I'm worried about Amira. I think she may be in danger. May I come in?'

Frau Erlichmann unlocked the double-glazed door and ushered Hart inside.

'I'm truly sorry…'

'You've already apologized once, Baron. There is no need to do so a second time. I am a light sleeper. You are depriving me of nothing I particularly value. Please sit down whilst I fetch my housecoat.'

Hart sat down. The full significance of Amira's unlikely silence was only gradually dawning on him. He recalled Amira's comments about the unlikelihood of Wesker ever switching off his phone. The same thing applied to her, surely? She was a journalist. And a good one. She would remain contactable under virtually all circumstances. All he could hope for was that she had switched off her phone because she was staking out the factory and didn't want to give the game away. But why would she be staking the place out in the middle of the night? He knew Amira. She was not a passive investigator. She believed in getting her hands dirty. He was a fool not to have thought all this through before. A fool for having allowed himself to be sidetracked, yet again, by Effi's overwhelming sexuality.

Frau Erlichmann sat down in front of him. She had brushed her hair and plumped her cheeks, and now she settled a shawl over the shoulders of her housecoat to counteract the night's chill. She gave a small inclination of the head, encouraging Hart to begin.

Hart let the retained breath hiss from between his lips. 'This may seem like a crazy question to ask you, especially at this time of the night, but do you have access to a car?'

'A car?'

Hart nodded. 'I believe Amira may have gone to investigate Effi Rache's factory in Gmund. You remember what was written in the letter you translated for me? About Hitler's final superweapon? What he called his *wunderwaffe*? Amira believes that Udo Zirkeler may be using the factory to try and recreate the Tabun clone – Trilon 380 – that Hitler's scientists succeeded in distilling in the final moments of the war. That a formula for Trilon accompanied the letter I found in Effi's strongbox, and that Zirkeler somehow got hold of it.'

Frau Erlichmann gave Hart an old-fashioned look. 'And Fräulein Rache has nothing whatsoever to do with this? You are certain of this fact? Even though the factory is hers? And even though the original letter was addressed to her grandfather?'

'I believe not. No. I believe it's been Zirkeler all the way down the line. Amira's assistant back in London – and a stringer her paper sometimes uses in Germany – has done some serious background research on him. We now know that his grandfather was a sergeant major in the SS – and that this man committed suicide on the final day of the war, just a few hours after he heard that Germany was about to surrender. We also know that his son – Zirkeler's father – was in bed with some extreme right-wing groups from about the mid-1960s until his death. Also that he was briefly imprisoned for GBH against a Turkish immigrant, who he claimed had insulted him, but that he was subsequently let out of jail on a technicality and the charge expunged from his record. Who knows what that sort of background does to a man? That sort of bottled-up resentment?'

'And Effi Rache? What did her background do to her?'

Hart stiffened. 'She's been extraordinarily open with me, Frau Erlichmann, even to the extent of showing me the Holy Lance and allowing me free access to it. These are not the actions of someone who is out to recreate a *wunderwaffe* nerve agent. Wouldn't you agree?'

'We'll put that aside for the time being, Baron. Please, go on. There is more you have to tell me. It is written all over your face.'

Hart laughed. Frau Erlichmann might suffer from detached retinas, but she didn't miss much. 'A little over an hour ago, some instinct drove me to slit open the protective gilding on the Holy Lance. Please don't ask me where the instinct came from, because I couldn't tell you. But I did discover a small phial containing a manuscript hidden inside the shell. The text is written on vellum, and, technically speaking, quite legible. But I am unable to make out any of the words. I can't tell whether they are in German or Latin or Double Dutch, as the Gothic script is entirely unfamiliar to me.'

'What has this to do with what Fräulein Amira is doing?'

'Nothing. And everything. I don't know yet.'

'And you need the car to drive to the factory and check up on Fräulein Amira?'

'Yes. Either that, or I was going to ask if you could call me a taxi?'

Frau Erlichmann sat up straighter in her chair. 'At two thirty in the morning? Bad Wiessee is hardly Munich, Baron. And Fräulein Rache's laboratory is in an isolated location. There would be questions.'

Hart no longer knew what to say. He had the overwhelming impression that he had somehow succeeded in botching everything he had ever set his mind to. Frau Erlichmann must think him mad. Because here he was again, following up Amira on the one hand, and a probably illegible scrap of vellum on the other, with Effi Rache steaming up from behind to challenge for the lead. He was like a jumbled-up bag of fireworks someone had inadvertently ignited with a discarded cigarette.

Frau Erlichmann felt in the pocket of her housecoat and brought out a pistol.

Hart reared back. For one horrifying moment he thought that she might be about to shoot him.

Frau Erlichmann placed the pistol firmly on the table between them. 'I think the time has come when you may need this. It was my father's. It is a Roth-Steyr model from 1907. I must warn you that it is a little rusty, and has probably not been used in my lifetime. My father carried it through the Great War, however, and it saw good service. The magazine is in the handle, I believe. I don't know how many bullets there are left. Nor where my father kept his spare ammunition. But I want you to take it with you anyway. It might serve to frighten the sheep.'

Hart picked up the pistol. He released the magazine with some difficulty and checked the load. There were three bullets left. The retaining spring was rusted solid. 'I'd rather not, if you don't mind. It will probably explode if I fire it.'

Frau Erlichmann pretended not to hear him. 'There is an Auto Union in the downstairs garage. I cannot guarantee the battery, but the car is facing outwards. If you open the garage doors as wide as possible, you should be able to jump-start the car down the hill. A male friend of mine uses it to drive me to the doctor, dentist, oculist or hearing specialist whenever needed. All the things that generally beset people of my age and make our lives so interesting. The keys are hanging on a hook at the back of the garage, near the rear entrance you will use from the house. Take them. When you have located Fräulein Amira, bring her back here. I shall have translated your message by then. All I need you to do now, Baron, is to hand me my Latin dictionary and my magnifying glass.'

FIFTY-EIGHT

The car was an Auto Union 1000 saloon. It was painted a sickly green colour. At first glance it reminded Hart of an upturned bowl of mushy peas. When he got over his initial shock, he estimated that the vehicle dated back to around 1960, give or take a few years. But the bodywork and trim were intact, and the engine, when he tried the ignition, turned over sweetly, once he had remembered to use the choke.

He drove out of the garage towards the main road. The streets were deserted. Whatever passed for nightlife in Bad Wiessee had put itself to bed long ago. Frau Erlichmann had given him detailed instructions on how to reach the factory, so he turned down by the new casino and northwards along the lake's edge. The moon was at its fullest, and its glow shadowed the car like a wartime searchlight as he headed towards Gmund.

Fifteen minutes took him to the large farmhouse, Gut Kaltenbrunn, that Frau Erlichmann had given him as a marker. The turnoff to Effi Rache's factory was less than a kilometre down the road. Hart pulled down a track about half a kilometre short of where he estimated the factory to be and turned the Auto Union round to face the road. It was a useless precaution. At nought to sixty in around a minute and a half, he suspected that he wouldn't be going anywhere fast – even if the hounds of hell were on his trail.

He switched off the headlights and got out of the car. Looking around, he soon realized that he would have no need of the torch Frau Erlichmann had lent him – thanks to the full moon, everything was lit up with a ghostly white light as if in the aftermath of an unexpected snowfall. Hart elected to take the torch with him anyway, just for the added sense of security it gave him to be holding something in his hands. He tapped the pocket holding the pistol superstitiously. The damned thing looked like a fancy cigar lighter. If he ever got to aim it at someone, they would probably burst out laughing.

He set off for the factory on foot. Three hundred metres down the road he came upon a hire car, parked in a lay-by. He tried the doors. Locked. He switched on the torch and looked inside. Nothing. The car was as clean as the moment it had been picked up from the rental agency. Hart had little doubt that it was the hire car Amira had told him about. He switched off his torch and hurried onwards.

When he found himself approaching the factory turning, he broke away from the road and cut through a small plantation of pines that led down towards the lake edge. As he dodged through the trees, he felt a burgeoning sense of urgency, as if some primeval instinct was cutting in and taking over.

Hart sensed the factory before he saw it. The building was lit up like an oil refinery, the glow from a series of arc lights reflecting back off the trees in front of him like the after-effects of a forest fire. He sank to his knees and crawled to the edge of the treeline. Spotlights reflected off the half-dozen assorted vans and cars parked in a fan formation near the front entrance.

Hart cursed beneath his breath. Was Amira still hidden up here on the periphery somewhere, watching what was happening? Or was she down near the lion's den? Hart wished he had a long-lens camera with him so that he could photograph the cars and their number plates. But he had not even thought to bring a pen and a notebook. And his pay-as-you-go phone would be less than useless at this distance for taking snaps. Maybe if he got closer?

The factory had been built tight up against the lakeside, so Hart was forced to make a complete semi-circle, keeping well out of the light bath emanating from the security lamps. No sign of Amira. One part of him had been half expecting her to call out from whatever hiding place she had chosen for herself. Another part of him acknowledged that the chances of her still being out here on the hillside were a thousand to one.

He checked his watch. Three thirty. He had maybe four hours leeway before Effi woke up and began to wonder where he had gone.

Hart looked around for guards, or a watchman, or someone coming out to relieve himself. But the outside area was clear. Whoever had arrived in the cars was inside the factory.

Hart chose his approach carefully. He would come in from the direction of the lake. A raised walkway ran down from the factory towards a boathouse. A sailing boat with a shipped mast floated a little way out, attached to a mooring buoy. An electro-boat was tethered on one side of the jetty, and a wooden rowing boat on the other. The boathouse gates were shut and locked, so Hart had no idea what might be inside. There was no wind to speak of, and the lake was as flat as glass.

Hart crept down to the shoreline and eased himself in amongst the reeds. Within seconds he was up to his knees in mud. He tried to flatten himself on top of the mud and crawl, but it soon became clear that he must either sink into the morass or swim. Hart acknowledged *force majeure* and allowed the lake to carry him away from the reed bed. Once he was out into the open channel, he struck for the jetty, keeping his head just above the surface of the water. The night was warm and the water was temperate. He would dry out eventually.

Two minutes later he was in place. He cross-handed his way along the hull of the electro-boat, ducked under the end of the jetty, and swam round the boathouse. He had decided long before that the lights were less intrusive on the side of the jetty where the rowing boat was tethered.

When he was safely ashore, but still in the lee of the jetty, Hart began to crawl. He felt achingly vulnerable. The factory was built on two storeys. He would be as good as invisible from the ground floor, but anyone stepping out onto the second-floor balcony could not fail to see him.

After what seemed like an eternity of slithering, Hart pressed himself tightly against the outer shell of the building and addressed his second problem – how to get inside the factory. He craned his neck upwards and outwards to check for opened windows. Nothing.

Hart dropped to his knees and began crawling round the periphery of the building. He felt all sorts of a fool. Maybe Amira was watching him from the treeline and wondering what the hell he was doing? At any given moment he expected Udo Zirkeler to walk round the factory corner and kick him in the head. Or maybe come up behind him and kick him in the balls. Frankly, he deserved it. A more inept sneak thief there never was.

Hart had already borne down on the shattered glass with the full weight of his leading hand before he realized what it was. He squeezed his damaged hand between his free arm and his flank and rocked in silent agony. When the first wave of pain began to wear off, he scrabbled around in his jacket pocket and retrieved his wringing wet handkerchief. Great, now he would probably get an infection to add to his disastrous start. Pneumonia, an infection and Weil's disease. He picked out the worst of the broken glass and wrapped the handkerchief tightly round his throbbing hand.

Hart craned his head to see where the glass had come from. Someone had smashed through the door pane above him. Amira? It had to be. It was hardly likely that a total stranger would choose exactly the night Amira was staking out the factory to conduct a break-in. And what would he be after, anyway? Swimming-pool chemicals? Sauna tabs? Detergent?

Hart lurched to his feet. He pressed himself as tightly as he could against the wall and poked his head round the shattered doorframe, feeling ridiculously vulnerable. Like an ant on a sheet of white paper. What with the moon and the floodlights, anyone stationed on the perimeter of the factory would be able to see him more clearly than they would even in the daytime. He needed to get inside. Fast.

When he was quite certain that no one was present in the room beyond the door, Hart took off his sodden leather jacket, laid it over the shattered frame, and scissored his way inside. He shrugged the jacket back on again for warmth. He was already shivering despite the relative balminess of the night. His hand had gone from just throbbing to painfully aching.

Hart avoided the residue of broken glass inside the doorway as best he could and squelched across the factory office towards an open door on the far side of the room. The office lights were off, but the glow from the next room illuminated a haphazard pile of cardboard boxes that had toppled down and were now half-blocking the exit.

Hart came at the doorway from an angle, intending to use the boxes as camouflage. Halfway across the floor he began to pick up male voices from the room beyond. He ducked behind one of the fallen boxes and tried to discern what was being said. But the voices were too far away, and his German too basic, to make any useful inferences.

Hart crept as close to the door as he dared. It was only then that he saw the blood. It was lit up by a direct shaft of light, which was somehow managing to find its way between two of the boxes. Hart reached down and touched it. It was drying fast, but it was still damp enough to leave a ghostly imprint on his fingertip.

Hart edged back into the shadows. What had happened here? That it was Amira's blood he had no doubt. Why else was her phone not switched on? Had the boxes fallen on her? Or had she been surprised after breaking in? Maybe she had cut herself climbing over the doorframe, just as he had, and was still at liberty somewhere? Whatever had happened, she was in trouble. The mass of cars and the three o'clock in the morning strobe-lit exterior of the factory attested to that fact. Hart knew that he must contact the police. Now. And to hell with Amira's scoop.

He took out his phone and checked for a signal. The VDU screen was a uniform grey, like a television set once the channel has gone dead for the night. Hart gave the phone a shake and tried again. He was now able to make out a definite waterline behind the plastic shield. Damn it to hell. He'd been immersed in water for more than thirty metres with the phone still in his pocket. What had he expected? It was a cheap over-the-counter job. Hardly waterproof. The sort of crap that wouldn't even survive a four-foot drop from a tabletop.

Hart put the phone back in his pocket. Maybe it would shake itself like a dog later on and come back to life? In the interim, he needed to do something. He could hardly sit here on the floor until someone found him.

Hart looked about. Straight above him was an old-fashioned transom window, designed to allow light to filter between the warehouse and the office. Hart stood up and began to construct a stepladder out of the boxes, layering first four, then three, then two, so that he'd have something resembling a pyramid to climb up on. Some of the boxes were surprisingly heavy, as though they contained sacks of chemicals. The hefting restarted the bleeding in his hand.

When he was satisfied that the structure might hold his weight, Hart eased himself up the boxes until his eye was parallel to the transom. He now had a perfect view of the interior of the warehouse. He counted a dozen men in the room beyond, standing about fifty feet from him. Udo Zirkeler was at the centre, dressed in some sort of black uniform. He was shouting at one of the men and pointing to something on the ground below them. But Zirkeler's body was masking the object he was pointing at.

Hart shifted to one side to get a better look. Just as he was settling into a more strategical position, he felt the boxes below him shift, as if one of them was only partially filled and had given way under the deadweight above it. Hart threw out an arm to steady himself against the transom frame, but it was too late. The boxes collapsed like a deck of cards, with Hart leading the way.

A split second before he fell, Hart was able to see that the object curled up on the ground at Zirkeler's feet was Amira Eisenberger.

FIFTY-NINE

Hart didn't hang around to see what effect his fall would have on Zirkeler's men. He sprinted back through the office, straddled the door, hovered for a moment between the lake and the forest, and chose the lake. He could hear his pursuers pounding across the warehouse floor behind him. He had counted twelve of them. If he headed for the forest, they would encircle him. The lake was his only chance.

Hart made for the jetty. He pounded over the slats and threw himself into the electro-boat. Zirkeler and his gang were fifty yards behind him and closing fast. Hart cast off the mooring line, switched on the motor, and then rammed the shift into forwards. The electro-boat inched away from the dock. A brisk walk would have been faster.

One of Zirkeler's men took a running header from the jetty behind him. He hit the water in a classic racing dive. In three strokes he was nearly up to the stern of the electro-boat. Hart threw the fluke anchor at him. The anchor glanced off the man's shoulder. The man snatched hold of the anchor line and began to pull himself, hand over hand, towards the retreating boat. Hart picked up the emergency oar and brought it down hard on the man's head. He went under.

Hart heard the roar of a powerful marine engine from inside the boathouse.

'Oh shit.'

By this time, the electro-boat was riding almost parallel to the moored sailing boat with the shipped mast. Hart knew that he had only moments in which to act. He stripped off his belt and secured the electro-boat's steering wheel to the forwards shift lever. He estimated that the electro-boat would pass within about five feet of the moored sailing boat. Hart waited for the right moment and then slipped into the water, keeping his silhouette as low to the gunwale as he could. Zirkeler's men were manhandling open the boathouse doors. Maybe they wouldn't see him?

Hart paddled round to the far side of the sailing boat and ducked under its hull. The unmanned electro-boat continued on at a stately five knots in the direction of Tegernsee. Hart offered up a heartfelt prayer to the Lady of the Lake.

A thirty-foot Riva Slipper Launch roared out of the boathouse, packed with Zirkeler's men. Twenty seconds took it past the moored sailing boat and out into the lake.

Hart struck for the shore, the Riva's wake buffeting him from side to side as he swam. The picture of Amira lying curled up on the ground at Zirkeler's feet was replaying itself in his head. He reached the jetty and sprinted up the plank-board walkway towards the factory. He didn't bother looking behind him. Whatever would be, would be.

He reached the shattered door. Zirkeler and his men had left it wide open. Hart took the pistol from his pocket and held it out in front of him. He sidestepped round the door. There was no one on guard in the outer office.

Hart strode the length of the room, hesitated for a moment by the door where the boxes had collapsed, and then charged through regardless.

Two young men were standing over Amira. He recognized them from the Gasthof zur Hirschtal car park. They'd been the ones accompanying Zirkeler when Frau Erlichmann's grandson and his friends had staged their piece of theatre.

Hart waved the pistol at them. 'Both of you. On the floor. Now.'

Jochen looked across at Sibbe. He spoke in German. 'What do we do now? He has a pistol.'

Hart replied in English. 'What you do now is you lie down on the floor with your hands and legs spread out like starfish. Wounded or unwounded. It's your choice. I haven't got time to argue with you.' Hart levelled his pistol at the boys to back up his threat. 'You're furthest away.' He pointed the gun at Sibbe. 'You get it first. And don't pretend you don't understand me. That's the way to dusty death.' He kept the barrel moving between the two of them so that neither of the boys could get a close look at it.

When he saw them begin to drop, he sank to one knee and felt for a pulse on Amira's neck. But the throbbing from his damaged hand and the residual cold from his swim meant that he could feel nothing.

'What did you fuckers do to her?'

Sibbe was already stretched out on the floor. He looked relieved to be taking orders again. He craned his head backwards to answer. 'We didn't do anything to her. It was Lenzi. He lashed out at her in the dark and knocked her out. It was lucky you came in when you did. Udo was talking about putting her in a cage and locking her in the laboratory. Like a human guinea pig. We weren't happy with that. But Udo never listens to us about anything. It's just a waste of breath talking to him.'

Hart's stomach was knotted with anxiety. He felt almost nauseous. 'I want you to get up again. Both of you. You're going to carry her out to the cars between you. She needs a hospital. Fast.'

Jochen shook his head. 'You'll never make it. Udo will come back. Then he will kill you both. Then he will kill us for letting you take her.'

'Pick her up, I said.'

Jochen was the first to get up. He shrugged and signalled to Sibbe. A brief shake of the head as if to say, 'Why bother? We're doomed either way.'

Hart saw the movement. 'Pick her up. If you don't, I will shoot each one of you in the knee.'

'Then you will never get her out of here.'

'But I'll have the satisfaction of knowing that you are both crippled for life.'

Sibbe helped Jochen to his feet. Both boys were white-faced. Sibbe reached down and took Amira's feet. Jochen took her shoulders.

'Right. Get a move on. I can hear the Riva coming back.'

The two boys carried Amira towards the main factory entrance.

Hart kept darting looks behind him. He expected Zirkeler and his men to come running into the warehouse at any moment. He had counted nine on the Riva. Ten with Zirkeler. Ten too many.

When they were out by the cars, Hart made a quick inspection for keys. Not a single car was unlocked.

'Head up towards the road.' He waved with his pistol.

'Believe me. This is not a good idea. Udo will be mad as hell.'

'I am mad as hell already.'

'But you are not Udo.'

Hart shepherded the two boys and their burden up the track towards the main road. He was counting on Amira having her car keys on her. The Auto Union, he knew, would be less than useless in a road pursuit.

Hart heard the clatter of boots on the wooden slats of the jetty. Zirkeler and his party were less than a hundred metres behind them, heading for the rear of the factory. Hart and his party still hadn't been seen, thanks to the false darkness at the edge of the spotlighted area.

'Move, damn you!' Hart hissed at the two boys.

As they reached the crest of the hill, the four of them were bathed in headlights from the road. Hart threw up his arm to shade his eyes. Had Amira managed to call the police before she was attacked? Maybe whoever was heading towards them would agree to spirit him and Amira away?

The car approaching them slewed across the track, effectively blocking them in.

Hart straight-armed the pistol out ahead of him. 'Get out of the car. Now. Keep your hands in the air where I can see them. Don't touch the ignition.'

Hart reached the driver's side of the car. All his concentration was on whoever was inside.

The two boys behind him exchanged glances. They laid their cargo almost tenderly onto the ground and sprinted away from the factory and towards the main road.

Hart let them go. It was probably the most sensible move the two of them had made in their entire lives. Now he had only the man in the driver's seat to think about.

'You.' He waved his absurd pre-First World War pistol at the driver, who was already halfway out of the car. 'You follow them. Do not head towards the factory. This way you don't get shot.'

'*Ich spreche kein Englisch.*' The man was grinning.

Hart brought the barrel of the Roth-Steyr down across his temple. The man pitched forward onto the gravel. Hart grabbed the collar of his shirt and dragged him away from the car, towards a drainage ditch. The man was still struggling, but ineffectually.

Hart doubled back and gathered Amira in his arms. She was moving almost languidly now, like a person drifting in deep

346

water. 'I've got you. I'm getting you out of here. You're going to be all right.' His voice lacked conviction. Its susurration was almost lost in the pre-dawn emptiness.

He cast a backwards glance towards the factory. Men were getting into cars and doors were slamming. There was to be no more pursuing him on foot. Everyone had seen the headlights on the hill and knew what they might portend.

His new car was a nondescript Ford. On the upside, he estimated that it was a good forty-five years younger than the Auto Union. On the downside, it probably boasted about one hundred brake horsepower. Some of the cars he had seen parked in front of the factory would be double that.

Hart gunned the engine and headed towards the highway. He could see the reflection from the headlights behind him swooping and skating off the trees above his head.

When he reached the main road he turned left, back towards Bad Wiessee. Effi would know which was the nearest hospital. And her house had been specially designed to keep out intruders – she'd told him as much, and explained some of the security workings to him. Hart was a realist. He knew that trying to outrun six or seven more powerful cars than his own was a lost cause. They'd have him off the road in under two kilometres. Better to head for somewhere he knew. He and Effi could barricade themselves upstairs whilst they were waiting for the police.

He also remembered noticing what had looked like a shotgun cabinet in Effi's father's study. He would get the key from her. From the top of the stairs, with a suitable barrier in place, the three of them could fend off a small army.

SIXTY

All the lights were on in Effi's house. The place looked like the Château de Chambord during a *son et lumière* show.

Hart glanced down at the dashboard clock. Five in the morning. Far too soon for Effi to be out of bed. She must have woken up, found him gone, and hurried downstairs to look for him. It was inevitable, really. Sometimes it was as if he and Effi were so physically attuned that when one was unexpectedly gone from a room, the other would come looking for them. It was a condition Hart was unused to, but one that he found he unexpectedly liked.

Either way, Amira's presence was going to come as a real test for them both this early on in their relationship. He hoped that Effi would understand. On the face of it, his ongoing connection with Amira didn't betoken much loyalty to Effi. But Hart was sure he could explain that away. His greatest problem was that he owed each of them his trust. Effi was his now, but Amira had been his then. Both women had claims on him. Maybe he could have played things a little differently, in retrospect? But he'd never been renowned for his emotional tact.

He pulled up as close to Effi's front door as he could and pocketed the car keys. He stuck the pistol into the back of his trouser band and covered it with his jacket – it would be pointless worrying Effi unnecessarily. He hurried round to the passenger side of the Ford to help Amira out. At first it looked as though she might be about to straighten her legs on her own, but it soon became clear that she had no sense of balance. If Hart had not held her, she would have pitched face forwards onto the ground.

So far Amira hadn't uttered a sound. Nor had she acknowledged Hart's presence either by look or by gesture. Hart suspected that she was, at the very least, badly concussed. He'd dealt with such concussions before. An ice pack and a good night's rest usually did the trick. But if there was internal bleeding or a fracture to the skull, the whole thing became considerably more complicated. Hospital would be the only answer.

He tapped in the code to Effi's front door and hustled Amira inside, supporting her dead weight with his free arm. He kicked the door shut behind him and heard the comforting click as the automatic security lock slid into place.

Effi was standing near the kitchen area in her nightgown. 'Johnny. What's happening? Who is this woman?'

'I'll explain later. I promise. But she's badly hurt. You need to call the hospital first, and then the police.'

349

'Was she in a road accident?'

'She's been shadowing Zirkeler, Effi. One of his men caught her and punched her in the head. My guess is that she crumpled like a rag doll and hit her head again going down. Either that or the bastard kicked her for good measure. She's been out for well over an hour. She needs a doctor fast.'

'Following Udo? Why was she following Udo?'

'Because she thinks he killed her partner. Wesker, the man at the Alpenruh. Effi, please make the calls.'

'Why don't we drive her to the hospital ourselves? It's just across the lake in Tegernsee. It will be quicker.'

'No. Zirkeler is just behind us with about a dozen of his men in tow. We don't have the time.'

'Udo is coming here?'

'They'll be here any moment. Give me the keys to your father's gun safe. Then we must go upstairs and barricade ourselves in. You told me all your windows are security glass, didn't you? It'll take them a hell of a time to break their way in through that. We should be okay.'

'But Udo has the door code.'

'He what?'

'I told you. He organizes security here. He has all the codes for all my properties.'

'Jesus. Can you override the codes?'

'I don't know how to. I'm sorry.'

'Then make those calls.'

'Of course.'

'Where do you keep the gun-safe keys?'

'In the top right-hand desk drawer. But there is only a squirrel gun left. And probably no ammunition. After my father died, I sent all his guns to an auction house in England. I have never shot at anything in my life. So there seemed no point in keeping them. They would only have needed cleaning.'

Hart stumbled across the drawing room with Amira pressed tightly against him. He could hear Effi talking urgently into the phone. At one point Amira's knees buckled, causing both of them to lurch onto the floor. Hart was just able to throw out an arm and steady her before she struck her head for a third time.

He unlocked the gun case and looked inside. Effi had been telling the truth. There was an old .410 squirrel gun in there and nothing else. Hart scrabbled around for some cartridges. He found two, wedged tightly against the inside doorframe as if they had been overlooked – or as if the box had simply rotted away around them. Hart rolled the ancient wax-paper cartridge near his ear – it crackled. Not promising.

Hart took the gun and the cartridges out of the safe. He squatted down and allowed Amira to fold forwards across his shoulder. When she was safely in place, he started towards the stairs. Effi ran over to join him.

'Have you made the calls?'

'Yes. The police say they will be here in ten minutes. The ambulance is on its way too. The police know me, so they know it is no hoax.'

'Good girl. We must get upstairs, then you must help me to push the spare bed across the stair opening. Zirkeler won't know how much ammo I have for this thing. At a distance it'll be less than useless. But close up it's potentially lethal. Especially if we get a few of them clogging the staircase. With luck we can hold him and his people at bay until the police arrive.'

'But I can't believe he means this woman any harm, Johnny. It must be a misunderstanding. Maybe she fell over and hit her head? And why are you involved? I don't understand. Do you know her?'

'If Zirkeler didn't mean her any harm, why was he intending to place her in a cage and use her as a human guinea pig at your factory? I got this information from two of his men. They didn't seem too comfortable with the whole idea either.'

'My factory? What was she doing at my factory? And what are you talking about? Human guinea pigs? Cages? Have you gone mad?'

Hart started up the stairs with Amira over his shoulder. 'This woman is a journalist, Effi. For a major British newspaper. Wesker was too. They are preparing a story on extreme right-wing groups in Germany. Not mainstream parties like yours, but the offshoots of them. The crap adhering to the edges.' Hart stopped and eased Amira into a better position on his shoulder. The past few hours had exhausted him. He was puffing like a shunt locomotive. 'Zirkeler is seriously crazy, Effi. You must realize that by now. When I saw him at the factory he was running around dressed in a frigging SS uniform. As if the Second World War had never ended. The man is two pecks short of a bushel. Amira thinks he's using the place to recreate some sort of nerve agent that

Hitler's scientists discovered at the end of the war. God alone knows who he intends to use it on. But he needs to be stopped now, before it goes too far.'

They reached the head of the stairs. Hart carried Amira into the main bedroom and laid her out on the bed. He piled a load of blankets on top of her to keep her body temperature up. Then he checked the .410. It had a single barrel with no obvious rust pits. So far so good. He loaded it. He prayed to God that it was set to full choke, because otherwise the squirrel shot would disperse after five yards and be worse than useless, despite what he had told Effi.

'Effi, come here. You can help me with this spare bed. We need to drag it out into the hall and across the top of the stairs.'

'Is Udo armed?'

'I don't know. I never got that close to him. I don't think so. Otherwise he would have taken a shot at me when I stole the electro-boat.'

'The electro-boat?' Effi squinted at him. She seemed on the verge of saying something, but then visibly changed her mind. 'What else has Udo done that you know of?'

Hart took hold of one side of the mattress and nodded at Effi to take the other. 'He killed my father in Guatemala.'

'Your father?'

'Yes. My father suffered from bipolar disease. What they used to call manic depression. Part of the time he lived under the name of Roger Pope, and part of the time under the name he was given when he was picked up as a child by some GIs during the war – James Hart. Zirkeler crucified him. Then he returned a few days later and killed my father's long-time mistress and her driver. That's how your political party got hold of the Holy Lance. Zirkeler conjured up some bullshit for you about a man in Portland, Oregon, who had inherited the Holy Lance from his father, an ex-GI, and then felt guilty keeping it. But he actually stole it from my father, who got it directly from my grandparents after the plane they were on crashed. The bastard's been hiding behind you and your political party all the time, Effi. And now you tell me he has the codes for all your buildings, the whole thing makes even more sense. How often do you visit your factory?'

Effi shook her head. The colour had started to return to her face. 'Hardly ever. Maybe once a year. I have a manager there who runs it. I get reports. My accountants check the figures. I keep the factory more out of a sense of duty to my late father than as any ongoing concern. And because it employs a dozen people in an area of low employment. That's the only reason I still have it. I've never been remotely interested in that side of my father's work.'

'Well, Zirkeler certainly has. He's been using the factory under your nose, Effi. Employing his own people to work there. Amira must have stumbled in and found him.'

Hart and Effi finished manhandling the spare bed frame out into the hall. They could hear the arrival of Zirkeler's phalanx of cars in the front drive. Hart estimated he had two minutes at the most, whilst Zirkeler's men encircled the house and decided what to do next.

'How long ago did you call the police?'

Effi shrugged. 'Nearly ten minutes now. They will be coming in from Rottach. You will hear the sirens soon.'

'Take this, then.' Hart handed Effi the .410. 'I'm going to check on Amira. She mustn't fall asleep. That would be the worst thing for her. If Zirkeler comes through that front door, fire over his head. Here, this is the second cartridge. You break the gun like this, pick out the old cartridge, and slide the new one in here. You'd have to hit someone straight on in the face to kill them, so it's really not that dangerous. It'll just make Zirkeler and his men a little more cautious than they would otherwise have been, and maybe buy us a few more minutes. Hold the second cartridge back for when they get closer. But I'll have returned by then.'

Effi turned the gun on Hart. She pointed it directly at his head. 'You mean when they get closer like this? From this distance, Johnny? Then it would be dangerous?' Effi's blue eyes were as cold as ice. The shotgun was mounted tight against her shoulder. Her legs were slightly apart. It was the stance of an experienced shot – someone who has been stalking and shooting game all their lives. Not someone who was picking up a shotgun for the very first time and feeling uncertain how to use it.

'For God's sake, Effi.' Hart started towards her. 'You never, ever joke with guns.' He stretched a hand out to turn the shotgun away.

Effi took a pace backwards. She motioned at him with the tip of the barrel. 'You stand still. Don't move.'

Hart could feel the first cold fingers of doubt encircle him. He took a deep breath. Effi was frightened and panicking. He had come back to her house in the middle of the night with a strange woman in tow, talking of viruses and violence. It was natural for her to have lost confidence in him. It had to be that. So he must shake her out of it. There was no other way.

'I can hear Zirkeler and his men at the door. We need to pull together now, Effi, or we're dead. Zirkeler has already murdered four people to my certain knowledge. Stop playing silly games and give me the gun.' He took another step towards her.

Effi levelled the shotgun at Hart's crotch. 'If you move again, I will blow your precious cock and balls that you love so much to kingdom come. Will that convince you, Johnny? This is definitely not a game. Not any longer.'

SIXTY-ONE

Frau Erlichmann had finished translating the manuscript Hart had found hidden in the Holy Lance's broken shaft. It had been less difficult than she expected. The message had been written in a script halfway between Old High German – what she knew of as *Althochdeutsch* or AHD – and Middle High German, with a bit of Latin and Greek thrown in for good measure. She had not been able to translate all the words, but she believed she had got the gist of it.

She knew that she ought to go back to sleep now, or else she would be exhausted by morning. But she found that she could not. From the moment Hart had left her house, she had begun worrying. Had it been a mistake to give him the pistol? An unnecessarily dramatic gesture, based on some absurd wartime regression? She had been tempted a number of times during the night to call the police, but surely if Hart felt he needed that sort of help, he would have told her?

Finally, when she could stand the tension no longer, she

called her grandson. Thilo was a sensible boy. She had been so proud of him and his friends when Hart had recruited them to frighten the Rache woman at the Gasthof zur Hirschtal. He would know what to do.

'Omi, why are you calling me in the middle of the night? I was asleep.'

'I'm sorry, Thilo. But I am worried.' Frau Erlichmann pressed the loudspeaker switch on her telephone. Suddenly she could hear her grandson sighing, throwing off the covers of his bed, plonking his feet on the floor. She refused to let embarrassment curb her tongue. She was far too old to stand on ceremony. 'Very worried, in fact.'

'What are you worried about?' Thilo shuffled on his slippers and checked his alarm clock. The noise was magnified tenfold at the other end of the line. 'You shouldn't live alone in that old house. You should come and live with Papi, Mami and me. Do you want me to come over later and visit you?'

'I want you to come over now. I think I have done something rather stupid. Two hours ago I gave the baron your great-grandfather's pistol. And I lent him my car.'

'You gave him a gun? And your car? In the middle of the night?'

Frau Erlichmann closed her eyes. She needed to concentrate. She owed it to the baron to get her point across without diluting its effect. Thilo was a sensible boy. She needed to treat him as such. 'The baron thinks that the Zirkeler creature killed my guest, Herr Wesker. The woman he used to be with, Amira Eisenberger – the one he was involved with before he

358

started this nonsense with the Rache woman – has gone to the Rache factory to investigate.'

'Amira Eisenberger? The journalist?'

'She is a journalist, I believe. Have you heard of her?'

Thilo sucked in his breath. 'Do you know how famous Amira Eisenberger is, in our circle? She has been covering the civil war in Syria since the beginning. She was in Bosnia, Iraq and Afghanistan. In Europe she specializes in extreme right-wing politics and fascism. She is one of the best-known journalists on the planet.'

Frau Erlichmann sighed. 'No, I did not know that. The baron can sometimes be a little reticent with the truth. I only know that he thinks she may be in trouble.'

'What sort of trouble?'

'Quite serious, I think.'

There was a lengthy silence down the line. For a moment Frau Erlichmann thought Thilo might have been cut off. Then she heard crashing noises through the telephone loudspeaker as he stumbled around his bedroom gathering up his clothes.

'I'm going to collect up a few of my friends, Omi. People who think the same way I do. Then we are coming down to see you. We will go to the factory first, as it is on our way, and then on to you. Meanwhile, you must call the police. Promise me you will do that? Sepp Unterbauer is a sergeant now. Ask for him by name. Papi says his mother used to work for you during the sixties, before she got married. Remember?'

'How can I call the police? I have nothing whatsoever to tell them. And if I call them, they will stop the baron and imprison him for carrying an illegal weapon and we will both go to prison. And this may all be *quatsch* anyway. An old woman's imaginings.'

Thilo laughed loudly down the phone. 'You may be an old woman, Omi, but I have never known you to imagine anything.'

SIXTY-TWO

Udo Zirkeler's men spread through the ground-floor level of Haus Walküre like a horde of locusts. Hart had a grandstand view of the bedlam from his position behind the makeshift barricade he and Effi had constructed at the top of the stairs. Thanks to the Z-bend construction of the staircase, they weren't as yet visible to the men below.

Hart motioned at the shotgun Effi was pointing at his chest. Then he pointed towards the spare bed frame blocking the stairwell. 'Shall I take this down for you? I might be tempted to kick it onto Zirkeler's head otherwise. And I wouldn't want you to shoot me for such a pathetic reason as that.'

'Leave it where it is. I don't want you moving.' Effi's concentration was fixed on Hart. She seemed entirely unmoved by the crashing and banging coming from downstairs as Zirkeler's men quartered the house.

An unwanted mental image came to Hart of what it must have been like for Jewish families when the SS or the Gestapo came to round them up in the middle of the night. Or for the East German intelligentsia when the Stasi came to call. All thugs were alike, he decided. They clattered and shouted and wrecked things. They imposed themselves.

Hart turned his back on the chaos happening downstairs and faced Effi. They would reach the first floor soon. He wondered idly what form his death would take. A beating? A tumble down the stairs? Or would he and Amira be taken to another place entirely and involved in a fake road accident? He was sorry now that he had borrowed Frau Erlichmann's vintage Auto Union. It was unlikely, given their present situation, that she would get it back in quite the same pristine condition as before. 'You didn't call the police, did you, Effi? Or the ambulance service? You were just talking into a dead phone.'

'You are joking, surely?'

Hart gave a hollow laugh. 'Yes. The joke does seem to be on me, doesn't it?' He met Effi's eyes directly for the first time since she had turned the shotgun on him. 'I vanquished all my doubts about you, Effi. I suffocated them at birth. All my doubts about your party. About your politics. About your Nazi antecedents. I wouldn't listen to my friends. I wouldn't even listen to my own bloody instincts when every bone in my body was screaming "red flag" at me. How does it feel to pull the wool over someone's eyes so categorically, Effi? Does it give you a sense of power? Of dominion? I was so desperate to believe you were who I wanted you to be that I steered my own people in the wrong direction in order to protect you. What a fool you must have thought me.'

'That's the understatement of the year. But you've got one thing wrong, Johnny. You weren't desperate to protect me. You were desperate to get inside my pants. I've rarely met a man as cock-driven as you. Men like you ought to be made to carry a warning sign. "Idiot on the prowl."'

Hart shook his head from side to side like a man who has been sucker-punched in a bar brawl. He used the movement to disguise a quick glance down the stairs. Udo Zirkeler was striding up the staircase towards them, a broad grin on his face. Hart knew that if he was to have any chance of getting his point across, he needed to do it in a hurry.

'Amira Eisenberger may be bleeding internally, Effi. If you don't get her to a doctor soon, it may be too late. She's a world-famous journalist. You do realize that, don't you? You might be able to duck out from under the other murders done in your name, but not this one. Her newspaper will crucify you if anything happens to her. You'll never be let alone. They'll bring you and your party down one way or the other. Don't let Zirkeler destroy you. Do something decent for a change. You can still pull this back from the brink if you act now. Shoot the bastard.'

Udo Zirkeler pushed the bedstead to one side and squeezed through the gap between it and the stair head. His SS uniform looked obscene against the studied modernity of Effi's show house. Like a scorpion on a piece of nougat, Hart decided.

Zirkeler clocked the situation between Effi and Hart and signalled to his men to wait downstairs for him. His smile was the smile of the victor.

'Eisenberger, you say? That's a Jewish name, isn't it? She

will be no great loss to humanity, then. My grandfather used to call the Jews "worm-eaters". You know why?'

Hart shook his head. 'No. But I suspect you are about to tell me.' He was still looking at Effi. Urging her with his eyes to turn the gun on Zirkeler. But he knew she wouldn't. He felt disgusted with himself. With his own witlessness. With his self-serving blindness. He deserved to die. But Amira didn't.

Zirkeler gave Hart his best Burt Lancaster grin. 'He saw a group of Yids one day scratching in the ground during a train stopover in Poland. This interested him. So he went over to take a look. The Yids extracted some wriggling red worms from the hole they had made. Fifteen centimetres long, he said. Like miniature snakes. Then they ate them. Just threw them down their throats like savages. Like you would throw back an egg. He told me their Adam's apples rose and fell like jackhammers.'

Hart stared at Zirkeler. He could feel himself seething. This was the man who had crucified his father. Who had returned to Guatemala to kill two innocent people because they might know something to his disadvantage.

'That's what happens when you starve people, Udo. That's what happens when you strip them of their humanity and brutalize them.'

'Jews have no humanity. You are labouring under a delusion.'

Hart took a deep breath. His right eye began to tick. All his attention was focused on Zirkeler. He needed to control himself and keep a lid on his temper, or Amira was lost. 'So, now that we've got that bit out of the way, may I ask what you intend doing with us?'

'What do you think?'

Hart shrugged. His neck felt as if two vices had been attached at either side of his trapezius muscles. 'So that's why you want your men to stay downstairs? Are you sure they will go along with you so easily? I suspect most of them will never have killed before. How can you be certain they won't lose their nerve at the last moment and turn you in to the authorities? This is Germany, Udo. Not Guatemala. And Amira Eisenberger is a celebrated journalist. There's a crucial difference between beating someone up and killing them. One is called GBH and will fetch you five years, tops. The other is a capital offence and will get you life.' Hart began to shout so that the men downstairs could hear him. 'This man is going to kill us. Are you going to stand by and watch this? You will be a part of it. Killing sticks to a person. You'll be accessories before the fact. You can say goodbye to your families. Your loved ones. Your lives.'

Udo Zirkeler snatched the .410 from Effi's hands and upended it, just as Hart had hoped he would, preparing to strike him in the face with the butt.

Hart dropped to one knee and drew the Roth-Steyr from beneath his jacket.

Zirkeler froze. Effi backed towards the bedroom.

'Stand still. Both of you.' Hart swung the gun barrel in an arc. 'Udo, order your men outside. And tell them to shut the fucking door behind them.'

Zirkeler laughed. 'Why would I do that? I recognize the type of pistol you are holding. It's a Roth-Steyr. Must be a hundred years old if it's a day. If you fire it, it will blow up in your face.'

Hart could feel his throat cramping with tension. When he spoke, his voice came out in a hoarse whisper. 'Then why aren't you turning that .410 round, Udo? Two seconds would do it. I can't tell you how stupid you look standing there with your crappy little uniform and your inverted squirrel gun.' Hart straightened up from his crouch. He took a step backwards so that he would be out of range if Zirkeler changed his mind and tried to swing at him. 'Drop the gun now, Udo. I would dearly love an excuse to kill you.'

Zirkeler glared at Hart. He stretched the wait to about half a minute, as though a part of him expected Hart to back down and lower his pistol out of sheer funk. Then he slowly unfolded his hands and placed the .410 on top of the upturned bed.

Hart backed up to the stair head so that the men downstairs could see his pistol. 'Clear out of the house. All of you. The police are on their way. If you get out now, you've got a chance of not being caught up in this. If you stay put, you'll go to jail. It's a simple choice.'

Hart counted the men out the door. He made it seven. He tried to work out how many might be left inside, bearing in mind the two who had run away and the two he had injured near the factory. But it was useless. He could still be one or two out. He didn't dare usher his prisoners downstairs for fear of being bushwhacked.

'Effi. Throw me your phone.'

'I left it downstairs. Do you want me to go and fetch it?'

Zirkeler laughed. A single, vulpine bark. 'What do you think of your girlfriend now, eh? Do you mean to send her to jail too? Or are you simply going to shoot her? The police aren't coming. We both know that. Everything is still to play for here.'

Hart could see Zirkeler struggling with whether it was worth risking a malfunction of the pistol or not. The shotgun was on the far side of the bedstead, about three feet from his left arm. Hart remembered the rusted spring in the Roth-Steyr's ammunition clip. The three remaining bullets might have been in place since 1918. The bastard was probably right – it would blow up if used. Or simply misfire.

He waved the pistol at Zirkeler. 'Back away.'

'No. We are staying here. You will have to shoot us.'

Amira lurched through the bedroom door. Her face, save for a livid bruise on one temple and a three-inch graze on her chin, was as pale as a shroud.

Zirkeler turned round to face her. 'Ah. The Jewess.'

'Amira, stay where you are. Don't move.'

Amira stumbled forwards into the hallway, toppling to one knee.

Zirkeler twisted in place. At first it looked as though he might be going for the shotgun, but he went for Amira instead.

Hart gritted his teeth and pulled the trigger. Nothing happened. The hammer was rusted solid. Hart tried to force it backwards with his thumb, but to no avail.

Effi sprinted past him, heading for the .410. Hart tripped her up. She struck the floor with a crash and went sprawling. Hart reached for the stock of the .410 and swung the shotgun round.

Zirkeler was holding his SS knife to Amira's throat. 'Another impasse. No?'

Hart felt the absurdity of his position begin to overwhelm him. All these people are living in a fantasyland, he told himself. And I'm a part of it. I'm standing in a house in Bavaria wielding a squirrel gun, whilst a man wearing an SS uniform is holding a knife to Amira's neck. How did I get here? What am I doing? How do I get out of this without killing someone? Or getting killed myself?

Effi picked herself up off the floor. 'How could you do that to me? I'm carrying your baby. You might have given me a spontaneous abortion.'

Hart's brain began to fizz and pop inside his head. 'My baby? What are you talking about?'

'I missed my period. And I never miss them. So I did a test. I was going to tell you later today over a bottle of champagne. You shouldn't have thrown me to the floor like that, Johnny.' Effi's voice had reverted to the tone he knew so well. A tone that promised the world and all its treasures to whoever succeeded in gratifying its owner. 'You must think of our son's future now. This woman is almost dead. Let Udo dispose of her. Then you can join us. Marry me. Give him your name. What is her life compared to ours?'

Zirkeler let out another of his barking laughs. 'He's made you pregnant, has he? And you want him to marry you? That's rich. I'm so happy for you both. You know she let me fuck her too, Englishman? You're not the only one who's pulled that particular chain. Far from it.'

Effi ignored him. 'This baby is yours, Johnny. You're the only man I've known these past few weeks. We made this baby the first time we made love, when I was at the peak of my fertility cycle. I wanted your son. Now I want him to carry your name. To be a baron like you. The hereditary guardian of the Holy Lance.'

Hart felt like upending the shotgun and sucking on the barrel. He was faced with Zirkeler's grinning face on one side, and Effi's earnest one on the other. They were both equally mad.

There was a sudden commotion outside the house. Shouts. Curses. The sound of running feet on gravel. Hart craned his head to one side so that he could see downstairs.

Two of Zirkeler's men sprinted towards the front door from where they had been hiding. He had been right about the shortfall in numbers then. The two had been lying in wait for him. He'd have been ambushed if he'd ventured downstairs.

'You see? The police are here.'

'Not the police. They don't arrive by osmosis.' Zirkeler's body language suggested that he was dealing with a congenital idiot. 'Someone else is joining the party. Maybe that old bitch at the Alpenruh called in some of her leftist friends? I knew I should have killed her when I had the chance.' Zirkeler glared at Effi. Then he twisted the tip of his knife so that it drew blood from Amira's neck. 'Tick tock. Tick tock. Tick tock. Time is running out for your little Jewess.'

Hart straightened up. 'How do you want to play this?' Despite his words, all he could think about was that Effi

369

was pregnant. And by intent. She'd drawn him into her web right from the outset. She was like the Lorelei, luring sailors to their doom on the Rhine. No wonder she'd found him so devastatingly attractive. He couldn't have presented himself better if he'd tried. He'd been a title with a cock attached.

'What you do is you put down the shotgun. You know you can't risk using it. The spread would hit your Jewess. I shall count to ten. On ten I'm going to slice through your girlfriend's carotid artery. Then I'm going to throw her at you.' Udo Zirkeler moved into a more comfortable position behind Amira, so that his entire body, save for his feet, was hidden behind her.

Hart shot Zirkeler's left foot. It was situated about eight inches from Amira's leg. Zirkeler had been about to tuck it in, but hadn't yet shifted his weight. Hart was a countryman by birth. He had shot game all his life. He knew that a shotgun spread starts tight and then expands later. At under seven feet, it is still tight as a drum.

Zirkeler screamed.

Hart sprinted towards him, reversing the .410 as he ran.

Zirkeler's hand holding the knife dropped briefly to one side.

Hart smashed the .410 stock into Udo's face. Then he felt something heavy land on his back. It was Effi.

The four of them – Effi, Zirkeler, Amira and Hart – rolled onto the floor in a bloody, tangled mass.

Hart tried to wrest the knife from Zirkeler's hand. Amira was flailing around like a rag doll between them.

Zirkeler was a stronger man than Hart, despite the wound

to his foot. Hart felt himself beginning to be turned over. He realized, to his horror, that Effi was doing some of the turning. Hart quickly overcame any scruples he might have about hitting a woman and struck backwards with his elbow. He heard Effi grunt. But still she held on.

Zirkeler took the opportunity to lunge at Hart with his knife. Hart twisted away from the blow. The point of the knife glanced off the collar of Hart's leather jacket and skidded past his neck. Effi cried out behind him. Hart felt something spray onto the back of his head.

Beneath him, Amira began to struggle for air.

Hart brought both his forearms down on Zirkeler's knife hand.

Zirkeler dropped the knife. He wriggled out from beneath Amira and dragged himself to his feet. He was still mobile. The stiff leather of his SS jackboot had taken the worst of the squirrel-gun blast.

Hart threw out an arm and gave Zirkeler's leg a glancing blow. Zirkeler fell with a crash against the upper edge of the stairs. He twisted round and made a grab for the Roth-Steyr, which had fallen out of Hart's pocket in the fracas. He thumbed back the rusty hammer – something that Hart had failed to do – and fired directly at Hart's face.

The pistol exploded. Zirkeler began to scream – a series of long, wet howls, like those a wolf will make just after he has killed. Zirkeler's face looked as though it had been encased in a red plastic bag.

Hart crab-walked backwards across the floor. His face

and torso were covered in Zirkeler's blood. Two of Zirkeler's severed fingers lay in his lap. Hart skittered them off as though they were still alive.

Zirkeler sat at the top of the stairs waving the stump of his pistol hand and screaming. The niveous glint of his teeth shone through the breech where his mouth should have been.

Hart dragged Amira away from where Effi lay. Effi's hands were twitching as if she were dreaming. Her upper body was surrounded by a widening pool of blood. Hart would remember later how beautiful her blood had seemed – pristine, like the surface of the lake in the moonlight a few hours earlier.

Effi appeared to be looking through him, her face framed by the blood as if in a surrealist painting. Hart caught himself wondering how a woman blessed with the features of an angel could be so evil? What trick of fate had triggered the aberration that had turned such beauty into madness?

He knelt beside Effi and pressed his finger deep into her carotid artery, where Zirkeler's knife had nicked her. It was the only way he knew to staunch arterial blood.

Effi's legs began to drum on the ground.

Hart began to cry. With one hand still on Effi's neck, he reached his other hand across her body and laid it gently across her stomach, like a blessing. He felt her hand briefly rest on his – like a child's hand will do when it is half asleep – and then fall away. Her lips moved. He pressed his head close to hers and listened for what she had to say.

'I hated you,' she said. 'I loved you.' And then, 'I'm sorry.'

Hart caressed her hair with the back of his hand. 'Take care of our child.'

He felt the pulse beneath his hand weaken and then stop. He looked up, his face contorted with grief.

Zirkeler was struggling to his feet, using the banister as a crutch. One eye was hanging on a thread down his cheek and one of his ears was missing. What was left of his mouth hung open inanely, as if he were about to ask a question but had forgotten his original point.

Hart stood up and strode towards Zirkeler. He could hear shouting from downstairs. The sound of approaching feet.

He slammed Zirkeler in the chest with both his hands.

Zirkeler threw his arms in the air and toppled backwards. His head struck the stairs about eight feet down. He did a reverse somersault, his legs flailing above him. When he reached the bottom of the staircase, he lay still.

SIXTY-THREE

Hart was ordered to leave Amira's bedside at two in the afternoon, just fifteen minutes after the hasty departure of the lawyer her newspaper had sent down from Munich to check her copy for libel. Fräulein Eisenberger needed her rest, he was told. Her doctors also failed to understand why she persisted in speaking endlessly on her phone despite such objects being banned in the hospital. They were a danger to medical equipment. Didn't these English people know that? Neither did they understand why Fräulein Eisenberger kept relentlessly tapping at her computer whilst still visibly ill. Patients should be patients. Thinking for oneself under such circumstances was forbidden by decree.

In the end, one of Amira's doctors insisted that she be tranquillized by intravenous drip. She had a severe concussion, he told Hart, albeit with no internal bleeding. But a concussion nonetheless. The hospital did not wish to be sued by her newspaper because their patient had suffered unnecessary swelling or traumatic brain injury. The publicity would be catastrophic.

For a few moments, standing forlornly outside the hospital gates, Hart did not know what to do with himself. The thought of Effi and their unborn child ate away at him like acid. What had constrained her to act the way she did? Had she been mesmerized by Zirkeler? Or was it she who had done the mesmerizing? The thought of the beautiful, vital woman he had known being buried in a casket six feet beneath the ground, with his child still inside her, was almost more than he could bear. How could she have brought this on herself? She had been given everything – only to throw it all away because of some insane sense of fidelity to a flawed and foregone history.

Hart hadn't dared confess his real name to the German police during the course of his six-hour interrogation. He had decided to continue using his Johannes von Hartelius alias until the publication of Amira's detailed piece about the LB triggered the case for his exoneration. The local Tegernsee police force, overwhelmed by the ramifications of the case, had requested to see his passport, had given it a cursory viewing, and then kept it. They would no doubt run it through Interpol eventually. But the hold-up bought Hart some precious time. With his luck, when the Germans did finally cross-check his identity, Scotland Yard would drop the murder case against him and open up a brand-new case involving the use of a false passport by a man masquerading as himself.

Finally, pretty much by default, Hart found himself boarding the Bad Wiessee ferry. He sat in the same place, on the same boat he'd shared with Amira the day before. But everything looked different now. Then, he'd fancied himself in love. Now, with the benefit of hindsight, the main emotion he had been experiencing had probably been lust, twinned with just a little vainglory. He was an Aries. A man-child. A mythologizer. He had welcomed Effi Rache's seduction of him as his due. No. That still didn't cover it. In the final analysis, he had seduced himself.

He disembarked at the Bad Wiessee terminus and started up the hill towards the Alpenruh. He hadn't been able to visit Frau Erlichmann in the direct aftermath of what had taken place at Haus Walküre, but, thanks to her grandson Thilo and his friends, he knew just how much he owed her. She had acted like his fairy godmother throughout. And as his conscience.

It was at her request that Thilo and his friends had gone, first to the factory, and then on to the house, where they had engaged in a pitched battle with Udo Zirkeler's private army. That had been the origin of the commotion he had heard coming from Effi's garden, and which had succeeded in drawing the last of Zirkeler's men from their hiding place. Now Zirkeler's 'apostles' were locked up, and the factory sealed inside a cordon sanitaire.

Hart paused halfway up the Alpenruh hill. He was struggling for air. It was only then that he realized that he had not slept for thirty straight hours. He lingered for a moment by the bridge, taking deep breaths, trying to regain his equilibrium. He looked across at Effi's house. It was surrounded by a small army of police vehicles. He recalled how innocent it had seemed at first viewing, surrounded by its lush cattle meadows and its wild bird cover. He remembered all the things that he had done in that house. The words he had said. The emotions he had felt. They all seemed so hollow now. As if someone else had been inhabiting his body and using his mind.

He glanced up towards the Alpenruh. A solitary figure was standing on the terrace, her face turned towards the afternoon sun. Frau Erlichmann. Hart raised his hand and waved at her, but she did not see him.

He continued up the track. When he was about fifteen feet away from where she was standing, she started. He called out and identified himself, and her face changed.

'Ah. Baron. I didn't see you. I was enjoying the feel of the sun on my face.' Frau Erlichmann made an apologetic movement towards her eyes. 'Come. Let us go inside and take some coffee. It is well past three o'clock. I have made a *mirabellenkuchen*. The plums come from that tree over there by the shelter.' She fluttered her hand, but it was plain to Hart that she could not make out the tree herself. 'It is a good tree. It produces more and more mirabelles every year. Just like Pandora's box.' She laughed in delight at her own image. 'I have covered the cake in walnut *streusel*. It is your favourite, if I remember?'

'Yes. It is my favourite. That, and the marzipan kirsch *Stollen* you made when we first met. Thank you.'

377

Hart followed Frau Erlichmann into the *esszimmer*. The smell of the house enfolded him like the memory of a perfect past he had inherited from someone else and arrogated to himself. He caught the bittersweet smell of ground coffee. The odour of chopped walnuts, cinnamon and other spices. The scent of air-dried hams and salamis. The smell of beeswax furniture polish, and of the apple, cherry and cedar wood logs stacked inside the *Kachelofen* alcove in readiness for winter, and chosen specifically for the scent they would give off.

'May I stay here for a few days, Frau Erlichmann? Just until Amira is well again and fit enough to travel? I am a little tired.'

'You may stay as long as you like, Baron. My hotel is empty, as you know. And my maid has little enough to do. Are you and Fräulein Eisenberger going to be together again?'

'It seems unlikely.'

'I'm so sorry.'

'Don't be. One makes one's own bed in this life. I seem to have contrived the apple-pie version for myself. I feel like a perfect fool.'

Frau Erlichmann didn't answer. Instead, she busied herself making their coffee. First she set the pot into boiling water. Then she fixed the filter in place and wet the grounds. Then, slowly, she dripped the parboiled water through the filter.

Hart watched her with a half smile on his face. He felt a sudden sense of freedom in her presence. A sense of infinite possibility. If she could lead her life, at close to ninety years of age, with such elegance and grace, surely he should be able to contrive something similar at the age of thirty-nine?

'This cake is quite wonderful.'

'Thank you, Baron.'

Hart sat back in his chair. He gazed around the room. At the endless rows of antlers on every wall. At the green-tiled *Kachelofen* with the neat piles of logs beside it in their dedicated alcove. He looked at the ancient pine floorboards, worn to burnished mahogany by a thousand feet. At the French windows leading out onto the terrace, with their dark green shutters folded neatly out of the way. At the waist-high panelling which strayed onto the windowsills and surrounds of each bow window, as if the carpenter who had made it could not bear to sign off on his work.

'You can't possibly leave this place. It can't pass into other hands. It would be a tragedy.'

'Everything changes, Baron. Nothing remains the same. We cling to the past at our peril.'

Hart nodded at her. But his thoughts were elsewhere.

Frau Erlichmann inclined her head towards him. She spoke gently, as if to a child. 'What have they done with the Holy Lance?'

Hart reached down for the bag beside him. He pushed aside the cake plates and laid the Lance on the table between them. 'I stole it. Just before I left Effi's house and confronted the police. I also stole my grandparents' photograph. I don't think anyone will care. The Viennese authorities think the Lance is a fake, anyway. They are convinced they have the real thing at the Hofburg Palace.'

Frau Erlichmann shook her head. 'This is not a fake, Baron.

I can assure you of that. This is the real Lance.'

'How can you be sure?'

'Because the strip of vellum I translated for you leaves no room for doubt. It is in the form of a letter. Written by your ancestor, Johannes von Hartelius, to his direct descendants in the male line. I shall tell you why he did that in a minute. The letter is dated Boreas, 1198. Boreas is one of the Anemoi. He is the Greek God of the freezing north wind that heralds winter. He is called the Devouring One. He had snakes instead of feet, and he blew the winds out of his mouth through a conch shell. He could turn himself into a stallion and father colts. All that the mares he mated had to do was to turn their hindquarters towards where he blew, and they would be impregnated without the need for coition. He lived in Hyperborea. Which is the place beyond the north wind. A place of exile, Baron. A place beyond the pale.'

'Why are you telling me this? What are you suggesting? That he was exiled?'

'Be patient, Baron. Age teaches us patience.' Frau Erlichmann raised her magnifying glass and studied the strip of manuscript in front of her. 'The ancients understood the importance of symbols. They expected their readers to be literate in such things. Not everything can be written down in black and white.'

Hart sat back in his chair. 'I'm sorry. I am dog-tired. It makes me tetchy. Please continue. I want to hear what my ancestor has to tell me.'

Frau Erlichmann shook her head. 'No. You will not want to hear this.'

'Read it to me. Please.'

Frau Erlichmann remained silent for a long time. At one point Hart began to wonder if she had drifted off to sleep. But when he looked closer he could see her lips moving. He realized she was praying.

Finally she looked up at him. Her eyes were kind. The eyes of a mother. 'The letter goes like this: "I, Johannes von Hartelius, Baron Sanct Quirinus, hereditary guardian of the Holy Lance, lawful husband of Adelaïde von Kronach, lawful father of Johannes, Paulus, Agathe and Ingrid von Hartelius, former Knight Templar, exonerated from his vows of chastity and obedience by Frederick VI of Swabia, youngest son of the Holy Roman Emperor, Frederick Barbarossa, acting lawfully in the name of his brother, Henry VI of Staufen, do dictate this letter on the day of my execution, to be placed inside the Holy Lance as a warning to all those who may come after me."'

'His execution?' Hart leant across the table. His face was pale with shock.

'Yes, Baron. His execution.'

'Why? What did he do?'

Frau Erlichmann addressed the manuscript again. 'This explains it better than I can, I think. "Swayed by my unlawful love for Markgräfin Elfriede von Drachenhertz, intended lawful daughter of the king, and former lawful wife of Elfriede von Hohenstaufen, military governor of Carinthia, I turned against my king and misused the Holy Lance, which had been placed in my care. In doing this, I refused to heed Horace's warning, passed down to me with the guardianship of the Lance. *Vir bonus est quis? Qui consulta patrum, qui leges iuraque servat* – He is truly a good man who observes the decree of his rulers and the laws and rights of his fellow citizens. Instead, I purposefully misunderstood the words Catullus handed down to all unvirtuous men – *Mulier cupido quod dicit amanti, in vento et rapida scribere oportet aqua.* I thus deserve my fate. May God have mercy on my soul."'

'What does he mean, Frau Erlichmann? What is he saying?'

'He is saying that "the vows that a woman makes to her fond lover ought to be written on the wind and in the swiftly flowing stream".'

'I do not understand.'

'Oh, Baron. No man has ever understood this. What Catullus is saying is that a woman will tell her besotted lover whatever she thinks he wants to hear.'

Hart sat still for a long time, staring into his coffee cup. 'Is there more?'

'No. Need there be?'

Hart sighed. 'What was the name of the woman who betrayed him?'

'He betrayed himself, Baron. Your ancestor had only himself to blame.'

'The name, Frau Erlichmann. Please tell me the name. I sometimes misunderstand your German pronunciation.'

'Elfriede von Hohenstaufen.'

'No. Tell me what her married name would have been.'

'Markgräfin Elfriede von Drachenhertz.'

'Elfriede Rache?'

Frau Erlichmann smiled. It was the serene smile of one who has seen everything, and who is content that their time should come. 'Only you can decide that, Baron. Only you can know such a thing.'